K-POP
CONFIDENTIAL

Don't we all dream of being 'discovered' and turned into a star? I know I did! But as ever, the reality is a little more complicated.

In *K-Pop Confidential*, our hero Candace is forced to confront the cost of her dream. Can she be true to herself in an industry determined to turn her into an idol? And then romance comes knocking . . .

Stephan Lee knows the world of K-pop inside out and this novel is brimming with authenticity, romance, rivalry and – of course – music. Prepare yourself for fame and fireworks!

BARRY CUNNINGHAM
Publisher
Chicken House

PS If you're new to K-pop, there's a super-helpful K-POP K-DICTIONARY on page 345 (if a word is in bold, the definition will be in there)!

K-POP
CONFIDENTIAL

STEPHAN LEE

2 Palmer Street, Frome, Somerset BA11 1DS
www.chickenhousebooks.com

Text © Stephan Lee 2020

First published in the United States by Scholastic Inc.,
557 Broadway, New York, NY 10012.

First published in Great Britain in 2020
Chicken House
2 Palmer Street
Frome, Somerset BA11 1DS
United Kingdom
www.chickenhousebooks.com

Cover art © Erick Davila 2020
Cover and interior design by Yaffa Jaskoll and Helen Crawford-White
Inside images © Shutterstock
Typeset by Dorchester Typesetting Group Ltd
Printed and bound in Great Britain by CPI Group (UK) Ltd, Croydon, CR0 4YY

The paper used in this Chicken House book is made
from wood grown in sustainable forests.

3 5 7 9 10 8 6 4 2

British Library Cataloguing in Publication data available.

PB ISBN 978-1-913322-29-8
eISBN 978-1-913322-54-0

For Umma and Halmuhnee. 사랑해.

PROLOGUE

GIRL IN REFLECTION

I bet I've stared at my reflection in rehearsal-room mirrors just like this one for hundreds and hundreds of hours.

Usually while I'm soaking in sweat, wishing my toes would just fall off from all the blisters and torn nails. Or watching myself try to wink and toss my hair and smile at the exact right time while our dance coach – 'The General' – screams at me for always being half a beat behind.

Now, as I huddle in this room with twenty-four other female trainees – all of whom have been training much, much longer than I have – my reflection looks like me, but she's me through a Snapchat filter. She looks as if long locks of silvery-purple hair have grown naturally from her head her whole life. She looks like she was born with other-worldly blue eyes that can pierce your soul. She looks like she's never had a pimple on her spotless, dewy skin.

1

She would never let on that her scalp is burning from the bleach, that her eyes are itching from the contact lenses, and that under those layers of 'natural-look' K-beauty make-up, she looks like she hasn't slept in weeks – because she hasn't.

This girl is me, but she's not exactly. She's still Candace from New Jersey. But this version of me knows how to push through pain, through bruises and bleeding feet and homesickness and inhumane diets. She knows how to rise above criticism and insults, keep her eye on the ultimate goal. She's left friends, said goodbye to family, flown all the way to Seoul. She's been picked apart by rooms full of executives older than her dad.

On top of all that, I haven't held my phone in three months. I've been *through* it.

Behind a closed door, the CEO of S.A.Y. Entertainment and top executives and investors are deciding the final line-up of their new super-hyped girl group, the female version of the most famous K-pop boy band in the world, SLK. Girls are praying, pacing around. Others are rocking back and forth, talking to themselves. Most are already crying.

Weirdly, I feel totally calm. I step closer to the mirror to get a better look at my familiar but unfamiliar face. It hits me how much I want this. I've earned this. I've given up everything for this.

I deserve this.

I believe, with all my heart, that I'm about to become a K-pop idol. And whichever other girls they choose, we're going to slay. Not just in Korea, or Asia, but the entire globe. It's my destiny. I can feel it in the roots of my unicorn-purple hair.

PART 1

CANDACE PARK OF
FORT LEE, NEW JERSEY

CHAPTER 1

ARE YOU THAT UNICORN?

Four Months Earlier . . .

One of my greatest talents in life is 'air-bowing'. It's the orchestral equivalent of lip-syncing, except it's not a cool skill and never will be. There will never be a TV show called *Air Bow Battle*.

The Fort Lee Magnet Symphony Orchestra is kicking off the Spring Performing Arts Showcase with a rousing rendition of 'Spring' by Antonio Vivaldi (a bit on the nose, I know). I keep my bow hovering a centimetre above the strings while I sway my body back and forth, curling my upper lip as if I'm smelling something nasty, all to give the *impression* that my whole body is overcome with the swelling emotions of the music – even though I'm not actually making a sound. It's better for everyone if I air-bow. If I can't be heard.

If it were up to me, I'd blast my viola up into space. It was Umma's idea, when I was five years old, for me to take it up. Since not that many kids choose the viola, she thought it would be easier for me to stand out and get accepted to the prestigious youth orchestras, which would look great on college applications.

Well, the joke's on her. Ten years later, I'm at the very back of the viola section with my equally untalented stand partner, Chris DeBenedetti. And let's be very real: violas are already the backup dancers of orchestras. We're essential, but no one's checking for us. The violins are the glamorous lead singers who get all the best parts, all the money notes. The cellos are the sexy, mysterious, brooding ones with the most Instagram followers.

Violas are the Michelle Williams of Destiny's Child of string instruments . . . except not iconic or best friends with Beyoncé.

It's only when we all stand up for our bow after the song is finished that I can see Umma and Abba in the audience. Abba is clapping frantically, giving a standing O, while Umma is taking tons of flash photos of me in my hideous orchestra uniform (a frilly white blouse and green ankle-length skirt). I smile miserably, getting blinded, until we can all sit back down to watch the glee club performances, which are what the audience actually came for.

Unlike every high school movie stereotype, the glee club is actually full of the coolest kids at Fort Lee Magnet. It's considered the easiest of the required arts classes, so it's packed with popular girls and jocks, including my older brother, Tommy.

The glee club has so many members that for this showcase, they've broken up into performance groups. For the opening number, Tommy and twenty of his bro friends strut on to the stage in neon tank tops, sweatbands and high socks; the students in the audience, especially the girls, go nuts. The dudes give an ironic performance of the boy band classic 'What Makes You Beautiful' by One Direction.

The dudes aren't good singers; they're making a joke out of it, shouting off-key while doing all the standard boy band moves, like tracing hearts in the air, pointing at girls in the audience, putting their hands on their chests and winking. But they're so unselfconscious about looking stupid that I have to admit it's legitimately pretty cool. Tommy and his friends from the baseball team stand out at the front, Tommy in the centre. I see my best friend Imani in the front row, literally swooning – she's always said my brother is her 'primary thirst object', which is too gross and cringey for words.

I don't know what it is about seeing Tommy and all those guys up there, but I'm suddenly balling up my hands into fists. A fantasy of breaking my viola against the floor flashes in my mind.

It's all so unfair. *I'm* the one who can sing – at least I think I can, even though I only ever sing alone in my room. So why does Tommy get to jump around in silly clothes, getting cheered on by the whole school, while I'm hidden away in the back of the orchestra?

No matter how many times I've begged Umma to let me quit viola and focus on singing, she won't budge. The last time I brought it up, she shouted *'Bae-jjae-ra!'*, which literally means *'cut my stomach open and let me bleed to death!'* Super dramatic, but basically, it's the Korean equivalent of 'over my dead body!'

What's even more unfair is that I'm pretty sure I'm not allowed to do glee club *because* she knows I'd take it seriously, unlike Tommy. 'Singing is something you can do on your own time,' she once told me. 'Singing is not a dignified art. You have to bring the sound from inside of you with so much effort – everyone can see how hard you try.'

Umma's bias against singing is so weird – she's actually a good singer herself. Umma and Abba both went to a prestigious music college back in Korea, which is how they met. Abba was studying to become a conductor and Umma was studying vocal performance. But I also know neither of them finished and they moved to America soon after they dropped out. Neither of them works in music now – they run a convenience store in Fort Lee – so I know Umma's music dreams went wrong somewhere, but she'll never talk about it. It'll remain one of those Family Secrets, probably for ever.

I put my viola on the floor – a big no-no according to Mrs Kuznetsova, the orchestra conductor – and slump in my seat. Will there ever be a time when I'm the one singing and jumping around onstage, not worried what anyone thinks? Probably not until after high school, when I'm somewhere far from my family. In the meantime, I'll just have to bide my time for a few more years, playing the role of the quiet Korean girl who takes all Advanced Placement classes and gets good grades and plays a classical instrument and never complains.

After the showcase, Imani and Ethan come over. It's a Friday night and we're doing what we love most: hanging out in my room, stuffing our faces and watching YouTube vids.

It's not like we're total rejects, even though we *are* in all the Smart Kid classes together. It's just that, more than parties or football games, we prefer hanging around each other, reacting in extra ways to all the weird things we're obsessed with: *RuPaul's Drag Race* clips we rewatch over and over, *mukbang* videos, beauty vloggers we make fun of but secretly love. ('A little goes a long way,' Ethan likes to say, pretending to dab highlighter on his cheekbones. 'And don't forget your cupid's bow!')

After we watch a tiny *mukbanger* demolish eight packs of Nuclear Fire Noodles in under four minutes, Imani commandeers my computer. I know what she's about to pull up: SLK's performance of 'Unicorn' from last week's *Saturday Night Live*.

'I love, love, love SLK!' says Ethan, as the host, Jennifer Lawrence, introduces them.

'Duh! What excuse for a human being wouldn't?' says Imani.

I shrug. 'I guess they're all right.'

'OK, *this* excuse for a human being.' Imani flashes me a shady look. 'Dude, sometimes I think I'm more Korean than you are.'

I mean, Imani *is* literally slurping kimchi straight out of the jar at this very moment. Not even I can eat kimchi like that – I like it with food, especially curry rice or black bean noodles, but it's too funky for me to eat it by itself.

'I'm super glad that an Asian group is so popular and on magazines and all,' I say, 'but their music seems a little . . . manufactured?'

'Girl, bye,' says Imani, closing the jar of kimchi and moving back to my bed to hug my giant whale pillow, MulKogi. ('*mulkogi*' means '*water-meat*', or '*fish*' in Korean). 'Like American pop

9

music *isn't* manufactured? Anyway, each of those SLK guys can really sing and rap – One.J wrote a ton of their biggest hits himself. And that choreography is *banging!*'

'Yeah, look at that, Candanista,' says Ethan, totally transfixed. 'One Direction used to just stand onstage and, like, *maybe* jump around – these guys *serve* it.'

OK, so I'm not sure why I'm lying to my best friends right now – I probably need to go to a therapist to get to the bottom of it – but I'm actually a *huge* SLK stan in secret. I've watched hours of their Korean **music show** performances and their reality show, *SLK Adventures*, on YouTube. And ever since SLK made it big in America, I've started following other K-pop groups, especially QueenGirl, who are touring with Ariana Grande right now. Nothing would make Imani, the biggest K-pop stan I know, happier than being able to obsess over it with me. But for some reason, I'm self-conscious about it. Isn't it so *expected* for the Korean girl to be super into K-pop?

On-screen, the five boys of SLK move in perfect sync, even when they're doing literal backflips. Each guy rocks a different shade of brightly coloured hair – they clearly spend just as much time on make-up and wardrobe as any girl group. In their own way, they're all really hot, especially One.J, the member who's always front and centre. Everything about his face seems created in a lab to be as telegenic as humanly possible: his brooding eyes; his candy-coloured lips; his chiselled, V-shaped jaw. Somehow, none of his moves seem rehearsed. When all the boys run their hands through their hair, it looks as though One.J is doing it spontaneously, just to feel himself, and the other four boys saw how awesome it looked and decided to copy him.

The *SNL* crowd totally loses it when the boys break into the Unicorn dance. 'Unicorn' is amazing, even though the chorus, the only part of the song that's in English, doesn't completely make sense: 'Baby, now I believe in unicorn/You're the girl I been searching for/Searching under all the ra-ainbow/Baby, all I know/You're my one-in-billion unicorn.'

By the end of the song, the three of us are dancing around, singing at the top of our lungs. Imani whips her hair back and forth, Ethan does a duckwalk and I move my body with no regard for rhythm or dignity.

'OK, fine,' I pant when the song is over. 'This song is super catchy.'

Right after the *SNL* performance, 'Unicorn' starts back up again. We're ready to shriek out the song all over again, but it's not the music video – it's an ad (so many ads, YouTube). The words 'ARE YOU ONE IN A BILLION?' flash across the screen. Then:

S.A.Y. ENTERTAINMENT
THE COMPANY THAT BROUGHT
YOU THE NO. 1 GLOBAL SENSATION SLK
IS LOOKING FOR ITS FIRST-EVER GIRL GROUP

Cut to a clip of the SLK boys smouldering directly at the camera, the light glinting off their shimmering cheekbones.

WE'RE SEARCHING FOR THOSE GIRLS
WHO CAN SING, DANCE AND RAP LIKE SLK

ARE YOU THAT UNICORN?

Each of the SLK boys says into the camera, seductively, 'Are you my unicorn?' I get a warm, queasy feeling in my stomach when it's One.J's turn.

GET DISCOVERED AT
THE S.A.Y. GLOBAL AUDITIONS
ROYAL OAK THEATER IN PALISADES PARK, NEW JERSEY
19 APRIL

I burst out laughing. 'Are they auditioning singers or looking for dates for the guys?'

Imani isn't laughing; she's staring at me. 'You should audition, Candace.'

I don't dignify this with a response. 'And Palisades Park? Is that a glitch? Why would a K-pop label recruit in *Jersey*?'

Ethan isn't laughing either. 'Well, Jersey *is* where the suburban Korean kids live.' He gestures to me as if to say, 'Exhibit A.'

'You should audition,' Imani repeats, all serious.

'Ha ha.' I roll my eyes. 'Could you see *my parents* letting me quit school to be in a K-pop group? Besides, do I look like an idol to you?'

Imani runs her eyes over my busted bare feet, holey jeans and oversized black hoodie. 'No, not at all. But you've got something to work with under . . . all of that. Besides, do you even know how big this is?! S.A.Y.'s the most powerful entertainment company in K-pop right now because of SLK. A girl group version of SLK would be *lit*!'

'And you can *sang*,' says Ethan. 'Even with "Unicorn" just now, your vocals were low-key slaying.'

'Dude, I've always told you,' says Imani, 'you have the voice of an angel. You need to share that with the world.'

Imani has said stuff like this to me before. It's a sweet compliment, for sure, but for some reason, my eyes get a little moist.

There's something about K-pop's popularity that scares me a little bit. I have no problem openly fangirling over my favourite American artists, like Ariana and Rihanna, because they're nothing like me – I can love them from afar. But now that SLK has graced the cover of *Vanity Fair* and QueenGirl has performed with Cardi B at the VMAs, it's all become a little too real. Maybe kids who look like me *can* become stars too, if they've got the talent and can put themselves out there. Deep down, I think I could be talented enough. But brave enough to go for it? Definitely not.

I glance at the Barbie-pink guitar in the corner of my room. It was my dad's gift to me for my twelfth birthday, which he bought in that dad-ish way of thinking all girls love hot pink (and I kinda do). Abba taught me a few basic chords and, unlike the viola, I learnt the guitar immediately, as if it were a long-lost part of my body – I think maybe it's because I've always thought of guitar as a tool for singing. I watched YouTube tutorials on fingerpicking and learnt how to play early Taylor Swift songs. Now my guitar is my prize possession, the first thing I'd grab in a fire.

I only ever play it in the privacy of my room though. I sing tons of covers, plus a couple of my own original songs. I sometimes film myself, and I've even considered posting a couple of videos to YouTube – like me singing an acoustic version of 'Here

With Me' by Marshmello featuring Chvrches – but those videos are just files on my computer, sitting on my cluttered desktop among AP Lit papers and Bio lab write-ups.

'Hmm,' I say. 'Maybe I'll think about it.'

'Dude,' says Imani, opening a bunch of new tabs on my computer, 'I think you're seriously underestimating how amazing K-pop is. It's not just one kind of thing. Let me be your girl group tour guide.'

Imani shows us music videos – or 'MVs', as they're always called in K-pop – featuring all sorts of girl groups, like Queen-Girl, Blackpink, Twice, Red Velvet, Everglow and ITZY. I've watched tons of SLK MVs, but I haven't paid as much attention to the female groups. Not like this. The visuals and the choreography are mind-blowing, and the girls are out-of-control beautiful, but there are all kinds of genres and influences, including hip-hop, reggae and EDM.

As she shows us all these videos, Imani explains the difference between **Girl Crush** versus **Cute Concepts** in K-pop girl groups.

She also explains the rules of K-pop like she's explaining the kingdoms of *Game of Thrones*. There are only four big entertainment companies in K-pop, S.A.Y. being one of them, and they recruit all over the world – Korea mostly, but also Japan, China, Thailand and the States, usually in Los Angeles. They're looking for talented kids, for sure, but talented kids who play a particular role that every K-pop band needs.

'So it's all a formula?' I ask.

'I mean, that's not *all* of it,' says Imani, 'but yeah, K-pop is kind of an idol factory. The companies hit up schools, auditions, malls

14

and, lately, YouTube and social media. If the kids they recruit aren't super talented when they're recruited, the companies will make sure they *become* super talented. There's this whole hardcore "trainee" system they have to go through before they debut, usually for years. The vast majority of trainees *never* debut after spending their whole childhoods training. It's totally *Hunger Games*.'

Umma pokes her head in. When Ethan's in my room, I'm not allowed to close the door, even though Umma knows there's nothing to worry about. 'Are you kids having fun?'

'Yes, Mrs Park!' Imani and Ethan pipe up.

'Imani is just tutoring us in Advanced Placement K-pop,' cracks Ethan.

'I *will* be quizzing you both,' Imani jokes.

'How fun,' says Umma. I can see a smidge of disapproval in her face. 'Imani, your sister is here to take you and Ethan home. I'll pack some kimchi to take with you.'

'Thanks, Mrs Park!'

After Imani and Ethan leave, I can't stop watching more girl group MVs. I never knew how many types of girls you could be as a K-pop idol – a cutesy girl, a rebel, a fashion queen or all three in one. Why have I never thought of it as a possibility for myself?

Well, that's a dumb question. There are so many obvious reasons I could never dream of being a K-pop idol. For one, my Korean is horrible; I never had to go to Korean language school on Saturdays like the Korean kids I know from church. Secondly,

I definitely can't dance. Like, I can't even pump my fist, *Jersey Shore* style, to a basic beat – it's that serious.

And of course, my parents would shut down any talk of being a singer before it even started. Umma's drilled it into mine and Tommy's heads that there are only three, maybe four, respectable fields we can go into as adults: medicine, law, business or academia – in that order. Being a singer is far down the list, probably between murderer and drug dealer.

I finally click out of YouTube and grab my guitar, making sure my door is closed. I hit record on my laptop cam.

I know this video will just clutter my desktop like all the others, never to be uploaded. I still like to record though, because – this is weird and super dark – I think if I ever got hit by a school bus or something, I'd want to leave these videos behind, so people would know: *Candace could really sing. Candace had something to say all along.*

I play the opening chords of a song I've been writing for a while, called 'Expectations vs Reality'. I sing softly:

Expectation:
I don't do confrontation
I don't get invitations
I live in my imagination

Reality:
You think you know me
But there's a lot you don't see
Wait till I become who I'm meant to be

OK, I know the lyrics are corny, and my rhymes might not be tight like *Hamilton*, but I'm baring my soul here.

I'm not the girl who speaks up
But one day I'll really blow up
One day you'll hear this song
And know that you were wrong
Cuz your expectation's not my reality

'Wow, how beautiful!'

I shriek and almost drop my guitar. Tommy's head is poking into my room. He's wiping away fake tears.

'Go away!' I scream, throwing MulKogi at him.

Tommy catches MulKogi easily. 'No one understands Candace! Candace is so deep!'

I shove Tommy's face out of my room and shout into the hall. 'Umma! Abba! Tommy's spying on me again!'

'So sorry, so sorry,' Tommy says in a Korean accent, bowing to me and cracking up. 'I'll be *really* sorry when you "blow up" and your song is number one!'

I slam the door and apologize to MulKogi telepathically for throwing him. MulKogi responds telepathically, 'Well, Tommy deserved it. *He* gets to be in glee club and you don't?!'

Steaming, I text Imani.

OK. I wanna audition.

I sit down at my computer and edit the video of my singing, cutting off the very end where Tommy so rudely interrupted. I click the mouse angrily, as if it were Tommy's face, and open my YouTube account. For the first time ever, after all the thousands of videos I've viewed in my life, I upload my first video to my channel. There I am, CandeeGrrrl0303 (don't judge me, I created this account in junior high), with a single video of me singing and playing a guitar.

Just because Umma is afraid of her own voice, based on some failure she had back in Korea before I was even born, doesn't mean she can silence mine.

I click publish.

When I look at my phone again, Imani has already responded to my text.

YASSSSS!!!!!!!!!!!

CHAPTER 2

ONE IN A BILLION

Imani and Ethan have my arms locked in theirs to show their support – and to keep me from running. I'm their prisoner. Without them, I would have bounced the moment I saw the crowd. Hundreds, maybe thousands, of kids and full-on adults have shown up to audition.

At first, I thought this audition was just for S.A.Y. Entertainment's first-ever girl group, but according to the signs everywhere, they're also looking for male singers for their upcoming boy group, which they're calling 'SLK 2.0'. The line stretches from the movie theatre lobby, out the door and into the parking lot, snaking around the building.

I'm shook. I didn't know there were this many K-pop fans on the whole East Coast, let alone in New Jersey. It's mostly Asians, but I'm pleasantly surprised to see there's pretty much every kind of human in the crowd. There's a local news team filming people doing the 'Unicorn' dance – it's basically where you make a horn against your forehead with your finger while doing a complicated gallop. It's sort of like PSY's 'Gangnam Style' dance, except when the SLK guys do it, it's cool and kind of sexy.

I gaze up at the giant posters of SLK plastered all over the multiplex. There are five members: ChangWoo, the leader and 'dad' of the group; YooChin, the swaggy Main Rapper; Joodah, the one with the really adventurous fashion sense; Wookie, the funny one who almost looks like a regular dude; and of course One.J, the **Centre**, **Visual**, **Face** and *maknae* of the group.

In some posters, the five of them look icy and a little scary, like vampires from *Twilight*, their skin shining white, their lips glistening blood red, their eyes glowing a fiery gold. In others, they look sunny and teenage-dreamy, like the ideal, puka-shell-wearing boyfriend you fantasize about meeting at summer camp but never actually do.

For a second, I get lost in One.J's gaze in one of the scary-sexy posters. His smouldering stare. His perfect, slightly parted lips.

I shake myself out of my trance – Imani and Ethan do too – when we finally get to the sign-in desk after waiting in line for more than two hours. The girl at the desk, who's wearing an SLK T-shirt, asks snippily, 'Are all three of you here to audition?'

'No, just this K-pop idol right here,' says Imani.

The girl glances at me sceptically and hands me a sign-in sheet. 'Next,' she drones.

We move along to the holding area right outside the auditorium where the auditions are going on. I sit on the floor and start filling out my sign-in sheet, which is in both English and Korean.

Name: Candace Park

Name in Korean (if applicable): Park Minkyung

Age: 15

Height: 5 ft 1

Weight: Don't know. Also, RUDE!

Skills (Acting, Dancing, Singing): Singing

Other Skills: Guitar, songwriting, once ate 3 Chipotle burritos in one sitting

Favourite Western Musicians: Ariana Grande, Rihanna, Justin Bieber

Favourite K-Pop Musicians: SLK, QueenGirl, Blackpink

Imani peers over my shoulder. I expect her to tell me to take my answers more seriously, but she just says, 'Cute. You're showing personality. Oh, and your picks for fave K-pop groups are super solid. You learn quickly, my young Padawan.'

I turn my sheet in to the can't-be-bothered sign-in girl, who gives me a number to pin to my clothes: 824. I take this as a good sign – my birthday is 24th August.

Ethan takes out his phone to film me. 'How does it feel knowing you're about to be chosen for the girl version of SLK?'

I hold up a peace sign and flash the cutesiest, most squishy-faced smile I can, my imitation of the perfect K-pop idol.

'None of that's gonna happen,' I say through my exaggerated grin. 'I'm going to sing my song, get rejected and pretend I was never here.'

'Boo, you're no fun,' says Ethan, putting down his phone.

I look around. The movie theatre, closed to the general public for the day, is full of kids who look like they belong at an anime cosplay convention: tons of heavy eyeliner, neon hair, chokers, pale gothic make-up. Others are more hip-hop, all baggy jeans and chains. Everyone's practising their breakdancing or doing vocal warm-ups, putting their whole bodies into singing a cappella versions of K-pop hits like 'Loser' by Big Bang or 'Love Whisper' by GFriend. I've never felt so out of place. I'm skipping *SAT tutoring* to be here.

Sensing how nervous I am, Imani says, 'Let's do Diversity Hands for good luck.'

Diversity Hands is one of our inside jokes, spoofing a photo in this brochure our school guidance counsellor Mr Torrence has in his office about Celebrating Diversity. We put our hands together and admire the differences: Imani's deep-brown hand, Ethan's pale, sorta hairy hand and mine. I don't know why people say Asian skin is yellow, because it's not, but it's definitely different from the other two.

'Well, would you look at that,' says Ethan in his Lame Dad voice.

When my number is finally called, Ethan helps me strap my pink guitar around my shoulder. Me and two other auditioners file into the auditorium, where we stand on a mini stage in front of the IMAX movie screen. After my eyes adjust to the spotlight shining on me, I make out three people in the audience: a cameraman filming us; a dude in hip glasses and a sweater vest; and a fierce-looking woman in a business suit with a neutral smile frozen on her face. The woman, I can tell, is the one I really need to impress.

'On behalf of S.A.Y. Entertainment, Manager Kong thanks you for coming out to audition,' says Glasses McSweatervest. Manager Kong must be the fierce-looking woman. 'I'm Brandon Choi, and I'll be your translator today. You'll have up to one minute to sing, dance or perform a monologue, based on your chosen skill. When we stop you, it means we've seen enough – please do not continue. First, we have number 822, Ricky Towns-hend, who will be singing . . . "Jebal". Is that right?'

An African American boy with pink hair steps forward. After doing a silent little prayer, Ricky starts singing an insanely sad ballad in perfect Korean. Even with my basic understanding of the Korean language, I know *'jebal'* means *'please'* – or more intense than *'please'*; it's more like, *'for the love of God, please!!!'* (Umma often yells at me, *Jebal, practise your viola!*). From the very first note, Ricky kills it. Not only is his Korean better than mine, but he brings aching emotions to the lyrics. When he's done, I have chills and can't help but start clapping until Brandon the translator shoots me a sharp look.

Next up is a Korean American dude with cornrows who decides to perform a rap he wrote himself. His calls himself Antikdote, and his skills are about as good as his name. Manager Kong and Brandon the translator stop him after ten seconds.

I'm up third and last in the group. I step forward.

'I will be singing an acoustic cover of "Bad Guy" by Billie Eilish,' I say with a nod of my head. I can't do a deep, proper Korean bow because of my guitar.

I can hardly see Manager Kong or the translator, just their silhouettes. I hold my breath and strum the first chord.

23

When I start singing, I hear myself rushing a little bit, but I can't help it – I suddenly feel self-conscious about my song choice. My voice sounds thin to me, probably because I haven't sung above a whisper in years. I probably look like a twelve-year-old with my pink guitar. No one would believe me claiming to be the 'make your mama sad type'. I should have chosen a Carly Rae Jepsen song or something.

I only expected to sing the first verse and chorus, but I don't hear anyone stop me. Or maybe they're yelling at me to stop, but I haven't heard them because it's like I'm outside my body – my brain's turned off and my fingers are moving by muscle memory. For the instrumental break during the song, I actually stop singing and just whistle while slapping my guitar for the beat.

At the end of the song, I stop kind of abruptly and my brain registers once again that I'm standing in an empty movie theatre auditioning for a K-pop group. I bow once more. It's completely silent, and I step back to my spot next to Ricky and Antikdote.

'Good job,' Ricky whispers to me.

'You too,' I whisper back.

Manager Kong and Brandon mutter to each other. I realize my whole body is literally shaking. One stream of sweat trickles down my temple.

Brandon the translator finally clears his throat. 'Thank you to all of you for coming out today. We appreciate your time and hard work, but we're looking for very specific qualities today. All of you are dismissed . . .'

Ouch.

I never expected anything to come of this audition, but still, my heart melts like a Salvador Dalí clock and drips into my stomach.

I start to follow the other two offstage when all of a sudden Brandon says, 'Except 824. All of you are dismissed except 824. 824, please remain on the stage.'

I let out an involuntary squeal. I swear, the translator was being extra on purpose, pulling one of those reality show fake-outs.

I stay put and wave sadly to Ricky – he really needs to become a singer somehow, whether or not it's in K-pop – before I focus on my next task. If they want another song, I've memorized how to play 'Since U Been Gone' by Kelly Clarkson.

'Please put your guitar down,' says the translator.

Shoot. OK, I can totally sing a cappella.

I lay my guitar on the floor, all naked and vulnerable, which I hate doing to my baby – this ain't my viola.

'Manager Kong thanks you for that creative rendition of "Bad Guy",' says Brandon. 'What song would you like to dance to?'

Uh-oh.

'Dance?' I say. 'Sorry, I think there must be some kind of mistake. I only signed up for the singing audition.'

Silence.

'Well, any K-pop idol is going to have to dance.'

By any means necessary, I must avoid dancing in front of these people. 'I'm sorry . . . is this Manager Kong talking, or is it just you?'

'Excuse me?' says Brandon.

I didn't mean to sound bratty, but I heard myself.

25

'I'm sorry, I just don't understand why I need to dance for a singing audition.'

Brandon and Manager Kong confer in Korean. He turns back to me and says, 'You don't have to do anything too crazy. We just wanna see you . . . groove to the music.'

'*Groove?*' I say, at a total loss. 'I'm sorry, I don't understand the assignment . . .'

Before I know it, 'Havana' by Camila Cabello starts up on the movie theatre speaker system. I feel the bassline in my liver.

I freeze.

I literally forget what it's like to be a human being with a body that's connected to my brain. A full verse goes by and I still haven't moved.

Do something, Candace! I scream at myself in my head.

I see the silhouettes of Brandon and Manager Kong shift in their seats. I see the red light of the camera recording this humiliating moment. Suddenly, it's like I'm watching myself from outside my body – I see myself doing finger guns.

What am I even shooting at, other than my chances at a K-pop career? Now, to my horror, I'm doing the cabbage patch. Then the sprinkler. Then the floss. All the lame dances I saw Tommy doing at Aunt SoonMi's wedding in Franklin Lakes last year.

With no other ideas, I imagine what a *RuPaul's Drag Race* contestant would do when she's about to lose a Lip Sync for Your Life and she's desperate to pull a flashy stunt, fast. I can't do a flying split or a death drop or tear off my wig. But I *can* do what almost passes for voguing.

I make forceful gestures with my arms like I'm an air traffic controller in a bad mood – my attempt at waacking. Then I crouch down to a squat and try a duckwalk, which I've seen Ethan do effortlessly a million times, but I quickly realize I don't have the thigh strength to pull it off. The music cuts abruptly just as I'm falling backwards on to my butt.

'Stop!' the translator yelps. 'Manager Kong and S.A.Y. Entertainment thank you for your time.'

I clamber to my feet, totally humiliated. I bow in Manager Kong's general direction and mumble 'thank you' in formal Korean: '*Gamsamnida.*' I grab my guitar and leg it out of the auditorium, sweeping my hair over my face to hide the fact that it's probably as red as a pot of boiling *kimchi jjigae*.

CHAPTER 3

UNKNOWN CALLER

Monday, I feel like I'm dying inside all day. I can't concentrate in AP Bio or Lit, and it's not just because my phone is blowing up non-stop with random spam calls from an unknown number, getting me in trouble with my Bio teacher, Mr Delacorte. At lunch, I can barely swallow down two bites of mac and cheese.

Why didn't I take the audition more seriously?

It's been hitting me every two seconds that this whole K-pop thing actually could have changed my life. I should have tried harder. Why did I try to make it into a joke?

I should have known they'd ask me to dance. Of *course*. I acted like I was too cool for K-pop, when really, I'm not too cool for literally anything. I play the viola, for crying out loud.

After school, Imani, Ethan and I go to my family's convenience store – creatively named Park Family Store – to study for our World History test tomorrow. Abba brings us a plate of

Umma's home-made *yakgwas*. We sell them at the store and the customers love them. They're Korean honey cookies, one of my favourite snacks – stretchy like toffee, chewy like soft-baked cookies and greasy like doughnuts. Imani and Ethan love them too.

'Yasss, *yakgwas* are the *jjang*!' Imani exclaims, reaching for a cookie.

Abba laughs. Imani's appreciation of all things Korean never fails to bring my parents joy. 'Imani,' says Abba, 'are you having bubble tea loyalty card?'

'In fact, Mr Park, I do have my loyalty card,' says Imani, pulling an unused card out of her pocket.

Ever since our store started selling bubble tea – probably the best business move my parents ever made – we've been giving out buy-ten-bubble-teas-get-one-free punch cards.

Abba takes Imani's card, punches ten holes in it all at once and tosses the little bits of paper in the air like confetti. 'Free bubble tea for Imani!' he cheers. Imani bounces up and down and squeals in over-the-top glee as the paper rains down on the table. This is her and Abba's shtick. It's so adorable it makes me sick.

Umma brings out Imani's free oolong milk bubble tea, her favourite, and a peach tea for Ethan, who's lactose intolerant. She leaves a bit of paper at the ends of the straws, so it's like a cap – an Umma touch. 'What are you kids watching?' she asks.

'Just some K-pop videos,' pipes up Ethan before taking a long sip of tea.

SLK is on their Rebel World Tour and just had a concert in Singapore, and the **fancam** videos have popped up all over YouTube.

'Again? Candace, you like this kind of thing too?' asks Umma, pursing her lips.

'Some of it's kind of cool,' I mumble, shrugging.

When she turns around, I scowl at the back of Umma's head. It occurs to me that if she'd actually encouraged my talent instead of treating it like some shameful secret, if I'd taken voice and dance lessons instead of years of useless viola lessons, I would have had the confidence to nail my audition. I'd probably be getting ready to spend a summer in Seoul.

Abba laughs approvingly. 'I am very surprise Candace is liking Korean music,' he says in English. 'I am always thinking Candace is one hundred per cent American girl.'

'Candace is becoming as big of a K-pop stan as I am,' says Imani, in bliss.

Umma swivels around in alarm. I look away quickly.

Imani shows us a bunch of videos of SLK members Joodah and ChangWoo cuddling each other playfully onstage. 'Aww, JooWoo's **skinship** is really becoming a thing on this tour,' says Imani, combining their names.

'"Skinship"?' asks Ethan.

'That's going in the K-Dictionary!' says Imani, turning to the back pages of her World History notebook, where she's writing up 'Imani's Advanced Placement K-Pop K-Dictionary', full of all the jargon and terminology I should know now that I've decided to embrace K-pop.

I heave a sigh, remembering my audition, how quickly I was rushed off the stage. I want to forget about it and focus on my latest discovery: the MV for 'Stun Me Stun You' by QueenGirl.

Seeing those four girls slay while looking fierce beyond words –
especially the lead singer, WooWee – never fails to give me life. I
take my phone from my bag and turn it on.

'I have forty-seven missed calls from an unknown caller,' I say.

'Probably a creeper,' says Ethan. 'Or a secret admirer!'

'Don't answer,' says Umma from behind the counter. She adds
in Korean, 'You can't just trust strange people these days.'

$$\rtimes\!\mathbb{C}$$

Two nights later, my total agony over my audition hasn't gone
away. I try to force it out of my head now that AP exams are
coming up, but the memory of not having a dance prepared for a
K-pop audition makes me want to slap myself.

Over a dinner of *bulgogi* and *ssam*, the conversation at the table
is, of course, all about Tommy's upcoming SATs and my AP
exams. I sigh loudly at the predictability of it all as I roll up a
loose, messy *ssam*.

'What's that lifeless sigh about?' Umma asks in Korean.

'Nothing,' I say, sighing again.

After dinner, Umma gathers Tommy and me around her
phone for our weekly Wednesday night phone call. She has
Harabuji, our grandfather in Korea, on KakaoTalk Video, Korea's
most popular messaging app. I get on my tippy-toes and Tommy
crouches down so we can both fit in the screen. Tommy still hasn't
showered after baseball practice, so he reeks of BO. Harabuji's
face is wobbly on-screen.

'*Anyunghaseyo*,' we say in unison.

'*Uh*,' says Harabuji in his gravelly voice. 'Is it you, kids?'

'Yes,' we say in formal Korean.

I'm not sure if this is something just our Harabuji does, or if it's something all old Korean people do, but it's always struck me as weird that Harabuji always asks 'Is it you?' while looking right at us. It might also be because we're always talking through the phone and he can't see us well. The phone is shaking in his hand. He doesn't look like his usual self – the whites of his eyes are yellowish and his skin has a greyish pallor.

Harabuji points to his chest. '*Nah-neun nu-gu-jee?*' he asks us. *Who might I be?*

'Harabuji,' Tommy and I say in unison.

A look of surprise and delight comes over Harabuji's face. '*Orlchi!*' he bellows.

In Korean, '*orlchi*' means '*that's right!*' or '*attaboy/girl!*' It's something you say to little kids when they do something precocious, like carry a heavy bag of laundry down the stairs by themselves.

This is about as deep as we go with our conversations with Harabuji, probably thanks to the language barrier. It's sweet that Harabuji seems genuinely overjoyed when we're able to correctly identify him as 'Harabuji', even though we're way too old for this to be very impressive. I think he'll always see Tommy as six and me as five, the ages we were the only time we met him in person, the one time he flew here from Seoul.

After saying goodbye to each other several times, we hang up. I give the phone back to Umma, who's doing the dishes in the kitchen with Abba. 'Is Harabuji OK?' I ask. 'He seems a little ... different.'

Umma sighs. 'Harabuji is very sick,' she says, preoccupied.

I wait around for her to say something else. How sick is very sick? Isn't anyone going to go visit him?

But that's apparently the end of the matter. 'Go study,' says Umma. 'If you don't get a five on your AP Biology exam, *kun-il natta.*' *It'll be a huge problem.*

After flipping through my AP Biology practice book for a few minutes, I open up YouTube to get another K-pop fix. The little bell icon in the top right corner has a red dot next to it. I have an alert. Someone new has commented on my video.

I bring up my video, which now has twelve views – I'm sure all from Imani and Ethan and people related to them. The first two comments, I've seen before:

ImaniCharles2003: YAS KWEEEEEEEN
EthanEmery627: You're my Korean Taylor Swift!!!!
😈 🎵 ♥♥♥♥♥♥♥♥♥♥

Then there's a third comment, one I haven't seen yet. It's from a user named S.A.Y. Entertainment. And it's written in Korean.

I swallow a gallon of air. My heart is racing as I sound out the Korean letters (I can't read Korean without moving my lips). After a minute, I work out that it says: *We have been trying to call you, but you will not answer your phone. Do you have KakaoTalk?*

I click on the S.A.Y. Entertainment username to make sure it's the *actual* S.A.Y. Entertainment. Sure enough, it takes me to the official S.A.Y. channel – the channel where SLK's music videos, all of which have over a billion views, get posted.

I go back to my video page, where I respond to the comment in English: *Sorry I've missed your calls! I don't have KakaoTalk but I'll download it right now.*

I can't believe what an idiot I've been – the unknown calls were from S.A.Y! My fingers tremble as I grab my phone. I download KakaoTalk. Even though Umma and Abba use it all the time, I've never had a reason to download it myself.

The very second I activate KakaoTalk, I get a new message alert, which sounds like a baby saying 'peekaboo!'

Warm greetings.

It's in English but from a Korean username, which I sound out as *Kong YeNa*.

This is Manager Kong from S.A.Y. Entertainment.

No way. NO way. The lady from the auditions. The all-business lady in the suit who didn't talk.

I type out awkwardly using the English alphabet:

Anyunghaseyo!

I'm screaming noiselessly and hopping around my room as Manager Kong types for a really long time.

Finally:

I have arrived back to Seoul. I showed the video of your audition to members of the company.

Oh my God. I really wish she hadn't.

> The company executives were very interested. Are you available to speak now?

Am I? I lie down flat on my back on the floor and press my feet against my door. Since I don't have a lock on my door, this is my bootleg way of getting some privacy.

I type,

> I am.

Instantly, my phone is chiming a sing-songy tune. It's a KakaoTalk video call. I hold the phone above my face and answer, hoping Manager Kong doesn't think it's weird that I'm sprawled out on the carpet. Manager Kong appears on my screen, sitting in what looks like a brightly lit conference room. Unlike when I saw her in person, she's barefaced and dressed casually in a black T-shirt and cap.

'*Anyunghaseyo,*' I say, straining to lift my head in a bow.

'Hello, Candace,' she replies in Korean. 'It's good to finally talk to you.'

I don't know how to respond. I'm good at understanding Korean because that's how Umma and Abba have always talked to me, but when it comes to forming sentences on my own, I'm a mess – I've always responded to my parents in English.

So I just say '*Neh,*' which is a formal yes, and an all-purpose silence-filler.

'I was very impressed with your audition,' says Manager Kong. 'You have a very unique, pure voice.'

'*Gamsamnida,*' I say.

35

'Your dancing . . .'

I giggle apologetically. 'Oh, that . . . I'm sorry,' I manage to say in shaky Korean.

Manager Kong grins a little. 'You showed no skill level, but I appreciated how you tried. You showed off your charms.'

I lift my head off the floor in another bow.

'Of course, if you ever hope to debut, you'll have to train very hard. At S.A.Y., we don't find kids who already have all the star qualities. We find kids with potential and make them practise, practise, practise. Very soon, we're debuting our first-ever girl group. I would like to offer you a spot in our trainee programme. We already have many talented female trainees, but our CEO thought we needed another Korean American. Out of more than three thousand people who auditioned in New Jersey, you were the only one who fit our criteria. So what do you say?'

Manager Kong speaks incredibly fast and to-the-point. I don't understand all the words she's saying, but I fill in the meaning in my head of what I'm *pretty sure* she's saying. She checks her watch as she waits for my answer, not realizing that she's turned my entire world upside down.

I clear my throat and say, 'Umm . . . I'm still in school.'

The cold, hard reality falls on my head like a cartoon anvil: Umma and Abba would never in a trillion years let me skip or delay any schooling whatsoever for any reason, let alone to go off on a wild trip to Korea to become a K-pop idol. The reason our family never has any money for anything extra, other than Tommy's sports stuff, my dumb viola lessons, SAT tutoring and computers for homework, is that Umma and Abba are saving every dollar to send me and Tommy off to the best colleges we can get into.

'What grade are you in, tenth?' asks Manager Kong impatiently.

'Yes.'

'Don't American students get summers off? Must be nice. Our CEO wants to choose the final line-ups for the new boy and girl groups at the end of summer. Of course, I think four months of training before debut is way too short, but idols have pulled it off before. If you fail to debut, and you probably will fail – nothing against you personally – you can go back to America and start school again. If you do debut, we can discuss schooling. There are some exceptional international schools in Seoul. So?'

'Umm.' I clear my throat. 'Can I speak to my parents and then get back to you?'

'Fine,' she sighs, seeming annoyed that I didn't agree on the spot to fly to the other side of the world and sign my life away to a Korean music company. 'We can offer you and a parent plane tickets to Seoul, and housing – a trainee dorm for you, a company apartment for your parent. Being a trainee will cost you nothing. You can have your parents call me directly if you want.'

I lick my parched lips. 'Is there a particular time I should call?'

'Call whenever. No one at S.A.Y. ever sleeps.'

I try to read her face to see if she's joking, but she's already hung up.

My head spinning, I get back to my feet. All week, I've been thinking life would be perfect if only I'd passed my audition. Now that I have, I realize I have an even more impossible mission: convincing Umma to let me go.

CHAPTER 4

BAE-JJAE-RA

When I tell Imani and Ethan the news the next day after school, they react exactly as I expect them to. Both scream at the top of their lungs. Ethan does a random headstand. Imani shakes me frantically while shrieking, 'I knew it, I knew it, I knew it, I knew it!'

We're in our usual hang out spot on the grassy knoll outside the cafeteria. It's a beautiful, hot day and seasonal allergies abound. A bunch of Robotics Club kids are making their robots fight each other a few metres away.

'Don't get too excited,' I say. 'As I said at the auditions, my parents will never let me go.'

'Girl, bye,' says Imani. 'You always do this, Candace.'

'Do what?'

'Let your inner saboteur get the best of you,' says Ethan.

'My what?'

'Your inner saboteur,' he repeats. He gets back to his feet, his face flushed, and shifts into his stage monologuing voice. 'The Great RuPaul defines the inner saboteur as the voice inside your head that stirs up your fears, holding you back from trying the things you truly want to do.'

'Listen to Mother RuPaul,' says Imani. 'And Ethan, I guess. Your inner saboteur is alive and well.'

'You keep it healthy on a diet of excuses and low self-esteem,' cracks Ethan.

My friends are totally savage.

'Oh, please.' I scoff, but I feel pinpricks behind my eyes. 'That's not me at all.'

'Really?' says Imani, arching an eyebrow. 'Then why didn't you take the S.A.Y. audition seriously?'

'And why are you still playing that godforsaken viola?' adds Ethan.

'You guys don't get it,' I say. 'You don't know the mother I have.'

'Actually, I do, and she's a literal saint,' says Imani.

'She has a copy of *Battle Hymn of the Tiger Mother* with all the pages dog-eared!' I say, waving my arms wildly.

Imani raises her hands in surrender. 'I'm not gonna fight you on this,' she says. 'I already dragged you to that audition. But I am *no one's* trusty black sidekick.' Ethan lets out an emphatic *Mm-hmm*. 'However,' says Imani, grinning, 'if you do decide you want to go for this – *really* go for it – I'll help you convince your parents. Persuading people is my superpower.'

'And think – if you're a trainee at SLK's company,' says Ethan, 'you'll definitely get to meet One.J!'

)||(

I wait until after church that Sunday to talk to my parents, despite all the frantic KakaoTalk messages I'm getting from Manager Kong.

> I need to know very soon.

> An opportunity like this won't wait for ever.

> Do you have any idea how many kids in Korea would die to be in your position?

After church, once they've changed out of their Sunday best into regular clothes, tends to be when Umma and Abba are in the best moods. Since they don't have a social life during the week, church is like my parents' version of recess. After hours of praying, eating and laughing with all their friends, they're tired out and happy.

I gather Umma and Abba in the living room, announcing that I have something important to tell them.

Right away, Umma is suspicious. She asks, 'You're not going to tell us something strange, are you?'

I can't honestly tell her that I won't. 'Just sit down next to Abba please.'

I stand in front of our TV, which I have my computer hooked up to, and take a deep breath before delivering my carefully rehearsed introduction.

'I've gathered you here today because I want to ask you guys for something that might surprise you. That's why I must ask you kindly to promise not to ask questions or speak until I am finished.'

'I promise,' says Abba right away.

Umma picks at a piece of lint on her sweatpants.

'Umma, I'm looking at you. Say you promise.'

After Abba prods her with his elbow, Umma says, 'Fine, Candace. I promise.'

'Thank you.' I clear my throat. 'So, because what I'll be discussing is complex and multifaceted, I've prepared some visuals to paint a clearer picture.' I turn on the TV. The first PowerPoint slide is already queued up. It's an adorable photo of five-year-old me standing onstage with my fellow kindergarteners, singing 'Away in a Manger' at a church Christmas pageant.

Abba flashes a huge smile and Umma clutches her chest. So far so good.

'I, Candace MinKyung Park, was born in Newark, New Jersey, on 24th August. And as far as I can remember' – I switch the slide to a photo of me dressed as Rapunzel from *Tangled* on Halloween when I was nine, singing 'When Will My Life Begin?' – 'I've always carried a love of music – of singing, especially – in my heart.' I'm not looking at Umma, but I can *feel* her aura darken. 'Whatever talent for singing I possess, I owe it to you, Umma and Abba – I know both of you were once, and still are, brilliant musicians.'

I flash a photo of six-year-old me crying my eyes out while playing a tiny viola – for some reason, Umma and Abba have always found this photo of my genuine anguish particularly adorable. Even now, they can't help but let out an '*Awww*.'

'When I was very young, I was allowed to sing to my heart's content – with the sort of pure innocence and joy only available to children.' That line is all Ethan. 'However, somewhere along the way, I lost that joy. All my life, I was strongly discouraged from pursuing the vocal arts, and instead forced to study the viola – an instrument for which I have neither talent nor passion.'

I switch the slide to my orchestra portrait from seventh grade, peak awkward phase, looking tragically miserable posing with my viola in my hideous uniform.

'Being so bad at the one thing that takes up the majority of my extracurricular time has not only harmed my self-esteem, but it has likely harmed my college chances. What kind of university would be impressed that I've stuck to an activity that's brought me no acclaim?'

My eyes dart to Umma's face. She looks stricken. Horrified. I tell myself this just means my plan is working. I press on.

'Lately, my heart has been screaming for an outlet for my long-hidden desire to sing.' Another Ethan line. 'Just last week, I must confess that I disobeyed your rules, but it was for the ultimate good: I skipped SAT tutoring to go to an audition for a K-pop company at Palisades Park.'

I hear my parents gasp. Umma says, 'What is this—'

'Umma, I said I'll take questions and comments afterwards.'

I switch the photo to a selfie of me, Imani and Ethan among the crowd of hopefuls in the multiplex parking lot. 'Yes, I realize this was wrong, but I knew I would be banned, judged and ridiculed had I told you about my plans. I sang in front of a manager from S.A.Y. Entertainment who flew all the way from Korea to find American talent. Last Monday, she reached out to tell me that out of three thousand people who showed up to audition, I was the only one they chose.'

I explain what a big deal S.A.Y. Entertainment is, how legit it is. I show a photo of SLK – not one of their scary-sexy photos but a nice, clean-cut photo of them in schoolboy uniforms posing in a classroom.

I flash a slide of bullet points:

WHY CANDACE SHOULD BE A K-POP TRAINEE THIS SUMMER
- ♥ Candace will learn a lot of Korean.
- ♥ Candace will make a lot of new friends from all over the world.
- ♥ Candace will gain confidence from seeing Asians become beloved idols. She has not seen enough of this growing up in America.
- ♥ Candace has dutifully suffered playing the viola for ten years.
- ♥ S.A.Y. will provide free airfare and lodging in Seoul for the summer.

The final point, which Imani thought of, is such a good clincher that I give it its own slide:

- ♥ **There is a belief among college admissions officers that Asian applicants don't stand**

out from the crowd. So many have high grades, test scores and play classical instruments much better than Candace ever will! A summer as a K-pop trainee is a unique experience that would make AN EXCELLENT COLLEGE ESSAY.

I end with a photo of me receiving my pink guitar from Abba on my twelfth birthday. My eyes are twinkling with delight and the flames of the candles.

'Thank you for your time,' I say, taking a huge breath. 'Are there any comments or questions?'

Silence. Abba claps awkwardly. Umma is looking off to the side with her arms crossed. That's OK. I expected resistance.

'Umma – you look like you might have something to say.'

Umma spits out, '*Bae-jjae-ra.*' *Over my dead body.* 'This is ridiculous.' The Korean phrase she uses for 'ridiculous' – '*maldo andwae*' – literally means '*these aren't even words*'.

My cheeks are blazing like hot coals under slabs of sizzling *galbi*.

'Why?!' I shout. 'What's so ridiculous? I never ask you for anything. I've never been allowed to do what I really want and I get good grades and I've never complained.'

'You've complained plenty,' says Umma.

'How come Tommy gets to be who he wants and be a sports star and you've never said anything? I get better grades. Is it because he's a boy?'

'How could you say that?' Umma asks in an urgent voice.

44

'That's not why at all. It's because Tommy's sports can help him get into a good college. Help his future.'

'Maybe my singing can too!' I shout.

Umma sucks in her lips. She nods to herself, steeling her nerves.

'If I'm being completely honest, Candace,' she says softly but firmly, 'you have a decent voice, but it's so hard to stand out as a singer. Do you know how many amazing singers and performers there are in Korea? You're such a shy girl and those idols have so much charisma and confidence . . .'

I'm shocked into silence. I've never been so hurt in my life. Abba finally gets to his feet.

'Candace,' he says in Korean, 'I have to say, I'm concerned as well. I've read things in the papers about those idol companies. There's so much corruption and those trainees are so mistreated . . . There are **slave contracts**, I've heard of abuse . . .'

I barely hear Abba. My fury at Umma is bubbling over.

'You're the reason I don't have any confidence,' I say to her, my voice shaking. I'm not even sure that's true, but it feels true in this moment. 'You've tried to take away my one true passion, the only thing that makes me special. Why would you do something so mean to someone unless you hate them? You're angry at *me* because you never became a singer.'

Umma's mouth falls open. She looks completely devastated. The bitter taste of guilt rises to the back of my throat, but I swallow it down.

'This is all too much, Candace,' says Abba. 'Let's talk about this later.'

'Fine!'

I storm to my room and slam the door. I lie on the floor and press my feet against the door. I hear footsteps. Someone turns the doorknob, but I put more strength in my legs. A knock.

'Candace, open this door,' says Umma gently.

'*Bae-jjae-ra*,' I shout.

I know I'll regret saying this to Umma one day. But I glare at the ceiling, realizing I'm not actually mad at Umma; I'm mad at myself. This isn't about viola lessons or not getting to join glee club or not going to Korea to train. This is about being honest about what I really want for once in my life. This is about me being brave.

I pound the door with my foot. I scream even louder, '*Bae-jjae-ra!*'

CHAPTER 5

EYE OF THE SNAPPER

At dinner that night, Umma brings the boiling-hot pot of *doen-jang jjigae* to the table with her bare hands – her skin is seriously made of dragon hide. I want to apologize, but I remember: this is my first time declaring what I really want. I'm not going to back down.

Abba brings out the whole steaming marinated red snapper with the face and tail and everything still attached. This is probably disgusting beyond words to most people, but Tommy and I have this thing where we fight over who gets to eat the fish eye because Umma told us it was good luck when we were little. But tonight, Tommy gets no competition from me. He plucks out the snapper's gooey, grey eyeball with his chopsticks – 'Yoink!' – and pops it into his mouth.

Everyone dips their spoons into the same *jjigae* pot but me. Umma and Abba praise Tommy for his team winning his baseball match. Game. Whatever.

I sit at the table not touching my food, glaring at everyone.

'What's *your* problem?' Tommy asks. 'You've been acting weirder than usual.'

I seethe in silence as Umma studiously ignores me. When no one says anything, I answer loudly, 'My *problem* is, Umma and Abba are stomping on my dreams and ruining my entire life.'

'Whoa. Drama,' Tommy says. He scrapes off a huge slab of tender snapper meat with his spoon. 'What happened?'

'What *happened* is, I put myself out there for once in my life, auditioned for a girl group at SLK's K-pop company, defied all odds and was the one singer out of thousands who passed the audition, and now *Umma's* not letting me go to Korea to train.'

Tommy freezes mid-bite. His mouth is full of food and there's a lone grain of sticky rice clinging to his bottom lip. 'Seriously?' he asks.

There's a silence around the table. Suddenly, my eyes water and my cheeks are volcanic. Again, shame rushes into my blood. Seeing my family's faces – the fact that they now all know that I think I could possibly become a K-pop idol, that they know I *want* such a thing – is so horrifyingly embarrassing.

'It's stupid, I know,' I say quietly.

'Actually, that's pretty cool,' says Tommy.

'Really?' I stare at Tommy, totally shocked.

'Yeah.' He's already devoured half of the snapper, which was about the size of a corgi. 'I mean, I'm not that surprised. You're obviously a really good singer.'

'I am?'

This may very well be the first compliment Tommy has ever given me during my fifteen years on this planet.

'I mean, yeah,' he says. 'Everyone knows that. Plus, I hear you through the wall all the time. That song you wrote ... the "Expectations and Whatever" ... it's a little cheesy, but I can see people paying money to hear it. Not a lot, but some.'

Umma finally comes to life, waving this whole notion away. 'Don't encourage such nonsense,' she snaps. 'Those Korean music companies are evil – they ruin lives. Most of them never even pay their idols and work them like crazy.'

Imani has prepped me well for this debate. 'The companies are getting a lot better about that,' I say. 'Besides, S.A.Y. is the most successful company in Korea and can afford to pay idols once they debut. They're known for being one of the good ones. I mean, look at SLK.'

Umma purses her lips. 'Candace, you're very talented at singing. I've always known this about you. But why does it need to be anything more than your hobby? Do you know how lucky you are that all you have to do is work hard in school? That's all you have to do to have a career where your thoughts and skills will be your value, unlike your *abba* and me.'

Her face droops with sadness. I wonder what Umma thinks her 'value' is. I want to tell her that despite the things I yelled at her last night, her value has nothing to do with what she does. She's the most valuable person in the world because she's Umma.

She taps the table once. Her face instantly snaps back to her usual determined expression. 'The fact is, Candace, that becoming a singer isn't going to help your future – like I said last night, it's not like Tommy's baseball, which can help him get into a good school, which will help him get a good job. Your *abba* and I work so hard so you can do something respectable and useful to others. It's an opportunity we never had.'

Abba clears his throat. He has a sad, contemplative smile on his face. He pats Umma's hand. '*Yubboh*,' he says, *dear*. 'That's not why we work so hard, you know that. We work so hard so Tommy and Candace can live for what makes them truly happy. *That's* the opportunity we never had.'

I bite my lips to hold in my tears. Tommy pats my shoulder awkwardly with one hand while continuing to stuff his face with his other.

'Candace, don't cry,' Umma says sternly. 'Look at me.' She puts down her chopsticks and searches my eyes. 'This is really your passion?'

I nod. Sobs stuck in my throat, I manage to get out my prepared argument. 'Umma, just give me the summer, please. The S.A.Y. exec says they're a few months away from debuting their new girl group. Then, if I don't get picked to debut – and of course I won't—'

'Yes, you will,' says Umma. 'If you go, of course they'll pick you. Who's more talented or special than you?'

For a second, I'm totally overwhelmed by this unprecedented vote of confidence. I stare at Umma in wonder.

Abba says, 'Candace of course has the talent.'

'All right, all right, let's not go crazy here,' says Tommy.

'But Candace,' says Abba, 'there's so much you don't under-stand about Korean culture and the Korean mindset. As an

American girl, you can't know. Things are difficult for young people in Korea right now. Getting into colleges and getting jobs is so competitive there and it'll be the same for debuting as an idol. I think you'll be surprised just how hard a Korean trainee is willing to work, whether or not they have your natural gifts. To them, becoming a K-pop idol might not just be a dream or a passion like it is to you. It might be their only hope at a future.'

'I would work so hard,' I say. 'Harder than I've ever worked in my life.'

Umma picks up her chopsticks again, grabs the last hunk of snapper meat left and puts it in my rice bowl.

'I'm not saying yes,' she says with a sigh. 'We have to think about it and we certainly need to talk to someone at S.A.Y.'

'Totally,' I say, nodding eagerly. I can't contain the biggest smile as I take my first bite of dinner.

CHAPTER 6

INTO THE NEW WORLD

I still haven't got a yes, but the following week, Umma and Abba speak over KakaoTalk with Manager Kong for hours at the kitchen table as I try to listen in from the living room. After their long video calls, Umma and Abba go on and on about what a nice person Manager Kong is. This confuses me, because Manager Kong strikes me as a lot of things, but nice isn't one of them.

S.A.Y. sends over their trainee contract for my parents to look at. Both my parents, but especially Umma, hate signing contracts and this one is literally seventy pages long. Umma asks the ladies in her Bible study group if anyone knows a lawyer in Korea and it turns out Deaconness Min, my friend Jinny's mom, has a cousin's wife's brother who understands the crazy-complicated Korean entertainer contracts. Umma convinces him over KakaoTalk to look at mine and he says it's pretty standard. Yes, the company will totally own my time while I'm a trainee, but it doesn't try to pull any insane tricks, such as keep kids under contract for seventeen years, like some of the smaller K-pop companies might do.

What really worries Umma and Abba is a clause in the contract that says S.A.Y. can delay making a decision about the final girl group line-up way past late August and during that time, I'll still be trapped in the company as a trainee. Umma and Abba insist on changing it so I'm allowed to leave S.A.Y. if they haven't made a decision by August 29 – the day before the first day of my junior year at Fort Lee Magnet.

Umma and Abba stay up late one night to negotiate this point with Manager Kong and the S.A.Y. lawyers. The lawyers put up a huge fuss, saying that they can't agree to that, that they've never made an exception like that for anyone before in the history of the company. But Umma and Abba are adamant.

For an entire week, S.A.Y. goes completely silent.

To my surprise, I'm actually kind of relieved. There's something comforting about being able to continue with my regular life, knowing I had the talent, knowing S.A.Y. wanted me, without *actually* having to go to Seoul to prove myself.

But I also know that there's a fire within me that won't let me admit this out loud. When Umma and Abba check in with me, asking if I still want this, I keep saying yes.

Finally, on a Sunday afternoon, S.A.Y. calls Umma and Abba back. While we're still in our church clothes, they sit me down at the kitchen table.

'S.A.Y. has agreed to our deadline of twenty-ninth August,' says Umma, pressing her lips together firmly. 'Their only condition: if you quit their trainee programme before that date and they still haven't chosen the girls to debut, we will be billed for the full cost of your training, which will be tens of thousands of dollars. I don't tell you that to say you can't quit early – if they mistreat you or you're unhappy, we want you to quit right away. We will find a way to pay the price. We just want to make sure you're serious about this. That this is really your dream.'

I'm shook. In no scenario did I see this working out. I nod my head slowly.

We work out a plan – or really, they do, as I listen with my mouth hanging open: the day after my last AP exam, I'll fly to Seoul with Umma. Umma will stay in an apartment in Seoul, paid for by S.A.Y., the entire time I'm training at the facilities. Umma will take that time to take care of Harabuji, whose condition is getting worse; he'll probably have to be moved to a hospital. For the first month, I won't be able to see Umma or even leave the training facilities at all while I get acclimatized to trainee life. After that, I'll be able to spend Saturday nights and all day Sunday with Umma each week, but that will be the only break from training I'll get. Back home, Abba will take care of the store by himself with help from Tommy, who's staying in Jersey for the summer for football camp.

'Does this sound good?' Abba asks.

Suddenly, I burst into tears. I sob in Korean, 'Yes, this is everything I want.'

Umma and Abba are shocked by my reaction. 'Why are you crying?' asks Abba.

'I'm crying because I'm so happy,' I blubber, even though that's not exactly true. I'm crying because I'm amazed they're willing to let me do this. I'm crying because I can't believe I thought Umma kept me away from singing because she didn't love me enough.

Umma comes around the table and holds my head against her body. 'We just want our Candace to be joyful,' she says.

Every night for the next three weeks, I have a panic attack about how much my family is sacrificing to let me go. My parents are going against everything they believe about parenting, and the American dream, to let me do this. I feel so grateful and unworthy that most nights, I cry myself to sleep. I can't help but think a huge reason Umma is going through with this is so she can take care of Harabuji in Korea. There's nothing good about Harabuji being sick, but it *is* making all this feel like it's really going to happen. Knowing this fills me with too much guilt to handle.

I study for my end-of-year exams harder than I've ever studied in my life and I end up acing them, even Honours Precalculus, the exam I was most worried about. I get fives on my AP Bio and Lit exams. I do extra work at the store. I even practise the viola a little.

Before she's off to volunteer digging latrines in Paraguay for the summer, Imani schools me even harder on K-pop history, going all the way back to the beginning of the modern hip-hop era, with H.O.T. and S.E.S. and Shinhwa from the nineties. I cram as much Korean language as I can, watching K-dramas with Umma and Abba after dinner most nights – they couldn't pay me to watch them in the past.

When S.A.Y. sends over a packet of fifty song lyrics I should know before I arrive (twelve of them are American songs, three of them by Ariana Grande, thank goodness), Umma even goes over them with me during slow moments at the store. 'You need to understand the meaning of every word to know how to perform it,' she says while we dissect the lyrics for 'Into the New World', Girls' Generation's debut single from 2007. 'This song is about beginning a journey that's sure to be long and uncertain, yet moving forward with courage, knowing you have a heart full of hope and love.'

'Wow, really?'

I've watched the 'Into the New World' MV with Imani, who told me it's a girl group classic that I'd probably have to sing a bunch of times as a trainee. But it struck me as a bubblegum pop song sung by nine adorable, smiley girls who looked like they were in the fifth grade. I had no idea it was so deep.

'Make sure you're thinking about that meaning when you sing the chorus,' says Umma. Then she clears her throat and sings the lines for me.

I'm speechless. I've only heard Umma sing a handful of times in my life; she barely sings above a whisper during hymns at church. Her voice is rich, coats my ears and raises goosebumps on my skin. I'm so glad she's coming with me on this journey, just like the song says.

Just after she finishes singing, a tired-looking blonde woman comes in to buy some ibuprofen and order a taro bubble tea. Umma mixes the tea for her like nothing happened.

Tommy, Abba, Imani and Ethan all come to Newark Airport to see us off. I almost wish they wouldn't. What if this is a total disaster and I have to come back in a week, full of shame? I mean, I'm probably going to fail: I speak terrible Korean and I can't dance!

But even scarier, what if I actually get picked? Will I have to enrol in a Korean international school in September? Will this be the last time I see these people in a long, long time?

After Umma's two massive suitcases are checked in – one is entirely full of random things that are better and cheaper in America that our Korean relatives and friends want, like Starbucks coffee beans, multivitamins and batteries – it's time to say goodbye. Tommy leans over to hug me, draping his long arms around me. As always, he smells like deodorant and BO. 'Are you going to come back some evil K-pop nightmare?' he asks.

'Probably,' I say.

Imani and Ethan have gifts for me. Imani gives me a handmade book, titled *Imani's Advanced Placement K-Pop K-Dictionary*, decorated in glitter and stickers. 'Since you're not going to have internet in there, this is your K-pop Google, with the Imani touch.'

Ethan gives me a cute pencil tin covered in photos of SLK, Blackpink, QueenGirl, Twice, 2NE1 and Girls' Generation. 'To help you visualize and actualize who you're going to be some day,' he says.

'How am I going to survive over there without you guys?' I say, blinking a lot.

'That's easy,' says Imani. 'When you're really going through it, think to yourself: What would Imani do?'

'That and remember to silence that inner saboteur,' says Ethan.

Imani beams at me proudly. 'Shall we do one last Diversity Hug?'

We huddle up and press our foreheads against each other. I'm really gonna miss these two weirdos.

Now it's time to say bye to Abba. 'Do well over there, but not too well,' he jokes, pinching my nose; everyone says we have the same nose. 'Have fun and learn a lot, OK?'

'OK, Abba.'

I strap my pink guitar on to my back. Umma and I each take one handle of my overstuffed duffel bag – half of it is just MulKogi – as we step on to the escalator. I look back at the people I'm leaving behind and my heart swells. Imani and Ethan are jumping up and down and cheering and holding up V fingers like K-pop fangirls. Tommy has his arm around Abba's shoulder. Abba's wiping his eyes on his sleeve.

Umma grasps my arm suddenly, looking as unsure as I'm feeling inside.

'Candace,' she says, short of breath, 'you said this experience will make a good college essay, right? I'm doing the right thing by letting you go?'

'Of course,' I say, forcing myself to smile confidently. 'I can handle this.'

CHAPTER 7

KOREANS EVERYWHERE

My first few hours in Seoul, I think my brain might explode from sensory overload. Umma seems just as overwhelmed – her eyes pop out over every little thing, from the miles-long bridge we have to cross in our cab to leave Incheon Airport to the grand, sprawling skyline in the distance. She repeats over and over, 'This is so different from the last time I saw it.'

As for me, the thing I can't get over is how *Korean* everything is. Koreans, Koreans, everywhere. My part of New Jersey is one of the most Korean parts of the United States, but it's such a weird feeling to know wherever I go, there's absolutely zero chance I'll be in the minority. We drive through what Umma tells me is Gangnam – from the PSY song! – and everywhere we look, there are billboards of flawless, smiling women advertising make-up, fashion brands, *soju* and plastic surgery.

And then I see him.

'Umma, look!' I exclaim, pointing up at the sky.

There's a massive video ad of One.J in LED lights holding a sports drink called Elektro Hydrate blasting from the side of a skyscraper. One.J's face must be thirty metres tall. One.J winks and flashes a bright white smile, which fries my retinas. My insides feel like they've turned into the creamiest, most refreshing frozen yoghurt. Could One.J be any more perfect?!

'*Nah-lee ga nasseo,*' Umma says wearily. *Everyone's gone nuts for him.*

I see flocks of kids in school uniforms, most of whom have the classic Korean schoolkid bowl-cut hairstyle, laughing and gossiping. I wish I could tell what they're talking about. Perhaps their favourite idols or how mean their teachers are – just like me and my friends. I think how they look like me but seem so foreign – how if things had gone a little differently, I could easily have been one of them.

When we finally get to the corporate housing where Umma will be living, I notice that the neighbourhood isn't nearly as swanky as Gangnam. I expected the S.A.Y. corporate apartments to be a little nicer, but they're short grey buildings that are blackened with smog. Inside, her apartment turns out to be a tiny one-bedroom with a peeling fake-tiled floor and no space for a dining table. Still, it's cosy enough.

As soon as we put down our bags, Umma grins and claps her hands. 'So! We're here! What should we do first? We can go to a cool cafe – Korea has the best cafes in the world. Or we can go shopping in Myeong-dong or see Gyeongbokgung Palace. We can even go to Lotte World!'

I tell her I don't really feel like doing anything. I just want to learn the fifty S.A.Y.-approved songs and stay close to her – if we go anywhere, I want to see Harabuji, who's been moved from his apartment to a hospital. We have less than twenty-four hours before I have to report to the S.A.Y. headquarters; Manager Kong's been blowing up both our KakaoTalks, saying I'm losing precious training time the longer we delay.

Umma seems relieved and surprised. 'There's such a fun city out there and you want to see your *harabuji* first? What a good granddaughter.'

Before we leave for the hospital, Umma fixes her hair and puts on lipstick and makes sure I'm wearing an unwrinkled shirt – it's our first time seeing Harabuji in person in a long, long time. We take the bright and clean subway to get to Harabuji's hospital, which is full of friendly nurses and stressed-out doctors. As stupid as this sounds, I still can't believe how *everyone* I've seen on the way here is Korean.

When we get to Harabuji's room, he immediately shouts, 'It's you!'

Umma runs to his side and hugs him gently, avoiding the tubes in his nose. 'Abba!' she shouts, wiping her tears.

Harabuji laughs and says in his deep, scratchy voice, 'Why are you crying? Seeing you two makes me very happy.'

He turns to me. The parts of his eyes that should be white are a bright, shocking yellow, but his smile is still cheery and energetic. We go through our whole *'Nahn noogoo-jee?'* – *Who might I be?* – routine, the same one we've done every week for as long as I remember.

'*You're Harabuji!*' I say. '*I'm Candace!*'

Umma gives him updates on Tommy and Abba and tells him I'm here to become a *gasu* – a singer – which apparently is news to him. He looks at me in wonder. '*Wah!*' he says. 'Just like your mom. Your mom is the best singer, you know that?'

'Ah, Abba, that was so long ago,' says Umma, embarrassed.

'Candace! Sing something for your *harabuji*,' he says, clapping his hands.

I laugh awkwardly. I hate being put on the spot like this, but I figure I better get used to this if I'm going to be an idol trainee. And how can I say no to my sick *harabuji*? I close my eyes and sing a few lines of 'Into the New World'.

Harabuji's yellow eyes are glistening when I finish. '*Wah*, how amazing. And you even sang in Korean. Yes, this talent of yours runs in our family. Yes, you're going to be a famous, beloved *gasu*. I know it.'

He nods to himself, totally certain about this fact, and I bow my thanks. I hope the people at S.A.Y. are this easy to impress.

)|(C

After a sleepless night – me in the bed, Umma on the couch – the day arrives. Over breakfast, Umma is already asking me what I want for lunch. She offers to cook me a massive feast of my favourite foods or take me to a *jokbal* restaurant. But I don't want anything fancy. My stomach is rumbly with nerves anyway. 'How about black bean noodles?' I say.

I start stuffing my clothes into my giant duffel bag, but Umma takes everything back out to refold it. 'Do it nicely,' she says. I start to complain, but I stop myself – I know that soon enough, I'm going to miss these Umma touches.

'Oh, I almost forgot,' Umma says. She goes to the kitchen and brings a stack of *yakgwas*, wrapped prettily in blue plastic and tied with a ribbon. 'I couldn't sleep last night, so I made these. Your favourite.' She buries them in my duffel bag, deep under all my clothes.

'I don't think I can take those in there,' I say, remembering Imani's warning about how strict K-pop diets can get.

Umma waves away my worries. 'Just tell them they're a reminder of home. I'm sure they'll understand.'

I take the *yakgwas* out of my duffel bag and put them inside my guitar instead – actually *inside* the sound hole, behind the strings, where hopefully no one will be able to find them.

When we leave the apartment, I have my guitar strapped to my back and Umma lugs my duffel bag for me. The whole subway ride, which takes us across the Han River, Umma squeezes my hand silently.

When we get off at the Hongik University station, I can tell it's a hip neighbourhood. There are young people bustling everywhere: lovey-dovey couples in matching outfits zipping by on mopeds, board game cafes, karaoke rooms, PC rooms, tons of adorable coffee shops – including a poop-themed cafe with mugs shaped like toilets! – skincare boutiques, street performers and vintage record stores, all stacked up on top of each other everywhere you turn.

We find a black bean noodle shop instantly – there are, like, seven on each block. We can't look each other in the eye because we know we might start crying.

I look at my phone instead. All the way from Paraguay, Imani has KakaoTalked me a link to a story on the blog Koreaboo. Apparently, QueenGirl, my favourite girl group, is in the middle of a huge scandal that all of K-pop fandom is freaking out about: 'QUEENGIRL MEMBER ISEUL ADMITS TO DATING HYUNTAEK OF RUBIKON!!'

I type back:

> Ugh who caressssss

In all my time following K-pop, one thing I've never understood is fans' obsession with idols dating, and why dating is always equated with scandal, no matter how innocent. I scroll through the Koreaboo article, which speculates that the future of Queen-Girl and RubiKon, a lesser-known boy band, is in jeopardy. Even WooWee, the Main Vocal and Centre of QueenGirl and probably the hottest female idol in K-pop right now, may lose her contract – all because her bandmate Iseul and HyunTaek got caught holding hands in public. They're two ridiculously attractive, consenting adults and QueenGirl is killing it right now. What's the big deal?

Umma brings me back to reality. 'Even though they won't let me see you for the first month,' Umma says, 'remember that I'll just be a subway ride away. The first month will fly by anyway. You'll learn so much and meet so many new friends. You won't miss me at all.'

Umma nods her head firmly. I know she's convincing herself

more than me.

We walk to Sangam-dong. The S.A.Y. headquarters isn't hard to find. I was expecting a cool building, but I wasn't expecting a massive, gleaming glass skyscraper jutting into the atmosphere in the middle of an expansive plaza of other glass skyscrapers.

The lump that's been growing in my throat all day is practically choking me by the time we walk into the lobby, which is swarming with men in expensive-looking suits and women in black business outfits, all walking fast and typing on their phones. Dozens of screens flash news shows, stock market numbers, K-dramas and SLK MVs. There's a long line in front of a futuristic coffee bar called Cafe Tomorrow.

A woman breaks off from the swarm and struts right up to us. 'Candace?' she says.

I don't recognize her at first. Umma lets out a surprised yelp and we both bow. Manager Kong is not wearing any make-up, but her skin is spotless and smooth. She's dressed in a casual (but still chic) black tracksuit and a baseball cap, both emblazoned with the S.A.Y. logo.

'Welcome, Candace. Welcome, Mrs Park,' she says with a big smile. 'So glad you made it OK. Are you ready, Candace?'

I'm so not. It all feels so sudden.

'Manager Kong, can we have a moment?' asks Umma, gesturing to me.

'Of course,' says Manager Kong, her smile disappearing as she steps away to tap furiously at her phone.

Umma holds my face in her hands.

'Candace.' She bites her lip to keep from crying. I do too. 'I need to say one last thing to you, OK?' She looks into my eyes intently, her face on the verge of crumpling. 'If anyone in there bothers you or hurts you, please find a way to tell me.' I try to pull away from her; I don't want to lose it right here in the lobby, but she squeezes my hands tighter. 'I hope they know that your *abba* and I are leaving our hearts behind in this building.' She gestures to the soaring lobby ceiling. 'Make sure they treat you like you're someone's dearest. That's what you are.'

'All right, Umma.' I break away and pick up my bag again. If I don't run inside now, I'll grab on to Umma's leg and hold on for dear life, like I did on my first day of preschool. 'I'll be OK. I love you.'

Umma runs her fingers through my hair one last time. 'You are worth so much,' she tells me. 'No one in there can decide your value.'

I nod and rush to join Manager Kong, who scans me through the turnstiles with her security card, which she's wearing around her neck. She explains to a guard that I'm the new idol trainee, that I'm here to surrender my phone. Surrender my freedom.

I hand over my phone like I'm handing over my heart. I'm going to miss all those *Friends* and *Queer Eye* episodes that got me through the fourteen-hour flight. As the guard inspects my duffel bag and my guitar case closely, rifling through all my underwear and T-shirts, I hold my breath – but to my relief, he doesn't look *inside* the guitar itself. He disappears into a back room with my phone. I turn back one last time and see Umma standing alone. She looks like the only real person in this lobby, which is as sterile as a space station with all its monitors, flashing lights and important people rushing around. Her eyes are full; she has a hand on her chest.

I step into the mirror-walled elevator. Manager Kong pushes the button for the ninety-eighth floor. I lean against the corner, picturing Umma going back to that dark little apartment alone. I scrunch all my facial muscles to keep from crying.

'Don't look so sad,' says Manager Kong. She sounds almost bored. Her reflection looks at mine. 'The best thing anyone can do for their family is to become someone. That's what you're here to do.'

PART 2
THAT TRAINEE LIFE

CHAPTER 8

THE *UNNIES*

We're greeted on the ninety-eighth floor by S.A.Y.'s giant logo and huge framed photos of each member of SLK, One.J.'s perfect face smouldering from the middle. For a second, I forget my sadness and nerves – it's like One.J's gaze releases a ball of butterflies inside me. The reality that I'm in the hallowed halls that made One.J the perfect being that he is sweeps over me.

I shake myself out of One.J's spell and run to catch up with Manager Kong as she leads me past glass-walled offices and conference rooms where very hip, well-dressed people are working. The building is ridiculously nice, which I wasn't assuming it would be – Imani told me even some of the biggest superstar idols had to train in cruddy basements. Manager Kong answers my question before I have the chance to ask. 'We're a part of ShinBi Unlimited,' she says. 'That's why we're in this amazing building. You're very lucky to be a trainee at S.A.Y. and not somewhere else.'

She explains further that ShinBi Unlimited owns hundreds of other companies: TV networks, grocery chains, film studios, home appliance lines and all sorts of random industries, even companies that make missiles and tanks for the Korean military. S.A.Y.'s corporate offices and trainee centre occupy the top three floors of ShinBi Unlimited's headquarters because, as Manager Kong says proudly, trainees are ShinBi's most prized assets – not because K-pop brings in the most money, but because idols, especially SLK, are the image of the company, facing not just Korea but the entire globe.

My whole body's tingling. I truly thought being an idol was just about singing catchy songs and looking fierce in MVs, not representing a bajillion dollar corporation and a whole country.

'That's why our standards for idols' behaviour are so high,' says Manager Kong, 'and why our number one rule for trainees is: absolutely no dating. Not other trainees, not regular boys, no one.'

'I understand,' I pant as Manager Kong scans us through another security clearing.

Manager Kong goes on, 'In Korea, K-pop idols belong to the fans, to the country. Think of it as you're in a serious, committed relationship with your fans. It's not like Hollywood, where dating around and bad behaviour are celebrated. Imagine how ruinous it would be to your own reputation, to your group and to the entire company if you're caught cheating on the Korean people. You must always maintain a pure image.'

Whoa. OK, got it – K-pop fans are intense about their fandom. This explains why fans are freaking out so hard about Iseul and HyunTaek.

K-pop **dating bans** aren't actually a big deal to me. Since I've never dated a boy before – unless if you count freshman year, when I 'dated' Ethan for a week before he came out – I'm not about to start while I'm locked away in a girls' dorm for three months.

'This is S.A.Y.'s corporate floor, where all the offices are. You'll come here for Language class, special meetings and monthly assessments only. This is also the floor where our junior trainees practise.'

We pause next to a big practice room where dozens of freak-ishly adorable little kids are doing cutesy K-pop moves. Seriously, each one must have been selected from a child modelling agency.

'The juniors go to regular school and live with their families, obviously. Many of your fellow trainees have been with S.A.Y. since they were the age of these little ones. The two floors above us are the training facility for senior trainees, where you'll be living and practising. Those floors are separated down the middle – the north side is for boy trainees, south for girls. They have separate stairwells, elevators, separate security. It's impossible to get from one side to the other, so don't you dare try. Think of those floors as two slabs of tofu that have been cut down the middle with a knife.'

'I understand, Manager Kong,' I say in my most obedient voice.

'The only interaction you'll have with boy trainees is with a few in your Korean Language class, but even that will be closely supervised by Teacher Lee, who's extremely strict. Understand?'

'I understand,' I say.

To calm myself down, I wave to one of the junior trainees. Her whole face brightens. She and her friends rush closer to the glass wall to bow and wave to me frantically. My heart swells . . . and breaks a little.

'Isn't that cute?' says Manager Kong, cracking a smile. 'They think you're somebody important.'

I wave goodbye to the adorable trainees as Manager Kong leads me past a nondescript door. If Manager Kong didn't point it out, I wouldn't have seen it at all. 'Behind that door is what we call the Fantasy Factory. There's a whole team of some of the most talented Korean stylists, costume designers, set designers and other artists in there creating **Concepts** for MVs and world tours for our artists, plus the two new groups that haven't even been chosen yet. They're the ones making sure our artists have the most innovative and awe-inspiring Concepts the world has ever seen.'

I nod appreciatively and say, '*Wah!*'

She leads me up a dark stairwell. There's so much new information that I'm getting light-headed.

'There are fifty boy trainees hoping to debut in SLK 2.0,' she says, 'and fifty girls trying to debut in our first girl group. And this is after we've cut hundreds of trainees already. The girl trainees are divided into ten teams of five girls each. Each team has elements that CEO Sang wants in the final line-up, but he'll choose only the best of the best. Every month, there will be a trainee assessment, where CEO Sang will make important decisions.'

At the top of the stairs is a sturdy metal door – it looks like it belongs on a submarine or in a bank vault – with a pink number '99' on it. I sound out the Korean words under '99' and realize it says *'female practice-people'*. Or 'girl trainees'. Manager Kong scans her ID card and I have to help her open the door – it's super heavy.

Floor ninety-nine is much less fancy than the corporate floor. It looks kind of like a college dorm, a hallway of doors decorated with girls' names and photos.

'You'll be on Team Two,' says Manager Kong. 'You're lucky. Up until recently, I wouldn't have been surprised if CEO Sang decided just to make Team Two the final group – everyone knows Team Two has some of the most promising talents and Visuals. But then we lost a member.'

A dark look comes over Manager Kong's face.

'Lost her? How did you lose her?' I ask.

She brushes me off. 'Not important. Anyway, instead of just moving another trainee into Team Two, I decided to recruit a brand-new girl. Team Two knows they're special and they're getting complacent. I wanted to find a girl who'd really challenge them.'

I'm totally confused. What about my audition would make Manager Kong think I'd be a *challenge* to the top girls?

'You're in the best hands with Team Two. I manage five of the trainee teams, so I won't be able to supervise everything. You're the *maknae*, so you'll learn a lot from your *unnies*. There's even another American girl on the team.'

Before I can ask anything else, we've arrived at Team Two's dorm. Manager Kong knocks on the door twice and throws it open before anyone responds.

The dorm is smaller than my room at home, but there are two

sets of bunk beds plus one other bed and no windows. It looks like a very girly bomb has gone off, scattering mounds of tops and pants and make-up and skincare products all over.

Amid the piles of debris are three of the most gorgeous creatures I've ever seen. They jump to attention and bow to greet Manager Kong.

'Girls, listen up,' says Manager Kong. 'Welcome your new Team Two member, Park Candace.'

I give a deep bow, hinging my body at ninety degrees. I say *'Anyunghaseyo,'* the formal word for '*hello*'.

The girl in the far corner, who looks kind of like a cartoon character, flashes me a twinkly smile. She's wearing heavy eyeliner and has two bushy pigtails streaked with pink and blue that look like they're straight out of an anime. A girl who's rocking black lipstick and a black trucker hat that inexplicably says POWDER PUP lifts her chin at me; she has the one non-bunk-bed. And the most stunning girl of all, whose long cascading locks of hair have been dyed a delicate strawberry blonde, barely even looks at me as she mumbles, *'Anyung.'*

'Candace is your *maknae*, your little sister, and she has a lot to learn from you. You're probably thinking of her as your new competition, but it will only reflect well on you to be good *unnies* to her. Understand?'

'Yes, Manager Kong,' say the girls in unison.

Manager Kong looks around the room. 'Where's Aram?'

'She's doing her beauty routine,' says Powder Pup Hat with a grin and eye roll, cocking her head towards a door in the back of the room.

Manager Kong rolls her eyes too and says, 'Of course. Anyway, meet upstairs in Practice Room Twenty-Four in ten minutes. Be nice to Candace. And *jebal*, clean this room!'

Just like that, Manager Kong leaves me alone with my new *unnies*. I'm so intimidated, I'm afraid to move.

'That's your bed right there,' says Powder Pup, pointing to the bunk above Strawberry Blonde Princess. I would never have known the bunk was free, since it's piled with junk.

I bow to Powder Pup. It's weird bowing to girls who are only a little older than me. At home, I only use formal language with Koreans my parents' age and even then, they let you get away with not-totally-perfect manners. But Umma and Abba warned me that in a K-pop company, I should always use honorifics, address older female trainees as *unnie*. No one's going to cut me slack on manners for being foreign.

I step on to the bunk bed ladder and carefully clear a spot on my mattress to put down my guitar. I peek down at Strawberry Blonde Princess. 'Sorry to bother you,' I say in a soft voice. 'Is any of this stuff yours?'

She doesn't look up. She's sitting on her bed, her glossy milky-white legs stretched out in front of her, hyper-focused on her fingernails, which are shaped into pointy claws, each a different shade of glittery neon.

I clear my throat. '*Unnie*, I don't want to move anything if it's yours.'

Still no response. Next to Strawberry Blonde Princess's bed, I spot all seven *Harry Potter* books, plus *Daring Greatly* by Brené Brown and *The Life-Changing Magic of Tidying Up* by Marie

Kondo. I perk up. This must be the girl from America.

She looks like she'd ignore me in the hallways if we went to the same school, but I can't say how relieved I am that I'm rooming with someone I can speak English with. The fact that she likes wizards and self-help books is icing on the cake.

I point to the *tidying up* book. 'I've read that one too,' I say in English. 'If it's not too much trouble, I'm gonna have to ask you, *unnie*, to tidy up just enough so I can put my bag down.'

I giggle nervously at my own stupid joke. Strawberry Blonde Princess's eyes dart up at me with a look of pure confusion.

'I'm sorry, are you talking to me?' she asks loudly in Korean.

She pulls out her earbuds. I didn't see them under her curtain of luscious tresses.

'Oh, yes, sorry. I was just admiring your taste in books. I've read all of these too. Harry Potter's dope.'

She leans away from me as if I'm some raving lunatic. 'Are you speaking to me in English?'

'Oh, I'm sorry,' I stammer, switching back to Korean. 'I just saw you had books in English, and—'

'Were you an orphan adopted by Americans or something?' she asks, brow furrowed. 'Your accent is so ... mixed up.'

'No,' I say, mortification nuking my cheeks. 'I'm from the States, but my parents are Korean. And alive.'

Powder Pup cuts in, 'Don't mind Helena, she's messing with you.' She smiles. So Strawberry Blonde Princess has a name. 'Helena's as American as they come – from a place in California called Newport Beach.'

Powder Pup's Korean accent is so strong it sounds like she's

78

saying 'Newport B-word'.

'My name is Binna, by the way,' she says.

'And I'm JinJoo!' pipes in Anime Pigtails, who's been practising vocal scales. She has a great voice.

I don't know how to express how thankful I am that Binna and JinJoo are being nice to me. I bow for, like, the twentieth time since entering the room.

'I *actually* don't speak any English, even though I understand a lot,' says Binna in a distinctively deep voice.

'My parents speak to me in Korean so I understand it pretty well,' I explain. 'But I grew up talking back to them in English, so I'm not the best speaker.'

Binna nods. By Korean standards, Binna is the least conventionally pretty girl of the three – her skin isn't milky white, and she has a sturdy, square jaw – but in a way, she's the most striking. She has an aura. I instantly feel at ease.

'Well, we've been told not to speak any English with you,' Binna says. 'Helena is the type to follow rules – when they suit her, that is.'

Just then, another girl emerges from the bathroom, her face glistening. This must be Aram. She says, 'So when's the new Westerner getting here?'

Binna catches Aram's eye and she realizes, startled, that I'm right here. I immediately go into a deep bow and when I come up, I get my first direct look at her face. My mouth falls open.

This is, hands down, the most stunning girl I've ever seen in my life. About two seconds earlier, I would have said that about Helena, but Aram is from-another-universe beautiful. If Helena would be the prettiest girl in any high school, this girl is a fairy-tale queen, Maleficent's fairer, younger Asian rival. With her sharp cheekbones, marble skin and electric-blue **circle lenses**, it's impossible to guess how old she is – she could be anywhere from sixteen to thirty.

'Aram, this is Park Candace,' says Binna.

Aram sizes me up from head to toe with her Siberian husky eyes. She lets out a snort as if to say, *Oh, so I had nothing to worry about* and turns away without a word, her silky, jet-black hair swishing in the air. Suddenly, I want to curl up in a ball and call Umma to come pick me up.

Binna sighs and chuckles. 'You'll have to excuse the girls, Candace. The trainee whose bed you're taking over was like a sister to us for the past two years. She got cut from the company yesterday, which was a shock. It'll take us a while to get used to the new dynamic.'

'*Yesterday?!*' I ask, shocked. Manager Kong left that part out. 'Why did she get cut?'

'I don't think any one thing,' says Binna, shifting uncomfortably. 'EunJeong was a great dancer, a great singer—'

'Oh, a really good singer,' adds JinJoo.

'She was really hard-working too,' says Binna. 'She was one trainee everyone thought would debut, no question. But sometime in April, she just seemed to get burnt out, lost her fire. It was very subtle, but everyone noticed. None of us thought they'd just cut her though. It was brutal.'

I do some mental maths and realize S.A.Y. announced the auditions in Jersey in April. Why did Manager Kong think I could have anything to offer that these girls don't?

Binna finally comes over and sweeps Helena's stuff off my bed.

'Hey!' says Helena.

I put down my giant duffel bag. I'm so thankful to Binna I could cry.

CHAPTER 9

BIG PROBLEM

I've barely closed my eyes when I'm shaken awake at four a.m.

'Hurry up,' says Binna. 'We're supposed to be at the gym already.'

'Seriously?' I blink up at the harsh fluorescent lights. I'm not exactly tired – all the adrenaline and stress from yesterday comes flooding into today – but still, the last thing I want to do is get out of bed to exercise.

I drag myself upstairs behind Binna to the gym on the hundredth floor, which is spacious yet packed with fifty girls stretching, lunging and sprinting on treadmills. 'Fire-Eyed Girl' by SLK is thumping. These girls are going *hard*. Some of us, including me, look like the walking dead, but others, like Aram, look as if they got eleven hours of sleep in a bathtub full of coconut milk and rose petals.

Right in the middle of the gym is a boy in an orange T-shirt doing bench presses, grunting loudly with each rep.

'Binna,' I whisper urgently. 'How did a boy trainee sneak in here?'

Binna looks around, puzzled, then laughs when she sees who I'm talking about. 'That's not a boy trainee. That's JiHoon-*oppa*. He's one of the junior managers. He assists Manager Kong and Manager Shin.' She whispers, 'Watch out for him, he's the biggest jerk.'

'Why is a boy a junior manager on the girls' side?' I ask.

Binna shrugs. 'I think JiHoon-*oppa* has connections at this company or something.'

JiHoon doesn't look much older than any of us, although he must be. *Oppa* is the male version of *unnie*, what girls are supposed to call their big brothers or any boy who's older than them. But *oppa* can have another meaning, depending on how it's used; something a girl might call a guy to flirt with him. Just laying eyes on JiHoon once, I can tell he's the type of guy who'd like having fifty pretty girls calling him *oppa* a little too much. I vow never to give him that satisfaction.

Binna has me do an exercise where I lean over and crawl with my hands on the floor. 'To improve your strength and flexibility,' she says.

JiHoon struts right up to us. 'You're the new girl,' he says to me.

I can't bring myself to bow to him – there's something about his whole vibe I really don't like. I nod my head slightly. He walks in a circle around me, breathing wheezily through his mouth. I can feel his gaze slithering all over me.

'You're not overweight,' he declares, 'but you have no shape.'

Ex-squeeze me?! Binna sighs heavily as she lowers herself into the splits but doesn't say anything.

I want to clap back at JiHoon, *Well, you're shaped like a fire hydrant – is that the ideal shape for guys?* But it's too early in my K-pop career to put an authority figure on blast, so I get up and let JiHoon make me do so many squats I feel like my butt's about to fall off.

As sweaty as I am, I don't even get to take a shower after the workout, because as Team Two's *maknae*, I'm the last to use the bathroom and Aram spends a full twenty minutes on her beauty routine. When Aram finally emerges from the bathroom as glamorous and fresh as a Glossier ad, she says, 'It's your job to clear the drain after all of us have showered.'

I wanna snap, *Clean it yourself, fam!* But instead I bow meekly.

Our bathroom is tiny and the shower isn't separated by a door or even a curtain. The water just splashes all over the sink and toilet and drenches everything, including the toilet paper, so the whole room is always as humid as a Florida swamp, and there's a drain in the middle of the floor, blocked by a massive mound of black and strawberry blonde hair. Even though it probably smells like flowery shampoo, I pinch my nose and hold my breath as I pick up the half-a-metre-long clump and plop it into the toilet.

The cafeteria is on the hundredth floor, the top floor of the entire ShinBi headquarters. It's split down the middle by a glass wall –

the knife through the block of tofu – so the boys and girls can see each other during meals. Occasionally the trainees will bow to each other through the Gender Glass, but mostly, the boys and girls ignore each other because everyone's dead tired and the orange-shirted junior managers, including a still-sweaty JiHoon, are keeping watch.

Breakfast is sweet potatoes and boiled eggs – a far cry from my favourite breakfast, which is sausage, egg, and cheese McGriddles. Even though the junior managers watch us like hawks, we're pretty much free to take whatever portion we want. I take one sweet potato and two eggs. JiHoon scowls from next to the serving line, his arms crossed, as if daring us to take more.

I spot Binna and JinJoo, who wave me over. They're sitting at a table with two girls I haven't met yet. I eye how much other girls are eating. JinJoo has only half a sweet potato and no egg on her plate. Binna has one full sweet potato and two eggs, just like me.

Binna and JinJoo introduce me to the other two girls. BowHee is from Team One. She's as small as I am and has big buck teeth, giving off strong tomboy vibes despite her long ringlets of violet hair. 'Hi! You must be the American! What year were you born?'

I wince, but Abba told me that it's normal for Korean people to ask you your age right when they meet you – it tells them how to talk to you, whether to use formal language (*jondaetmal*) or casual (*banmal*), and how to treat you in general.

When I tell her, BowHee exclaims with a laugh, 'Ah, so you're the *maknae* of this table!' For a person so tiny, BowHee's voice is surprisingly husky and loud. For some reason, I have a mental image of her kicking boys in the shins on a school playground.

The last girl bows wordlessly to me. She has a bowl cut and thick glasses and reminds me of a cute cartoon turtle – not an idol type at all, which makes me like her right away.

'That's RaLa!' pipes BowHee. 'She's from Team Six and never talks!'

Through the Gender Glass, I see the boys eating in their identical half of the cafeteria, except their breakfast looks way better than ours: porridge, scrambled eggs and sausage. I briefly catch eyes with a *super*-cute boy, taller than all the boys around him. Not everyone here looks like an idol yet, but this guy definitely does. I might be wrong, but he nods at me.

I quickly look back down at my sweet potato, thinking of Iseul and HyunTaek – their promising K-pop careers in jeopardy, just for being caught holding hands.

I ask Binna why the wall is see-through in the first place – why even tempt us by letting us see but not talk to each other? Binna shrugs and says it's probably because the company thinks girl trainees will eat less if boys are watching.

My mind reels over how messed up that is. But I have no doubt that Binna's exactly right.

I spot Helena and Aram at a table with what must be all the most gorgeous girls from the other teams. 'Are those the Plastics?' I ask.

My whole table laughs. Thank goodness they've all seen *Mean Girls*.

'We call them the Visual Table,' says JinJoo, giggling behind her hand.

I blink at her, confused. But then I remember how Imani explained that every K-pop girl group has a Visual member, the one the company decides is the most beautiful.

Looking around the cafeteria, I realize that the girls at my table look the least like typical idols; if this is K-pop high school, we're the geeks. That's probably why I feel so at home.

A female junior manager drops my weekly schedule off at my table. I gasp out loud.

CANDACE (TEAM 2) TUESDAY SCHEDULE
4.00 a.m. – 5.00 a.m.: WORKOUT/SHOWER
5.00 a.m. – 5.30 a.m.: HEALTHY BREAKFAST
5.30 a.m. – 11.30 a.m.: KOREAN LANGUAGE CLASS
11.30 a.m. – 12.30 p.m.: HEALTHY LUNCH/FRESH AIR
                 TIME
12.30 p.m. – 7.30 p.m.: TEAM 2 GROUP PRACTICE
7.30 p.m. – 8.30 p.m.: HEALTHY DINNER/FRESH AIR TIME
8.30 p.m. – 12.00 a.m.: TEAM 2 GROUP PRACTICE/SELF
                 PRACTICE

My schedule changes up a little day-to-day – I sometimes have something called 'Behaviour and Manners Class' and on Saturdays I have a five-hour 'Dance Class With Miss Yoon' – but the six hours of Korean Language class and the nine hours of practice and the inhumane amount of sleep are every day except for Sunday.

How am I going to survive one week of this, let alone three months? Normally, I'm super grumpy if I get anything less than eight hours of sleep and I'm really worried that Manager Kong somehow forgot what a terrible dancer I am. And when I think of the literal cost of me failing and how much my parents sacrificed to bring me here and how excited my friends are . . .

BowHee gives my shoulder a sympathetic pat. 'The first few weeks are the hardest! You'll get used to it eventually.'

'Yeah,' says JinJoo cheerily, 'I had so many meltdowns my first month, but now look at me.' I can barely understand her because her mouth is full of her own pigtail. Her half sweet potato stays untouched.

For my first Korean Language class, all of us foreign, non-native Korean speakers file into a bright white classroom with no windows on the corporate floor. Boys and girls are escorted in separately by junior managers. The classroom is literally split down the middle by a Gender Line: two strips of tape – one pink and one blue – girls on one side, boys on the other.

I'm assigned a seat at the very front of the class. Right across the boy–girl divide from me is a boy who has to sit sideways because his legs are too long to fit under his desk – it's the super-cute boy from the cafeteria. He flashes me a friendly smile; I look away quickly, remembering Manager Kong's lecture about how getting friendly with a boy will ruin my future and bring down the entire company and lead the world into a fiery apocalypse.

Teacher Lee enters the room, greeting the students in a voice that's way too energetic for five thirty a.m. Everyone jumps to their feet to bow. 'Good morning, Teacher Lee.' Teacher Lee, who barely looks older than some of the trainees, motions for us to sit back down.

Right away, Teacher Lee gives me kindergarten teacher vibes. She has an innocent, dimpled face and wears an outfit that looks like it was taken off a life-size doll: a plaid dress with a Peter Pan collar and Mary Jane shoes with knee-high socks. When she sees me, she says, 'Oh yes, we have a new student today, don't we? Park Candace, is it?'

I nod and stare at my desk. I haven't felt first-day jitters like this since ... ever.

'Welcome, Candace-*shi*. Why don't you stand up and tell us the year you were born, where you're from, your main K-pop skill and ... your favourite food?'

I stand up and look around the room for the first time. There are two lines of desks. Four boy trainees and six girls, including me ... and Helena. In the back, Helena shoots me an evil look for no reason I can think of.

My heart races; everyone's going to laugh at my crappy Korean. For the first time ever, I curse my parents for not forcing me to go to Korean school on Saturdays.

I begin with a bow. 'Hello, everyone. My name is Candace. I'm from New Jersey and I'm fifteen years old. And ... I'm not sure what my main K-pop skills are yet. I've been a trainee for less than twenty-four hours.' This gets a little laugh. 'But I like to sing and play the guitar. And what was the last one? Oh, yes. My favourite food is ... *jokbal*.'

There's another titter around the room. Long Legs applauds

my answer. 'An American girl who loves pig's feet,' he cracks. 'I'm in love!'

Everyone laughs. Blushing, I sit back down and Teacher Lee says, '*Wah!* Candace, your Korean isn't as bad as I was told. You just need some more confidence.'

I look up at her and smile. I have no idea why Manager Kong warned me about how strict Teacher Lee is.

The rest of the class stands up to introduce themselves to me too. On the girls' side there's ShiHong, a tomboy with a pixie cut from Shanghai; Luciana, a stunning Brazilian Korean with the thickest, shiniest, most wig-worthy hair I've ever seen; a girl from the Philippines named Zina; and a girl from Osaka named Hina. Then there's Cho Helena from Newport Beach, of course. Helena's main pop skills, according to her, are 'dancing, singing, rapping, Visual *and* charisma'. Her favourite food is mangoes.

When it's the boys' turn, I listen while keeping my eyes fixed on my desk until it's Long Legs, whose name turns out to be YoungBae. He's the same age as me. He's from Atlanta and has only been training for two months.

The class starts up. It's not a regular Language class like you'd take in school; everything's framed in terms of our future careers as K-pop idols. Teacher Lee asks, 'Helena, if I'm a journalist who wants to know where you went to school, what do you say?' (Helena says in perfect, prim Korean that she went to elementary and junior high in a sunny private school next to the ocean.) Teacher Lee asks YoungBae, 'If I were a fan who asks where your first job was, how would you answer?' ('Well, dearest fan, first I would thank you for being a fan – I love nothing more than my fans. Then I would tell you I worked at a movie theatre. The best part of the job was getting to watch *Fast & Furious 8* sixteen times in one summer.')

I actually didn't know the word for 'movie theatre' until YoungBae put it into context in his American accent, which is just as strong as mine. I write down not only the new vocab, but also, for some reason, I write 'YoungBae <3s Fast & Furious' and underline it.

'Candace, I'm a variety show host who asks where your parents work,' says Teacher Lee. 'What do you say?'

I freeze up. I rack my brain for the word for 'convenience store' – I've obviously heard Umma and Abba say it millions of times, but it doesn't come to me. 'They own a place that sells items,' I say like a three-year-old. 'Their place that sells items also sells bubble tea.'

'*Daebak!*' exclaims YoungBae. 'I love bubble tea.'

The six-hour session actually goes by pretty fast. After the first two hours, Helena and a couple of the more fluent trainees leave for other practice sessions. By the final hour, YoungBae and I, the most beginner-level language students, are alone in the classroom.

For the last fifteen minutes, Teacher Lee lets me and Young-Bae chit-chat in Korean together, since we 'probably have a lot to talk about', because we're both from America. We stare at her incredulously; this much interaction between a boy and a girl is definitely not allowed. But she just points to her eye, then points at the door.

Just like that, I decide Teacher Lee is my favourite grown-up at S.A.Y.

I get my first decent, close-up look at YoungBae. Even under the gross fluorescent lighting, YoungBae's face glows. He has pouty, kinda heart-shaped lips, a fresh haircut that's buzzed on the sides but tousled and swoopy on top. He's wearing a white shirt that's halfway tucked into his holey jeans.

All this is to say: YoungBae is young and totally bae.

He's also definitely not shy. 'So, Candace-*shi* . . . is that the name you want to debut with?'

I shrug. 'I don't know. I don't think there's another Candace in K-pop, so probably.'

'That's cool. There are a few other K-pop YoungBaes, so the company might make me change it.'

'You can go by your American name if you have one.'

YoungBae smiles. 'There's no way I can use my American name. It's the worst name. It's so bad that I go by "YoungBae" even in America.'

'OK, now you *have* to tell me.'

'Promise you won't laugh?'

'Promise.'

'All right.' He pauses. 'It's Albert.'

I burst out laughing.

'You promised you wouldn't laugh!'

'I'm sorry! But Albert is *so* not an idol name.'

'Yep, it's unfortunate. What is it about Korean American parents giving kids old-people names?'

For the first time, I forget that I'm in a K-pop training facility, or even that I'm speaking Korean. It turns out YoungBae and I have a lot in common: we both play guitar; we both like *jokbal*; we

92

both go to big Korean churches back home. In fact, YoungBae got discovered when a S.A.Y. recruiter found a YouTube video of him rapping about Jesus in his church's praise band.

A chime sound effect comes from the speakers in the wall, signalling the end of the session. Teacher Lee waves goodbye cheerily and says, 'Good job today, Candace.'

YoungBae shoves his books into his backpack. 'Well, good to meet you, Candace.'

Out of nowhere, Teacher Lee pounds her desk, turns bright red and shrieks, 'THE TWO OF YOU, FOR THE LAST TIME, NO TALKING!'

I practically have a heart attack. I make a note to self: watch out for Teacher Lee, because she's clearly a two-faced psycho.

But then I realize YoungBae's manager and Manager Kong have arrived to escort us to our next lesson. On my way out, I turn back to Teacher Lee when the managers aren't looking. She smiles and shrugs at me in apology.

Manager Kong attends my first Team Two group practice. We sit cross-legged on the floor as Manager Kong writes each of our names on the whiteboard next to a bracket. Then she writes the word 'PROBLEM' in huge English letters across the top. For a second, I'm convinced she's referring to me, the big PROBLEM.

'Girls, this is the song I've decided you'll be performing for your next monthly assessment,' she says. '"Problem" by Ariana Grande and Iggy Azalea.'

There's a squeal of excitement. '*Daebak!*' says Binna.

Aram looks horrified. 'Another song in English? We already did "Worth It" last month.'

'Well, since it's our American friend's first assessment, I figured we should do something in her comfort zone,' says Manager Kong.

Aram flashes me a stunningly beautiful glare. I bow apologetically, but I have to admit, I'm relieved.

'Now, this song has a very challenging vocal line and because it's so energetic, the dance will also have to be hard-hitting,' says Manager Kong.

Oh, *snap*. Stupidly, I haven't been thinking about the possibility of singing *and* dancing at the same time, even though that's literally what being a K-pop idol is all about.

'That said,' says Manager Kong, 'who wants to be Centre?'

Four hands immediately shoot up in the air. I notice that the girls cover their armpits in a show of modesty.

'Candace, you're not interested?'

I shake my head. I know from Imani that the Centre is extremely important. They should embody the essence of the song in some indefinable way. In an MV or live performance, it's the Centre's face that'll be the camera's focus at the beginning and end. But I have exactly zero confidence that I can carry a performance of this or any song.

'*Really*. Huh,' says Manager Kong.

I keep my eyes down and shake my head again.

'Suit yourself. Binna, you were Centre for "Worth It", so let's give someone else a turn. Aram, you were just complaining about the English, so put your hand down. Helena and JinJoo, let's have a sing-off to decide.'

I lean forward; I'm eager to hear what these girls can do. Helena and JinJoo jump to their feet to sing a line from the hardest part of the song, the pre-chorus. Helena's voice is clear as a bell, but she cheats by switching to falsetto on the high notes. JinJoo sings the same line, but much more powerfully. She has a thick Korean accent, but her voice is money, a cool throwback to old-school diva vocals, like Christina Aguilera or Mariah Carey in her prime.

'*Wah*, I think Ariana suits JinJoo really well,' says Manager Kong. 'JinJoo, let's make you Centre this time.'

JinJoo does a happy dance. Helena looks *livid*.

'Candace,' says Manager Kong, 'let's hear you sing the same line. Just so we know what we're working with.'

I feel the pinpricks of cold sweat breaking through the skin of my armpits. Other than at my audition, I've never actually sung in front of strangers before. Besides, I'm so used to singing at barely above a whisper in my room; with an Ariana song, you have to go full volume or go home. I stand up, hiding my trembling hands behind my back. *Here goes.* I squeeze my eyes shut and let loose on a song I've heard millions of times but have never actually sung.

I open my eyes to everyone making an O shape with their lips. Binna, JinJoo and even Aram slow clap. Helena looks angrier than ever.

'*Daebak*, this is why I picked you, Candace,' says Manager Kong, giving me a thumbs up.

A nuclear blast of heart-eye emojis detonates in my brain as I sit back down. Manager Kong assigns the rest of the roles on the whiteboard.

JinJoo: Centre, Main Vocal, Sub-Dancer
Binna: Leader, Main Dancer, Main Rapper, Sub-Vocal 3
Helena: Lead Dancer, Lead Rapper, Sub-Vocal 1
Aram: Sub-Vocal 2, Sub-Dancer
Candace: Lead Vocal, Sub-Dancer

I can't describe how giddy I feel seeing my name up there with assigned roles – I remind myself that 'Main' is above 'Lead' in K-pop language, which is super confusing, but still, being part of a real singing group is thrilling. This is how Tommy must feel being on sports teams.

My giddiness flames out fast though, because Manager Kong says we should focus on figuring out the dance before adding vocals.

The song blasts from the speakers and Binna tries out dance moves in front of the mirror, making up choreography as she goes along. The rest of the girls hang back and try to copy what Binna's doing, which seems impossible to me. It blows my mind how she's making up such legit choreo on the spot. After going through the song only three times, she's already created a full routine. 'Looks good,' says Manager Kong, before leaving to check on other teams.

'All right, everyone,' says Binna. 'Let's give this a shot!'

What comes next is the most torturous seven hours of my

entire life. It's not just the physical exhaustion of twisting my body into positions it's never attempted before or using muscles I never knew I had. What really gets me is the pure humiliation of not being able to do the simplest thing. The very first move of the routine, before the beat drops, is all of us putting our hands on our hips and jutting them out – a simple *America's Next Top Model* pose. But immediately, Binna catches me messing it up in the mirror.

'Oh, Candace, it seems you're a little behind the beat,' says Binna.

'Am I?' I ask.

'Yeah. Just three, two, one, POP! And really POP that hip. Oh. Does your hip not want to pop? That's OK, let's try it again. OK, now you're a little ahead. Really exaggerate that movement. POP! Oh, gosh. That's not it either.'

No joke, we spend an entire hour starting and stopping the song while Binna tries to get me to do that one pose right. Aram is tugging her lustrous black hair in frustration. Helena is throwing hatchets at me with her eyes. JinJoo is off in her own little world, staring at her reflection, mesmerized by her own pores.

Every time Manager Kong comes back to check on us, she's stunned by my lack of progress. 'Candace still hasn't got the first move right? Is that even possible?'

Somehow it is. I can't explain why I suck. Just like my little stubby fingers weren't built to fly over viola strings, my body wasn't built to move to music. I just zone out, dissociating my mind from my body, letting my arms flail and hips do everything except POP.

Eventually, Helena and Aram put in their earbuds and practise on their own, JinJoo hasn't moved in hours and even Binna, who apparently has the patience of Mother Teresa and Michelle Obama combined, starts to get a little frustrated. 'What's going on here, Candace? You can tell me.'

'I don't know,' I say quietly, letting my hair cover my face. 'I just can't do it.'

'Come on. Lift your head. Look at yourself in the mirror when you move. How's your brain supposed to know what your body's doing if you don't look?'

I can feel myself shutting down. I can't bear to look at my body while it looks this stupid. If my body is my instrument, it's clearly broken. This song I used to love starts to sound like the soundtrack to my tragic demise; the line 'I've got one less problem without ya' sounds like a demon whispering in my ear.

I look dumb, like something's seriously wrong with me. I can't explain why I can't do the simplest thing. We skip forward to other moves, but nothing's working. I can't. Maybe I should just shut down in all my dance rehearsals so they'll kick me out. If they kick me out before I quit, my parents don't have to pay for my trainee costs. Coming here was a huge mistake.

At the end of the seven-hour group practice, Manager Kong checks in again. Helena says, 'We didn't get to practise as a group at all because of her. Can't we trade her to one of the other teams?'

Manager Kong ignores her and fixes me with an intense look. 'Candace. Look at me.'

I unstick my eyes from the floor.

'Is being an idol really what you want?'

I nod, even though I'm not sure it's true any more. I don't think I can survive another six-hour session after dinner before going to bed at one a.m.

'Find a way to get better,' says Manager Kong. 'Otherwise . . . *kun-il-nasseo.*'

We'll have a big problem on our hands.

CHAPTER 10

DAEBAK

My first week, I don't think I get more than three hours of sleep a night, but I can't exactly say I'm tired. Panic keeps me on high alert at all times. Whenever I think of Umma or Abba or Imani or Ethan or even Tommy, there's a stab of actual, physical pain in my chest.

Luckily, there isn't much time to think about them. So many new things are being thrown at me every minute. New Korean vocab, new faux pas I need to avoid, new dance moves I can't do, new people I need to bow to, new adults who are screaming at me about whatever it is I'm doing wrong.

One morning, I get screamed at in the cafeteria for showing up to breakfast wearing a ratty old strappy vest top and my comfy plaid pyjama bottoms – my I-wish-I-were-still-in-bed, I-don't-give-a-damn outfit. Manager Kong, who's pacing around patrolling how much we're eating, takes one look at me and snaps,

'How can you be so shameless!' She shouts me into the hallway as the other girls stare with their hands over their mouths. At first, I think it's because I took three boiled eggs. But then she yells, 'What are you thinking, showing your shoulders and your chest when the boys can see through the glass?!'

All the girls, even some of the boys on the other side of the Gender Glass, turn to stare. YoungBae looks at me, alarmed.

I'm so humiliated and confused. It's apparently totally fine for girls to wear the teensiest, tiniest skirts – skirts so short that the cafeteria provides 'modesty blankets' for girls to spread across their laps when they sit down. But wearing a strappy vest top is unacceptable?! It's not like I even have much cleavage to look at in the first place.

All sorts of other little things baffle me too. There are no tampons available, just pads. (When I ask one of the junior managers, SeoHyun-*unnie*, if there are any tampons to use instead, she looks at me like I've asked for a condom or something.) Or why the light switches are on the outside of the bathroom. Someone always turns the light off while I'm sitting on the toilet; I suspect it's Helena, being petty for no reason.

Another strange thing: I climb up to my bed every night to find garbage on my pillow. Brown banana peels, apple cores, sanitary pad wrappers. This must be some cruel Korean hazing ritual. My bed is right next to the bathroom, so it'd be more effort to climb up to my bunk than to just toss it in the trash can. Again, Helena is my prime suspect.

I'm so stressed I don't even feel hunger pains, even though I know my stomach is empty. Our typical meals in a day:

Breakfast: boiled eggs, sweet potato
Lunch: salad with no dressing, Greek yoghurt
Dinner: fishcakes, radish soup, purple rice
Dessert: choice of fruit

Girls are allowed to take *one* piece of fruit from the cafeteria after dinner as dessert – an apple, a tangerine or a banana. We line up by age, so I'm always one of the last and since they're the most filling, the bananas are the most popular and always gone by the time it's my turn. I'm usually stuck with a tiny little tangerine, which I inhale in seconds as soon as I get to our dorm. I then throw the peel in the trash can, like a civilized person.

Dance rehearsal doesn't get any better. Manager Kong keeps repeating, *'We have a big problem on our hands, Candace,'* when she sees me miss every beat. At a certain point, Binna has to move on to helping the other girls learn the full choreo, while I just back into the corner of the group practice room, knowing there's no hope of keeping up. Every now and then, Binna will check back in with me by raising her fist and shouting, *'Hwaiting*, Candace, *hwaiting!'*

I'm not sure what she's saying at first, but I put together that she's saying *'fighting'* – there's no real *F* sound in the Korean alphabet. It basically means *'Put forth strength!'* or *'You can do it!'* I raise my fist and mumble *'Hwaiting'* back, but the word sounds meaningless coming from my mouth.

My total meltdown in dance practice is bringing me down everywhere else. I'm usually a good student, but in Korean

Language class, every time Teacher Lee calls on me – 'Candace-*shi*, can you name all the provinces of South Korea?' I have to say, 'I'm sorry, I don't know.' I'm too distracted by my anxiety to listen to any of my lessons. I keep picturing how and when I'm going to be kicked out of the company. The purse of Umma's lips when she sees she was right – that there really *is* no future in singing for me.

Even YoungBae looks concerned. 'Yo, is everything OK?' he whispers across the Gender Line one day while Teacher Lee's back is turned. I nod, even though I'm chewing on my knuckle so hard it's bleeding.

The only thing propping up my sanity, other than my brief conversations with YoungBae, is our daily Fresh Air Time on the roof, which we have after lunch and dinner. The roof is dope, actually. Cobblestone paths, purple flowers (lilacs, I think?), potted trees for shade and plenty of wooden benches. The real highlight though is the spectacular, panoramic view of Seoul, the Han River and green mountains all around. The mountains have a different shape from anything I've seen in America – it's like they were written in a totally foreign alphabet against the sky.

A three-metre wall of Plexiglas separates us from Seoul, so no one can fall or jump off, I guess. The only ugly thing up here is a concrete wall, once again separating the boys' half from the girls' half – it's the top of the knife cutting into the tofu. There's a door right in the middle of it, but it's made of rusty metal and locked with a key card scanner. Sometimes we can hear the boys yelling on the other side, probably playing handball or something.

BowHee likes to lead me, Binna, JinJoo and RaLa in taekwondo, but I can't bear to engage in any more coordinated movements than I have to, so I follow along half-heartedly while we chit-chat.

'Candace, where in America are you from?' asks BowHee, jabbing the air with her fist.

'New Jersey.'

BowHee's face brightens. '*Daebak!* Isn't that right next to New York?'

'Yes, I live not too far away,' I say.

Truthfully, I go into the city maybe three times a year, max. And usually just to Koreatown while Abba does something boring, like buy a new cash register.

'*Daebak.* I am Carrie Bradshaw,' says BowHee, giggling. She kicks the air with the strength of an ill-tempered ostrich and screams, 'KYAHHHH!' I barely lift my leg.

'Forgive me,' I say, 'but I've been wondering ever since I got here – what does "*daebak*" mean? Everyone says it a lot.'

They're all amused by this question. Binna says, 'This is a very important word to young people in Korea. "*Daebak*" means' – she switches to English and gives two thumbs up – '"very, very excellent".'

I laugh. It feels so good to laugh; I feel a tiny bit of my crippling anxiety leave my body. I like these girls so much already. Even RaLa, who I've never heard say a word, gives off good vibes. 'Well, in that case,' I say, 'you guys are all *daebak*.'

Maybe the encouragement I'm getting from these new friends, and YoungBae in Language class, will be enough to motivate me to survive until the assessment. Then, right after that, I get to visit Umma for the first time.

I can do it! I think, punching the air.

'Hey, nice front jab, Candace!' shouts BowHee. 'You've come to life!'

CHAPTER 11

THE GENERAL

No one in Korea gets Saturdays off, least of all K-pop trainees. Much to my dread, it's my first session with Miss Yoon, aka The General. Binna explained to me that The General was a member of StarLady, an OG girl group from the nineties that helped set off the whole K-pop craze. Now she's the choreographer and head dance coach for S.A.Y. and she came up with SLK's viral 'Unicorn' dance that the whole world is doing. In other words, she's kind of a big deal.

When we get there, The General is finishing up with a boy trainee team. We crowd outside the glass door to watch.

My heart does a pop-and-lock when I see YoungBae front and centre of the group. The General is shouting out the beat as the boys dance *and* rap to 'Ridin'' by Chamillionaire. The five boy trainees are all amazing, but YoungBae is the best dancer, almost as good as Binna, going all out, pounding at the air with his fists, his sneakers flying across the floor in a white blur. He even does the full rap solo, risqué lyrics and all, without missing a beat. A Jesus rap this is not.

When the boys' rehearsal ends, they all give The General bro hugs, as if she's one of them. YoungBae is soaked in sweat. He's wearing a tank top so skimpy and loose he might as well be shirtless. His shoulders are wide and taper down to a narrow waist, making a hot V shape – his torso's basically the shape of a Dorito. Even though he has a six-pack, he looks like he'd be soft to the touch. And even with his hair dripping, he still has that perfect wavy lock draped over his forehead.

'Candace, wipe your mouth, I can see you drooling.'

I jump, startled. I brush the back of my hand over my lips, but they're dry. Helena smirks at me. Aram tries to hide a laugh.

When the boys file out of the practice room, we all bow to each other.

The boys mutter apologies for being so sweaty. YoungBae says, using formal language, 'Hello, Candace-*shi*.'

My cheeks are burning and I don't dare look him in the eye.

'Ladies, let's get going. Hurry up!' shouts The General, clapping her hands.

This practice room still smells like boy sweat, but it's way fancier than the rooms upstairs. This one has ten-metre-high ceilings and giant photos on the wall of S.A.Y.'s biggest K-pop stars. There's MegaloMaxx, a hip-hop duo. JinKo, a super famous solo ballad singer my parents love. The only women are A-list actresses from S.A.Y.'s drama division, including Jeon DanHee, the star of a crazy-popular K-drama called *My Spiky Pearl*, which

I found on Netflix before coming to Seoul. It's about an out-spoken country bumpkin who marries into a rigid **chaebol** family. Super cute.

Of course, SLK takes up the most wall space, looking awesome as always. One.J's face is taller than three of me. I silently apologize to him ahead of time for making a fool of myself in his presence.

'Gather around me, ladies,' says The General. She really does look like a drill sergeant, with her black tank top, studded belt and military stance. 'As you know, the debut date is in sight. CEO Sang is going to pick five girls out of the fifty girl trainees. It's time to get serious. Up until this point, we've all been playing around.'

I look around at my teammates, whose eyes are blazing with determination. I seriously doubt there's been much playing around.

The General tells us that our next monthly assessment won't be held in the usual main conference room; it'll be held in the *Popular 10* studio down on the third floor. The girls let out a collective gasp; *Popular 10* is a music show that airs on one of ShinBi's broadcast networks, YNN. It counts down the ten most popular MVs each week and features tons of live performances. Then she tells us that in addition to our fellow trainees – including the boys – who will be watching each other's performances, there will be a few extremely important VIPs in attendance.

We all squeal in excitement. Before I can stop myself, I'm bouncing up and down too. I know everyone's thinking the same thing: we're going to meet SLK!

'Yes, you should be excited,' says The General, pacing with her arms behind her back. 'SLK is taking a break from their sold-out world tour to give CEO Sang their opinions on all of you. And – this information doesn't leave this building – as One.J is preparing his second solo **Comeback**, he may or may not be selecting a girl trainee to appear in his MV.'

Helena screams. Aram's and JinJoo's knees buckle. Binna and I grab each other's hands.

The General booms, 'This means you'll have to work harder than you ever have.'

'YES, MISS YOON!' we all shout in unison.

'This means fighting through pain and self-doubt.'

'YES, MISS YOON!'

'All right, ladies. Let's get your weight.'

My limbs go rigid. My teammates jog to the corner, where there's a digital scale. We're not going to be weighed in front of each other, are we?

But that's exactly what's happening. Helena hops on first. The scale flashes a number in kilos – I don't know the kilos-to-pounds conversion, but I know the number is tiny. I refuse to say her exact weight here, because it shouldn't be anyone's business, but The General compliments her on her 'self-control'. Aram's number is even smaller, which The General says is very good, but she'd like to see Aram gain some definition and strength in her arms and legs. Binna's is higher than the other two, but barely. The General says she's getting too muscular, that she needs to do more running and lay off the weight training.

JinJoo's curvier than the rest of the girls. In America, a lot of people would say she has the sexiest figure out of all of us. But I know by K-pop standards, she's downright chubby, which is honestly ridiculous beyond words.

'JinJoo,' says The General in a serious tone when her number comes up. 'How are we still having this problem? What does this say to CEO Sang? You're showing him you're not committed to one of an idol's most important responsibilities: taking care of her Visual.'

JinJoo is on the verge of tears. 'I don't know how this can be. I've been watching what I eat so closely. I didn't drink water today. I've even been spitting as much as I can to lose just a little more weight.'

I'm shook to Shakespearean levels – I'm shooketh. How totally barbaric that grown people are allowed to judge teenage girls on their weight, with no concern for physical or mental health. I think of how horrified my guidance counsellor at Fort Lee Magnet would be.

But when it's my turn, I don't deliver the passionate mono-logue that's going on in my head. All my teammates turn to me. There's no choice: I step on the scale and hold my breath. I have no idea what The General might say. Fast metabolisms run in my family, but I don't consider myself either skinny or overweight. One of Umma and Abba's greatest joys is watching Tommy and me eat a lot, so I've never thought about dieting.

My number means nothing to me, but The General clucks her tongue.

'So you're the new girl, huh?' she says.

I say yes in the most formal way I know how.

'Your weight is technically not horrible, but since you're so short, we should really aim to lose two kilos by next month.'

Is that a medical opinion? I want to ask. I cover my stomach with my arms. To add to my humiliation, The General says, 'Besides your weight, your proportions aren't pretty. You won't look good when you're dancing. We need to find a way to make you look longer and more beautiful.'

I don't even have time to stew over this, because out of nowhere, The General blows a deafening whistle. She makes us strap five-kilo weights around our ankles – they look like little packs of dynamite. 'We practise while wearing these so at performance time, you'll feel easy and light,' The General explains to me. As a warm-up, she has us run in circles around the practice room singing 'Into the New World' at the top of our lungs. Without warning, she'll yell one of our names and peg a heavy medicine ball right at us so we have to stop and catch it. It's to improve our 'stability' while singing.

As we run and shout the lyrics – I'm so glad Umma went over this song with me – The General explains, 'When you're performing live, you have to be an expert multitasker – know which camera you're looking at, your intricate choreography, your expressions. If you're lucky, you'll also be distracted by thousands of fans going crazy for you. Throughout all of this, you can't be distracted from your breathing or singing. For now, don't worry about sounding good. Just don't let anything distract you from your breath.'

This cruel form of torture combines three of my least favourite activities: musical chairs, dodgeball and running in circles with weights strapped to my ankles.

Binna and Helena are pros at this, catching the balls with ease without a break in their screaming of the lyrics. JinJoo jams her finger on her first catch and Aram stops singing completely whenever it's her turn. 'WAKE UP, ARAM!' The General booms.

I'm so out of breath just from running that I'm barely panting out the words. At first, the weights don't make a huge difference, but after only a minute, I can barely lift my feet off the floor. The first time The General shouts 'CANDACE!' she has such a beastly look on her face, like she's really trying to kill me, that instead of stopping to catch the ball, I scream and dive out of the way. The ball slams into the wall behind me. The General zooms over to me and shouts in my face, 'What's the matter with you, *geopjaengi*?! Why don't you have any energy?!'

While she's so close to me, I whisper, 'I'm sorry to bring this up, but I'm having cramps from that time of the month ...'

I'm not lying. Umma taught me exactly how to say this phrase in Korean in case I ever need an instructor to go easy on me.

But this is the wrong instructor to use it on.

'ME TOO, YOU BRAT!' The General screams right into my face. 'DO YOU THINK IDOLS NEVER HAVE THEIR TIME OF THE MONTH RIGHT IN THE MIDDLE OF THEIR PROMOTIONS?! NEVER USE THIS EXCUSE WITH ME AGAIN. AND DON'T LOOK SO SURPRISED THAT I STILL GET MINE, I'M STILL A YOUNG WOMAN.'

Helena and Aram giggle into their hands.

'Into the New World' replays ten more times and each time the music stops, I run away from the ball and get screamed at by

The General. The one time I don't move away fast enough, the ball nails me right in the ribs. All the air leaves my lungs and I crumple to the floor, choking and coughing. The General stops the music. Everyone crowds around me. 'Are you OK?' Binna asks.

I blink up at the faces hovering over me. A drop of someone else's sweat plops on to my face. I'm seeing spots, my legs are searing and I'm gasping for air.

'See this, kids? Come over here,' says The General to Helena and Aram. 'This is what it looks like when the spirit of a regular girl leaves a body, leaving room for the spirit of an idol. It's a pathetic sight, right?'

'It is, Miss Yoon,' says Helena.

Oh, shut up, Helena! I'd say if I had any air in my lungs.

The General continues, 'It's a painful process. Let Candace be your reminder of how much you've already transformed and how much you have left to go.'

As I get to my feet again, I wonder: was this what Manager Kong meant when she said I was recruited to motivate the other girls? Am I an example of how weak they used to be and everything they *shouldn't* be if they want to be an idol?

One.J's towering face peers down at me. I can't help but think he's silently judging, wondering who I am to think I could possibly reach the heights that he has.

After our drills, Binna shows The General the choreo she's come up with for 'Problem'. The General likes it, but she adds extra steps and formation changes to make it even more intricate.

When the rest of us stand up to join, The General is on me like avocado on toast (*mmm, avocado toast*).

'HEY, WHY DON'T YOU ANSWER ME? IS IT A LANGUAGE ISSUE? DO I NEED TO BRING IN A TRANSLATOR?!'

'YOU CALL THAT A HAIR FLIP?! I'VE SEEN YOUR PRESIDENT'S HAIR MOVE MORE GRACEFULLY!'

'CANDACE, WHAT'S SO INTERESTING ON THE FLOOR? LOOK UP!'

By the end of the five-hour session, I've had it. Not only are my body and brain exhausted, my entire sense of self is exhausted. I feel as if I've never done anything right and will never do anything right again. I almost want to tell them that I'm not always this worthless – I'm a good student, I'm helpful at my parents' store, I'm a good friend, I'm actually somewhat articulate when I speak English. It's just this one thing I'm completely hopeless at.

Manager Kong arrives to escort us back upstairs. Immediately, The General gives her an update: 'This is not going to work out with Candace. I think you're going to have to tell CEO Sang it was a mistake to bring her here, especially this late.' Her voice is hoarse and raspy. 'I've worked with many trainees with no skill level, but not one with no will. Even if I saw a light in her eye, a greed for getting better . . . but I don't see that either.'

Manager Kong groans.

I would give anything to disappear right now.

Even Helena and Aram look concerned; this is bad. 'Candace,' says Manager Kong, 'am I really going to have to go to CEO Sang and admit I made a mistake going all the way to America to hold an expensive audition just to find you? He'll scold me to death, I could lose my job . . . but I'll do that if it means you can't waste any more of our trainees' or instructors' valuable time. Team Two deserves better.'

I lose it. Tears and snot explode from my face like a tsunami through a dam. I don't know what to say. All I would say is, *I'm sorry, I'm sorry, I'm sorry*, but I'm sobbing so violently that I'm convulsing – with every gasp for air, there's a sharp pain in my ribs where I got hit with the medicine ball. I can't speak.

Then I feel a hand on my back.

'Manager Kong, I will practise with Candace one-on-one. It's my fault as Leader that I haven't spent more time with her.'

I look up, shocked. Binna gives me a resolute nod.

'Do you really think that will help anything?' Manager Kong asks.

'I do. I think Candace's only problem is that she doesn't believe she can do this. But she's extremely smart and has the ability – I know that from the short time I've spent with her.'

I dry my face on my sleeves and blink up at Manager Kong. 'I promise to work hard and get better,' I whimper.

Manager Kong cracks an almost sympathetic half-smile. 'Be grateful your *unnie* is willing to take the time – she's the best dancer and Leader in the company.'

Binna wipes my remaining tears with her thumbs and tucks a strand of hair behind my ear. I realize it's the first time anyone's touched me since I've arrived here. What could I have possibly done to deserve this kindness?

CHAPTER 12

SUNDAY

I'm shell-shocked after that practice. I'm emptied out. I'm a scooped bagel.

It's early evening, not even dinner time, and I'm lying in my bunk, turned to the wall, while the other girls pack. There are fruit peel and Korean sheet mask wrappers in my bed, but I don't bother throwing them in the trash; I just lie among them.

Trainees who have family nearby, which is almost everyone, get to spend Saturday nights at home and they don't have to come back until late Sunday evening. Every cell in my body is desperate to follow them out of the building to see Umma, but I also understand why they won't let me leave the building during my first month – if I left now, I definitely would never want to come back.

Someone nudges me. I turn over. Binna has her Powder Pup hat perched atop her head. 'Rest up now,' she says, 'because when

I get back, you and I are going to practise until we drop dead. Hear me?'

She winks. I nod and smile weakly.

Aram and JinJoo also pack up and go, leaving me and Helena alone in the room. I figure Helena has nowhere to go since her family's back in California. She's right below me in the bottom bunk. She's listening to music on her headphones so loudly that I can tell she's listening to Post Malone. I want to lean over and say something, anything. *I like Post Malone too. What's your favourite Friends episode? Do you have siblings?*

While I'm still working up the courage to interrupt her music, she gets up and leaves. Probably to go practise for hours and hours on my own. What I really wanted to ask her, as a fellow foreign trainee, is: *When does it get easier?*

When I wake up, it's four p.m. on Sunday. How is it possible I've slept this long? In all the chaos of my first week, I've forgotten that I'm still horribly jet-lagged. I haven't slept properly since I arrived. Once my feet hit the floor, suddenly the aches and pains of the entire week hit me at once. My ankles and knees are on fire. My legs are so stiff I can barely move them enough to walk. My head is throbbing.

The girls' half of the cafeteria is empty except for JiHoon, Helena and Luciana from Language class; most of the lights aren't even on. When I approach Helena and Luciana's table, Helena's eyes glint at me like a pair of razor blades, so I detour

117

and take my tray of rice, salad and four strips of cold fishcake to a table by myself, right by the Gender Glass. Sitting there in the dark, cold cafeteria, an emptiness sweeps over me. Will I really survive a whole summer of this?

But right then, YoungBae puts his tray down half a metre away from me. We nod at each other but nothing more. I stare ahead, but I can practically feel YoungBae's body heat through the Gender Glass separating us. We both sit there as long as we can – even him being in my peripheral vision makes me a little happier. Just as I'm picking up my tray, YoungBae suddenly presses his mouth up against the glass, puffs out his cheeks like a blowfish and crosses his eyes.

I burst out laughing. He looks so stupid and cute – I can totally picture him as that goofy kid who put his mouth on the tanks on the school field trip to the aquarium. JiHoon has to come running over to ruin the moment though. He thwacks the glass right where YoungBae's mouth is and shouts, 'Knock it off, *imma*!' I can totally picture JiHoon as that bully on the school field trip who pounds the tanks to scare the fish.

That little moment lifts my spirits enough that I decide to do something bold – borderline crazy.

I go looking for Helena after dinner, a secret weapon hidden in the pouch of my hoodie. I walk down the hall of practice rooms, peering in each window until I spot Helena, rehearsing the dance breakdown of 'Problem' by herself. I knock on the door until she finally hears me. She turns to me with a resplendent smile, as if she's expecting a friend – I'm knocked backwards, by her beauty and her unexpected good mood – but the smile vanishes when she sees it's just me. I let myself in anyway.

'Hi, *unnie*,' I say shyly, bowing my head. 'I thought you might need a break.'

I have a cold barley tea from the cafeteria. I extend it to her with both hands. She snatches it from me.

'I don't need as many breaks as you seem to,' says Helena.

I accept the shade with another humble bow. I'm disappointed that she's still refusing to speak English with me, even when we're alone.

'I can learn a lot from your work ethic,' I say. 'I hope to win your respect gradually.'

'Hmph,' she says as she downs the barley tea in one gulp.

I take a deep breath, steeling my nerves. 'It seems we got off on the wrong foot, didn't we, *unnie*?'

'Why should that matter? We're here to train, not be best friends. There's just something about you I don't like, that's all.'

I wince. There are lots of ways to say you don't like someone in Korean, but the words she chose – '*nae maumae ahn dureo*' – strike me as unusual. I could be wrong, but I think the words literally mean something like, '*you don't fit into the shape of my heart*'.

I clear my throat. 'That may be so, but I thought since we're both from America, we might have some things in common. Be able to help each other out.'

Helena rolls her eyes. 'You really don't see it, do you? There's no use in us getting close anyway. They're never going to debut more than one American girl in the group.'

'I don't think that's true,' I say, based on no actual knowledge. 'I'm sure the company will choose girls based on our individual talents, not where we're from.'

Helena clicks her multicoloured nails together impatiently. 'You're really naive if you think that. CEO Sang wants the group to appeal as globally as possible. They'll want to keep the group majority Korean, so that's three girls. They'll want one girl from Japan or China or South Asia, to appeal to the other big K-pop markets. That's four. CEO Sang is obsessed with breaking into America, but he only needs one of us to do that – SLK did it without *any*. So it's going to be you or me.'

I don't buy this reasoning at all. It can't be so cut and dried. 'Didn't Girls' Generation have two American girls?'

'Yes, but Girls' Generation had nine members. And there was only room for one in the end.'

'Well, we can be different,' I say. 'Besides, if they had to choose one, of course they would choose you. I just want things to be a little more pleasant between us.'

Helena flashes me hardcore side-eye. This is a risk, since Helena isn't one for breaking rules, but I bring out my roll of home-made *yakgwas* from the pouch of my sweatshirt.

Helena backs away. 'That?! We can't have that.'

'I know,' I say quickly. 'If you want me to throw them out right now, I will. But . . . my mom made these. They're my favourite and they're my only taste of home.'

I unwrap my precious *yakgwas* and hold them out to her, using every ounce of willpower to keep from devouring them all myself.

Helena considers them suspiciously, then breaks off a tiny piece and puts it in her mouth, chewing hungrily. She closes her eyes. 'Would you like any more?' I ask.

'No. It's quite good, but I shouldn't have done that. I'll have to dance for another hour to burn that off.'

I bow and wrap the cookies back up, hoping this is one step towards peace between us. 'If you want any more, just ask me. I keep them inside my guitar.'

I want us to have a secret together, in case that brings us closer.

Helena scoffs, putting her earbuds back in. 'I'm not going to want any more. *I* have some self-control.'

I bow and make my way to the door.

'And Candace? This is the second time you've interrupted me while my earbuds are in. Don't do it again.'

CHAPTER 13

EATING RICE CAKES LYING DOWN

'Let's get one thing out of the way: you don't have any talent in dance and you never will,' says Binna, looking into my eyes with her hands on my shoulders.

Way harsh, Binna. 'Gee, thanks. The General already made that very clear.'

We're in one of the individual practice rooms for our first one-on-one dance tutoring session. There's barely enough room for two people to dance without smacking each other in the face.

'No, Candace, I mean this as a friend. What I'm saying is, I can't give you talent, but I can help you build your skills. Skills will never fail you.'

I nod, but I'm doubtful. Many have tried to teach me viola skills and failed; why should this be any different?

'Second thing. If I'm really going to take you under my wing, you can't be afraid to look stupid in front of me. I can tell that's what you're afraid of when we're dancing with the group. I know we haven't known each other for long, but if we're going to debut together, we need to jump ahead in our friendship. You can even use *banmal* with me, if that helps.'

My jaw drops; it's a huge step, I've learnt, with Koreans, to be given permission by an older friend to speak *banmal*. '*Unnie*, I couldn't possibly ...'

'OK, fine, but just promise me you'll trust me like a friend,' says Binna, putting out her pinky.

I hook mine in hers. 'I promise.'

Binna cues up 'Problem' on the sound system, which has all fifty S.A.Y.-approved songs preloaded. I've come to loathe this song; the saxophone run that loops through the whole song has started to sound like the herald of my doom.

'Just go nuts, Candace,' shouts Binna over the music. 'Move your body!'

I nod my head. Shift my weight from foot to foot. This is already so cringey.

'Come on!' says Binna. She starts flailing her limbs wildly and popping her booty. It's probably her best effort at dancing badly, but she still looks awesome.

I look at my awkward self in the mirror. I tell myself to wave my arms around like an idiot, but I can't explain it – it's physically impossible. I'm convinced that when I look like an idiot, I'll look like an idiot to end all idiots. That whatever I do will be wrong. That she'll take one look at me and say, 'Never mind, I give up. There's nothing I can do with *that*.'

Binna pauses the song. 'Hmm. This is all mental, Candace.

Tell me – what did you do at your audition? Clearly, Manager Kong saw *something*.'

I turn red. 'Oh, that. No, that was a fluke. I made a fool of myself and fell on my butt.'

'Well, do that again, now.'

'I can't. I think I could only do that then because I'd already given up. I just pretended I was dancing around with my best friends. Here, everything's so—'

'What are your best friends' names?'

'Imani and Ethan.'

A pang of homesickness throbs in my chest.

'Close your eyes and pretend I'm Imani and Ethan,' says Binna.

I close my eyes. I'm back in my room. Imani's slurping kimchi straight out the jar. Ethan's being extra, as always. I cue up 'Problem' on YouTube. Imani's whipping her hair. Ethan's twerking against my bed. Then he does a duckwalk. I'm jumping around, doing my faux-vogue moves, acting out the lyrics whenever I can. During the sax loops, I pretend I have an invisible sax in my hands and play it passionately.

When I open my eyes, the song is over and Binna is rolling on the floor laughing.

I knew it. She might have told me she wanted me to look like an idiot, but when she actually saw it, it was too much.

She wipes tears from her eyes and looks up at me. 'Candace, that was so good.'

I make a face and shake my head.

'No, I'm serious! You can move and you have a lot of charisma.

124

That saxophone – oh my goodness, you have to do that in the actual **Stage**. It'll kill. And I can see you like doing voguing and waacking moves. That style isn't common in idol choreography, but I can put some into our routine.'

We get down to business. She tells me to go ahead and mess up – 'mess up big', she tells me. Every time I almost clobber her in the face with my arm or fall while doing a turn, she shouts, '*Orlchi!*' as if I'm doing her the world's biggest favour. 'We can turn too much energy into a good performance,' she explains, 'but we can't make a performance out of no energy at all.' Throughout our five-hour training sesh, she repeatedly shouts, 'We're having fun! We're having fun!' And after a while, it becomes true. I'm having fun.

At the end, we plop to the floor, exhausted. Binna gives me a high five. 'Pretty soon, you'll nail this choreography. It will be like eating rice cakes lying down.'

'What?!' I say.

'Ha, I suppose you wouldn't know that saying. It means that all this will become easy for you some day.'

'Oh, I see. We have a similar saying in English. We just say it's "a piece of cake".'

'Hmm.' She puzzles over this. 'Just "a piece of cake"? But don't you need to know what kind of cake?'

I burst out laughing. 'Huh, that's a really good point.'

CHAPTER 14

THE SECRET WEAPON

For my first Behaviour and Manners class, Manager Kong has to escort me down to the fiftieth floor of the building, where Madame Jung's expansive, bright white office is. As Manager Kong explains in the elevator, Madame Jung is the Head of Global Communications of ShinBi Unlimited.

Madame Jung is the most put-together human being I've ever seen. I'd guess she's older than Umma and Abba, but it's hard to tell – her face is totally lineless and covered in make-up so white she looks vampirish. She's dressed in chic, head-to-toe black.

Madame Jung barely looks up when I walk in. She's answering emails at her immaculately organized desk. There's a breathtaking view of the Seoul skyline behind her.

'Come in, Miss Park,' she says. 'Sit down.'

My hands folded demurely in front of me, I take a seat. I sit as straight as I possibly can and cross my legs knee over knee.

'I hate everything about the way you're sitting,' Madame Jung says with a sigh. 'You're slouching like an American. And why are your legs crossed? Crossed legs are so unattractive. Ugh, I didn't mean you should spread your legs. Glue your knees and ankles together and angle your feet to one side, I don't care which side. Not great, but better.'

Madame Jung proceeds to ignore me for what feels like an eternity. She taps away at her keyboard. She takes two calls. I sit absolutely still, frozen in position. My back and shoulders start to ache. I wonder if that's just my Proper Korean Lady muscles growing stronger.

'When you're meeting an important person or appearing in public as a K-pop idol' – it takes me a second to realize she's talking to me again – 'you're representing not just yourself but the hope of the Korean people. You are a manifestation of the best this country can produce.' She takes her eyes off her computer to give me a thorough sizing up. 'You need to work harder on your appearance. This isn't America, where you can just walk around like a slob. Being your best-looking self is a sign of respect and character, do you hear me?'

'Yes, Madame Jung,' I say, my voice trembling slightly.

Madame Jung reaches under her desk and brings out a gift bag. 'Your skin is naturally quite fair, which is lucky for you, but an idol should have bright white skin, as close to the ideal as possible.' She rifles through the gift bag and pulls out a very elegant white tube. It makes me think of Gwyneth Paltrow. 'Next time you come to see me, be wearing this BB cream–foundation combo. Korean beauty products are the best in the world, don't you agree?'

'Yes, Madame Jung,' I say, remembering all the ten-step K-beauty tutorials I've seen on YouTube with Imani and Ethan.

'This product is quite exquisite,' boasts Madame Jung. 'It's made by ShinBi's cosmetics line, GlowSong. It's make-up and skincare in one. It's so effective I no longer have to wear any other make-up. What do you think about that?'

My mouth falls open. What I'm really thinking is, *Lady, your neck is at least six Fenty shades darker than your face. No make-up, my butt.* Instead, I manage to croak, 'That is quite amazing, Madame Jung.'

With a satisfied smirk, Madame Jung extends the tube to me. I reach over to receive it with a bow, but Madame Jung snatches it back.

'Excuse you. In Korea, we accept a gift with two hands.'

'My apologies, Madame Jung,' I murmur, getting up out of my seat to receive the tube with two hands. But then Madame Jung snatches the tube back.

'Really? You're just going to receive it? Just like that?'

Is Madame Jung messing with me? What can I possibly be doing wrong?

She sighs. 'It's so rude that you're just accepting my kindness so easily. You should refuse my generosity three times. Say, "I couldn't possibly!", "This is too nice!" Because if I'm being honest, this *is* too nice of a gift. Go on!'

I sit back down and say, 'Oh my goodness, I cannot accept such a fine gift. Please give it to someone who really deserves it.'

Madame Jung sighs impatiently. 'I insist. You must use it to become more beautiful.'

After refusing two more times, I stand back up, bow deeply and extend both my hands. 'I will use this exquisite gift diligently so I can one day be as beautiful as you.'

Madame Jung scoffs. 'OK, OK, don't go too far.'

I nod, trying so hard to appear alert, show that I'm listening to every word.

'Why are you staring at me like that? Westerners are so aggressive with their eye contact – it's very off-putting, like you want something from me. When talking to a superior, make eye contact only ten per cent of the time. Look downwards.'

Another torturous fifteen minutes pass. 'OK, that's enough for today. Come back next week with a better face. And *jebal*, wear a dress or a skirt.'

I bow and walk as fast as I can to the sitting area to wait for Manager Kong to take me back to the girls' dorm. I close my eyes and repeat the last words Umma said to me in the lobby: *You are worth so much. No one in there can decide your value.*

It's not until Friday of my second week that we have our first formal singing lesson. Accompanied by Manager Kong, we file into a slick recording studio on the corporate floor, complete with mood lighting, sound absorbers on the walls, five music stands with mics and headsets arranged in a circle and a sound mixing booth where producers sit.

I'm excited and nervous. Excited because this is somewhere I can shine, and nervous because our vocal instructor's name is

Clown Killah. As Manager Kong explained, he's the right-hand man of S.A.Y.'s lead producer, Chang-y, and he's the primary music director of all trainee recordings. Based on a name like that, I'm expecting him to have a face tattoo or something. But Clown Killah turns out to be a clean-cut, cool-nerd type, with his shirt buttoned all the way to his throat, hipster glasses and fresh white hat – someone you'd be safe to introduce to your parents.

From the producers' booth, Clown Killah says, 'Before we get into "Problem", would you like to hear what I've been working on with Chang-y for SLK's next Comeback?'

We all go nuts. 'Yes, Producer Clown Killah!'

He plays ten seconds of a sick beat. It sounds thick and rich, literally like money – like sacks of gold coins being slapped on to a table over and over. The other girls fall all over themselves to express their enthusiasm.

'Mr Clown Killah, sir, this will surely be SLK's next **Perfect All-Kill** number one,' says Helena. 'I hope we're able to record a hit half as wonderful as this one if we have the great fortune to debut.'

Clown Killah chuckles and hands out our lyric packets that have been all marked up to show who's singing when. As the Main and Lead Vocals, JinJoo and I sing most of the verses and pre-choruses, while the others mostly harmonize. Then Binna and Helena share Iggy Azalea's rap break, which they've written their own Korean–English – Konglish – lyrics for.

When I sing my first lines, my entire body tingles. My team-mates widen their eyes at me in shock; Binna gives me a thumbs up. I've never heard my voice on top of a professionally produced track before and it's like my brain is doused in Diet Mountain Dew, my favourite soda.

'Candace, that was really, really great,' says Clown Killah. 'You fit right into the harmony they worked on for years. I was worried about this team after losing EunJeong, but now I'm thinking you might be Team Two's secret weapon. You have a very special *charisma* to your voice. So many people can imitate Mariah Carey, like JinJoo, but not everyone has your . . . uniqueness.'

My eyes dart to JinJoo apologetically. She looks panicked.

We sing the song at least twenty more times, starting and stopping a lot, mostly so Clown Killah can correct Aram's pitch or try to get Binna to sing more powerfully. Every moment is like heaven to me. This must be how Tommy feels on the baseball field (court?) and Binna feels on the dance floor. This is how it feels to know you're good at something and for everyone else to see it too. I can't help but resent Umma for keeping this feeling from me all these years.

'Wow,' says Clown Killah at the end of the session, blinking at me in amazement. 'Wow, wow, wow. I have to ask: wouldn't it be better if the Main and Lead Vocals were switched?'

'I couldn't possibly, when JinJoo is doing such a good job,' I say breathlessly, bowing. 'Thank you, Producer Clown Killah.'

Manager Kong looks up from her phone to beam at me from the corner.

'Listen up, girls,' she says. 'Just like Binna leads team dance practice, Candace is your new leader when it comes to vocals. When you're not with a producer, you can ask her for advice.'

I glance at JinJoo's colourless face again. She looks totally dazed, like her world has been turned upside down. I feel a complicated mix of excitement for myself and guilt towards JinJoo – JinJoo's been nothing but nice to me so far, but now I wonder if she's cursing the day I stepped into the S.A.Y. Headquarters.

Next to her, Helena's glaring at me with such fierceness it's as if she's trying to make my head explode with her mind.

Even though she's terrifying, I force myself to stare back until she looks away first.

CHAPTER 15

HOPE TORTURE

The following Monday, I actually survive group practice without Manager Kong yelling at me any more than the others. I practised on my own all day Sunday. I still can't keep up with the hardest parts of the choreo, but I've improved enough that Aram tells me 'You've worked hard!' afterwards, which, coming from her, feels as good as being told I've been picked to star in One.J's solo MV.

But JinJoo's sluggish the whole time, flinging her limbs like limp noodles to the point where Binna has to yell at her to get it together or leave. JinJoo manages to tough it out, but she's on the verge of tears the whole time.

It almost seems as if whatever confidence I'm gaining, I'm sucking it right out of JinJoo, like some parasite.

During our night-time Fresh Air Time, Binna and I are leaning against the Plexiglas, staring out over the streets of Seoul. It's crazy-muggy out – it's Korea's monsoon season – but the view is still incredible. Girls are chattering and singing behind us, but I spot JinJoo sitting on a bench alone, staring at the ground.

'Is JinJoo going to be OK?' I ask.

'Yeah,' says Binna. 'We all go through low times. Times when you want to quit.'

'I just feel so guilty. After what Clown Killah said—'

'Don't. This is your dream too.'

We look back at JinJoo's silhouette – it's hunched and tragic.

'I love JinJoo,' Binna says. 'I've trained with her for a long time. But sometimes I feel like I don't know her well either. She's a K-pop kid – her mom, who raised her alone, is one of those extreme K-pop parents. Before she could walk or talk, she was put in intense idol academies. Her mom even took her to get plastic surgery as soon as she turned fourteen.'

'*Seriously?*'

'Yeah. I mean, it's insane – even though JinJoo's Korean, she's more foreign to me than actual foreigners like you or Helena. Her idol training has been so intense her whole life that she doesn't know things everyone should know, like which political party our president is from. And she's never done certain normal things that everyone should do – go to the movies with friends or anything like that. I mean, I've been a trainee for ten years, but I've only been a live-in trainee for a year – before then, I finished regular high school and lived with my parents. But JinJoo's case is different – imagine the intensity of this, but it's been your whole life.'

I'm stunned. 'Binna – you've been a trainee for *ten* years?'

'Not at S.A.Y. But overall, yes. I started out at a small company, but I never got to debut. After a few years, I moved to one of the other Big Four companies and trained to debut with QueenGirl, actually. I was chosen to debut with them, but at the last second, the company recruited WooWee and she took my spot.'

My jaw falls open. WooWee, the Centre and Face of Queen-Girl? I try to picture Binna in QueenGirl instead of WooWee, but I can't. WooWee is my Ultimate **Bias** of female idols and I've been worrying what will happen to her if QueenGirl falls apart because of the Iseul–HyunTaek scandal.

'So after that,' continues Binna, 'I got traded to S.A.Y. right when they first started taking girl trainees, when it was still a small company. It was before SLK debuted and before it was bought by ShinBi.'

'I can't imagine training for that long,' I say. 'I've only been here for two weeks and it already feels like a lifetime.'

Binna turns to look at me, her black hair flowing in the wind. 'You know what it feels like? It's like *hwemang gomun*.'

'What does that mean?'

Binna explains each part of the phrase and I put together that it means something like '*hope torture*'. 'You never know if a company is going to pick you to debut, or tell you that you don't have the right Visuals to debut, or if they'll pick you to debut but cancel the group altogether at the last minute,' says Binna, staring far into the distance. 'All those things have happened to me. They keep your hope alive – they tell you, "Just practise harder, lose some weight, get plastic surgery". And all along, you have no certainty of your future and every year that goes by, the less likely it is that you'll ever debut.'

A heaviness forms inside me. I feel so unworthy, like I haven't suffered enough. But I know I want to be here too.

In the meantime, I vow to be a good friend to JinJoo. I go over to join her on the bench. I ask what her favourite Wookie rap verse is – Wookie is her SLK Bias, which is a *choice* – and she lights up immediately. It turns out, she has a lot to say if you take the time to ask.

CHAPTER 16

PEPERO

In the final hour of Language class, it's just me and YoungBae in the front of the class after all the more advanced students have left. Teacher Lee is giving a lesson on how we should speak to CEO Sang at our assessment. 'The two of you have me most worried about getting into a *sago*.'

I've always thought '*sago*' meant 'car accident', but apparently it also means having a cringey moment in public. A *train wreck*, I guess.

Teacher Lee tells us that, when in doubt, we should speak to CEO Sang using indirect sentence structure. It's a modest, highly respectful way to speak. If he happens to give us a compliment, we shouldn't just say, 'I've worked really hard and I'm proud of myself.' Teacher Lee makes an X with her forearms. 'Don't say that. Kanye West can say something prideful like that in America, but in Korea, our idols should say something like, "It seems to me that I may have worked really hard and it seems to me that I'm glad our Stage seems to have gone well.'"

My pen is flying across the lines of my notebook. My eyes dart to YoungBae. God, he's cute. His eyes are puffy, but that only makes him look more devastating and that swoop of hair over his forehead kills me every time. While Teacher Lee is writing sentences on the board, he slides a box from his jeans pocket.

It's a red box of Pepero, a popular Korean snack. My family's store back home sells them. They're these long, skinny cookie sticks lightly dipped in chocolate. *Delicious.* How did YoungBae get them?!

His eyes still on Teacher Lee's back, he reaches his long arm across the Gender Line to pass them to me. I shoot him a look. *I can't take that.* But he shakes it once, insistently. I turn back and check the door to see if any execs or managers are walking by – the coast is clear – and I grab the box, just to get it out of sight more than anything. I stash it in the pencil tin Ethan gave me and the moment it clicks shut, Teacher Lee turns back around.

'Any questions?' she says, smiling brightly at us.

'No, Teacher Lee!' YoungBae and I pipe up in unison.

At night, after the other girls have fallen asleep, I turn on the little light attached to the rail of my bunk bed and open my pencil tin, pretending I'm doing my Language homework in bed as usual. My heart races as I see that the Pepero is still there; it wasn't a 'trainee delusion' – a hallucination, which I've heard other girls talk about. I open the box and tip it, practically tasting the delicious sweet-but-not-too-sweet Peperos.

But no cookie sticks slide out of the box, which is surprisingly heavy. Instead, a plastic card with a long strap attached to it – one of those ID badges all the managers wear around their necks – falls into my hand. And then, out falls a phone. One of those old-timey cell phones people used to use before I was born.

Where did he get such things?!

I bite my fist to keep from squealing. The ID belongs, or *belonged*, to a surly-looking junior manager named Pak DongHo. It's really ballsy for YoungBae to steal one of these. I can't imagine the world of hurt I'll be in if anyone finds these highly contraband items.

This is all so crazy exciting – a cute boy likes me! I don't think this has ever happened to me before (unless you count the time Ethan and I dated for a week). A boy doesn't pass a forbidden box of Pepero to a girl across the Gender Line unless he likes her.

The ancient phone flips open, which is kind of cute. I find the on switch. The phone makes a jingly noise when it powers up. Aram shifts in her bed and I throw my sheets over my head as I look at the two new text messages in my inbox!

> (1/2) hello candace. this is young-
> bae the boy trainee. dont hav charger
> 4 this weird phone so pls check it 1x
> a day

> (2/2) security card can open roof
> door. will text u when safe 2 meet/
> when. this place drives me nuts lol

I'm so excited I'm holding my breath. I tap out a response – it takes for ever to type words on this number pad. I wish there were emojis on this old phone so I could communicate properly, but …

> How did you get this stuff? Why did
> you give it to me?

The odds of him having *his* contraband phone open right now are probably slim, but I wait for a while just in case he gets back to me right away. I check the battery, which is almost half-empty. Or half-full, I guess.

The phone vibrates twice. I muffle my excited squeaks with MulKogi.

> (1/2) many trainees died 2 obtain
> these items. jk but almost. & i gave
> u bc it seem like u need friend that
> time i saw

> (2/2) u on sunday in the caf. u
> looked like that scary girl from the
> ring. i kno what that feels like lol
> so . . .

A friend? So he just feels sorry for me. My heart sinks a little. I love Binna and JinJoo and some of the girls from the other teams, but as a new trainee from America, YoungBae's the only one who *really* knows what I'm going through. I tap:

> Got it. Excited:)

And immediately, YoungBae's response:

> ok turn off phone. check it 1x every
> night. gnite

I tap, 'Sweet dreams', which is literally the cringiest thing I've ever texted. I blame the weird phone and switch it off. I wrap the strap of the ID card around it and stash both on top of the ceiling tile half a metre above my head.

CHAPTER 17

MANNER HANDS

At five to midnight, I check the hall of practice rooms to make sure the coast is clear. Helena's practising in one of them, as always, but she's too busy practising her expressions – winking and pouting girlishly in the mirror – to notice me creeping past. I peek behind me to make sure JiHoon isn't lurking around like some henchman in a *Mission: Impossible* movie.

This is the *last* thing I should be doing on a night so close to the assessment. If I get caught, I'll be finished. But for some reason, *not* seeing YoungBae isn't an option for me. I hold my breath and run up the staircase that goes up to the roof. My palms are sweaty as I reach into my underwear to pull out the ID – I didn't put it in my sweatpants in case I ran into a junior manager in the hall and they made me turn out my pockets or something . . . which has literally never happened, but this place makes you paranoid.

I hold the ID to the scanner. The door clicks open. Out in the muggy night air, I expect an alarm to alert all the security guards in the whole building and then they'll come after me with flashlights and tasers. But without dozens of chattering girls, the garden is eerie and almost pitch-dark – I only see shadows in the city lights from below. All I hear is the whir of traffic in the distance.

I watch the rusty metal door in the centre of the concrete Gender Wall. It's hot out, but I'm so on edge that I'm actually chilly. I could be discovered by a junior manager or security guard or janitor at any minute.

I've been checking the phone every night and there's usually been a text from YoungBae saying, 'not tnite. manager is up my butt. dont respond save ur battery' but last night, YoungBae finally texted, 'ok can meet tomorrow midnite yay'.

But after twenty minutes of waiting, I figure something must have gone wrong. I turn to go back downstairs when I hear a loud click. The scanner on the Gender Wall flashes green. The door opens, and a tall shadowy silhouette walks through. I get ready to run in case it's an adult . . .

'Dude, you made it,' says the shadow in English.

'YoungBae?' I whisper.

'I was worried you'd chicken out.'

YoungBae steps into a pocket of orange light, which glints off his swoopy hair and illuminates his sharp jawline. I can feel sweat break through my forehead as my heart revs up.

'I'm the one who was waiting around for you,' I whisper. 'This is totally nuts.'

'Sorry about the delay. I'm in a lot of trouble with my manager right now, which is why we're up here. I got written up again.'

He unwinds a hose hidden behind a bonsai planter.

'What do you mean?'

'When I get written up before lunch, I get put on bathroom cleaning duty, which is the worst. When I get written up after lunch, I get put on roof garden watering duty.' He holds up his own ID badge. 'Mr Jeon, one of the janitors, lets me borrow this.'

'And mine?' I say, looking at the surly photo of DongHo.

'One of my teammates, WooChin-*hyung*, found it a while ago, and he passed it down to me when he got cut from the trainee programme last month. It never got deactivated, I guess. These cheap old bootleg phones, WooChin smuggled them in from outside for me. You don't want to know what I had to do for him in return ...'

'Oh no,' I say. 'What?'

He makes a gagging face. 'I had to massage his feet every night.'

'Oh, vom!' I say, laughing. Now that I know what YoungBae's gone through for me – trainee feet get disgusting and torn up. I mean, look at mine – I have renewed hope that I'm not being friend-zoned.

It feels unbelievably refreshing to be speaking English. I feel unburdened and light, like when I take the ankle weights off after one of The General's drills. We talk about the crazy practices we've been doing before the assessment in a few days. I learn that he's the *maknae* of his team too, and his *hyungs* – the boy version of *unnies* – hazed him at first too.

'What kind of shenanigans have your *unnies* been pulling?' he asks.

'Well, two of them keep throwing their garbage on my pillow every day.'

YoungBae laughs. 'Oh, snap. My *hyungs* did that to me at first too. It's some weird Korean rule where the *maknae* is supposed to throw out the garbage for their seniors. Your pillow though? That's just messed up. My *hyungs* at least had the decency to put their trash on my dresser.'

'How did you get them to stop?'

'I won my team's respect, eventually.'

'How?'

'First, I beat my meanest *hyung* YoonSoo in an arm-wrestling match and now we're cool as hell.'

'Yeah, I don't think that's going to work so well for me.'

'The other thing was my first monthly assessment. I pulled out some new moves, which seemed to go over pretty well. Once they knew I was taking debuting seriously and not just messing around, they stopped messing with me.'

'Ah. Well, my manager and The General told me I'm the worst dancer they've ever seen. They're having me stand off to the side doing nothing while everyone else does the dance break.'

YoungBae accidentally sprays water all over his crotch. 'Shoot!'

I laugh and he sprays me for laughing. I scream and run away. 'Stop it!'

'So sorry, my hand slipped,' he says, bowing deeply. Finished with the watering, he rolls the hose back up.

'I don't know what I'm going to do,' I say. 'I really think I'm going to get kicked out after this assessment.'

'Well, we can't have that,' says YoungBae, stroking his chin. 'If you're not the best dancer, you need to think of something else to help you stand out.'

'I think the best I can do is make the dance funny – make a lot of faces and stuff like that. But our Stages are so planned out. I don't think the managers or the *unnies* will appreciate me being all extra.'

'Go ahead and be extra. Kinda like this,' he says. Without warning, he drops to the ground and does a b-boy windmill, his legs slicing through the air like propellers, his foot whooshing centimetres from my chin. He jumps back up like nothing happened, not even breathing hard.

I applaud and YoungBae bows.

'Make your funny faces,' he says. 'We're trying to be K-pop idols, not, like, lawyers or whatever. Everyone expects you to be extra anyway, being American and all.'

I make a mental note: *BE EXTRA*.

I stop and look at him. 'Why are you standing like that?'

Now that he's done watering, YoungBae is standing with his arms crossed and his long legs spread wide apart, as if he's airing out his wet crotch.

'I learnt this in my Behaviour and Manners class. This is called Manner Legs.'

He tells me that since he's so tall, his Behaviour and Manners teacher – who, lucky for him, isn't Madame Jung – tells him it's good manners when he's talking to a lady to stand like this so he's

146

not towering over her like some creeper-giant. Manner Legs.

Honestly, I'm way into it. He's still towering over me, but it's adorable that he's trying. With his wide shoulders, he looks like a giant X.

'He also taught me something called Manner Hands.'

'Oh, I know all about Manner Hands,' I say.

I've seen photos of male idols posing with female fans at **fansign** events. They'll put their arm around the girl but not actually make physical contact – their hand will just hover ten centimetres over her shoulder, or her back if they're 'hugging.'

'Isn't that almost ruder than just touching someone?' I say. 'It's like you think girls are radioactive or something.'

'Yeah, there's a lot I don't really get about Korean manners,' says YoungBae. He spreads his legs wider, his Manner Legs getting even more manner-like, so we're almost eye to eye. As I look at his face head-on, I must be hooked by a gravitational pull coming from his lips or something, because I stumble forward – I swear, it's completely by accident. Before my lips can land on his, he catches me and laughs. 'You OK there?'

'Yeah,' I say, feeling my head. I'm a little dizzy. 'I think I'm just hungry.'

He's still standing with Manner Legs. He has one arm around my back, one hand on my shoulder. My hand is on his chest; he hasn't budged at all from me falling on to him – completely sturdy. It feels so good.

He smiles and we make eye contact for a long second. His eyes are turning into those adorable straight lines. But then he suddenly props me back up to a standing position and lifts his palms in the air. 'Oh, I forgot my Manner Hands. Manner Hands!'

We laugh, but inwardly, I'm thinking that I'll be fine if he decides to use Rude Hands next time. Or Rude Lips.

Or maybe it's on me to forget my manners first.

CHAPTER 18

ASSESSMENT

The period pads sewn into the armpits of my S.A.Y. schoolgirl uniform are really doing their job. It's seven a.m. on the day of the assessment and we're down in the *Popular 10* studio on the third floor. You can pinch the tension in the air with a pair of chopsticks. I watched a lot of *Popular 10* on YouTube before coming to Korea – it's one of SLK's favourite places to debut their Comeback Stages – and usually the studio is flashing with lights while Kim SeungBum, the movie star slash host, announces the most popular songs of the week with his catchphrase, 'Weeeeeee're popular!' But now the stage is totally dark. It's giving me abandoned carnival vibes or something.

Everyone's looking around the darkened studio to see if SLK's actually shown up. I spot YoungBae on the other side of the auditorium, sitting with his team. He looks adorable and hot – a confusing combination, I know – in his S.A.Y. schoolboy uniform, which is a navy blue blazer, purple plaid tie and fitted grey slacks.

I'm sitting between Binna and Aram, pumping a heavy flow of stress sweat into the pads, which were Binna's idea to take care of my perspiration problem. Manager Kong warned us that the entire assessment would take anywhere from thirteen to sixteen hours. We've been up for three hours already. CEO Sang apparently doesn't like girls with a lot of make-up, so we woke up at four a.m., trying really hard to use enough make-up to make it look like we're not wearing any.

At eight a.m., a thunderous clap of apocalyptic music crashes down on us. The stage lights up. The trainees scream in genuine terror and then cheer. A door in the back of the stage opens slowly, dramatically. Blinding sparks rain down from the ceiling as a man emerges from the door. Everyone jumps to their feet. The man has shiny, unnaturally jet-black hair slicked away from his forehead. Even though he's probably almost Harabuji's age, he's dressed in the trendiest outfit I've ever seen – half-moon sunglasses, skintight black jeans, a shirt made out of two clashing plaids sewn together, and bright silver shoes. Everyone gathered in the studio is screaming, jumping up and down, as if he were One.J himself.

This can only be CEO Sang.

'Thank you, thank you,' he says, motioning everyone to sit down. 'Trainees, on behalf of S.A.Y., I'd like to thank you for all your hard work during this intensive pre-debut period. I know some of you are at your limit – but I'm going to have to ask you to work even harder for the next couple of months.

'Just to explain to you how serious we are, let me start out by saying, S.A.Y.'s first girl group will be the most expensive, most hyped, most ambitious debut in world history. Not just of K-pop groups, but of any music group on the planet. With the record-shattering success of SLK, we can afford to shock the world with the most excellent girl group Korea can produce. This will be the girl group to kill all other girl groups. That's why the debut Concept of our new girl group will be ...'

A dramatic pause. '... world domination.'

An image flashes on the giant projection screen behind CEO Sang. It's a satellite image of the Earth, but the entire planet is being squeezed like a stress ball in the palm of a perfectly mani-cured female hand. At the end of each long, tapered finger is a pointy nail painted a different bright, glittery colour – each nail has the black silhouette of a girl printed on it, representing the eventual five members.

There's a collective *Wahhhh!* and gasp throughout the room. My stomach flips – it's a fierce, sick, iconic image. I search the silhouettes on the nails to see if any look like me, but none of them are a short chick with stubby legs – they're all just idealized, long-legged female figures in various Sailor Moon-ish poses.

I hear Helena from two seats over. '*Daebak*, that's my hand!' she whispers. 'I was wondering why the creatives wanted to photograph me squeezing a stress ball!'

Ugh. Suddenly I like the image a little less.

'We've been evaluating your progress closely to see how well you fit into this Concept,' continues CEO Sang. 'Because this is going to be the ultimate girl group, dominating in all categories, we're going to break all the rules. The first single, which our lead producer Chang-y and junior producer Clown Killah have been perfecting for months, was actually meant to be SLK's next Comeback title track.'

The reaction to this is the biggest of all.

'Yes, you heard this correctly. I'm delaying the most antici-pated Comeback in K-pop history to make sure this girl group's debut breaks records. Your *sunbaenims* in SLK have graciously sacrificed this guaranteed Perfect All-Kill hit for the good of the group and the good of the company. Why don't you all thank your *sunbaenims* right now?'

Aram squeezes my arm. I squeeze Binna's. We all turn to the back of the auditorium, where five figures in dark clothes have snuck in without anyone noticing. We can't make out any of their faces, but my heart explodes like a potato in a microwave. It doesn't feel real that I'm in the same room as SLK. We bow in SLK's direction to thank their shadows profusely.

'Now, without further ado, let's get started, shall we? I hope this taste of what's to come motivates all of you trainees to perform to your fullest – and this is your most important test yet.'

With that, the assessment finally kicks off. Girls are up first and the teams are performing in reverse, starting with Team Ten. CEO Sang takes a seat on a raised platform in the centre of the audience, *American Idol* style.

I'm fascinated, seeing the other groups' skill levels for the first time. Team Ten does a swaggy, spot-on version of 2NE1's 'I Am the Best'. Luciana, Helena's Brazilian Korean friend from Language class, is the team's Centre and Visual. Her dancing is powerful and seductive. RaLa on Team Six kills the rap from EXID's 'Up & Down' – now I understand why she's here.

Can I possibly do what these girls are doing? I'm blown away by the talent, nervous but thrilled.

After the groups perform, CEO Sang calls each team member to the stage individually to receive a critique in front of everyone. I quickly realize he's totally savage, like Simon Cowell on steroids. He doesn't just go in on trainees' skills ('SooJung, if I'd paid to see your concert, I'd not only ask for my money back, I'd sue for damages.'), he rips into their looks, which completely horrifies me ('MunHee, did you eat something salty last night? Why is your face so bloated?'). He makes some girls step on a scale, which broadcasts her exact weight on the big screen for everyone to see. For SLK to see. This whole process takes hours – some of the boy trainees, knowing they have hours before they perform, are falling asleep – but my outrage keeps me as wide awake as a can of full-sugar Red Bull.

My hands ball into fists as a dozen flaws he could potentially bring up about my body swarm my brain, leaving no room for the choreography I should be thinking about.

Before Team Three takes the stage to perform 'Abracadabra' by Brown Eyed Girls, Manager Kong whispers to us to follow her backstage to get ready. In the dressing room, Aram touches up her make-up. JinJoo practises her vocals. Binna and Helena stretch.

Suddenly, the insane reality of what I'm trying to do hits me all at once. I've never danced in front of a real audience before. I've never performed in front of a scary Korean CEO. And I've *definitely* never performed in front of the most popular boy band in the world.

I go up to Binna and tug on her wrist. 'Binna,' I whisper urgently. 'I'm going to mess up. I'm sure of it. I'll ruin this.'

She grabs my shoulders and looks me right in the eyes. 'No you won't,' she says.

'I will! If you asked me right now what the first move is supposed to be, I couldn't tell you.'

'It'll all come to you when the music starts up. We've rehearsed this for so long.'

'You're right, you're right,' I pant.

'Besides,' she says with a half-smile, 'if we mess up, we mess up. It's not the end of the world, is it?'

Try telling that to CEO Sang or Manager Kong, I want to say.

We line up at the wing of the stage. Right before Manager Kong gives us our cue to walk out, Binna winks at me and whispers, 'We're having fun!'

I might be imagining it, but it feels as if the cheers we get walking out on to the stage are louder than any I've heard so far. I wave. I don't dare look in the far corner in the back, where SLK is allegedly sitting – that part, I can't even begin to think about. I scan the boys' section to spot YoungBae's face, which is easy, because he's standing and shouting something; I'm hoping it's something like, 'CANDACE, I'M YOUR NUMBER ONE FAN!'

I'm so distracted by the audience that I run straight into Aram. There's scattered laughter and Aram shoots me a frozen smile of death. We haven't even done our intro and I've already messed it up. And Binna was wrong – messing up *will* be the end of the world, I'm sure of it.

Binna counts us down for the intro we've prepared and rehearsed a million times. 'Three, two, one . . .'

'*ANYUNGHASEYO!* WE ARE THE LOVELY AND TALENTED TEAM TWO!' we pipe in perfect unison, in the cheeriest, girliest voices we can muster.

'Very well,' says CEO Sang from the centre of the auditorium. His voice lasers from his platform straight into my **in-ears**. 'I've been looking forward to the great Team Two.'

Total silence encloses the studio. I hold my breath as the five of us get into our starting formation, with me on the end next to Aram, my hand planted on my jutted hip. For a brief second, I feel a surge of connectedness to the other four girls – even Helena – like I've never felt before in my life. A success or a disaster, we're doing this together.

Finally, the familiar horns of 'Problem' blare from the speakers and it's like I completely lose control of my body. I have the first line of the song and I bring my mic – when did I even grab a mic? – to my mouth and let it rip. The audience lets out a surprised 'whooo!' at the sound of my voice.

So *this* is why we practise around the clock. All thoughts, all plans, all mantras wipe themselves from my brain and my body is left to do the choreo that's been drilled into it over the course of four excruciating weeks. I'm completely, utterly, stupidly focused on what I'm doing. I see the other girls only in my peripheral vision. I have no idea if everyone is doing what they're supposed to do, or if *I'm* exactly where I'm supposed to be.

In the first pre-chorus, after JinJoo and I belt out a perfectly synced high G, the audience goes wild. By the time we get to the second chorus, I see that all trainees are on their feet – they haven't done that for any of the teams before us. I'm like Tinker Bell or Lady Gaga – my essence shines brighter the more applause I get. Energy floods into my limbs.

Then comes the dance break: the part where I'm supposed to stand awkwardly on the side singing my notes while the other four slap the **Killing Part** of the choreo.

But something comes over me. My hands curl around the imaginary saxophone in front of me and suddenly it's as if I'm possessed. My cheeks pufferfish as big as they'll go; my fingers fly over those invisible keys. I'm rocking my body back and forth, gettin' *down*. I'm so consumed by my air sax that I break away from my spot next to the other girls and shuffle across the entire stage by myself. I'm playing the crap out of my instrument and it's playing the crap out of *me*. The crowd goes wild – whether it's for the insane acrobatics Binna is doing a couple of metres away from me, or for my funky, nasty, bombastic sax solo, I have no idea – in the moment, I don't care. I just wanna blow with all the soul of Kenny G and Lisa Simpson combined.

After my riff, I come out of my trance and my imaginary horn evanesces into nothing. I run to join the girls for the last bit of choreography. I'm so high from adrenaline by the time the song winds down that I know there's no other choice: at the end of the song, I'm supposed to pose with my hand on my hip while all my teammates drop into cool splits, but now I've *gotta* whip out my surprise showstopper.

On the last beat, it's as if gravity reaches up and grabs me by the back of my schoolgirl blouse and pulls me to the floor with all its strength. All I see is the maze of lighting tracks on the ceiling, and there's a light twinge in my knee, which is folded under my body, when a swell of raucous applause and cheers washes over me.

I did the death drop – or at least what I hope to God was something resembling a death drop – right at the end. I started practising it after my rendezvous with YoungBae on Saturday. Something about his advice – to 'go ahead and be extra' – put this idea in my head. I've seen my favourite drag queens on *RuPaul's Drag Race* pull out the death drop during a Lip Sync for Your Life, doing a free fall backwards on to the ground while folding one leg behind you to absorb the impact. It doesn't require the flexibility of a falling split, but it can have the same wow factor.

I get to my feet slowly. My knee is aching and I'm seeing stars, but that's OK, because I'm also seeing all my fellow trainees, boys and girls, jumping up and down cheering. Even CEO Sang is clapping and grinning. I glance up at the far corner – the five shadowy figures who are allegedly SLK are jumping too.

I throw my arms around the nearest person – who happens to be Helena – and scream into her ear, 'Good job!'

'OK, OK, thanks,' she pants while pushing me away.

I jump on to Binna and squeeze her as tight as I can. 'Thank you!' is the only thing I can think to say.

'You did so well, Candace,' she gasps as we sweat on to each other.

'*Wahhhh!*' booms CEO Sang. 'This is what I've been waiting for right here!' he shouts.

The five of us bow profusely and chant in unison, 'Thank you, CEO Sang!'

'What the managers have been saying may actually be true – maybe I should just debut Team Two as it is now and call it a day.'

At this, the five of us scream and jump, hugging each other all over again. What sounds like a groan from the girl trainees and a collective '*Wahhh!*' from the boys swells throughout the studio.

'It looks to me that,' says CEO Sang, checking his notes, 'that . . . Candace, is it?'

I nod so violently my neck aches.

'Park Candace from New Jersey. New Jersey as in Tony Soprano.'

I have absolutely nothing to say in response, so I bow again and say, 'Yes, sir.'

CEO Sang goes on, 'I wasn't sure that bringing an American in at this late stage in the process was a good idea, but . . . Everyone besides Candace, please leave the stage for now.'

So my individual assessment begins. I step to the centre of the stage as the other four return to the wing.

'You have quite an impressive voice,' he says.

I bow deeply. '*Gamsamnida*. It seems to me that I may have worked really hard and it seems to me that I'm glad our Stage seems to have gone well.'

CEO Sang nods once. 'Your pronunciation is OK but needs a lot of improvement. Korean fans are very proud of our language and expect even *gyopo* idols to speak it well.'

I bow again. 'It seems to me I want to work even harder,' I say.

'Good. Now let's talk about your performance, Candace-*shi*.'

158

He tells me that my singing is excellent – strong, current and perfect for recording.

'However,' he says, 'your dance skills are still severely lacking – you were off centre and out of time. But still, I was looking at you. I very much enjoyed your . . . saxophone move.' There's warm laughter from the audience. 'And that interesting move you did at the very end – where you dropped to the ground – I've never seen any of my idols or trainees do that before. Was that move approved by Miss Yoon?'

I shake my head, my eyes fixed on the ground. But when I peer upwards, to my shock, CEO Sang is giving me a thumbs up.

'It reminded me of an American artist,' he says, 'the way you were willing to feel the music and be spontaneous onstage. Still, I want to see you improve your basics next time.'

Even though I decided hours ago that CEO Sang was a misogynistic monster, his approval has a magical effect on me.

'Now let's talk about your Visuals. You have quite a cute face. Next to your teammates Aram and Helena, you're definitely not a K-pop "goddess" type, but you have a bright, healthy vibe. I can imagine you being popular with the youngest fans.'

I'd give anything for him to stop talking about my looks. Cringey times a million.

'But I think you can take yourself to another level. Do you want to just be cute or do you want to be a fashion icon like Blackpink's Jennie? Or a living doll like IZ*ONE's Wonyoung? Or a **CF** queen like Red Velvet's Irene? I believe you should get a nose job.'

My head shakes of its own accord. '*Bae-jjae-ra,*' I blurt.

I feel the oxygen leave the room as there's a shocked gasp. I clamp my hands over my mouth.

I must have gone completely nuts. I really just said that out loud. I just told him to cut my stomach open – *over my dead body*. Not only that, I definitely didn't use *jondaetmal*. On the CEO! My K-pop career is over.

'What did you just say to me?' he growls.

I bow over and over. 'I am so, so, so sorry, sir. It just slipped out of my mouth.'

CEO Sang surprises me by smiling – but this time, it's ice-cold. 'I take it, however, that the sentiment is true? You don't want a nose job? Even though I would pay for it? Even though it'd take your Visuals to the next level?'

'If I'm being honest, sir, no,' I mumble, staring at the floor.

'And why is that, Candace-*shi*? Is it because you think your Visuals are perfect as they are now?'

'It's not that, sir,' I say. 'It's just that . . . I want to look like my *abba*.'

A tsunami of laughter from all directions crashes over me. I have no idea what I said that was so funny.

But then it occurs to me that with my imperfect Korean, I might have accidentally implied that I care so little about my looks that it's fine with me if I look like some *ajusshi* – a middle-aged man. I open my mouth to explain what I meant, but I realize I still don't have the vocabulary to express myself.

What I really want to say is that I got my nose from Abba – everyone says so. When we were little, Tommy used to call me 'potato nose'. I used to hate it and to be honest, I still don't love it.

I've fantasized about changing it into a perfect, refined, delicate Natalie Portman nose. But now I realize I'll never really do it – not to make some CEO happy, not to be part of some hyped-up girl group, not to have YoungBae or even One.J fall in love with me. Every time I look at my face in the mirror, I see Abba's nose. Just like Abba's, my nose gets wider when I smile or laugh. When you look at Abba's big, open face, what it tells you is, 'I won't judge you. You're already exactly as you should be.' What greater honour is there in life than having some of that quality of his right in the centre of my face?

'You truly have an American spirit,' CEO Sang says, 'but you need to learn some more of that Korean respect, Candace-*shi*.'

I bow and apologize over and over.

'But for now, keep your American directness going a bit longer, because I have an important question for you. As a brand-new member of the top team in the company, what are your impressions of your fellow Team Two members?'

This one's easy. 'Each one of them is kinder and more talented than the next,' I say.

'All right, all right,' says CEO Sang, waving his hand dismissively. 'We're not on a broadcast show. I actually want you to be honest. If I had to cut one member of Team Two today, who would it be?'

There's a scandalized murmur in the audience. My entire body clenches up.

'I couldn't for all the world cut one of my members,' I say. 'They're too talented.'

'Come on and answer the question, Candace.'

'I'd sooner be cut myself, sir.'

'Candace,' CEO Sang growls. 'If you don't answer the question, I really will cut you. You're being disrespectful. Give me an answer, now.'

Well, I'm screwed. At this point, I really do have to answer. I remember the lesson from my first session with Madame Jung: it's polite to refuse a Korean person up to a point, but on the third time, you should really give in.

I squeeze my eyes shut and say softly, 'It seems to me my choice would have to be Helena-*unnie*.'

There's a gasp. I open my eyes again slowly. CEO Sang's lion head rears back. 'Helena? But I consider Helena one of my very top trainees.'

'Well, then I would like to change my answer back to myself.'

'No, it's too late. Now I must know why.'

I can feel Helena launching heat-seeking missiles at me from her eye sockets. I stammer, 'W-well, it seems t-to me that Helena is great at all th-the idol skills, but it seems to me she's n-not quite the very best at any one thing . . . and isn't your goal to put together the ultimate girl group?'

To my shock, CEO Sang laughs as if he couldn't be more pleased. 'You're fiercer than you look, Candace-*shi*. A real *yeowoo*.'

I'm not sure, but I think he just called me a fox – basically the equivalent of a *she-wolf*.

'Thank you, Candace-*shi*, you've given me many fascinating insights. Now leave the stage so I can speak to your *unnie* Helena about all this.'

What just happened? My head is swimming as I head to the

162

wings of the stage, where my teammates are waiting. I can't look any of them in the eye, but I know it's Helena who clips my shoulder as she moves to centre stage to take her grilling from CEO Sang.

The moment I step backstage, Manager Kong grabs my wrist.

'What on earth was that?' snarls Manager Kong through clenched teeth. She tugs me into the green room, where the members of Team One, including BowHee, are warming up for their Stage.

'I don't know what came over me,' I insist. 'I'm sorry!'

'How could you betray one of your teammates like that?! One of *my* trainees?!'

'He asked three times,' I explain, staring at the floor.

'So?! Where are you getting this "three times" business from, you idiot? Would you quack like a duck if he asked you three times?'

'I'm not sure,' I answer honestly.

But I can tell Manager Kong thinks I'm being sassy. She jabs my chest with her finger. 'You need to learn some respect. You think because you can sing and your Stage went well you're a shoo-in to debut? You're a celebrity already?'

'No, Manager Kong—'

She ignores me and drags me into the elevator up to floor ninety-eight, down the hallways of the corporate floor, up the stairs, through the metal door to the girls' training facility, berating me the whole time, going on about how Helena has been working harder than me for years, that I'm not half the trainee she is.

Manager Kong shoves me inside my dorm and flicks the light on. I massage my wrist.

'This is over,' Manager Kong says coldly. 'You're done.'

What?

'I'm sorry, Manager Kong, but what do you mean "done"?'

'I mean pack your bags and get out of here. When I saw you that first time in New Jersey, I thought, *Oh, what a cute girl, what a unique voice.* You danced like a joke, but there was something in your face that made me think you were open and teachable. But now I know I made a huge mistake. I can't believe you would use *banmal* on the CEO of this company – it's so inappropriate I almost want to laugh. Not only that, you broke from choreography, and you could have thrown off your *unnies*. You call yourself a team player? You're a *ssagaji* American princess and you're dragging my other girls down.'

I'm seeing spots. I close my eyes, hoping this is a horrible nightmare. It takes effort to open them again. I can't believe all my hard work for this month – the worst and best month of my life – has all been for nothing.

'Well?!' screams Manager Kong. 'Get packing, *you little brat*!'

An adult yelling at you in Korean is a million times scarier than an adult yelling at you in English.

'You mean right now?' I ask. I check our clock. It's quarter to midnight. 'I have nowhere to go.'

'Not my problem. I'm coming back to escort you out in five minutes. I'm not missing any more of the assessment to deal with you.'

She slams the door shut and I'm alone.

CHAPTER 19

THE BIG BANG

I don't even have a chance to cry, because my brain is reeling, figuring out a plan for when I'm thrust out into Seoul alone. It's three days before Umma's expecting me and I have no idea how to get back to the apartment. Should I sleep in the subway station? Find a shelter for runaways? I have cash Umma gave me, but not enough for a hotel.

It takes me less than five minutes to pack up my entire life. I strap my guitar case to my back, stuff MulKogi into my duffel bag and take one last look at that cramped, stinky little dorm room. I hate everything about the room, but I realize that I'll come to miss it one day – that feeling of having everything on the line for a dream, of giving it everything you have from the moment you wake up at dawn to the moment you close your eyes late at night.

I won't be able to say goodbye to YoungBae.

I want to write Binna and JinJoo a note, but there's no time.

165

My stomach lurches as the elevator plunges down ninety-nine floors to the lobby.

I turn to Manager Kong shyly. 'I'm sorry to ask, but may I please get my phone back, please? I need to call my mom to come get me.'

'Ask security at the front desk,' she snaps.

She doesn't even get out of the elevator with me. She doesn't bother to look at me one last time before the doors close.

The lobby is an abandoned space station, an expanse of black stone floor. The monitors play twenty-four-hour news stations for no one. Cafe Tomorrow is darkened. A lone thick-necked security guard mans the curved front desk. He's watching some noisy variety show on his phone.

When I ask the security guard for my phone back, he tells me he doesn't have any phones.

'But I need to call my mom.'

'What's her phone number?'

I have no idea what Umma's Korean phone number is. She gave all her essential contact info directly to Manager Kong. Instead, I start telling the security guard my phone number in Jersey, so Abba can call Umma for me.

'Hey, stop messing around,' snaps the security guard. 'I'm not calling an American number. Go over there and wait for someone to get you.'

He nods to a cluster of modern but uncomfortable-looking sofas.

I don't know Umma's address. I don't remember the name of her neighbourhood – I just remember that it's across the Han

166

River. What if I go out into the Seoul night and get murdered or something? Does S.A.Y. really want to be responsible for a dead trainee?

I figure I know enough Korean by now to be able to find my way back by asking around and looking pitiful in front of adults. But not in the middle of the night.

Then I remember the phone YoungBae gave me – I left it in the ceiling of the dorm room. I really am an idiot.

When I'm curled up on one of the uncomfortable couches, using MulKogi as my pillow, the enormity of what just happened hits me. My whole time as a trainee already feels like a dream – was that real life? Did I really get that close to becoming a K-pop idol? Did I really just mess it up all because of my big mouth and bratty attitude?

After moaning into MulKogi's soft, plush belly for I don't know how long, I finally drift off into a restless half-sleep.

'Hey. Hey, you. Wake up.'

I feel something cold and wet on my forehead. *Huh?*

I open my eyes and see a pair of eyes staring back at me over a black **surgical mask** with a skull and crossbones on it. I scream.

I've been kidnapped. A creeper wants my organs.

I sit up, wiping the ice-cold numbing agent or blood or what-ever the hell that is from my forehead, only to see there are four more of them. An entire gang of creepers all in black, the same scary surgical mask. The words *don't let them take you to a second location* echo in my head and I bicycle-kick my legs at the air as hard as they'll go.

'Hey, calm down!' says the lead creeper, the one in the middle. He removes his mask. So do the others.

I see five familiar faces. Five extremely handsome faces. My mouth is open but all that comes out is a croak.

'You're the saxophone girl,' says the tall one on the right, puffing out his cheeks in an impression of me from earlier.

The short one in the middle – the one with the perfect piercing eyes and the delicately pointed chin – says, 'I can't believe you talked to CEO Sang like that. You have some nerve.' He holds his hand up to me, smiling.

I give him a high five and it finally hits me.

'You're One.J.' I point right at his face with a trembling finger. Then I go down the line, naming them. 'And you're YooChin. Joodah. Wookie. And ChangWoo.'

I'm such a weirdo.

'Yep, that's us,' chuckles Wookie.

The members of SLK look exhausted. They're not wearing any make-up and they're in street clothes, but they don't look anything like regular guys (except for Wookie – Wookie looks like any Korean dude anywhere). *These* are the five guys who shut down *SNL*. Who charmed Wendy Williams and James Corden and Jimmy Fallon. Who've graced the covers of *Vanity Fair* and *Esquire*. Who are Instagram's most followed celebrities. Who've given hope to hundreds of millions of young people around the world.

So *this* is what being star-struck feels like. It feels like a new big bang has gone off right before my eyes, creating a new universe. These five guys radiate a warm glow and I'm being drawn into their gravity. They all have that pull – even Wookie – but One.J is the centre of this constellation.

'Why are you out here on your own, Saxophone Girl?' says ChangWoo in his deep, chocolatey voice.

'Well . . .' I'm so ashamed and embarrassed I can't look at them, even though I really want to stare at them for days and days. 'I've been kicked out of the trainee programme.'

SLK bursts out laughing. Their laughs echo throughout the cavernous space lobby. Wookie doubles over, slapping his knees. I'm so confused.

'I'm sorry . . . but what's so funny?' I mumble slowly.

'Look. She has her bag and guitar case and everything,' gasps One.J to YooChin. 'It's so cute!'

Finally, One.J catches his breath. His disturbingly symmetrical face is flushed. 'Sorry, sorry. It's just that . . . it's very charming that you think you've actually been kicked out. Candace, was it?'

I'm about to crash to the ground like an ancient oak. One-freaking-J knows my name. I nod with my mouth hanging open.

'Candace, you haven't been kicked out.' He smiles the billion-dollar half-smile I've seen on countless posters and MVs. 'Your manager is teaching you a lesson. All of us have been "kicked out" of the trainee programme. We've all had to spend the night in the lobby.'

YooChin raises his hand. 'I was "kicked out" five times as a trainee.'

'Four times,' says Joodah.

169

'Twice,' says ChangWoo.

'Thirteen times!' pipes Wookie proudly. ChangWoo punches his shoulder playfully.

So I *don't* have to go back to Umma, admitting my failure? I *do* get to see YoungBae and Binna again?

'I'm not sure,' I say shakily. 'She was really, really mad.'

'Why, because you used *banmal* on the CEO?' says Chang-Woo.

'Or because you talked smack about that teammate of yours?' says Joodah.

They burst out laughing again.

'Oh my God, Candace, I can't believe you did that,' chuckles One.J. 'That *unnie* is going to kill you when you get back upstairs.'

Wookie is slapping his knee again. 'You were supposed to say something like, "I would cut this *unnie* because she's so great at everything that there'd be no room for the rest of us to shine". You can't say something that's actually true.'

ChangWoo, still laughing, says, 'When it was that *unnie*'s turn for her assessment, CEO Sang said, "Now that Candace mentions it, you really *aren't* the best on your team at anything. You're a good singer, but Candace is better. You're a good dancer, but Binna's better. You have great charisma, but Candace has you beat there too."'

Oh no. No, no, no. There are no words to describe how dead I am.

But also, CEO Sang thinks I'm more charismatic than Helena?!

'Ah, those trainee days,' says YooChin wistfully. 'Everything felt so life or death.'

'Well, it kind of was,' says One.J. He gives me a look that makes my butt crack sweat. 'Poor thing. You look traumatized by that assessment. Here, we got this for you.'

He hands me a Cafe Tomorrow cup of iced matcha latte, my favourite drink. (Magically, there's now an employee working at the cafe in the middle of the night.) He must have pressed this against my forehead to wake me up. I accept it with both hands and a deep bow. 'Thank you, One.J-*sunbaenim*.'

A whole entourage of adults in black – SLK's managers, I would guess – are milling around next to the security desk.

Every trainee upstairs would kill to be in my position right now: I'm having a drink with SLK!

I'm probably hallucinating, but it seems to me One.J is looking at me a lot more than the rest of the guys are. He smiles thoughtfully at me again, and – forget my armpits – I need double panty liners for my butt sweat.

They all mime saxophones. I laugh and try to hide my burning cheeks with my hair.

'A lot of the girl trainees are talented,' says One.J, 'but a lot of them are too rehearsed.'

'But that's what the trainee system does to idols,' says Chang-Woo. 'You learn important fundamentals, but part of being an artist is learning to forget what you learnt in training.'

'I've already forgotten everything!' says Wookie with a goofy grin.

Wookie really *would* be perfect for JinJoo. Two sweethearts.

One.J nods to my hot-pink guitar case. 'You play?'

'Yes,' I say, 'but nothing too serious.'

'I bet you haven't had a chance to play at all as a trainee.'

I shake my head. I know One.J is only a year older than me, but there's something about his stillness that's so powerful and grown-up, despite his baby face. ChangWoo and Joodah are in their twenties, but One.J is clearly the oldest soul.

'Yeah,' he says, 'it wasn't until after our debut and first two Comebacks were successful that CEO Sang finally let me and ChangWoo write our own songs.'

'I really love that song you wrote on the *Love Darkness* mini-album . . . "Flower Petal Romance". It's really beautiful.'

I hope I'm not fangirling too hard. One.J has literally millions of people telling him his songs are beautiful. But he simply nods slightly and smiles. 'Thank you. Do you write songs at all?'

'Yes, but nothing like you . . .'

'Why don't we hear one?'

My mouth goes as arid as a desert. 'It's so late . . . you just spent a whole day watching a hundred trainees perform, I'm sure you're exhausted—'

'We're used to not getting any sleep,' says One.J quickly. 'I wanna hear you play.'

Most of the other guys look tired, but Wookie claps his hands. 'Concert, concert, concert!'

I can't say no to SLK – and even though I'm scared, every part of me does want to show them what I can do. My hands are so unsteady that it takes me a long time to get my guitar out. I can feel the pack of contraband *yakgwas* shifting around inside it, but it shouldn't affect the sound too much.

I take a deep breath. 'Please don't expect too much.'

One.J sits up straighter. 'We will listen with joyful hearts,' he says.

OMG. As annoying as Korean formality can be, sometimes it's really sexy.

I strum the opening chords to 'Expectations vs Reality'. I haven't played in a month, but I never once worry about forgetting my finger placements.

The words all come back to me easily. I feel like I have a new grip on my voice I never had, as if it's a weapon. I'm now able to swing powerfully with it, stronger than when I was whispering softly in my bedroom.

When I finish, SLK applauds for me. *SLK* ... clapping for *me*. The managers and the thick-necked security guard clap from across the lobby too. Wookie gives me a standing O and shouts, 'Encore, encore!' I bow to all of them, beaming.

'That concept is really *daebak*,' says One.J. '"Expectations vs Reality". Does that phrase refer to how things aren't always how they look on the outside?'

Just as it was in SLK's interview on *The Tonight Show*, One.J's Korean accent when he's speaking English is adorably thick.

'That's exactly right, *sunbaenim*,' I say.

One of SLK's managers comes up to us. 'Sorry to interrupt,' he says, 'but you guys need to start preparing for your appearance on *Knowing Bros*. And I Kakao'd Manager Kong – she would like Candace back in her bed right away.'

Thank God. So I really *haven't* been kicked out.

I check the monitors. It's three a.m.

'Good talking to you, Candace,' says One.J, standing up. I stand up too. He's only a few centimetres taller than me, but his presence is massive. The other four have already faded into the background; they're satellites orbiting around him.

He puts his hand out for a shake. I take it with both of my hands and bow, the way Madame Jung taught me. One.J looks amused. Then he draws me a couple of centimetres closer and says softly, 'Listen. Since you obviously have talent as a song-writer, here's my advice to you: write one song every night. Even if you're exhausted and all you want to do is sleep, even if trainee life has drained your soul, even if all you want to write about is how hungry and tired you are, write a verse, chorus and bridge about whatever you're feeling that day. I can tell you're not meant to be just an idol. You want to be an artist too. Right?'

I nod and he releases my hand. I bow to all the members and managers, my head spinning from the events of the day. One.J thinks – or One.J *knows* – I'm an artist.

The security guard opens the glass doors for me to re-enter. I gather MulKogi, my guitar and my duffel bag. I promise myself to stop complaining. To practise till my voice goes ragged and my feet are bloody stumps. To not let some girl with fake strawberry blonde hair intimidate me.

I step back into the elevator and look at my reflection. I don't just want to be an idol. I want to be an artist.

CHAPTER 20

FOX

I'm woken up first thing the following morning, while my team-mates are still asleep, for an unscheduled meeting with Madame Jung. In her office, she's standing by her window with a file in her hand. Behind her, all of Seoul is cast in the hazy, majestic glow of dawn.

Does no one here sleep?!

Madame Jung approaches me slowly and perches on the edge of her desk, looking down her nose at me. There's no moisture in my mouth, so I gulp down dry air.

'Yesterday, the way you behaved towards CEO Sang – a brilliant businessman and image-maker – was unacceptable. Do you know what would happen to me if I used *banmal* with him? But for a little girl to do so . . .'

'I'm sorry, Madame—'

'I don't know if we want such a girl, who's studied the viola with nothing to show for it, who's only ranked number two in a New Jersey public school, to represent one of the most important corporations in Korea.' She leafs through my file. 'Both parents went to such a prestigious music conservatoire where only the elite and talented can go. Now they work at a convenience store in New Jersey. To fall like that, they must have made some pretty big mistakes, huh?'

My face is boiling. My hands are in fists. I tell myself to stay calm. Don't cry or yell. For the sake of my dream, keep it together.

'Stand up,' she says through clenched teeth.

I thought Manager Kong yelling at me was terrifying, but she has nothing on Madame Jung. I slowly get to my feet. Madame Jung walks back around her desk and pulls out a delicate wooden box with ornate designs on the lid. Inside is a pair of smooth rose-coloured stones.

'Take these, little girl. Go to that corner of the office and face the wall. Get on your knees and put one stone under each knee. Hold your arms over your head and keep them there for the next two hours – I'll tell Manager Kong you'll be late for group practice. As you feel your own discomfort, think of the discomfort you caused others with your disrespectful behaviour. Go!'

I don't move.

She snarls, 'Go on. What is this disrespect?!'

I look down at the floor and try to arrange my mouth into a placid smile. Somehow, a calm washes over me. 'It seems I'm not able to do what you ask, Madame,' I say gently.

Her ghostly pale face darkens a shade. 'Watch your tone, little girl.'

No matter what Madame Jung says, I know in my bones that I won't kneel. First of all, my right knee still hurts from my death drop. But on top of that, I think of Umma, Abba, Tommy. Imani and Ethan. And now Binna, JinJoo, YoungBae. I'm loved. No matter how rich or powerful this company is, no matter how powerful this woman is, I'm someone's dearest daughter and sister and friend. I'm not kneeling in a corner for Madame Jung just because she has a grand office and fancy title.

I force my quivering lips into a smile and say, 'It seems I'm afraid we can stand here all day, yet I still won't be able to do what you ask.'

I fold my hands neatly on my knees, keep my eyes downcast and sit absolutely still.

'*Tch*, look at this shameless *ssagaji* behaviour,' Madame Jung spits in disbelief, packing away her stones. 'This is why of all the things I do for ShinBi, marketing idols is my least favourite task. I have to convince the public that you kids are special, deserving of worship and adoration . . . when in reality, idols, and the trainees who desperately want to be idols, are the losers of this country. Bottom of the barrel, like my youngest son – I had to pull strings just to get him a junior-level job at this company. Most idols are just empty-headed losers who never had hope of scoring in the top percentile on the national university entrance exam.'

I start to say, 'It seems to me that isn't what I've seen,' but she cuts me off.

'Don't feel like you've won a victory today, because you haven't. I can make things harder for you. Now get out of my sight.'

When I get back to the dorm, none of my teammates seem the least bit surprised to see me. JinJoo hugs me and says, 'Welcome back!' Binna laughs when I say good morning.

However, in the gym, I see that everything's changed. The girls from the other teams stare at me, give me wide clearance as I pass, as if I have something contagious. JiHoon barks at everyone, 'Wake up, girls! Get working. Most of you looked fat onstage yesterday.'

Ugh. I can't with JiHoon – not today, Satan.

Back in our dorm after the morning workout, Helena keeps her back to me. I can't see her face; I know I'm in for it later. But Aram is downright friendly. Coming out of the bathroom after a shorter shower than usual, she says while towelling off her hair, 'Good job yesterday, Candace.'

I bow my thanks. For once, I have time to take a morning shower before breakfast.

As I walk into the cafeteria, I look through the Gender Glass at YoungBae. He lifts his hands above his head to applaud me. I laugh and give him an exaggerated bow. Aram whispers, 'Be careful, Candace!'

'Oh, right,' I say, composing myself and staring straight ahead.

I remember how YoungBae told me he won his *hyungs'* respect after the first assessment. Is it possible that I've won Aram's?

As we're lining up for our food, Manager Kong claps her hands. 'Ladies!' she shouts. 'Listen to me. I have an announcement to make.'

Manager Kong steps on to a table and everyone immediately quiets down.

'You all worked hard in preparation for the assessment yesterday,' she says. 'For that, we all thank you. CEO Sang was impressed with some of you, less with others. However, he does believe that among the girl trainees, there's a bit of a problem with self-control and discipline.'

I might be imagining it, but I feel forty-nine pairs of eyes landing on me all at once.

'That's why, until the next monthly assessment, S.A.Y. will be introducing a stricter diet.'

There's a panicked groan throughout the cafeteria. I can't imagine how our diets could get any more extreme than they are now.

'It's for your own good. Not only will the new diet improve your Visuals, it will test who's strong enough to debut. Do you think diets will get any easier for you once you're in the public eye? Do you know how harsh **netizens** can be? Take this as an opportunity to show us your inner steel.'

'YES, MANAGER KONG!' shout fifty hungry girls.

At our usual table, BowHee squeals, 'Are they trying to kill us?!'

'Oh my God,' says Binna. 'Now it's getting really real.'

'I'm dead meat,' moans JinJoo.

The menus until the second assessment are exactly the same as they were before, but portions are set – it's no longer all-you-can-eat-while-managers-are-silently-judging-you.

I remind myself that my first weekend outside the building is coming in just two days. When Saturday comes, I'll be with Umma, feasting on *jokbal* and black bean noodles and cheese-burgers. Until then, I have to survive Helena and one last session with The General. I can do this ... I *think*.

RaLa shakes her head gravely at her pitiful breakfast. 'Woman cannot live on sweet potato alone,' she says.

I feel a twinge of guilt – could this be all my fault?

Manager Kong joins our group practice to nail down our next assessment plan.

'Before anyone asks,' says Manager Kong, 'One.J has not chosen a trainee to appear in his video yet.'

My heart plummets. A part of me was wishing he would have shut down the search after I sang my song for him downstairs. But I'm being an idiot. One.J is the most popular singer on the planet right now – his superpower is making billions of girls (and boys) fall in love with him. There's no way I'm *actually* as special as he made me feel.

'One.J and CEO Sang want to see more before making a decision,' continues Manager Kong. 'And I don't blame them. While there were high points to your performance, it was sloppy and there was too much individual spotlight-grabbing.'

I hang my head in shame.

'The next assessment won't be in the studio. It'll be in the CEO's conference room. And I'm not talking about CEO Sang – I'm talking about CEO Im, the CEO of ShinBi Unlimited at large.'

Holy sheet mask. This CEO Im dude has to be one of the five richest people in Korea.

'*Daebak*,' gasps Helena.

'CEO Im, CEO Sang, top investors, top executives and top creatives will watch you perform up-close. There can be no mistakes, no watered-down choreography this time. And no funny business. Right, Candace?'

I feel Helena's laser-beam gaze searing into my face.

'Yes, Manager Kong,' I say with a bow.

'In addition to a team performance, CEO Sang wants each of you to prepare a two-minute individual performance. It can be whatever you want, as long as you shine to your greatest ability, whether it's singing, dancing or acting.'

'Acting?! *Daebak!*' squeals Aram. While I'm in Korean Language class every day, Aram and some of the other top Visual trainees take K-drama acting classes on the corporate floor. It's where Helena goes when she leaves class two hours early.

Manager Kong claps her hands. 'All right, let's get to work!'

Our group performance will be a Korean song – 'Red Flavor' by Red Velvet – which everyone is excited about. (I love Red Velvet the girl group even more than I love red velvet the cupcakes – my Bias: Seulgi.) But I've never performed a song in Korean, and now my teammates have to worry about my dancing *and* my Korean. But I tune out my inner saboteur and tell myself what I need to hear: I'm going to nail it. Like One.J said, I need to show S.A.Y. I have the will to become the perfect idol. No matter what, just debut.

All I can allow myself to think about is debut: eat (mostly

sweet potatoes), sleep (not nearly enough) and debut.

KIC

That night in bed, after I finish my Korean homework, I can't sleep for the second night in a row. I open my notebook and click on my bunk light. I think about what CEO Sang called me – *yeowoo*, or 'fox' – and wonder if that's what I really am. I scribble the first lines that come to mind:

> When I'm polite you say I'm not a warrior,
> When I'm forward you say I'm not a lady,
> But I'm neither, I'm a yeowoo.
> I'm sweet when I need to be, fierce when I need to be,
> Don't underestimate me, I'll turn your traps back on you,
> Cuz I'm a yeowoo, yeowoo, that's right, *negga yeowoo dah*.

I write some *ahwooooooooooooo* howls into the bridge, even though I think it's wolves that howl at the moon, not foxes. It doesn't matter though; artists can take all the creative licence they want.

I've been so wrapped up in One.J land that I've been neglecting YoungBae with my thoughts. Is it pathetic that I almost feel like I'm cheating on YoungBae with One.J?

I turn on the flip phone and, sure enough, there's a text. I'm already down to less than a third of my battery life.

> we need 2 talk ab that assessment.
> 3 a.m.?

CHAPTER 21

SYMMETRY

At ten to three a.m., I creep out of the dorm with the stolen ID, pretending I'm slipping off to sneak some late-night individual practice time.

The moment I arrive on the roof, YoungBae comes through the rusty door in the Gender Wall. Right away, he sweeps me up in a hug. My feet come all the way off the ground. Forget Manner Hands. My Rude Hands are firmly on YoungBae's shoulders.

'You were so awesome at the assessment!' he says. He puts me down and then drops to his knees, giving me worshipful bows. 'I'm in the Candace fan club.'

'You're so extra,' I say, laughing.

'You can sing, you're funny, you showed CEO who's boss – if he's smart, he'll debut you tomorrow.'

'Thanks. I mean, I really wish I could have watched your performance, but ...'

As I follow him around the girls' half of the roof garden while he waters the plants, I tell him everything that went down with me getting "kicked out" – everything except for meeting SLK.

YoungBae thinks my story is hilarious.

'I've been 'kicked out' twice already,' he says, cracking up. 'I didn't think someone like you ever would though. But I guess not even *I* have the guts to diss the CEO.'

'Really? Mr Rule-Breaker?'

'Nope. During my interview, my mind went totally blank – that dude is straight-up scary. But he didn't say much anyway. He just said I was handsome and I was a good dancer.'

'Oh, really? He said there was *nothing* about you that can improve?'

YoungBae frowns. 'He actually rushed through all the guy performances. All the guys on our side have been talking about how CEO Sang is way more interested in the girl group, since he already has the number one boy group.'

'Huh.' Now that he mentions it, I don't remember CEO mentioning the boys' debut at all. 'Well, that sucks,' I say, 'but I'd stan a group you were in.'

YoungBae's face lights up. 'Would I be your Ultimate Bias?'

'You have to earn that status. Right now, it's One.J.'

'Oh, come on!' he laughs, but it feels like there's actual jealousy in his voice. 'Now I have to be better than One.J?'

I shrug. 'I haven't seen you perform onstage. Seriously, the girls might be getting a bit more attention, but at least you're getting more food. We're all on an even crazier diet now. It's basically just sweet potatoes.'

'You serious?' YoungBae shakes his head. 'That's it. Next time, I'm bringing you some chicken.'

I get goosebumps all over my body and my mouth waters. Partly because chicken sounds delicious, but also, YoungBae sneaking me chicken is literally the most romantic thing ever.

'Thanks, *oppa*,' I say without thinking.

YoungBae's eyes widen. I clamp my hands over my mouth.

'Did you just call me *oppa*?'

'I don't know!' I say, my insides shrivelling up like salted slugs. 'That just slipped out. *Such* a cringey word.'

YoungBae rubs his chin thoughtfully. 'You know, no one's ever called me *oppa* before. I thought I'd hate it, but . . . I could get used to it. *Oppa*.'

'Oh, barf!' I say. 'Seeing how much you like it makes me hate it even more.'

'I *am* five months older than you. So I *am* literally your *oppa*.'

I mime vomiting. 'Gross! I have to go.'

He spreads his long arms. 'Give your *oppa* a hug before you go.'

'You're such a Neanderthal,' I say, but I go in for the hug anyway.

He's so warm. I've never touched One.J, but somehow I doubt he'd be as warm. He's too . . . other-worldly.

After I help him roll the hose back up, YoungBae goes back through the Gender Wall to the boys' side. Once the metal door clicks shut, I skip around the garden, whooping under my breath. A K-pop song blasts in my mind, a super girly, love-struck one – 'Ah-Choo' by Lovelyz. I try to burn off some of my love energy by doing a random cartwheel – I haven't done a cartwheel in years –

and I come down weird on my ankle. Ugh, now my knee *and* ankle are messed up, but I can barely feel either.

Downstairs, I skip down the practice room hallway as quietly as I can, running my fingertips along the walls. If YoungBae and I both debut, we can date in secret – we won't get caught like Iseul and HyunTaek – we'll meet backstage at music shows. We'll go to each other's concerts when we're both on world tours. Or, if we don't debut, we can try to make it as a duo in America (each with our own solo careers, of course!).

There's no way I can sleep now. With my adrenaline pumping, it's a perfect time to work on that 'Red Flavor' choreo while everyone's asleep. I burst into the nearest practice room on the left.

My racing heart stops in its tracks.

'Oh, sorry!' I say.

I see the back of a big dude in an orange T-shirt. There are two female hands with elaborate nail art running up and down the dude's back. The dude turns around. It's JiHoon.

He yelps, startled to see me. The girl peeks out from around his shoulder. It's Helena, her face as white as a sheet mask. 'Candace!' she shrieks.

Helena and JiHoon?! Making out? I'm so shocked that I can't move for a second. JiHoon rushes past me and sprints out of the room. I hear his sneakers squeaking frantically down the hallway. Helena covers her face.

My head's swimming – I'd be in huge trouble if I got caught meeting up with YoungBae, but Helena and a *junior manager*? I can't even fathom how quickly she'd be kicked out. Helena, who's thirstier to debut than anyone.

'Sorry,' I say quickly. 'I didn't see anything.'

I turn to leave, wanting to pull my covers over my head and never come out, but Helena yanks me back into the room.

'What are you doing, spying on me?' she hisses, digging her talons into my arm.

'No, Helena, I swear, I couldn't sleep so I wanted to practise—'

'I bet you're real glad you caught me, huh?'

'No, Helena, I swear. I have *zero* interest in telling anyone about this.'

It takes me a second to realize we're speaking our native language to each other for the first time since we met. Unlike with YoungBae, speaking English with Helena doesn't feel like sweet relief; it feels unnatural, downright creepy.

'Stop playing innocent for once, Candace,' she snaps, pointing one of her glittery claws a centimetre from my nose. 'I'll dog walk you for what you said about me to the CEO.'

I swat her hand away. 'Just leave me alone, Helena. Why are you so threatened anyway?'

She laughs in disbelief. 'Threatened?! By *you*? Don't get it twisted – you will never, ever debut with us. You speak Korean like a two-year-old, you're disrespectful and you're too short. No amount of training will fix that.'

It's my turn to laugh. 'OK, now you're reaching. This isn't the Universal Studios. There's no height limit in K-pop.'

'Everyone knows CEO Sang wants to debut girls all around the same height – you know, for symmetry? How dumb would we look onstage with a little runt at the end?' She smirks. 'We should start calling you *ggeutae*.'

I flinch. '*Ggeutae*', I know, means 'the end' – as in the dirty end of a vegetable you chop off and toss in the garbage.

I take a step closer to her. 'Or they could just make me the permanent Centre,' I say. 'You know, for symmetry? Like One.J in SLK – shortest in the middle.'

I can tell by the wave of terror rippling across Helena's face that she's never considered this possibility. She recovers her composure and grins again. 'Trust me, Candace, you're not Centre material. You don't understand what we've already been through and how much harder it'll be once we debut – not that you need to worry about that.' She turns dramatically, hitting me in the face with her flowery-smelling hair. She pauses in the doorway. 'By the way, if I ever see you sneaking off to meet a boy on the roof again, I'm gonna tell.'

A chill trickles down my spine. 'How do you know about that?'

'I pay attention to everything that goes down in here.'

I gulp. 'Are you sure you want to threaten me, Helena? After what I just saw?'

'You have no idea what you saw, *ggeutae*,' she snarls.

Helena slams the door behind her, leaving me alone in the room.

CHAPTER 22

RULES FOR LEAVING

At lunch, after Korean Language class, InHee the junior manager drops by my table. 'It's your first time leaving on a Saturday, right?' she asks.

I nod and my heart swells. Especially after last night's events, and that creepy session with Madame Jung, all I can focus on is getting out of this building and seeing Umma. I don't know if I can sleep half a metre above Helena for yet another night in a row – who knows what that girl is planning?

Things have been getting too intense. It seems surreal, totally impossible, that this evening I'll be able to see Umma, hug her. All that stands in the way is one more six-hour session with The General.

InHee hands me a green laminated card.

SATURDAY/SUNDAY RULES FOR LEAVING –
S.A.Y. TRAINEES, GIRLS.

1. Don't break your diet. Strictly forbidden foods:
   a. *Jokbal*
   b. Black bean noodles
   c. *Tteokbokki*
   d. Fast food
   e. Chicken
   f. Bread
2. No clubs, alcohol, smoking or drugs.
3. No **SNS**.
4. No dating. No being alone with boys that are not family.
5. Continue practising.
6. Do not bring attention to yourself in any way.
7. No *selcas*.
8. No unauthorized changes to appearance – no haircut, no hair colour, no tattoo, no piercing.
9. DO NOT TELL ANYONE S.A.Y. COMPANY SECRETS, NOT EVEN YOUR CLOSEST FAMILY. NO DETAILS AROUND TRAINING. NO SINGING OR HUMMING ORIGINAL S.A.Y. SONGS THAT ARE BEING DEVELOPED FOR FUTURE DEBUTS OR COMEBACKS. TRAINEES WHO BREAK THIS RULE ARE IN BREACH OF CONFIDENTIALITY AGREEMENTS AND WILL BE PROSECUTED TO THE FULL EXTENT OF THE LAW.

I can't help but LOL at rule 1. Those are the exact six foods I plan to gorge on the second I bust out of this building.

Down in the big practice room on the corporate floor, we're being weighed in for the week. I've lost three kilos since the beginning of training, which means nothing to me, but The General nods approvingly. '*Gosaeng mani haesseo*,' she says. I'm pretty sure this phrase literally means something like '*you've suffered a lot*', but instructors here seem to use it to mean '*good job*'.

JinJoo puts her hands together in prayer before stepping on the scale.

'Remember our deal?' says The General. 'If JinJoo doesn't make weight, all five of you are planking for ten minutes.'

We hold our breath as JinJoo steps on the scale. The digital screen scrambles numbers like a slot machine before spitting out her number. She's under The General's 'cut-off' weight by 0.2 kilograms.

We all scream and jump in the air. JinJoo collapses to the floor, crying tears of relief. '*Gosaeng JINCHA mani haesseo*, JinJoo!' says The General, pumping her fist. ('*You've suffered a TON*, or *REALLY good job!*')

The General gathers us around and says what she says every time: 'We're *really* not playing around any more.'

But this time, she means it. It turns out to be the hardest practice I've ever had. (The General has decided we'll perform our 'Red Flavor' Stage in stilettos, to show off our team's 'pretty lines' and 'femininity'.)

I bet Umma's already down in the lobby. She probably got there an hour early. She probably bought a matcha latte for me from Cafe Tomorrow, nothing for herself.

On the dorm floor, all the girls who are leaving for the day are already packed up, holding their bags and lining up in the hallway for a manager to open the high-security submarine door. For the first time ever, I'll be joining them. Despite the pain in my feet from the stilettos, the pain in my ankle from my cartwheel and the pain in my knee from the death drop – I'm such a mess – I'm grinning like an idiot.

But when we get back to our room, everything's wrong. The dresser drawers are all thrown open; clothes are scattered around. And JiHoon is sitting on my bunk, poking through my duffel bag that I've already packed for the weekend.

'What are you doing?' I demand.

'Random room check,' he says.

Binna tries to pull me back out of my room by the shoulders. 'They do this every now and then,' she says. 'To make sure we don't have any contraband.'

'WHAT DID YOU DO TO MY GUITAR?!' I shriek.

My guitar case has been thrown open and my guitar is lying face down, naked, on the floor. I break from Binna and race over to my hot-pink baby. I turn it over and my blood runs cold. All the strings are broken and the front has two deep cracks in it. My most prized possession, ruined! That jerk JiHoon must have stuck his meaty fist right into the sound hole to pull out . . .

'Looking for these?' JiHoon dangles my bundle of Umma's *yakgwas*, wrapped in blue plastic.

'You wrecked my guitar!' I scream, tears tickling the backs of my eyes.

Manager Kong walks into the room. 'What's going on in here?'

'Look at what he did!' I burst into tears, cradling the remnants of my guitar, the best gift I ever received.

JiHoon leaps off my bunk and bows.

'We didn't discuss room checks for today, JiHoon,' says Manager Kong.

'Well, it seems to me it's a good thing I took the initiative, because I found these.' He hands the *yakgwas* to Manager Kong with both hands. 'I can't even imagine how many calories are in these.'

'I haven't even been eating them!' I wail. 'I kept them as a reminder of my mom.'

Manager Kong opens the wrapping. Binna, JinJoo and Aram gasp. Helena crosses her arms, a smug look on her face.

'Do you know how forbidden these are?' asks Manager Kong. 'How did you get them in here?'

'She hid them inside her guitar,' says JiHoon, sighing gravely. 'Very cunning. You can't always trust an innocent-looking face.'

Yeowoo.

I point my finger at Helena. '*She* told him to look in here!'

'Me?' Helena says, her eyes wide with feigned ignorance. 'What are you saying?'

'Stop lying, *you little brat*!' JiHoon booms at me. 'Manager Kong, it seems to me there should be a severe punishment. Perhaps Candace-*shi* should be forbidden to leave the building today.'

'NO!' I jump to my feet. My guitar clangs back on to the floor, but it's already broken. 'You can't do that!'

Manager Kong wraps the *yakgwas* back up and stuffs them in her pocket. 'There has to be some punishment for this, Candace.'

'I'll clean everyone's bathroom for a month. I'll . . . I'll water the roof garden, I'd *hate* to do that! But please, let's decide later, my mom's waiting downstairs.'

I stuff the clothes JiHoon left strewn around my bed back into my duffel bag. Manager Kong's blocking the door, but I shove past her.

'Ouch! Candace, what do you think you're doing?'

I have to get out of here. I have to get out here. I can't stand to be in the same building as Helena, JiHoon or Madame Jung for another second. I can't breathe. I'm hungry, I'm tired, I'm in pain – not just my battered body, but I feel as if my soul's been beaten up too.

As I push past the girls who are lined up down the hall, I think of spending another Saturday night and all day Sunday alone and depressed again, with no one around but Helena. No way. I'm getting out of here. Nothing, not even a steel submarine door, will stop me.

I pound my fists against the steel door and shout, 'Someone please open this door!'

Dozens of trainees are watching me, stunned, their hands over their mouths, some worried, some laughing. But I don't care. I need to get out of here.

Then I think of the ID badge in the ceiling – JiHoon didn't find that. I'll go back and grab it, run back here and scan the door open. Everyone will see and they'll take it away from me and I'll probably get kicked out for real, but I need it. But when I turn back, I see JiHoon, his face red and ugly and angry, barging towards me. I can't get back to my dorm without getting past him. I'm trapped. Panic closes my throat and a cold sweat breaks through the pores of my forehead.

'PLEASE! OPEN! THIS! DOOR!'

I pound my fists against the steel door as hard as I can. I can't breathe. I'm gagging. My heart is knocking against my chest, begging to get out too. Am I having a heart attack?

Just when I'm about to collapse to the floor, I hear a click and a cheery digital chirp.

Manager Kong has appeared out of nowhere and scanned the door open. She pulls me into the dark stairwell leading down to the corporate floor and closes the door behind us. She searches my eyes and says, 'Breathe, Candace. Breathe. Yes, that's it. Don't worry, you're going to see your *umma* in a minute.'

Hearing this, my chest stops spasming and I slowly start to breathe normally again.

'I was never going to stop you from seeing your *umma* today,' she says, almost sounding nurturing, 'but we need you calm before we send you out to her. Got it?'

I nod. 'Am I kicked out of the programme?'

Manager Kong bites her lip. 'No. I can explain to the other managers that you really needed this weekend away and you had a little panic attack. But that didn't look good, Candace. You know EunJeong? The girl you replaced?'

I nod.

'Just before we had to ask her to leave, she had a similar incident, but worse. She was very talented but having a hard time in here, and she was pounding against this door, screaming to get out . . . but then she rammed her head against the metal door. She knocked herself out and there was blood everywhere. We had to call emergency services.'

I gasp. So that's why everyone gets awkward every time her name's brought up.

'I never liked the policy of restricting kids from leaving in their first month – getting out every weekend from now on will help your mental health greatly. Today was bad, but Candace . . . trainee life is tough because idol life is tougher. Are you sure you can keep going?'

'Yes, Manager Kong,' I say as firmly as I can.

Manager Kong takes me to a bathroom on the corporate floor so I can splash my face with cold water.

And sure enough, down in the lobby, Umma is waiting right at the security gate, holding a matcha tea with a bit of paper still covering the end of the straw – an Umma touch. She looks like brightness, like warmth, like love. I shout her name and we both burst into tears as I run into her arms like a little girl after her first day of preschool.

CHAPTER 23

JOKBAL

'They're not starving you in there?' Umma asks, concern tightening her features. 'Your face looks so small.'

'They have us on a healthy diet, but I'm getting enough to eat,' I lie, making my voice as chipper as possible. I know 'small' faces are considered ideal according to traditional Korean standards, but Umma sounds worried. 'Besides, we're getting so much exercise. I couldn't gain weight in there even if I ate a black bean noodle feast every night!'

Umma doesn't ask too many more questions – she's too shaken and overjoyed by how good my Korean is. The fact that I'm speaking Korean to her at all blows her mind.

We're walking arm in arm to the apartment from the subway. I know now that Umma's staying in the Yeongdeungpo neighbourhood, in case I'm ever *actually* thrown out of the programme in the middle of the night. It's a chill residential area with lots of groups of young women, probably college students, walking in groups. Umma's carrying my duffel bag and I'm carrying a box of spicy garlic KFC (Korean fried chicken, not Colonel Sanders) we picked up from Chicken Kyochon. That's just a side dish for the feast Umma's prepared at the apartment.

'And there's no one in there treating you badly?' she asks, holding my arm tighter.

'Nope!' I say brightly. I go on and on about how much I love my new *unnies* Binna and JinJoo, and how Aram is 'the most beautiful girl I've ever seen!' – all of which is true. Then I go on about how glad I am to have an American teammate, Helena. 'We're not supposed to speak English, but sometimes we do in private, just to feel like we're back at home.'

I'm laying the lies on thick, but I'm putting to words how things with Helena should be instead of how they really are – that she and JiHoon hate me so much that they conspired to break my guitar – and I know Umma would pull me out right away if she knew how intense things were getting. I don't want my family to have to pay the massive penalty for quitting early, and even more important to me than that: I want to debut. More than I've wanted anything. I thought I wanted this before I came here, but now, after I've learnt how low the lows can be and how high the highs are, I know for sure. There've been horrible parts and things I disagree with morally – maybe I'll write essays about the impossible body image standards for my college newspaper some day – but in the meantime, I'm willing to put myself through a whole lot more for more time onstage. More time in the recording booth. More time singing for One.J.

I got this.

Right when we get home, Umma lights up the stoves in the kitchen to make sure all the food is as hot as possible right before I eat it. I make sure she's not looking when I quickly take off my sneakers and put my sore, blistered feet into my fuzzy hippo slippers she bought for me to wear inside. Umma's done a great job making the drab apartment more cheerful; she has a magical touch for that kind of thing. Potted plants everywhere, colourful tablecloths, rugs and family photos in simple frames on the wall.

My knees aching, I sit on the floor at the fold-out dining table in the living room and Umma brings out enough food to make the table collapse under the weight. Spinach-miso soup, spicy fish eggs, *japchae* noodles, potato salad, kimchi pancakes, cod nuggets, sesame-oil-drenched spinach, spicy bean sprouts, *galbi jjim* and a whole platter of marinated *jokbal*. I can't believe Umma made *jokbal* herself; she's grossed out by it, doesn't even like looking at it – back home, it's a special Saturday thing for me and Abba to go eat it at our favourite Korean restaurant.

'Umma, how are we supposed to eat all this?'

'Just leave whatever you can't eat,' says Umma cheerily. 'I'll eat leftovers the rest of the week.'

With just the first few bites, I can feel myself get happier and stronger. Umma doesn't ask too many questions – she lets me crunch happily through the sinewy *jokbal*, I let her talk. Umma's been living her best life. She looks younger and happier than I've seen her in a long time, maybe ever. She's joined a church and she's been meeting up with friends she went to school with who she hadn't seen since she was younger than I am. She got a nice haircut and bought new pastel-coloured blouses. Abba and Tommy are fine back in New Jersey, and she's been visiting Harabuji every day; he's no worse and no better than when we saw him last, but he's been listening to K-pop girl group music – Blackpink and QueenGirl, especially – to learn more about what I'm doing. I realize it's probably the first month since Tommy and I were born that Umma's had any time off from the store.

What Madame Jung said pops into my mind: *To fall like that, they must have made some pretty big mistakes.*

I shake that lady out of my head.

After dinner, Umma puts me on KakaoTalk Video with Abba and Tommy, who are sitting at our dining room table back home. Abba waves frantically and shouts 'HI, CANDACE!' Tommy, his hair a wreck – it's eight a.m. in New Jersey – flinches and says, 'Abba, she can hear you.'

'*WAHHH*, CANDACE!' shouts Abba. 'YOU LOOK SO BEAUTIFUL! YOUR FACE IS SO SMALL!'

I wince and Tommy gives him crazy side-eye. Abba's called me 'cutie' before, never beautiful.

Like Umma, Abba doesn't seem to know what to ask about my time in a K-pop trainee programme; he just asks whether I'm eating enough, if I'm making friends, if I'm learning a lot of Korean, and I say yes to all of it. Tommy says, 'Why isn't your hair pink? Why aren't you making peace signs and giggling? Tee-hee!'

'Ha, ha, ha,' I say. 'You're very funny. I know for a fact that my training is a hundred times more hardcore than whatever you're doing at your football camp.'

'Doubtful, Candace. Highly doubtful.'

After we say our goodbyes – Abba looks like he's holding back tears and Tommy signs off with, 'Good luck, kid' – I take a long shower, where I see the whole bottom half of my body looks as if it's been run over by a truck from all the times I've fallen down during 'Red Flavor' rehearsal. Afterwards, I fall asleep early with Umma stroking my hair.

Eleven hours later, Umma shakes me gently awake for a breakfast of rice, egg, kimchi and a side of bean sprout soup. Then we explore Bukchon Hanok Village, full of ancient Korean buildings where you have to wear a traditional *hanbok* to get in. Afterwards, Umma and I share a delicious *patbingsu* – sweet red beans, fruit and milk on top of a mound of fluffy snow – at a 'flower cafe', the most Instagrammable place I've ever seen. Umma slides her phone to me. KakaoTalk Video is up again, but this time, I see a split screen of Imani and Ethan. I shriek with joy – the other customers look at me in alarm, but Umma just laughs. 'Surprise!' she says.

Imani is calling from the little school in Paraguay where she's digging latrines, Ethan from a cabin at his theatre camp in Lexington, Massachusetts.

My heart bursts seeing their faces. Since I'm not supposed to talk about what's going on at S.A.Y., I try to direct the conversation to how they're spending their summers, but Imani says, 'Forget us, I wanna hear about *you*! Have you met One.J and SLK yet?!'

I tap my chin and say in a sing-songy voice, 'Hmm, I can't say!'

I want nothing more than to tell them everything that's been going down. But while Umma's right here, I don't want to get into the details, good *or* bad. Umma would probably be almost as afraid of me doing *too well* at S.A.Y. as me being mistreated – it's best to keep up the illusion that this is nothing more than a summer activity.

I do give Imani and Ethan one juicy tidbit.

'Candace Park did a death drop?!' exclaims Ethan before clutching his chest and falling out of frame.

'I snatched *everyone's* wig with that move,' I say proudly.

Imani wags her finger and screams, 'Yasssssssss, queen!'

Before we hang up, Imani lowers her voice so Umma can't hear. 'By the way, check your YouTube channel, sis. I may or may not have posted your video in a **fancafe**. Byeeeeee!'

'Imani!' I say, but she's already gone. As soon as we get home, I run to open up Umma's laptop in the bedroom, remembering that S.A.Y. required me to shut down my social media accounts before I entered the trainee programme. I made my Facebook and Instagram private, but S.A.Y. never said anything to me about YouTube – even though they definitely know my channel exists.

I must be hallucinating. There must be a worldwide YouTube virus, because it's telling me my 'Expectations vs Reality' video has 84,532 views. My eyes race to the 2,797 comments, which are half in English and half in Korean.

[+734, -12] I heard rumours this girl is training for the female SLK that's about to debut! Amazing voice and cute Visuals. I hope she makes it!

[+158, -413] singing good. visuals just ok. just my opinion i do not think she meets S.A.Y. or SLK standard sorry

[+1,206, -29] I THINK I AM IN LOVE! I HOPE SHE DEBUTS!

[+47, -944] KEEP K-POP GROUPS KOREAN NOT KOREAN AMERICAN

Short of breath, I make the video private and slam the computer shut. I feel thrilled and violated at the same time. It's hard to fathom that so many people saw the inside of my room at home. They saw MulKogi on my bed in the background. They saw my pink guitar! (RIP.)

At that moment, Umma pokes her head in and asks what I want to do this evening. She suggests walking in the street markets in Namdaemun or shopping for face masks in Myeong-dong.

Suddenly, all I want to do is shut myself inside the ShinBi building and practise my butt off – make that one commenter eat their words about not meeting 'S.A.Y. or SLK standard'. And as much as I needed this time with Umma, there's a weird distance between us now. There's so much I can't tell her.

CHAPTER 24

MONOLIDS

With only two months until the final group members are decided, all the girls have stepped up their game. The individual practice rooms are packed until two a.m. For the next two weeks, I can't decide what's worse – the hunger or the lack of sleep. With the new ultra-restrictive diet in place, the hunger doesn't always feel like physical pain; it's more like an absence of will. Because I'm forcing myself to attack my training, to give it 100 per cent despite the hunger, what I no longer have energy for is resisting.

I hate to admit this, but hunger makes me a better trainee.

In a session with The General, I strap weights around my ankles and put high heels on my scabbed, nailless, bandaged feet. When I stumble on the 'Red Flavor' choreography and The General yells at me to run twenty laps around the practice room, I turn off my brain and just start running.

It's not just me though; all the girls are drained of energy. In our team practices, everyone practices so hard that the mirror fogs up with our body heat and sweat. There's nothing left over. The upside of this is that Helena and I don't have any more flare-ups. It's easy to just keep our heads down and practise. We only talk to each other when we absolutely have to, when we're adjusting the choreography or switching vocal parts.

The lack of sleep is something else – sometimes I feel like I'm losing my mind. One week, I drift off to sleep during Language class every single day. Teacher Lee has to gently shake me awake. My mood has been spiking and plummeting unpredictably and it's not even my time of the month. One day, The General tells me and Aram to swap positions, causing me to reorient and switch up all my choreography and a pit opens in my soul and swallows me up, and I feel desolate and hopeless, like I'm alone in a field of ashes. But only for a second. I feel good emotions more extremely too. On the roof during Fresh Air Time, I'm feeling totally loopy and JinJoo shares one of her random theories, something about lima beans actually being cauliflower seeds and I laugh so uncontrollably for so long I pull an ab muscle I never even knew I had.

On weekends, Umma's been noticing that I'm changing, that I'm quieter. 'It's not just that you've lost weight,' she says. 'The light in your eyes has changed.' One Sunday as we're carrying containers of potato porridge Umma cooked at home to Harabuji's hospital, she's nagging me so much, telling me I can quit and we can go home whenever I want, that I stop in my tracks and snap, 'Umma, I'm not as weak as you think I am, OK?! I'm fine!'

I immediately feel terrible and apologize, but her concern is becoming a burden.

My main saving grace is YoungBae. As punishment for the *yakgwas* and the scene I made, Manager Kong assigns me roof garden watering duties at two a.m. every night for the next month. So now the tables have turned: it's *me* texting YoungBae when I'm ready, borrowing an all-access key card from Mr Jeon, the custodian, and opening the big rusty door in the Gender Wall for YoungBae (while Teacher Lee's back was turned in Language class, I gave him back the ID he gave me so he can get on the roof himself).

Every night, I water the plants. YoungBae offers to do it for me, but I insist on doing it myself, since it's my punishment. He thinks it's hilarious that I've already got in bigger trouble than he has, joking that I'm the 'new bad girl of K-pop', which, I have to admit, I don't hate.

He's also been bringing me bits of food every night in his pocket. A few chicken strips wrapped in a napkin. A single breakfast sausage, a boiled egg. I pick the lint off the food and devour it hungrily, grateful for the real protein my body is screaming for. I know this is food out of his own mouth, food he really needs himself – he's almost thirty centimetres taller than me and the Main Dancer of his team – but he insists. 'I'm doing my part to end gender inequality in K-pop,' he says.

I think I'm falling in love.

But we still haven't kissed. There are times when we say good-bye for the night when I know we're about to, but I pull away. I've never been kissed in my life and I'm worried I'll be horrible at it, or that I have bad breath – eating so little has been giving me acid reflux and I'm constantly tasting something bitter in the back of my throat.

Instead, we're touching a lot. Like, *a lot* a lot. Manner Hands have long been forgotten. I'll burrow my face in his chest or let him wrap his arm around my waist while I'm watering the lilacs. Yes, he's hot as in insanely cute, but also he's so hot as in *warm*. Since I have no calories to burn, I'm constantly cold, even in the middle of muggy Seoul summer. And I'm so tired that I once legit fell asleep while standing up, leaning against his chest – I was probably snoring and everything. When I woke up, there he was, looking down at me, sturdy as a rock.

ЖC

After only two hours of sleep and a killer morning workout in which JinJoo and I pounded the treadmills, I sneak a thirty-second shower before breakfast. I pull half a metre of multihued hair out of the drain and flush it down the toilet. I grab my notebook and K-pop pencil tin – we have our epic vocab exam, where we'll be tested on three thousand words out of a possible six thousand. I'll have to jam a sweet potato down my throat and gulp down horrible coffee to get through it.

On my way out of the dorm, Manager Kong stops me in the doorway. She's carrying my big shiny pink guitar case and drops it off inside the room. The air escapes my lungs.

'Manager Kong, what's that?'

'Have you ever seen another guitar case this colour? I dropped it off at a speciality music store in Hongdae. You'd never know anything happened to it.'

The aches and pains leave my limbs and I shriek with joy.

'Manager Kong! It's really fixed?'

'It's better than new. Blindingly pink.'

'Thank you, thank you, thank you!'

'Don't thank me,' sighs Manager Kong, looking at her phone. 'Thank Helena. She insisted on paying for it; I just dropped it off.'

I'm at a loss for words. 'Helena-*unnie*?'

'Indeed.'

I want to throw the case open and tune the strings, inspect the neck and sound hole, but Manager Kong snaps, 'Hey! Don't you have an important test today? GET MOVING, *NOW*!'

A week before our second assessment, I have my first Loveliness Class with my team. Our first class will take all day because we're each getting a private consultation and makeover by Mr Oh and his hair and make-up teams, as well as a consultation with a stylist. As Manager Kong escorts us to the corporate floor, she explains to me that Mr Oh is the top make-up artist in Korea and has worked at many New York, Paris and Seoul fashion weeks on some of the most famous female stars in the world, including Gigi Hadid and Chanel Iman. He's now the mastermind behind ShinBi Unlimited's lead cosmetics brand, GlowSong.

For the first time ever, Manager Kong leads us through the nondescript door that she told me on my first day was the Fantasy Factory, the lab where all S.A.Y.'s incredible Concepts are created. Inside, we all gasp – it's as if we've walked into an airplane hangar. The whole floor is a maze of low, movable walls and black curtains, forming temporary 'rooms'. In one room, we see five dress forms wearing bedazzled performance outfits that seem to be made entirely of different shades of sparkling gemstones – rubies, emeralds, topaz, amethysts, white crystal.

She takes us into a room set up like a spacious beauty salon, complete with vanity lights and five swivelling chairs.

'Welcome, girls, welcome,' trills a graceful, slim person with long, jet-black hair that rivals Aram's in lustrous perfection. This must be Mr Oh, who takes my breath away. In a place that's so divided by strict gender lines, it's shocking – but a relief – to see someone who obviously doesn't care. He's wearing high-heeled cowboy (cowgirl?) boots and a pink cow-print western outfit, complete with a bandanna and vest. He looks like an Asian pastel-pink version of Woody from *Toy Story*. 'Aram, Helena, Binna, JinJoo, New Girl. Sit, sit.'

We all bow repeatedly and take a seat. There's a whole team of make-up and hair artists who march into the salon and immediately begin feeling our hair and inspecting our faces. 'What a beautiful team,' exclaims Mr Oh, walking around and peering at each of us intently. 'I've been working on boy trainees all morning. They were very handsome, but it's so much more fun working on girls. Let's play!'

Aram, Helena and JinJoo squeal in excitement. Binna and I flash each other worried looks. Mr Oh is so *fabulous* that I'm worried he'll make me feel plain and dull compared to all the gorgeous idols and Hollywood stars he's worked with before.

After he consults with Aram ('This one's already so lovely, all we need to do is bring out what's already here.') he comes up behind my chair and tucks my hair behind my ears. 'Hello, little one. How adorable you are.'

I bow in thanks.

'This one has a very fresh, innocent vibe – I can see her being called Korea's Little Sister,' Mr Oh says with a chuckle. 'Play around with some dewy foundation and bright cream blush to bring out these full cheeks,' he tells a young make-up artist. 'Have you ever had your eyebrows shaped, little one?'

'No, sir,' I say.

'I can tell,' he says with a good-natured laugh. He says to the make-up artist, 'Shave the brows.' Then he gets distracted by something on my face. A wrinkle appears on his otherwise perfectly lineless forehead. 'Oh, little one. You have **monolids**.'

I see my ears turn bright red in the mirror. Yes, I'm pure monolid: my eyes are like two holes cut out of a Kraft single with a knife, not a hint of a crease above or below. Even though most Koreans are born with monolids, they're not considered ideal. I've seen seen tons of trainees get double-eyelid surgery, both girls and boys. BowHee got it done one eye at a time and wore an eyepatch as it healed so she wouldn't have to take a break from training. I don't blame anyone else for getting the surgery, but for me it's the same as my nose: I want my eyes to look like Umma's and Abba's and Tommy's.

I hold my breath, expecting Mr Oh to pressure me into the surgery.

But instead he says, 'I personally think monolids are lovely.

Idol companies are so quick to suggest procedures. Good make-up can do everything that procedures can do, except the best part: you get to wipe it off. Right, little one?' He gives the end of my nose a little tap.

To my shock and delight, he tells the hairdresser that I should have white-blonde hair, 'to take her to the next level', to make me 'just a little unattainable'. I've always fantasized about having Targaryen hair but never thought about actually going for it – Umma would never let me and it seemed so drastic. But here I'm in the best possible hands. I nod cheerfully and say, 'Let's go for it!'

The hairstylist gets to work, bleaching my hair and lightening my eyebrows. It takes six hours, smells horrible and burns my scalp, but the time flies by because Mr Oh is so entertaining – he has everyone in the room laughing like crazy. He loves name-dropping and is a master of the humblebrag, saying things like, 'Oh my goodness, it's such a burden – I did Jeon DanHee's make-up just once, as a favour when her personal artist was sick, and afterwards, she says, "Mr Oh, I hate you – I'm loyal to my make-up artist, but now that I've had you, I'll always know what I'm missing!"'

At the end of the session, I'm transformed. I get out of my chair and look at myself up-close. I could stare at myself for the rest of my life.

I look like an idol.

My eye make-up in combination with the eyebrow shaping and lightening has changed my whole face – made the whole thing look symmetrical and satisfying and orderly, like a completed puzzle. The make-up is paler than I'm used to, but it's perfectly even and natural – I'm shining, spotless, bursting with health and radiance, even though on the inside I'm exhausted and hangry.

And the Targaryen blonde hair makes me look like the Korean Mother of Dragons. I look 'unattainable', even to myself. I can't stop pouting my Barbie-pink lips; I'm living my actual fantasy.

Helena and Aram didn't go through a transformation as drastic as mine, but they are enhanced versions of their already-beautiful selves – their skin dewier, their hair even more pristine. For JinJoo, the artists went experimental, leaning into her anime vibe – one of her big, bushy pigtails is electric blue, the other is full-on orange, and she has glitter stars and rainbows on her face. She looks awesome, like a manga-unicorn dream.

But when Binna spins around in her chair, we all die. We're dead.

'This is my favourite transformation of all,' says Mr Oh in a dramatic, hushed voice.

For Binna, Mr Oh went in a completely different direction from the rest of us; the ubiquitous Korean style of make-up is soft and 'natural', but Mr Oh used Western techniques seen on the Kardashians and drag queens: contouring on her cheeks and jawline, and going heavy with the highlighter on her nose bridge, high points and, yes, her cupid's bow. Binna's always liked dark lipsticks, blacks and even blues, but now she has a deep plum lip, which suits her perfectly. He gave a slight wave to her curtain of black hair, which cascades down her back. It's unbelievable how well this style works for Binna – instead of trying to downplay her unique, strong features that don't fit Korean ideals, Mr Oh played them up.

Binna looks at us shyly, waiting for our reaction.

'I'm sorry, Aram,' I say after a moment of stunned silence, 'but I think we have a new Team Two Visual.'

Aram grins. 'I must admit defeat when I see it.'

'You really think I look all right?' asks Binna. 'It's not too much?'

JinJoo shakes her head, misty-eyed. Even Helena manages, 'You look really nice.'

Manager Kong comes back and compliments us all enthusiastically on how great we look. 'Is this really my team?' she asks in wonder. 'You look like you've already debuted!'

Manager Kong ushers us into the next room, which is lined with racks of clothes along every wall. A team of wardrobe stylists swirls like a tornado of couture. I get clothes thrown at me with demands to 'try this on', and in minutes – the stylists already have all our measurements – I'm wearing the shortest skirt I've worn in my life (black leather), a silky black tank top (no cleavage) that exposes just a few centimetres of midriff and a long, dark green camel-hair coat that touches the floor.

It's way trendier and more revealing than anything I'd choose myself, and I've definitely never exposed my midriff, but for the first time in my life, I can see the faintest, ghostly outline of an ab muscle. Together, the five of us look like a girl gang that's ready to kick some butt.

The wardrobe, hair and make-up stylists herd us into a corner of the floor that's been turned into a makeshift studio full of hot lights and a bunch of people swarming around trying to look busy. We bow to a goateed, shiny-faced photographer named Mr Choi who Manager Kong tells us is a big deal: he shot SLK's last four mini-album covers, as well as plenty of female idols for *Vogue Korea*. He immediately has us stand in front of a white backdrop. Without asking any of our names, he barks at his assistants to rearrange us: Aram in the centre (of course), with me and JinJoo on the ends.

'You and you!' he says, pointing to Helena and Binna. 'Switch spots. You, the second prettiest one' – no one needs to be told he's talking about Helena – 'stand next to the short one.' That's me. 'You two have such contrasting vibes. I want you to play off each other.'

Without hesitation, Helena starts to use me as a prop, resting her hand on my shoulder, putting her face awkwardly close to mine, hugging me from behind – I try to nudge her away, but Helena is a natural-born poser, changing up her positions with every snap of Mr Choi's camera.

'MOVE YOUR BODIES!' Mr Choi yells. 'Change up your expressions, give me something to work with. Hey, scary one!' He means Binna – not in a nice way, although Scary was always my favourite Spice Girl. 'Your expression is too hard! No man will want you with a face like that!'

I'm so uncomfortable that I start sweating and a make-up artist has to come by every minute to powder my face. I wish Mr Oh had stayed for this photo shoot – Mr Choi is making us feel like dolls he's playing with.

'Hey, moon-face!' barks Mr Choi.

I feel all four of my teammates stiffen. I know that's a pretty bad insult, and he means JinJoo.

'Put one leg in front of the other, do *something* to make yourself look a little slimmer!' Mr Choi shouts.

JinJoo bows and apologizes, eyes glistening.

'Hey, short one! Move over to the end next to moon-face. Maybe you can hide some of her body with yours.'

Even in this very moment, I know I'll regret this one day – but I obediently do as I'm told without a word.

It doesn't seem possible to speak up – there are so many people in this studio that I've never seen before, all wearing black, all incredibly intimidating and much older than me. I feel so judged. Bright, hot lights trained on me, a famous fashion photographer pointing out my flaws, scrutinizing my every move and expression. None of the other girls are speaking up and neither is Manager Kong; she's tapping away at her phone.

But the main reason I don't say anything: I'm freaking hungry and exhausted. This whole Loveliness Class has been taking so long we've skipped lunch and dinner, and I'm in danger of fainting. When Mr Choi shouts at me to 'LOOK ALIVE!' and give him something to work with, I give him some poses I learnt from watching *America's Next Top Model*. I 'smize', I do the Broken Doll, I make a high-fashion-editorial hoop with my arms over my head. I feel like I'm being random, but Mr Choi is into it. 'Yes, short one, more of that, finally!'

Anything to make this shoot end faster.

$$\text{XIC}$$

Afterwards, back in the dorm, we kill an entire box of make-up wipes between the five of us. Without a word, Helena takes the trash bag full of dirty wipes to the garbage chute instead of me, which is a first.

We comfort JinJoo, calling Mr Choi a jerk and a chauvinist, but JinJoo insists she's fine, even though she takes an extra-long time to scrub the liner from her eyes.

I plop into bed, completely spent. As soon as the lights are out except for my little reading light, I hear sniffling and crying. It's not just JinJoo. It's Helena too, who got nothing but compliments. I get it – I want to cry as well. Even the fun parts of the Loveliness Class with Mr Oh were emotionally exhausting, having to look at yourself from every angle, having strangers poke and prod at your body, making judgements, silently or out loud.

But I still have my song to write. I've kept up the habit every night, even when all I have in me is a god-awful song about how much I hate sweet potatoes. Tonight, though, words come to me right away.

Monolid Girl
My eyes are wide open, they see just fine
Maybe your double eyelids make you see two
You can't tell what's real and what's just illusions

CHAPTER 25

QUEEN OF CUTE

My team and I wait around in a swanky, sterile waiting room on fiftieth floor for a full hour before our second assessment. I'm listening to Red Velvet's 'Red Flavor' for the ten thousandth time. I do the choreography in my head. I struggled with the Korean pronunciation at first, but Clown Killah explained the difference between singing in English and Korean in ways that helped a ton: Korean has such short, staccato syllables; you have to breathe differently and soften the consonants.

My teammates are all in their own worlds, mouthing lyrics. We're hyped up because Manager Kong gave us an extra protein shake this morning and a nurse came and gave us all B-12 shots just a few minutes ago.

The door to the conference room finally opens and out walk Manager Shin and Team Three, which has ShiHong from Language class in it. Team Three just performed 'I'm So Sick' by

Apink for the executives, and they're all wearing deconstructed tuxedoes. Our teams bow to each other and I try to read from Team Three's expressions how their assessment went, but they all have poker faces. ShiHong has permanent poker face.

For this assessment, all trainees have been told we'll get very little feedback, since CEO Im is a very busy man and he needs to see all ten girl trainee teams today. Once again, we're going in reverse order, starting with Team Ten. While the last assessment took more than twelve hours, this has only taken two so far.

Earlier this morning, we had another wardrobe session, where the stylists came up with a 'fruit and ice cream' theme, since 'Red Flavor' is an upbeat, summery song that calls out all things sticky-sweet: 'melting strawberries', 'peach juice', 'spilt ice cream'. I'm wearing a sequinned skirt (super, super short, of course) that looks like a slice of watermelon, one red sparkly heel and one green one. Aram's look is strawberry-themed, Helena is the ice cream, Binna is blueberry and JinJoo is peach. We all have huge bows in our hair. Mine makes me look like a toddler pageant contestant, but I'm glad – my hair has suddenly decided to self-destruct in the days after my bleach job and this obnoxious bow is covering my whole head.

A female executive assistant with her hair in a knife-sharp side-parting beckons us into the conference room. Manager Kong passes us our cordless mics; because the room doesn't have a full sound system, we won't have in-ears. We quickly put our hands together and shout, '*HWAITING!*'

Then we line up in order – Binna out front, Aram in the

centre, me bringing up the rear – plaster huge smiles on our faces and walk into the room just as we practised for five hours with Manager Kong: our heels barely making a sound against the hard wood, our fingers extended delicately at our sides, making sure to maintain a precise distance from the girl in front. My legs are coated in foundation *and* covered with nude stockings to hide my bruises. Our Concept for this performance is ultra-feminine; we have to maintain that aura from the moment we walk in until the moment we walk out.

Once we reach our positions at the front of the room, we each turn on one heel and stand with our legs elegantly crossed and bow deeply. Binna counts to three, and we say in high-pitched, delicate unison, '*Annyeong hashimnikka*' – the extra, *extra* formal word for '*hello*' – 'we are the lovely and talented Team Two!'

Standing there, my heart starts thudding like an EDM beat. We've never seen this room before, but Manager Kong described it in detail, even drew diagrams so we'd know exactly where each executive and investor would be sitting.

It's a spacious conference room with two walls that are all windows – we're bathed in soft, golden early-evening sunlight. A table takes up most of the room, so we only have a small space to dance. CEO Im sits at the head of the table; he's built like a line-backer and has the most massive, rectangular head I've ever seen, the size and shape of a SpongeBob SquarePants piñata. CEO Sang sits on his left side and Madame Jung sits on his right. Two investors sit beside them: CEO Rho of Elektro Hydrate, the sports drinks company, and the other, CEO Noh, heads a company that drills tunnels through mountains.

'Ah, the famous Team Two,' says CEO Im in a gruff voice. 'I've heard many good things.'

We bow many more times and giggle delicately. Even CEO Sang seems flustered and sweaty in CEO Im's presence. He says, 'Yes, these are five of our finest.' He flashes us a *don't mess this up* look. 'Whenever you're ready, girls.'

The cameras are on, filming everything to send to SLK while they're in Europe on tour. With even more at stake, I'm ten times more nervous than the last assessment.

The track we laid down with Clown Killah blasts throughout the room louder than expected.

But we're prepared for anything. We spring into performance mode. Unlike last time, my mind doesn't separate from my body. We've spent so many hours practising together that I know exactly where my feet are supposed to go, I know exactly where my *unnies* are in the formation without having to turn my head. When we do a series of lightning-fast synchronized kicks, my legs fly almost as high as the others'. I know exactly when I'm supposed to smile, toss my hair, pucker my lips, wink. It's hard to hear myself sing, but I know exactly what I sound like and when my cues are. Helena and I harmonize perfectly in the pre-choruses. JinJoo belts a crisp high G in the bridge. Binna kills the rap. And Aram, I'm sure, looks devastatingly good.

When we're finished, we end in pretty poses – I have my hands tucked under my chin and I'm fluttering my long (fake) lashes.

There's no applause, just as Manager Kong warned us. We maintain our bright smiles and try not to breathe too hard, even though this 'effortless' and 'hyperfeminine' dance is twice as exhausting as the hard-hitting dance for 'Problem'. We get back into our perfectly straight line and stand in our delicate way – legs glued together, knees slightly crossed, one heel slightly off the floor. As The General put it, 'Stand in a way so it *looks* like the slightest wind will knock you over, even though you're perfectly balanced.'

The executives at the table turn to CEO Im to say the first word. Finally, he rumbles, 'What a bright, wholesome perform-ance. Such attractive girls too.'

CEO Sang lets out a sigh of relief. 'Thank you. Yes, I also think they did an excellent job. Aram is our top Visual and she embodied the song perfectly as Centre.'

'Yes, she's quite stunning,' says CEO Im. 'She could become the nation's next CF Queen.'

'She would be perfect for one of our campaigns,' agrees CEO Rho.

Aram bows profusely in thanks. Madame Jung just smiles a frosty smile.

'Cho Helena and Park Candace are from America,' explains CEO Sang. 'They've turned out to be two of our hardest workers. Candace has only been with us for two months, but her dancing has improved dramatically. She also scored highest in her class on the Korean vocabulary exam: ninety-eight per cent.'

CEO Im raises his eyebrows and exclaims, 'Oh-ho! Smart girl.'

I can't believe what a big deal everyone's been making about this. Two days after the exam, Teacher Lee posted the class's scores, ranked in order. I was number one with a ninety-eight, Helena was number two with a seventy-four and YoungBae was *all* the way at the bottom with thirty-six per cent. The news travelled to Manager Kong, who presented me with the tiniest sliver of strawberry shortcake as a reward.

Our group photo, taken by Mr Choi, flashes on a projector behind us. My memories of how miserable we were posing for it are almost erased by how fierce we look. We turn our necks without budging from our 'delicate' standing positions and gasp. This looks like a real K-pop Girl Crush poster.

CEO Im nods his gargantuan head. '*Wahhh, cham meoshitda.*'

Which I loosely translate as '*Y'all look bomb-dot-com.*'

CEO Sang says, 'Note that the Concept of the photo is exactly the opposite of their performance Concept you just saw. These girls can embody all sides of being a female.'

I want to remind him that there's more to being female than Cute and Girl Crush, but I'll take any compliment I can get today.

After the group evaluation, we each go down the line doing two-minute solo performances, pre-approved by Manager Kong, for individual evaluation. Binna steps forward first, temporarily breaking from her elegant persona to slay a freestyle dance solo to 'Beez in the Trap' by Nicki Minaj. I want to *yas-queen* her, but I stop myself. The CEOs compliment Binna on her dancing, but Madame Jung tells her that she's too muscular and she should cover up her abs and arms more. It takes everything in my power to keep from rolling my eyes.

JinJoo almost blows out the windows with her rendition of 'Reflection' by Christina Aguilera. CEO Sang compliments her for losing weight but pushes her to lose more. Aram does a funny monologue from the K-drama *My ID is Gangnam Beauty*; her acting is completely over the top, but she's surprisingly funny. She gets the first applause of the assessment from all the men in the room. Helena sings 'Part of Your World' from *The Little Mermaid* a cappella, giving Disney princess vibes as always, and all she gets are comments on her pretty hair and smile.

I'm up last, and for my solo bit, Manager Kong passes me my guitar, pre-tuned. Manager Kong pre-approved my performance of 'Expectations vs Reality', but in that very instant, I decide to sing something different. I'm tired of pretending I'm a perfect girl who looks like I can be knocked over with the slightest breeze. Plus, that B-12 shot and all that protein is making me wanna She-Hulk out. I start playing.

I'm sweet when I need to be, fierce when I need to be,
Don't underestimate me, I'll turn your traps back on you,
Cuz I'm a yeowoo, yeowoo, that's right, negga yeowoo dah.

Then, for the entire chorus, I'm howling at a high, lilting pitch. I lose myself in the moment. I howl like I'm a fox in the Arctic tundra calling out to the moon – or is it only wolves that do that?

Baby, negga yeowoo dah. Baby, I'm a fox.

I close my eyes and see how high my howls can go. By the end of the chorus, I almost reach a whistle register, something I've never heard myself do before.

Ahwoooooooooo!

When I open my eyes, Manager Kong has her mouth open. The CEOs blink at me like freshly hatched chicks opening their eyes for the first time. Madame Jung glares at me with narrowed eyes.

I don't know what else to do, so I bow. 'Thank you for listening,' I say.

More silence.

Suddenly, CEO Im throws his head back and releases cannon blasts of laughter into the ceiling. CEO Sang takes that as his cue to laugh too. CEOs Rho and Noh join in.

The sanitary pads in my armpits are fat and juicy with sweat. What exactly is so funny?

Once CEO Im catches his breath, he says, 'To see such an innocent-looking girl singing such bold words!'

Madame Jung smiles stiffly, saying, 'Is this decent for a young girl?'

'And with a pink guitar,' says CEO Noh, gasping for air.

'This girl is the queen of Cute,' says CEO Im. 'Bold isn't always a bad thing for a young lady to be. You know that old saying: "A man can live with a *yeowoo* for a wife, but never a cow".'

The men at the table laugh even louder. My ears are burning. What does that saying even mean? And whoever said anything about being any of their wives? Some of them are almost as old as Harabuji.

'She has a good voice too,' says CEO Rho. He turns to me. 'You wrote this song?'

'Yes, sir,' I say, and I bow in thanks at the first real compliment I've received.

'Well, CEO Sang, you have your work cut out for you,' says CEO Im. 'This is the best team so far and I can see each has an element you'd want. If only you had five girls who could each sing as well as Candace, look as good as Aram, have the charms of Helena and dance like Binna.'

I glance at JinJoo, the only girl not mentioned, but she betrays no emotion other than pleasantness.

'But you see, CEO Im,' says CEO Sang, 'if there's one thing I've learnt about forming idol groups, it's this: a perfect group is destined to fail. You don't want five One.Js – you need a Wookie too. It's all about the right balance of strengths and flaws.'

CEO Im smacks the table. 'Well then, in that case, I think you might have your group right here.'

Even though not every part of our second assessment was awesome, Team Two is flying high that night about being called CEO Im's favourite girl trainee team, and the idea, as teeny-tiny as it might be, that it might be us five who get to debut. Since Helena fixed my guitar, I'm starting to see a glimmer of hope that we could be decent group mates.

I didn't even get scolded for singing a different song – Manager Kong said, 'I just wish you'd told me. I liked "Yeowoo".'

Back in the dorm, JinJoo says, all humble, 'If every group needs flaws like CEO Sang said, I guess I can be our group's flaws.'

We all say 'Nooooooo!' and make sure she dances around the

dorm alongside us to 'Unicorn' by SLK and 'Ddu-Du Ddu-Du' by Blackpink and 'Dumb Dumb' by Red Velvet and 'Fancy' by Twice. Finally, a girl from Team Three pounds on the paper-thin wall separating us and screams, 'SHUT UP, WE'RE TRYING TO SLEEP!' Binna shuts the music off right away and shouts back through the wall, 'Many apologies!' but the rest of us make just as much noise laughing.

Well after one a.m., the five of us are finally in bed and we do something we haven't done in all my time as part of this team: we talk through the night, as if we're at summer camp. We gossip about boy trainees we have crushes on. JinJoo admits to having a crush on this boy YoonChul with an eyebrow ring on boys' Team Four; Binna's into Noah, a half Canadian boy in my Language class; Aram isn't into any trainees, just ChangWoo from SLK. Helena claims she's so focused on practice that she 'doesn't have any eye for boys'.

'Ugh, Helena, you're *no-jam*,' says Binna.

'What about you, Candace?' asks JinJoo.

'Oh, I know,' says Aram, clapping once. 'She likes that cute boy – that funny one who does hip-hop dance, YoungBae.'

'That's right, that's right!' says Binna, seal-clapping. 'I've noticed the way you look at him in the cafeteria.'

'I do *not*!' I insist. 'I've only said a few words to him in Language class, that's it.'

'That's more than most of us get,' says JinJoo.

I wait for Helena to call me out – but thankfully, she stays silent.

'Well,' I joke, 'my heart belongs to One.J anyway.'

'That goes without saying,' says JinJoo. 'That's all of us. That's the entire world.'

'Duh,' says Aram. 'I don't like younger guys, but One.J? I'd be his *noona*.'

We all cackle.

'Obviously One.J is going to choose Aram for his solo MV,' says JinJoo with a sigh. 'To be Kim Aram for a day.'

'Oh, come on,' says Aram, although I hear the delight in her voice.

As I stare at the dark ceiling, I wonder if there's any chance in a million years One.J will pick me. Or even if One.J wanted to pick me, would the company make him choose one of the prettier girls without a broad nose and monolids?

$$\rangle\!\!\parallel\!\!\mathbb{C}$$

The next morning in the cafeteria, the sweet potatoes are particularly cold and tasteless. I'm tired and grumpy. My once-gorgeous Targaryen hair practically melted in my hands in the shower this morning. I found a single strand that had *eleven* splits – it looked like a cricket leg. (Mmm, even fried crickets sound tasty at this point.) The colour is still the same, but it's so thirsty it needs several beverages. Binna lent me her Powder Pup hat for me to hide my straw-like monstrosity.

As I struggle to swallow down pasty sweet potato, I say to Binna, 'I've always meant to ask you – what does "POWDER PUP" mean anyway?'

'Oh, you know – it's that American cartoon I love. *Powder Pup*

Girls. I made that hat myself.'

'Powder Pup?' I ask. Then I realize what she means. Suddenly, my spirits lift a little bit. 'You mean *Powerpuff Girls?*'

'Yeah, *Powder Pup Girls*. That's what I said.'

I crack up laughing for a solid minute while Binna stares at me, puzzled, asking, 'What's so funny?'

Manager Kong and Manager Shin interrupt my giggle fit. From the centre of the cafeteria, Manager Kong shouts, 'Girls! Listen up! We have three pieces of important news.'

The girls' half of the cafeteria goes silent immediately.

'CEO Sang and CEO Im were overall very pleased with what they saw at yesterday's assessment,' says Manager Shin, who manages the five girls' teams Manager Kong doesn't. 'CEO Sang could see that you've all suffered a lot and improved in the last month. That's why the strict diet is over – we'll go back to regular meals for the next month.'

The girls all cheer. I squeeze RaLa's and BowHee's hands, we're so excited. Back to decent portions!

'However,' says Manager Kong over the commotion, 'you'll need that energy, because your next assessment will be the final one before CEO Sang decides who gets to debut. For that assessment, each team will have to perform *two* Stages with opposite Concepts. And that assessment will take place in Seoul Olympic Stadium and be broadcast *live* ... for all of Korea – all of the world – to see on the YNN Network.'

There's pandemonium in the room. We're freaking out, holding on to each other. Some girls are actually sobbing – so many of these girls have been working towards this moment for years and years, their whole childhoods.

'It will be a three-part special showcase,' says Manager Shin dramatically, 'called *S.A.Y. 50*, for the fifty girl trainees who hope to debut.' I peer through the Gender Glass; the boys are getting the same news from their managers and they're all whooping and punching the air and jumping all over each other. I spot Young-Bae so overcome with emotion that he has his face in his hands.

I'm so happy for him. I'm excited for *us*.

'The first two nights of the showcase will be the Stages – CEO Sang and SLK will be serving as co-panelists, so all of Korea will be sure to be watching, and Korean fans will be able to vote on their favourite trainees.'

More screaming, more sobbing, more pandemonium.

'The third part of the special,' Manager Shin goes on, grinning, 'will take place the following week. It will be the live coronation of the final girl group. CEO Sang will take the judges' opinions and the nation's votes into account, but the final decisions will be his alone. It will be a magical moment K-pop fans around the world will never forget.'

The managers let all of us feel our feelings for a minute. I'm practically hyperventilating. Binna and JinJoo are openly weeping, hanging off each other.

This is real.

No matter what, in just another month, we'll know our fates, one way or another. I'll either be part of the most hyped K-pop girl group of all time, at the most powerful K-pop company, alongside the most successful boy band in K-pop history – or I'll be back at Fort Lee Magnet starting my junior year, with a full slate of AP classes, in the back of the viola section, air-bowing next to Chris DeBenedetti. Both options feel equally impossible. Straight-up surreal.

After we finally quieten down, Manager Kong says, 'There's also some bad news – not for you, but for your friends on the other side of the building. The boy group that's training – SLK 2.0 – will not be debuting as planned. CEO Sang believes the boys need a bit more time, and that the girl group should get the full attention of the public during such a high-stakes moment. Unfortunately, that also means half the boys are getting cut today.'

The girls gasp and we all look through the Gender Glass. I realize the boys weren't cheering earlier; they were shouting in anger and disappointment. Many are crying. I search for Young-Bae again – he's sitting on the floor with his knees drawn to his chin, sobbing. *Please* tell me he hasn't been cut.

'Oh, and one last announcement,' says Manager Kong. 'One.J has been generous enough to review your group and solo assessments overnight from his tour stop in Copenhagen. He has chosen one girl trainee to appear in his solo MV, which will debut just before the showcase. He'll be flying all the way back to Seoul to film three days from now with this trainee. And that trainee is: Park Candace.'

In that moment, forty-nine pairs of tired, bloodshot eyes swing to me, widened in horror and wonder and shooketh-ness. My arms go all tingly and I start seeing double. Suddenly, the shiny linoleum cafeteria floor is speeding right at my face.

CHAPTER 26

WHO MIGHT I BE?

'Harabuji hasn't been speaking this week,' Umma says, 'but he can understand everything we're saying.'

At the hospital, Harabuji looks awful, worse than ever before. The whites of his eyes are a dangerous yellow, the colour of poisonous frogs. His eyes follow me as I put a cool wet cloth on his forehead. Umma brings a spoonful of potato porridge to his lips, but he keeps them shut.

The thought occurs to me that while I was fainting over the news that One.J chose me over forty-nine other girls, Harabuji was here refusing to eat.

'Your *harabuji* always had a good appetite,' says Umma. 'The fact that he doesn't want to eat . . .'

I massage his oily ears between my fingers. Umma instructed me to give him plenty of contact, since old people who are bedridden don't get touched very much. 'His appetite will come back,

Umma. Look at his eyes – they're still sharp.'

Umma smiles at me with her whole face. 'Look at my mature Candace, taking such good care of her *harabuji*.'

I smile back, but I feel so guilty. Even as I sit here, I'm thinking about being in One.J's MV, picturing all the jealous eyes on me in the cafeteria. I've been starting to feel as if life inside S.A.Y. is the only real life – everything's so intense and new and dangerous and exciting in there – and everything outside it, this vast, bustling country, where my mom and grandfather are, where my ancestors are from, is just a distraction. Last weekend, we came here to the hospital and Harabuji was talking like normal, asking me, *'Nahn noogoo-jee?'* – *Who might I be?* – just like always. My mind had been so consumed by the report on TV that QueenGirl was officially disbanding due to the Iseul-HyunTaek scandal – all the members bawling their eyes out at a press conference, WooWee especially – that I just mumbled a vague response.

Now I realize that those might have been the last words Harabuji ever said to me.

'Harabuji,' I say, focusing on his eyes. I point to myself. *'Nah noogoo-jee?'*

He looks at me. The left corner of his lip twitches upwards slightly and he lifts his finger in my direction.

'That's right,' I say, clapping my hands. 'It's me, Candace.'

We don't go straight to the apartment from the hospital. Instead, Umma and I walk arm in arm through Namdaemun street food market, looking at all the steaming honey pancakes, red-hot *tteok-boki*, Korean corn dogs and fried pastries with salty egg yolks in the middle. Each piece of food is delicious and cheap and sold by an *ajumma* or *ajusshi* who's working extremely hard, hawking their offerings and ensuring each bite customers take is coated in the appropriate condiment, making it as delicious as possible. Most of the vendors' faces are tanned and worn – so far from the dewy, white ideal that's S.A.Y.'s standard. After so much time locked up in a K-pop trainee building, normal faces have become unusual to me. Unusual but beautiful. Interesting. Friendly. 'You have such a lovely daughter,' many of them say to Umma, and we bow our thanks.

Umma tries to run her hand through my damaged hair, but her fingers snag in the tangles. For the tenth time since she picked me up from the ShinBi Building, she clucks her tongue, saying, 'What did they do to you?' Her eyes settle on the bruise on my forehead, which I got from fainting in the cafeteria. I told her it came from tripping over my feet while dancing.

'Like I said before,' I sigh, 'they just wanted to see what I looked like with light hair.'

We take the subway back to Yeongdeungpo-gu. When we're on the familiar streets near the apartment, Umma asks, 'Did you ever find it strange that Harabuji always asked the same questions every time he saw you? "*Who might I be?*"'

'Yeah,' I say. 'It never gets old to him.'

Umma laughs softly. 'It's funny, because he used to ask me and your aunt SoonMi the same thing. But when I got a little older, I started to think it was odd, that he was treating me like I was younger than I was. I remember yelling at him, "Stop asking me the same childish questions every day! You sound simple-minded!" And after that, he never asked again. I've felt horrible about that moment. It wasn't until I was older that I realized why he constantly asked, "*Who am I?*", "*Who are you?*" It's not because he forgot, of course. It's because he grew up without a family.'

Umma looks at me to make sure I'm listening. I bury my mouth in the *wang-jjinbbang* she bought me.

'Like so many Korean people,' she goes on, 'when he was quite a bit younger than you, he was separated from everyone he loved, when the North and South border was suddenly drawn, and there was no way to cross it ever again. So I think, to him, when he had a family of his own, being able to look in our eyes every day – your eyes – and acknowledge each other's existence – ask "Who am I to you?" and be able to hear an answer he already knew – was always a miracle to him. It never got old.'

I look away quickly, blinking away my own tears.

'Candace, you're already so good. Just as you are. You don't need to become better or more impressive. I'm sorry if I ever made you think you did.'

I don't answer. I watch a street hawker scoop ice cream into cones shaped like fish mouths for a couple of European tourists. I know what Umma is saying is real and good and true, but there's a part of me that still doesn't believe her – doesn't *want* to believe her. If I'm already enough the way she says I am, I want to prove it. Figure it out for myself.

Back in the apartment, Umma mixes together her own concoction to treat my hair: mayonnaise, honey, sesame oil and eggs. It smells like one of Aram's farts and I beg her to take me to Olive Young so I can buy a name-brand hair mask, but she says, 'Chemicals are what got us here in the first place. You were perfect the way you were.'

CHAPTER 27

STORYLINES

Preparations for the showcase are a whirlwind right from the get-go. Not only do we have to prepare two Stages instead of one, we only have *three weeks* to prepare, since the final results broadcast is in a month and the performance broadcast comes a week before. All fifty girl trainees go down to the fifth floor to a giant banquet hall with all the tables cleared away. Managers Kong and Shin and all the junior managers stand next to a board on the wall with the twenty songs that have been cleared for broadcast – ten Girl Crush songs, ten Cute or ballad songs. The atmosphere in the cavernous room is tense; the stakes have never been higher and song choice is more important than ever.

Because I've been chosen by One.J to appear in his video, the managers decided that I also get to choose our final assessment song first for Team Two, which is a huge advantage – it's also another reason for the other trainees to hate me. At least my teammates and I, surprisingly, were in total agreement. From the Girl Crush column, I snatch 'Boombayah' by Blackpink, and under Cute/ballads, I take 'Into the New World (Ballad Version)' by Girls' Generation.

The trainees let out yelps of agony. I blush and bow in apology as I run back to my seat, covering my lap back up with my modesty blanket. Every K-pop fan knows these songs. 'Boombayah' is the quintessential Girl Crush song; there's no song that's more hard-hitting. And 'Into the New World (Ballad Version)' might as well be the national anthem for the youth of Korea.

In our Team Two meeting, we once again have to decide on positions. Binna's chosen as Laeader for both Stages, as always. When Manager Kong asks who wants to be Centre for 'Into the New World', I shoot my arm up into the air, along with Helena, Aram and JinJoo. Obviously, I should be Centre for this. It's a ballad that's all about the vocals, and JinJoo already got to be Centre for 'Problem'. Then Manager Kong asks who wants to be Centre for 'Boombayah', and I keep my hand down as everyone else's flies up. It's a rap-heavy, dance-heavy song – I just need to survive this Stage, not be the Centre.

'So,' says Manager Kong, 'the most obvious choice would be Binna for "Boombayah" and Candace for "Into the New World". But for an assessment that's this important, do we really want to do the boring, expected thing?'

Me and Binna look at each other as if to say, *Umm, yeah, kinda.*

'Let's make Candace the Centre for "Boombayah" and Binna the Centre for "Into the New World",' Manager Kong says with a grin. 'This *will* be a TV show, after all. We need to make some storylines. What's better than seeing two girls face their greatest weaknesses and overcome them?'

Binna and I look at each other, shooketh out of our minds.

OK, that's awesome in theory, but what if these storylines don't have a happy ending?!

$$>\!\!|\!|\!\!C$$

It's already the night before my shoot with One.J and I know exactly nothing about the plan. What's the song about? Where are we filming? What will I be doing? All I know is that I'm supposed to be ready to go at three thirty a.m. tomorrow morning.

Everyone's so frantic about the televised showcase that no one can answer my questions. All I know is that the shoot will be all day – I'll be losing precious practice time right as everyone's learning new choreography.

It's worth it, I know that. I get to be in a freaking *One.J MV*. Anything involving One.J or SLK gets a billion views on YouTube within a week. I get to be close to him for a day. Millions of girls would kill for this chance. It's just coming at the most stressful time of my life, and I can't help but still have this idiotic worry that I'm somehow 'cheating' on YoungBae by being in the MV.

I'll have hair and make-up in the morning, but I'm worried that the stylists will take one look at the dusty witch's broom on my head and throw their hands in the air and say, 'This girl is a mess! Someone call Aram to take her place!'

So I do the unthinkable. I go over to the Visual table during dinner and ask Helena for help. Her always-perfect strawberry blonde locks are proof that she's an expert in taking care of bleached, colour-treated Korean hair.

Helena glares at me like I'm a human-sized cockroach, and I can feel Luciana's gorgeous green-lensed eyes burrowing into me. But, much to my relief, she actually agrees.

'Fine,' Helena says, getting up from the table. 'I was going to offer anyway. No one should be in a One.J MV looking like that.'

I bow and thank her a million times.

'I'm doing this out of pity,' she says.

Back in the dorm, she changes into a bikini and comes into the bathroom with me. I don't have a bathing suit, so I just put on a black T-shirt and basketball shorts and sit on the toilet as she turns on the shower to wet my hair, soaking both of us. She puts on gloves and rubs a harsh-smelling clear liquid all over my scalp, not very gently at all.

'This is to heal your scalp,' she says. 'You have a ton of dandruff.'

'No, I don't,' I say.

I really don't.

'You know, white-blonde isn't good for you anyway,' says Helena. 'You don't have the bone structure for it.'

She's doing you a favour, I remind myself.

Helena empties an entire bottle of goop into her hands and rubs it into my brittle locks.

She shuts the shower off and twists my hair into a towel and wraps it on top of my head in a way that won't come undone – I've never known how to actually do that.

'OK. Just leave it in overnight and it'll be better by morning.'

'Thank you *so* much, Helena. I owe you one.'

'Hmm. You do, don't you?'

Maybe it's the treatment seeping into my scalp, but later, during our evening Fresh Air Time on the roof, I decide I want to ask Helena to come spend next weekend with me and Umma. I do genuinely feel bad that she never leaves the building, and I'm 100 per cent sure Umma would be happy to host a 'friend' of mine who doesn't have anywhere to go. Whether both of us debut or neither, it seems important to me, somehow, that we end our trainee experience on good terms.

Clusters of girls are practising their showcase routines or meditating or just pacing around – no one's truly relaxing. Binna, JinJoo and Aram are practising 'Boombayah' next to the blue hydrangeas.

'Hey, Centre, come join us!' calls Binna.

'One second!' I say. I spot Helena and Luciana in the corner by the lilac bushes, leaning on the rail, looking out over the city. I approach cautiously, not wanting to be a creeper. As I get closer, I hear Luciana say in deep, sexy, Brazilian-accented English, 'I still can't believe *she* was chosen to be in One.J's MV.'

'We should actually take it as a compliment that we weren't picked,' says Helena in English. 'They probably wanted someone One.J's fans wouldn't be too jealous of.'

I freeze. My blood runs cold. There's something hypnotic

about overhearing people talk smack about you. It's highly upsetting, but at the same time, you *have* to listen. I ease slowly on to a nearby bench nestled in the lilacs.

'Honestly, let her have this,' says Helena. 'It's not like she's actually gonna debut.'

'You said she did good in the last assessment.'

Helena scoffs. 'The bar is lower for her – she was "most improved". CEO Sang is just entertained by her because she's so clueless about everything, but at the end of the day, she doesn't fit the Concept. This group needs to be fierce – we can't have Dora the Explorer tagging along and bringing us down.'

Luciana laughs. '"Dora the Explorer". Girl, you're a mess.'

'I mean, think about it,' says Helena. 'The group *should* be you, me, our girl Aram and Binna – she might not be very pretty, but she's a good Leader and the top dancer. Imagine *Candace Park* in that line-up. It's all wrong. Not to mention, she's totally fake. JiHoon says his mom sees through the cute, innocent act too.'

JiHoon's mom?!

Helena goes on, 'JiHoon's mom told me she saw it from the get-go. Candace used *banmal* with the CEO. She's selfish and does whatever she can to stand out. Even in the last assessment, she didn't sing the song she was supposed to. She sang this *ridiculous* song instead . . .'

I've heard enough. I feel my pulse throb in my temples. It all makes sense now. I remember Madame Jung talking about her youngest son, a 'loser' who works at the company – JiHoon is that loser. Helena is 'dating' JiHoon to get closer to powerful people at the company, get insider knowledge. Helena's more calculated than I could have imagined. To think I was about to invite her to meet Umma.

Helena has shown me who she is. Now I believe her.

I storm across the roof to where Binna, JinJoo and Aram are practising. I join them. The 'Boombayah' choreo is harder than anything we've done so far, but I channel my fury into slapping each move, holding my towel on my head the whole time. 'Yes, Candace!' Binna shouts. Manager Kong's words echo in my mind:

Practising ruthlessly is the best revenge.

Actually, I don't think she ever said that. That's all my own.

CHAPTER 28

ALIEN

I'm shaken awake. Light is streaming into the dorm from the hallway. 'Candace, wake up,' hisses Manager Kong.

It's three thirty a.m., the morning of the MV shoot. I climb down from the bunk, but I'm totally disorientated and don't know what to do – what should I wear? What do I need?

Manager Kong reads my mind and whispers, 'You don't need anything.'

'I need to get dressed,' I say. 'I need to brush my teeth.'

'They'll have everything there. Just come!'

I follow Manager Kong out of the room in my pyjamas, slipping my sockless feet into my ratty sneakers as I go. I hear Binna whisper in the dark, 'Good luck, Candace!'

'Thanks, *unnie*!' I whisper back.

I run after Manager Kong down the hallway and through the corporate floor. It's in the elevator where I look at my reflection in the mirrored walls and see that I look like a total wreck – dark brown bags under my eyes, chapped lips, a zit on my forehead. I practised so hard last night that I fell into bed without washing my face. I still have the towel on my head. I snatch it off.

Manager Kong sees it at the same time I do. I shriek, and she gasps and clamps her hand over her mouth. 'What did you do, Candace?!'

It looks as if I'm wearing uncooked ramen on my head. It looks like it's been baking in the desert sun next to the tumbleweeds. It *is* the tumbleweeds. It's so much worse than before.

'Helena!' I scream. 'She did this!'

'What did you do?' Manager Kong moans again. 'This is ruined! What am I supposed to do with you now?'

She pulls me by the arm as she storms across the dark, almost empty lobby where a stressed-out twenty-something lady in glasses is waiting for us. I'm cursing Helena in my head. *Saboteur!*

The lady jumps back when she sees me. 'What's this?'

'This is Park Candace, the trainee who's supposed to star in the video,' explains Manager Kong.

'No, she's not,' says the lady.

'Yes, she is, Producer Kim,' says Manager Kong. 'She just had a . . . hair *sago*.'

Accident. Train wreck.

'Well,' snaps Producer Kim, 'can you go upstairs and grab a different girl?'

I look at Manager Kong, horrified. Tears of humiliation and rage brew in my eye sockets. This is exactly what Helena wanted. She's trying to destroy me.

244

Manager Kong bites her lip; I can see her mind whirring.

'No,' she says finally. 'One.J chose *this* one. We'll have to make this one work. Let me call Mr Oh for backup.'

Producer Kim frowns at me. 'Fine, let's go. Hurry up, *haksaeng. Ppali-ppali!*'

Sniffling and wiping my eyes, I run after the two women into a parking garage, where I get into the back of a nondescript grey van with tinted windows. Manager Kong frantically dials a number on her phone with one hand, starts the engine with the other. 'Yes, is this Mr Oh? I'm so sorry to wake you ...'

The tyres squeal as we peel out of the parking garage. Manager Kong drives like a madwoman through the streets of Seoul while Producer Kim briefs me on the day ahead. She addresses me as *'haksaeng'* – *'student'*. I half listen as a cold sweat breaks out all over my body.

Apparently, One.J's solo track is called 'Alien' – it's a nineties-style Korean ballad. Umma and Abba loved listening to this kind of ballad when I was little. I didn't understand the lyrics, but they were usually performed by a male singer with an *unreal* voice who could blast a nuclear high note for a full twenty seconds while literally sobbing. Back then, I thought those songs were depressing and only for old people – but now I can imagine One.J singing throwback style being totally *daebak*.

'We can never show One.J and a female love interest interacting directly in an MV,' explains Producer Kim. 'One.J's fans are too intense. It's for the girl's own safety.'

Say what?!

'Luckily, it fits the song's Concept for you two to be apart,'

Producer Kim continues. 'It's all about One.J remembering a girl from his past, who he went to elementary and middle school with. Now, One.J is a huge, global megastar, and this girl – that's you, *haksaeng* – is now a normal high school girl, doing normal high school things. Their lives are now so different that it's like they live on two different planets – One.J now feels like an "Alien" in her life. Sometimes, he secretly goes back to his home town to check on her from afar, but it kills him inside to know that they can never truly be together.'

I swoon a bit. It sounds super depressing and a smidge stalker-ish, but to think that I'll be the object of One.J's obsession . . . it's romantic enough to make me light-headed. Well, the carsickness isn't helping either.

Thankfully, we arrive at our destination: Dongtan High School. It looks like any modern suburban high school in America, except the parking lot is crowded with equipment trucks and trailers and the whole campus is bustling with yellow-uniformed students, and it's not even dawn. I'm embarrassed to be seen by kids my own age while I'm in my PJs, nasty sneakers and my crispy-crunchy hair.

Right as we walk into an empty classroom that's been turned into a makeshift dressing room, Producer Kim announces to everyone, 'This is Park Candace, the S.A.Y. trainee – she has a pimple on the right side of her forehead and her hair is unsalvageable.'

I want to say *How rude!*, but immediately, a crowd of adults surrounds me and I'm pushed into a chair. They gasp.

Manager Kong tells them, 'I've called Mr Oh. He's sent an emergency team – they're on their way with a *gabal*.'

Thanks to my three-thousand-word vocabulary exam, I know that '*gabal*' means '*wig*'. I relax now that I know Mr Oh has a plan for me. I'm actually looking forward to wearing a wig for the first time. Helena didn't get away with this; the fact remains that One.J chose me. Despite her efforts, I'm still here.

A make-up artist starts me off with a face massage, which feels so good I let out a creepy moan. The various brushes feel so good on my skin that I fall half-asleep as Producer Kim tells me my shot list for the day. In the morning, I'll be filmed doing regular schoolgirl things – raising my hand in a classroom, drinking at a water fountain, putting books in my locker. I'll also be in a lunch scene where I'm tripped by some mean girls and drop my tray. All that time, One.J will be watching me from afar. (Seriously, if it were anyone but One.J, this would be cringey beyond words.)

I'm suddenly wide awake. 'So One.J will be filming with me all day?'

Producer Kim breathes an exasperated sigh. 'No, he already filmed his parts of those scenes at a studio in Budapest. He's not arriving here until the afternoon, for a scene outside on the soccer field. You'll be crying in the bleachers after being bullied by the girls, and he's about to show himself to you and comfort you. But before he can reach you, another boy swoops in and comforts you first. One.J is left with mixed emotions: he's happy that you've found love, but he's also crushed it can't be him.'

'*Wahhhhhhh*, so romantic!' I squeal, startling a make-up artist so bad she pokes me in the corner of the eye.

I, Candace Park, who's never had a real boyfriend (well, aside from Ethan that one week), will have not one but *two* boys fighting over her, one of whom is the biggest K-pop star of all time. Is this real life?!

Well, no. But still! I squeal again until the make-up artist yells at me to stop moving.

Two hours later, the sun is streaming in through the windows and I wish I had my phone so I could take a million *selcas*; I've never felt cuter in my whole life. This look definitely beats the test makeover I got in Loveliness Class, because now I'm MV ready. My face is dewy, smooth, poreless and zit-free thanks to Glow-Song BB cream. (It's a touch too white for my tastes, but it's the Korean style). My eyebrows are straight and perfect and light brown, and I have a head full of lustrous, real-looking lavender hair thanks to Mr Oh's emergency wig team.

I hate to admit it, but Helena was kinda right – white-blonde wasn't quite right for me. Silvery unicorn-purple is my jam. My scalp itches like crazy under the wig, but . . . hashtag worth it.

I'm wearing a school uniform costume – a bumblebee-yellow blazer with navy trim, a navy skirt so short I have to wear **safety shorts** under and fresh white sneakers. The jacket is so yellow it's almost too much, but clashing with my purple hair it looks swaggy as anything.

Also, have my legs got longer?

When we start filming, I'm shocked by how many people it takes to film an MV with such a basic storyline. The shot of me raising my hand once in the classroom takes a whole two hours. There are four cameras, at least twenty production assistants, hot lights and a whole crowd of stylists touching me up and blotting me and adjusting my wig every two seconds. Mr Choi – the evil photographer – is actually the **P.D.** of the MV, but now he couldn't be nicer. In fact, everyone's nice to me on set. The dozens of extras playing my classmates – some of whom are my age, some of whom are fully thirty years old – all bow to me when they meet my eye . . . because I'm the star. It's so surreal being the highest-status kid in the room and not just the *maknae* of Team Two. Maybe this is how everyone will treat me after I debut and become successful. Like an *idol*.

Finally, we get to the soccer field scene. I've been looking around all day at the male extras, wondering which one of them will play my non-One.J boyfriend, but I'm supposed to start the scene by myself. I'm supposed to be sitting alone on the bleachers.

A crowd of producers and Manager Kong are staring right at me. P.D. Choi is standing on a ladder and yelling directions into a megaphone. 'All right, Candace! Look down at the ground and think of something really, really sad! And then, when you feel a hand on your shoulder, look up, full of hope that it's One.J, but it's not – it's a different classmate! And when you see his face, you're disappointed for a split second, but then you're happy, because you realize you can move on! We need all of those emotions in one look, got it?'

'Yes, P.D.-*nim*,' I say, although I'm quite sure not even Meryl Streep can convey all those emotions in one look.

'ALL RIGHT, LET'S GET ROLLING!' shouts P.D. Choi. 'OK, CANDACE, YOU'RE LOOKING AT THE GROUND. THINK OF THE SADDEST MOMENT OF YOUR LIFE! ROLLING IN ONE, TWO, THREE . . .'

I stare at the ground. I've never felt so awkward, sitting there on the bleachers alone, being watched by a crowd. The other scenes were kind of easy because I could pretend to be just one of many students, but this is different. There are so many eyes on me. What has the saddest moment of my life been? Not getting to sing for all those years? Having to play the viola? If those are the saddest moments of my life so far, I've lived a pretty good life.

I think of Harabuji in that hospital bed, not being able to speak. How I wouldn't exist if he hadn't been brave enough to escape from the North during the Korean War as a kid, losing his whole family. How much Umma and Abba have sacrificed to give Tommy and me a good life in New Jersey. How much they've sacrificed to let me be here, in the country of my ancestors, to try to fulfil a ridiculous dream.

The tears come.

'GOOD, CANDACE! GOOD! WOW!' shouts P.D. Choi.

My shoulders start to shake, my chest convulsing. I wonder if it's too much at this point – it's becoming an ugly cry – but P.D. Choi keeps encouraging me.

'OK, NOW YOUR CLASSMATE IS CROSSING THE SOCCER FIELD – DON'T LOOK UP YET. DON'T LOOK UP YET. HE'S CLIMBING UP THE BLEACHERS TO YOU. OK, HE'S TOUCHING YOUR SHOULDER.'

I feel a hand land on my shoulder.

'OK, NOW LOOK UP!'

I look up. The sun or one of the camera lights is shining in my eyes.

It's YoungBae. Beautiful as a dream. He's in his yellow blazer and navy tie. His hair is done neatly, that one lock curling over his forehead. His skin is perfect and radiant, his lips pink and glossy. Every good feeling comes flooding into my veins.

'ALL RIGHT, YOUNGBAE, SAY SOMETHING TO COMFORT HER,' says P.D. Choi. 'SAY ANYTHING, NO ONE WILL HEAR YOU.'

YoungBae grins. 'So, we meet again, Candace.'

'YoungBae?' I say, shook out of my mind.

'YES, GOOD AD-LIBBING, CANDACE. VERY SPONTANEOUS.'

'Yep, 'tis I,' says YoungBae. 'It's been a while.'

I've texted YoungBae a million times since I heard half the boys got cut – my battery's at just 10 per cent. YoungBae's still safe – thank God – but I haven't been able to get away this week, even late at night, to meet him on the roof.

'I'm sorry, I've been busy . . .'

'I get it,' he says. 'Your time is important, *sunbaenim*. Now you're acting? *Oppa's* very proud of you.'

I laugh and smack him on the shoulder. I wipe my tears.

'EXCELLENT! EXCELLENT, YOU TWO! WOW, WHAT CHEMISTRY. IT'S LIKE YOU'VE KNOWN EACH OTHER FOR A LONG TIME!'

'We haven't, sir!' YoungBae and I shout back at the same time.

P.D. Choi yells cut, and immediately we're separated. Young-Bae's manager, Manager Byun, shoos him to the opposite side of the bleachers and Manager Kong runs up to me alongside a team of make-up and hair stylists, who immediately begin touching up my foundation. Manager Kong looks overjoyed.

'Candace, that was amazing, way beyond what I expected!' exclaims Manager Kong, stroking my back. 'You haven't even had any acting classes. Are you OK?'

I nod. 'I'm just surprised to see that kid from my Language class,' I say.

'Ah, CEO Sang decided at the last minute this would be a good opportunity to show off one of our handsomest boy trainees instead of a random extra. Do you need a break?'

I nod.

'CANDACE NEEDS A BREAK!' shouts Manager Kong. I'm pretty sure this is the first break she's ever approved of me taking.

'OK, EVERYONE, LET'S FILM ONE.J!' shouts P.D. Choi into the megaphone.

One.J's here?!

Sure enough, across the soccer field, I spot a boy in a slick black outfit – definitely not a student at this fictional school – surrounded by an entourage of managers and assistants. The entire production crew turns and sets up a new shot around him.

I hear P.D. Choi shout, 'ROLLING IN ONE, TWO, THREE . . .'

The song 'Alien' blares from the field's loudspeakers as One.J lip-syncs from the centre of the soccer field.

We were once inseparable
But now we live on two separate planets
I've forgotten the ways of our old world
I can never truly return

My new home is a planet of screaming strangers
I can't bring you here, there's no oxygen
You'd hate me for the things I must do to survive
That's why I spare you by leaving you alone

Yet please know I still check in on you
Just to know that you're happy
In our shared language I'll send you signals
All the way from my distant star

I'm fanning my face. In the tradition of Korean ballads from the nineties, this song is exploding with emotion. One.J sings with range I've never heard from him before. In parts, he's practically wailing. The lyrics are so far beyond his seventeen years – I feel his love, his loneliness, despite his wealth and fame.

Even Manager Kong is clutching her chest by the end. 'This kid is something else,' she says.

After an hour of One.J filming, it's time for me and YoungBae to film my crying scene a few more times. One.J actually puts sunglasses on and watches us from a distance with his arms crossed. I'm so nervous and spent that I'm not as good as I was in the first take, but I still manage to shed real tears every time – only now, I'm thinking about the anguish in One.J's voice, even as I'm looking into YoungBae's eyes.

Once we have that scene in the can, we take another break before our final shot of the day. The crew brings a long folding table out on to the soccer field, where there's a lunch of sandwich platters that all the production people and One.J and his entourage crowd around. I'm exhausted and starving at this point. Manager Kong brings out a plastic bag with chunks of sweet potato and boiled egg for me to eat, as if I'm a preschooler on a diet. I glance over at YoungBae – I know I'll get in trouble if I stare too long – and see that he's eating a similar sad meal with Manager Byun.

Manager Kong asks, 'Tired? You can lean on my shoulder for a bit.'

I'm shocked by the offer, but I take her up on it. I rest my aching eyes.

But after what feels like a couple of seconds, Manager Kong is shaking me off. 'Candace, wake up,' she says.

When I open my eyes, One.J is smiling down at me with his entrancing eyes.

I jump to my feet and bow, adjusting my wig. '*Anyunghaseyo*,' I say.

'Thank you for your time today, Candace-*shi*,' One.J says, not moving his eyes from mine.

I bow three more times. 'Thank you so much for choosing me, One.J-*sunbaenim*.'

'It's my pleasure,' he says. '*Oneul gosaeng mani hasseunungataeyo*.'

Which means, '*it seems to me you've suffered a lot today*', or '*you've done a very good job today*', or both.

'What an honour it is,' I say. 'What a wonderful song you've written.'

'Those kind words mean a lot to me, coming from you.' He extends to me a plate with a sandwich on it. 'You must be very hungry and these are quite tasty.'

I look at Manager Kong for permission. She makes a face at me. 'Oh, thank you so much,' I say, 'but I couldn't possibly. I'm actually not hungry.'

One.J chuckles. 'Nonsense. You're a trainee – you're always hungry.'

I look at Manager Kong again. She says, 'Candace, your *sunbae* is offering you food. Don't be rude.'

I bow and take the plate with both hands. One.J and Manager Kong are watching me. One.J's managers and the producers are watching me. I know it's good Korean manners to let One.J see me take a bite and show him how much I enjoy the food he gave me – nothing makes Korean people (normal Korean people, not K-pop managers) happier than sharing food.

'I'll eat it with joy, *sunbaenim*,' I say.

In case Manager Kong plans to take the sandwich away after my one courtesy bite – my Manners Bite – I make it a big one and cram about half of the sandwich into my mouth at once. This ham might be the only real meat I have until this weekend, unless YoungBae sneaks some for me before then.

'*Umona*, look at this one go,' says Manager Kong, clucking her tongue disapprovingly.

One.J laughs. 'You must have been so hungry.'

I close my eyes as the saltiness of the meat, the creaminess of the mayonnaise, the pillowiness of the bread and the crunch of the lettuce come together in a perfect symphony of high-calorie deliciousness. I took such a gigantic bite that I've got a piece of the wrapper, but I don't care. I swallow down everything that's edible and, like a proper Korean lady, I turn to the side and cover my mouth with one hand as I fish out the piece of wrapper with the other.

'Ugh, Candace, watch your manners,' snaps Manager Kong. 'You got mayonnaise on your face.'

I hide the soggy piece of sandwich wrapper in my fist. I'm so disgusting.

'That was quite improper of me,' I say, genuinely mortified.

'Thank you, One.J, but she's had enough,' says Manager Kong. 'Candace, let me get you a napkin. And then let's get your make-up retouched.'

Manager Kong snatches the plate from me and throws it in the trash.

One.J's managers are watching us, so there's not much we can do or say. His eyes fixate meaningfully on my fist, which has the dirty piece of wrapper in it. I hide it behind my back – I'm such a slob! – but One.J looks meaningfully at me again and tilts his chin ever so slightly.

I open my fist and take a look. It's not a shred of sandwich wrapper. It's a note:

Here's my KakaoTalk

I look up at One.J again, amazed. His lip curls slightly as he turns away. Manager Kong and a team of make-up and hair people rush back over to clean me up. I put my hands behind my back and stuff One.J's number under my skirt into my safety shorts. Not romantic, but I have no other choice – my uniform slash costume doesn't have pockets.

I have One.J's KakaoTalk!

Daebak! How many people on this planet can say that?!

I can't stop smiling as Manager Kong wipes my mouth and my foundation is retouched.

But then I glance over at YoungBae again. Guilt rushes over me. Like a gentleman, One.J is offering him a sandwich too, which YoungBae gladly accepts with a handshake. 'Thanks, dude,' I hear YoungBae say in English.

Seeing them next to each other is such a worlds-collide moment. Fantasy versus reality. What would YoungBae do if he knew One.J gave me his KakaoTalk number? Is it cheating if we've never kissed?

I know there's no way I'm not going to use One.J's number; I need to know how it feels to text with one of the biggest celebrities in the world.

After the lunch break, we film the final shot of the MV. I'm hugging YoungBae on the bleachers, but this time it feels different. I can feel myself pushing away, trying not to let One.J see that YoungBae and I have a real connection. It works for the scene though – I'm hugging one boy, but my mind is on a different one. One.J is standing three metres away, reaching his arm in my direction, his face contorted in anguish. He lip-syncs the lines:

I'm sending you my signal
Please let me know you can hear it

'ALL RIGHT, CANDACE, LOOK RIGHT PAST ONE.J!' shouts P.D. Choi into the megaphone. 'YOU CAN FEEL HIS PRESENCE, BUT YOU CAN'T SEE HIM! YOU'RE SO CLOSE, YET YOU'RE ON DIFFERENT PLANETS!'

CHAPTER 29

PRIVATE LIFE

'We need to talk,' Umma says the moment she picks me up from the lobby.

'Why? Is it something about Harabuji?' I ask, panicked.

Umma's mad at me for some reason. We end up not talking at all on the entire subway ride to the apartment, but it becomes clear to me what this is about.

Plastered all over our subway car is the same ad: the whole planet being squeezed in Helena's glittery, manicured hand, the five silhouettes of female idols printed on the nails; *S.A.Y. 50 LIVE SHOWCASE* in sparkly pink letters; and the dates:

21 August: TOP 50 TRAINEE PERFORMANCES WITH SPECIAL APPEARANCES BY SLK NIGHT 1

22 August: TRAINEE PERFORMANCES WITH SPECIAL APPEARANCES BY SLK NIGHT 2

The moment Umma slams the apartment door shut, she shouts, 'Why didn't you tell me it's getting this serious?!'

'What do you mean?' I say. 'They're deciding who gets chosen on twenty-eighth August – that's a day before the deadline you set.'

'But it's going to be aired on live TV? We didn't discuss this! Millions of people are going to see you.'

I get a sweet yoghurt drink out of the refrigerator. 'Wasn't that the point of all this?'

'No. The point of this was for you to come here, learn some Korean culture, sing and dance like you wanted. That's it!'

I finish the yoghurt drink in one gulp and plop down on the couch. I turn on the TV. Bad timing. At that exact moment, a CF for the live showcase blares. I'm not worried though. I've done nothing wrong.

'Wow, Umma,' I say sarcastically. 'So you only let me come to Korea because you thought I had no chance to debut? It's great knowing you believe in me.'

Umma storms over to me and shows me her phone. 'Look at what your aunt SoonMi sent me.'

All the way from Franklin Lakes, New Jersey, Aunt SoonMi sent Umma a KakaoTalk link to a YouTube video . . . with my face on the thumbnail. My heart races. It's a fifteen-second teaser for One.J's 'Alien' MV. I can't believe they edited this so quickly!

It's a slo-mo shot of me in the school hallway, clutching my books to my chest and looking tragically sad. The sunlight is streaming through my flowing purple hair. I seriously look like a legit star of a teen K-drama. One.J is hiding right around the corner, leaning against a wall of lockers, looking tragically lovestruck. We never filmed in the hallway together – they must have spliced together footage of me with footage of One.J in the studio in Budapest. That's *Hallyu* magic for you!

'*Daebak!*' I exclaim.

I scroll through the comments for a second. An icy sensation blooms in my gut when I see, 'WHO IS THAT UGLY GIRL WITH ONE.J?' and 'THAT GIRL BROKE MY ONE.J'S HEART. I WILL KILL HER!'

Whatever. Haters are the price of stardom.

'Why didn't you tell me you were going to be in a One.J music video?' Umma demands.

I can't believe she's not the least bit proud of me. 'I only filmed it this week. Anyway, they told me not to tell anyone.'

'And you didn't tell me? I'm your mother.'

'Maybe I knew you'd react exactly like this,' I say, moving to the bedroom. 'Do you have any idea what a big deal it is to be in a One.J MV?'

'Why should I be impressed by him? Why is One.J any more important than Candace Park?'

'Umm, maybe because he's one of the biggest stars on the planet? And his music gives millions of kids around the world hope?'

I fall face first into the bed, pretending I'm about to take a nap. I still have Umma's phone. My heart racing, I try to look casual as I send a KakaoTalk to One.J's number – I memorized it backwards and forward.

> Hi. This is Candace. I'm using my mom's phone.

Umma follows me into the bedroom. I delete the Kakao right away.

'Candace,' Umma says. 'Now that you've appeared in this MV, and after you're on TV . . . it's going to be harder for you to go back to America to be a regular girl.'

Shockingly, One.J responds right away.

> Hi. ^__^ I figured. I'll keep this brief. Meet at 6 p.m. at Hongik University station, entrance 6?

> Please delete this.

> OK!

I delete both messages. That's only in an hour.

'Candace,' says Umma firmly. 'Stop Kakao-ing Imani and listen to me. Did you hear what I said?'

I bury my head under a pillow. 'Yes, I heard you. Have you ever considered that I don't want to go back to being a regular American girl? I like it here.'

'I must not have heard you right. We're getting on a plane to Newark on twenty-ninth August and you're starting school the next day.'

'Maybe, maybe not,' I say.

Umma snatches the pillow from my face. 'Excuse me?!'

'I like it here! I know this may shock you, but I might make this group. And even if I don't debut, I'm going to be miserable going back home and being the same person I was before.'

Stricken, Umma takes a step back. 'I've heard you loud and clear. You don't have to do orchestra next year. You can do glee club. You can take singing lessons—'

'Umma, you've never even seen me perform! There are people at S.A.Y. who think I have something special and that makes me *happy*. But you only care that what I do fits your standard of what's "respectable". I'm not going to quit like you did!'

I can't believe I just said that, but I also can't believe we're having this argument again. I've changed so much since we last had it in New Jersey, but Umma's exactly the same. I storm out of the bedroom.

Umma calls after me, 'You have no idea what I went through! And I've seen your feet! I see your hair, I see your eyes, how skinny you've become. They're going to use you, they're going to squeeze everything you have from you!'

'Maybe I have more in me than they can take.'

I grab Umma's spare Tmoney card for the subway.

'Where are you going?'

'I'm going to go hang out with Binna and JinJoo,' I lie. 'We have to squeeze in all the practice we can for the showcase. I'm really serious about this, Umma.'

'You don't have a phone or anything.'

'I know enough Korean to get around now. Anyway, I won't be long.'

I walk out the door, half-surprised Umma doesn't come running after me. I feel queasy about lying to her, but I've learnt a tough truth this summer: just because your parents love you and want the best for you doesn't mean their plan for you is right. If I did exactly what Umma wanted, I'd probably major in Economics in college, or something else I have zero interest in, then drag myself through law or business school, miserable for every second of it. On the other hand, S.A.Y. doesn't *actually* care about me at all – not as a living, breathing human being – but if I do exactly what they tell me to for just a little bit longer, there's a chance I can have a life beyond my wildest dreams.

It's all so backwards and messed up, but that's life, I guess.

I end up walking to Hongik University station, asking directions the whole way. There are countless well-dressed girls my age or a little older out for a fun Saturday night, arm in arm with a boyfriend or friend, who are happy to point me in the right direction.

At Hongik University station entrance 6, there are other kids just like me, checking their phones and waiting to meet up with friends or dates or whoever.

I'm cold with nerves. The last time One.J saw me, I was a purple-haired dream girl; right now, I have on a plain white blouse, jeans and my usual ratty sneakers. At least my hair isn't a total disaster, thanks to the GlowSong hair masks Mr Oh sent me after the MV shoot. I figure One.J knows that most trainees don't have date-night clothes, but what if he arrives in a limo and we go to some swanky secret restaurant where you need a password to get in?

The clock above the station says 6.23 p.m. I've been stood up by a global K-pop superstar. It was too much to hope for. Maybe I'll get some black bean noodles to go for Umma, to apologize for being such a brat.

But just as I'm about to step on to the escalator down into the station, I hear a frantic, high-pitched horn beeping. I turn. There's a guy all in black – black jacket, black jeans, black helmet – driving a moped scooter type thing, putting his feet out as it comes to a wobbly stop at the curb. I can't see his face, but I'm suddenly positive it's him. I can't picture One.J on a scooter, and I've never seen someone so awkward driving one.

The blood in my veins is fizzing like soda – it's a sensation I've never felt before in my life. I run up to the helmeted dude.

'One.J?' I ask quietly.

The helmeted dude shouts, 'Ahwoooooo!'

I'm confused for a second, but then I realize he's singing the chorus of 'Yeowoo', my song that got me chosen for his MV. It's definitely One.J!

He awkwardly props the moped on its kickstand, opens the seat compartment and pulls out a surgical mask for me – identical to what I saw him wear before, except the skull and crossbones is bright pink – and a helmet. It's a little creepy that he's not talking, but I put it on my head, and instantly I feel like I'm underwater, enclosed from the city.

I ignore everything my parents ever told me about strangers and get on the back of a motorized bike with a boy I don't really know. I hesitate about Manner Hands – but One.J guides my hands with his around his narrow waist. He nods his helmeted head at me. I give his abs a slight squeeze – I feel him flex them

264

once – and I nod back. The bike purrs to life under me and we almost speed straight into a parked taxi, but One.J swerves just in time. I scream in my helmet as we weave between two buses to speed through a yellow light.

After the wobbly start, we're speeding down the road and I let out another scream. The lights of Saturday in Seoul streak past us like lasers, and I hold on tight as we turn on to a bridge over the Han River, where the world opens up. The sun is starting to set and the sky is hazy and blushed. On the other side of the river, we come to a quiet neighbourhood, where the streets are made of uneven cobblestone and laundry hangs from clothes lines stretched over the alleys.

We stop in one of the secluded alleys, at a nondescript restaur-ant that literally looks like a hole in the wall – there's no door. One.J pulls off his helmet. He has on his surgical mask and a red bandanna around his forehead, but his eyes and the point of his chin are unmistakably him.

'Are you hungry?' he asks. I see his grin behind the mask.

'Always,' I say.

The restaurant is old-fashioned; we have to take off our shoes (luckily, I'm wearing decent socks) and the customers, mostly middle-aged *ajusshis* who are cheers-ing loudly, sit on the floor at low tables. One.J bows to the waitress, an *ajumma* in a stained apron, and she takes us to a private room with a traditional Korean sliding paper door.

Once we're alone, sitting on the floor, we take off our masks and One.J lets out a relieved sigh.

'Ahhhh, that's better.'

I'm face to face with One.J, alone. Under the unflattering fluorescent lights, I can actually see his face is caked with make-up, even on his day off. He's still ridiculously cute though, especially with that red bandanna.

I remember my session with Madame Jung about eating and drinking. I quickly pour his water first from the jug on the table with two hands, then my own. One.J sets out the silverware.

'Oh, *sunbaenim*, you should let me do that,' I say.

One.J laughs. 'S.A.Y. teaches foreign trainees the strictest version of Korean manners. Let's just be informal today and have fun – none of this *sunbae–hoobae* stuff, OK?'

'OK.'

'I know this place isn't exactly a cool Saturday night spot,' he says, looking around at the dingy little room. There's an electric fan in the corner and a fly buzzing around. The racket of *ajusshis* playing a rowdy drinking game comes through the paper door. 'But I know the owners quite well, so we can order whatever we want . . . even if it's not on the menu. Are you in the mood for *chimaek*? You know, without the *maek*?'

'I love KFC,' I say.

Chimaek is chicken and *maekju*, or fried chicken and beer, an insanely popular combo in Korea. The waitress pokes her head in and One.J barely has to say a few words before she nods and leaves us alone again.

'Anyway, sorry I was late picking you up,' says One.J. 'I had to take a long route. I started thinking I was being followed by *sasaengs*.'

I've never heard the word before.

One.J must notice the blank look on my face and explains the *sasaeng* phenomenon to me. They're obsessive fans who will stop at almost nothing to insert themselves into idols' private lives (the word literally means '*private life*'). 'They make up a tiny, tiny percentage of fans,' One.J emphasizes.

SLK has about a thousand *sasaengs* in Korea and thousands more around the world – but they have a huge impact on his life. He has *sasaengs* who've quit their jobs, dropped out of school, gone into debt in order to hire '*sasaeng* taxis' – special cabs that will charge $600 to follow him around all day; they'll buy first-class tickets so they can be on the same flight, where they'll take photos of him and his bandmates sleeping. Some don't necessarily want him to like them – they want him to *remember* them, even for bad reasons. He's been slapped and spit on by *sasaengs* at fansign events. One even gave him a letter written in blood.

One.J sees the terror on my face and says, 'Don't worry. Male idols get way more *sasaengs* than female idols.'

'Hey, are you saying I can't attract *sasaengs*?'

'I'm sorry, I didn't mean to imply . . . you will have many, many *sasaengs*, a whole army of *sasaengs*. You will have stacks of letters written in blood. Look at me, I couldn't help but put my Kakao in your sandwich. That's very *sasaeng* behaviour.'

We laugh. An entire feast of fried chicken in different sauces arrives on the table. Instead of beer, we share a bottle of *saida*. One.J shouts, '*Geonbae!*' (Korean for '*cheers!*'), holding a piece of steaming, sticky, spicy chicken out to me. I touch his chicken with mine. '*Geonbae!*'

'I have to ask,' I say, swallowing the delicious chicken, 'why did you pick me for your MV? Why did you give me your Kakao?'

I might as well be begging, *Tell me you like me!*

He thinks about this seriously – everything about him is so serious – as he sucks a chicken bone completely clean.

'I see myself in you,' he says.

Not as romantic as I'd hoped, but OK; I'll take it.

He explains, 'Well, I don't see myself as I *actually* am in you. But more how I *wish* I could be. Ever since I saw you at that first assessment, I thought, *this is a girl who will never lose sight of who she is.* Being an idol, your name no longer belongs to you, your body no longer belongs to you. It belongs to the company and to the fans. There are constant scandals over nothing, criticism over nothing. Yet because I am not my own, I have to apologize for all of it, without ever knowing why.'

I think of Umma's words: *they're going to squeeze everything you have from you.*

'This may be too personal,' I say, 'but do you regret it sometimes? Being an idol?'

'I regret it *all the time*,' says One.J too quickly. 'The costs *are* too high. My advice to you is: don't debut. Do something else. Do the thing your parents want you to do.'

Ugh. One.J's on Umma's side too?

'But,' One.J says, a glint in his hazel-lensed eye, 'if you're anything like me, you won't listen. There was no convincing me otherwise when I was a trainee. And you know what? Even though I regret it, I wouldn't take it back – does that make sense?'

I nod. I think of everything that happened to get me to this moment, right here.

'I think so,' I say. 'It's like ... the road you're on is difficult and full of obstacles, but when you look behind you at where you've been, you see that the road was beautiful, in its own way, all along.'

One.J makes an O with his mouth. '*Wahhh*, Candace. You're so deep.'

'Well, I'm thinking poetically these days. I've been writing songs every night, just like you told me to.'

One.J does the high-pitched 'Yeowoo' howl and cracks up. 'You know, that's what really sealed the deal on choosing you for my MV – the song you wrote for your second assessment will be a Perfect All-Kill one day. Mark my words.'

'You really think so? I have to say, the vast majority of songs I write are awful. I wrote one called, "*Jebal*, Let Me Sleep", and one called "I Hate You, Sweet Potato".'

'Oh, those sound like masterpieces compared to some of mine. During my trainee days, I wrote one called, "Why Can't I Poop?"'

I lean forward, rest my chin in my hand and say, 'Can you sing a little of that one for me? It sounds beautiful.'

After dinner, One.J takes me to a raccoon cafe in Hongdae. One.J says, 'I'll be safe in here. No one expects an idol to go somewhere so touristy.'

Over iced matcha lattes, One.J gives me advice for idol life if I end up debuting.

'Buy your own in-ears,' he says, lifting his mask just enough to put the straw to his mouth. 'The ones they give you at music shows are super unreliable, and it's a disaster if you can't hear yourself.'

He tells me to keep up with the trends, like doing **finger hearts** on camera. He gives me advice on how to manage CEO Sang, who he calls a *kkondae* – a bossy old man who thinks he's always right.

After we're done with our drinks, we go into the raccoon room, where there are two regular raccoons and one albino raccoon climbing on a jungle gym. We feed them little strips of dried squid. One.J puts one on my head and soon enough I feel paws pitter-pattering on me. I have to say, even though they smell like pee, raccoons are adorable. The raccoon reaches with one of its weirdly human five-fingered hands and lifts One.J's mask for a second. I gasp and pull it back down, looking around.

'No one saw,' I say.

'Good,' says One.J. 'That's my last piece of advice. Keep up a safe level of paranoia.'

One.J parks the scooter two blocks from Umma's apartment and walks with me. With each step, I feel like I'm getting tiny electric shocks to the brain. *One.J from SLK is walking me home.*

A block away from the building, I stop. 'We shouldn't go all the way to my door,' I say. 'Paranoia, right?'

'Very smart,' he says, grinning. 'It seems to me that this is where we part.'

We stand for a second, awkward. I hug myself and rub my arms, as if I'm cold, even though it's sweltering out. We both look around. The whole block is dark and quiet, except for a drunk businessman staggering home across the street.

One.J suddenly fixes me with an intense stare. '*Hokshi* . . . may I kiss you, Candace?'

Electricity shoots through me. I nod. One.J steps closer and pulls his mask down off his face. I do the same. The moment before One.J's lips touch mine, YoungBae's face flashes in my mind, but in the next moment, all I can do is close my eyes. One.J's lips touch mine. The kiss feels sweet, tastes a little like *chimaek*, and for some reason, it feels . . . room temperature. When I open my eyes, all I see is One.J's perfectly made-up famous face, smiling his famous smile, only for me to see. All I can do is giggle a little bit, and he does the same.

I put my mask back on – I'm going to keep it as a souvenir of this night, I decide – and he puts on his. We bow to each other awkwardly, and we turn and walk in opposite directions.

All I can think is that it felt a bit like a Manners Kiss. Maybe I blew it. I *was* super nervous. But still, I skip down the street. My first kiss was with the most popular K-pop idol of all time.

The next day, Umma and I visit Harabuji in the hospital, where he's sitting up, speaking and eating potato porridge. 'Praise God!' Umma says. Instantly, I feel the chill between Umma and me thawing a little.

'Candace,' Harabuji says between loud slurps of porridge, 'I've been seeing the CFs. Is my granddaughter going to be on TV?'

I glance at Umma before saying, 'Yes, Harabuji. I'll dedicate my performance to you.'

'*Wahhh!*' says Harabuji, grinning. 'What a blessing. It makes my heart bubble over to know you're pursuing your dream.' He looks at Umma. 'You know, most parents of my generation didn't want their children to go into the arts. But it's always been my belief that when Korean parents impose their will on children, it dims their *gi*.' *Life force*. 'Don't you think so, daughter?'

Umma looks caught off guard. 'I suppose so,' she says, wanting to change the subject.

But I'm not going to let her. 'Umma, why did you and Abba quit music?'

She gives me a warning glance. 'Candace, let's not talk about this now.'

'I've been wondering about it all my life,' I insist.

I assume Umma's about to make an excuse and leave the room, but Harabuji sits up slightly and looks at her expectantly, like a little boy waiting for a bedtime story. She sighs and lowers herself into the bedside chair.

'Your *abba* and I met when we were both students at a prestigious music conservatoire in Seoul. You know that part. But I was the only student from the Gangwon-do district they ever accepted. All the students there were from good families, who'd received music tutouring their whole lives, except for me. I got in through a singing audition. Did you know that?'

I shake my head no.

'Your mommy?' Harabuji says to me in English. 'Number one singer!'

'Everyone at the school could tell I was from the country,' Umma goes on, frowning, 'from my face to my clothes, my taste in food, the way I spoke. They also found out I came from a broken family. My mother left my family when I was very young, leaving your *harabuji* to raise me and your aunt SoonMi alone. This was extremely scandalous in Korea back then, because in some old ways of thinking, the daughter carries the shame of her mother. Because of this, I was alienated at this school. Treated as an outsider, the lowest of the low. Only your father was different. He always saw the equal value in every person – it was just in his nature. That's why we fell in love.

'At first, we dated in secret. But when we finally decided to tell everyone, your father's parents were furious. They refused to keep paying for the school. He was from a good family and he was one of the most talented students, on his way to becoming a renowned conductor.'

'I had no idea,' I say.

'Very sad time,' Harabuji says, shaking his head.

'It was a big scandal,' she says, 'and suddenly, your father's music prospects in Korea evaporated. When we married, your *abba*'s family cut all ties – it's the reason you've never met that side of your family – but the last favour they'd do for their son was to get us sponsored for an American visa.

'In America, we vowed to do something more practical than music. We worked in restaurants, we cleaned offices. When we had Tommy and we opened the store, we were working so hard to survive, and music was the furthest thing from our minds. But then we had you. It was clear from very early on that you'd inherited our talent and love of music – particularly singing. That worried me. I didn't want you to have to go through what I went through. When people see you sing, they're not just seeing your skills. They're seeing your face, your clothes, the way you carry yourself. They're not just hearing sounds, they're hearing the meaning you bring to words – where you come from, your pain, your hope. And when I opened myself up like this, they couldn't hear my music – they only saw what was lacking in my instrument, and the only instrument I could play was myself.

'So when I saw how beautifully and expressively you sang, I thought – couldn't she just as easily put that talent into a classical instrument? Isn't it more respectable, isn't it *safer*? And for so many years, because you were so calm and obedient, I assumed you were OK. But now, as I've got to know you as your own person, not just my little girl, I understand you're different from me. Not only is your talent greater; your courage is greater.'

Harabuji is wiping his tears. Umma hops to her feet to adjust his pillow and start clearing his tray. 'Candace, promise me something. If you debut and stay behind in Korea, check in on your *harabuji* – no excuses, OK?'

'I promise,' I say, my throat tight.

'I trust you now, Candace. You've matured so much.'

After we get off at the station in Sangam-dong, I say to Umma,

'We have plenty of time. I want to do something fun with you before I go back.'

Umma looks surprised. 'Don't you have to get back early to rehearse for the showcase?'

'I'd rather go to a *noraebang*.' A karaoke room.

'A *noraebang*? You've done nothing but sing this summer!'

'Never with you though.'

After a little more insistence – I ask her three times – she finally agrees, and I encourage her to pick songs that mean something to her. I'll try to join in if I can, but I really just want to listen. She picks songs that sound familiar to me from her and Abba listening to them in the car, in our store, but I never bothered to listen too closely until now. Songs like 'Dear J' by Lee Sun-hee, 'Sad Fate' by Nami, 'Where Are You?' by Yim Jae-beom. Of course, she sings beautifully, with a strong yet vulnerable voice – she could teach me a lot about conveying emotion through songs.

I understand almost all the words now, but even the words I don't understand stir a part of me that's always been there. The part of me that's Korean. The part of me that's my mother's daughter.

CHAPTER 30

THAT'S ME! THAT'S ME! THAT'S ME!

A week and a half before the showcase, film crews invade S.A.Y. Cameras are here to capture our practices, our makeovers, the moments before we fall asleep. Madame Jung, as the Head of Global Communications at ShinBi Unlimited, has been making frequent appearances in the girls' trainee facilities. Under her watchful eye, the facilities have been scrubbed to the point of sparkling for the cameras.

She'll snap at girls passing by, 'Fix your face! Stand up straight!' And to me: 'Mind your manners, Miss Park. I'm watching you extra closely. And cover your hair – it's a mess!'

The cameras barge into Team Two's session with The General while I'm royally screwing up part of the 'Boombayah' choreo. The General stands up even straighter than usual and claps her hands and yells, 'Come on, girls, let's stop playing around!'

There's a part where we have to lean over, grab our knees and whip our hair extremely fast. Blackpink only does four hair whips, but to show that we can do more than top idol groups, we're supposed to whip twice as fast, eight times in the same four count, as if we're Beyoncé dutty-wining at the Super Bowl. Immediately after that, we have to do three sensual body rolls while lowering ourselves into a crouching pose – almost the splits – then, right on the beat of a drum blast, slap the floor as hard as we can. We have to go all out in full She-Hulk mode, while also being perfectly precise and looking hot. It's the hardest thing I've done so far.

Helena is particularly amazing at the lightning-fast hair whips – I don't know how her neck can take it. Her strawberry blonde ponytail twirls so fast I can actually hear it slicing through the air. Me, whipping my head as fast as I can, I can only do five turns with my neck – Binna's Powder Pup hat I'm borrowing is in no danger of falling off – and afterwards, I'm so dizzy that I'm stumbling around, too disorientated to go directly into the sexy floor-slapping move.

After my fifteenth time screwing it up, The General shouts, 'CANDACE! This is not acceptable. This is the Killing Part and it needs to be perfect – you're destroying it for the whole team.'

'I will help her between now and the showcase!' pipes up Helena, grinning for the cameras.

OMG. I truly want to punch her in the face right now. When has Helena *ever* helped me?

'Actually,' I say, 'Binna has never failed to help me learn a move this whole time despite my lacking dance skills. I'm sure with her amazing leadership, I'll learn this in time.'

Binna gives me a fist bump. 'We'll get it, don't worry,' she says.

The problem is, I really don't think I'll learn this in time. So much can go wrong: wardrobe malfunctions, in-ear malfunctions, malfunctions in general. And worst of all is having to keep track of which camera to look at. Taped all over the rehearsal-room mirror are sheets of paper that say 'Camera 1', 'Camera 2', all the way up to 'Camera 11'. Once we get to Seoul Olympic Stadium, there will be several cameras on each side of the stage, the middle, further back in the middle of the auditorium, two overhead ones that zoom from wires in the ceiling, and one that pans back and forth on a track right in front of the stage.

A producer from YNN flashes a laser pointer on the sheets of paper, indicating which camera will be on us at any given time during the actual performance. During the Killing Part dance, it switches almost every second so the cameras can capture every awesome angle.

'IF YOU'RE EVER CAUGHT LOOKING AT THE WRONG CAMERA, YOU'RE DEAD!' The General screams, always helpful. 'YOU WILL LOOK LIKE AN IDIOT IN FRONT OF THE WHOLE WORLD!'

When we walk into Clown Killah's studio, I'm blinded by the lights of a camera crew and One.J's radiant smile.

Aram, Helena, and JinJoo scream, cry and point as if One.J were Pennywise or something. Binna knows One.J from her early trainee days, so they hug without touching – full Manners Hands. I'm shocked too, but I have to force the crazy fangirl reaction for the cameras, pretending I haven't already kissed those iconic lips. The blood in my face turns to molten lava as he smiles at me and greets me by name, thanking me for appearing in his MV.

Turning on his full celebrity charm, One.J explains that he's visiting all the teams' recording sessions as a performance coach. We let out a gasp at this good fortune.

As we start up, I couldn't be happier to be singing a group song with zero dancing for once. We're rehearsing and laying down the track for 'Into the New World (Ballad Version)'. As the Centre, Binna has to take the Main Vocal parts. Making it even harder, Clown Killah has decided we'll be singing a cappella.

One.J says, 'Look at the girl you're harmonizing with and *feel* the lyrics together – that's this song's choreography.'

Aram and I make eye contact when we harmonize on the first chorus; her dazzling, shy smile gives me a head rush. ('That's better!' Clown Killah shouts.) JinJoo and I wink at each other when we sync up perfectly for the second pre-chorus.

I force myself to gaze at Helena and smile beatifically when our parts line up. I haven't spoken to or looked at her, except for the cameras, since returning from One.J's MV shoot wigless. In fact, no one on our team is really talking to her after they saw how she tried to sabotage me.

I give Binna an encouraging nod as I gently pass her my ascending line of the bridge, setting her up to blast Taeyeon's iconic, belting high note – the Killing Part of the whole song.

Binna's voice is sweet and clear leading up to the note, but right as she's about to unleash, no sound comes out – just a hollow exhale.

Clown Killah tears off his headphones in frustration. Binna buries her face in her hands; it's at least the twentieth time in a row she's wimped out on the note.

'Binna-*shi*, what are you so afraid of?' asks One.J gently. 'It seems to me you're able, but you're backing away.'

'It seems I won't be able to do it,' mumbles Binna, hiding her face from the cameras with her hair.

'Unfortunately, that's not an option,' sighs Clown Killah. 'Let's stop for today and record that part next week. Binna, until then, practise to within an inch of your life. Your sisters are relying on you.'

I whisper to her that I'll help her hit that note if it's the last thing I do and she flashes me a weary smile. After all those hundreds of hours she helped me with dancing, it's the least I can do. We gather our lyrics packets to leave. But Clown Killah stops me. 'Candace, stay behind, please.'

My teammates look at me, alarmed; now that we're so close to the end, everyone's more paranoid than ever about any sign of preferential treatment. Now I get to be almost-alone with One.J again?!

'I just need to work with you on your Korean pronunciation a bit,' he explains. He turns to the camera crew. 'Will you please give us some privacy? This will be boring.'

The other girls, satisfied, bow and leave with the camera crew. I'm a little disappointed – I thought I made a ton of progress on pronunciation during 'Red Flavor'.

When we're alone, Clown Killah says, 'I was fibbing, Candace. Your pronunciation's great. We were hoping you could do us a favour.'

One.J winks at me and my heart melts.

Clown Killah comes out of the mixing booth to hand me a lyrics packet. The title at the top is 'I'm Every Girl'.

I'm stunned. 'Is this the group's debut song?'

'No,' says Clown Killah. 'This is a promotional single written by me and One.J. All of you trainees are going to perform as a group at the beginning of the *S.A.Y. 50* showcase.'

'Oooh,' I say, nodding. I'm imagining the group performance at a beauty pageant, just like in *Miss Congeniality*. 'It's such an honour that we get to sing such a song, thank you, Mr Clown Killah.'

'We don't have time to record every trainee, so I'm going to record you and stack your voice so it sounds like a crowd of girls. We thought your voice was the most versatile for this song.'

Daebak. I'll be singing solo times fifty!

My heart racing, and hyperaware that I'm being watched by One.J, I take a second to sound out the Korean lyrics. The Concept of the performance is that all the S.A.Y. girls are split into three categories: Cute, Sexy and Girl Crush. There are three verses, one for each type, and the three groups will take the stage at different times for their verse. I'll be in the Cute group (of course). But I'll be recording all three.

Clown Killah cues up the beat. Honestly, it slaps. It's dubsteppy and a little EDM. When he points to me, I start singing the 'Cute verse'.

The last gem in the mine, that's me
The rare mushroom in the forest, that's me
The lost page of the book
The white whale on the hook
THAT'S ME! THAT'S ME! THAT'S ME!

I'm almost doing a Minnie Mouse impersonation, with all the squeaks and lilts. (The lyrics are cleverer than they seem – the Korean words for *gem* and *mushroom* rhyme.) For the Sexy verse, all I do is lower my voice and make it a little throaty – Britney Spears with a cold.

They say the colour white
Is all colours and no colours at the same time
Isn't that the case with me?
I'm every girl but no one girl like me exists
THAT'S ME! THAT'S ME! THAT'S ME!

And then for Girl Crush, it's an easy talk-sing rap soaked in stank and attitude.

Bare-faced or full make-up
Ten steps, three steps, no steps
Makes no difference when I come up
I'm a geisha, a warrior, a princess, the president
I'm GI Jane, I'm Barbie, I'm Ken
THAT'S ME! THAT'S ME! THAT'S ME!

Then the choruses are basically an electronic dubstep break-down with me chant-singing in English.

I'M LIKE NO OTHER GIRL
BUT I'M EVERY GIRL IN ONE
I'M EVERY GIRL
EVERY GIRL
EVERY EVERY GIRL
I'M EVERY GIRL IN THE WORLD

'*Wahhhhh*,' says Clown Killah, snapping his fingers. 'You're making this so easy.'

We record five more times straight through, then clean up my Korean pronunciation a bit on the verses, and we're done faster than I could have expected. By the end, Clown Killah and One.J are high-fiving each other.

'Listen, *hyung*,' says One.J to Clown Killah once we've finished recording. 'Can I have a word with Candace? In private.'

Clown Killah laughs uncomfortably. 'That's a little weird. Why?'

'I need to give her some important performance advice, *hyung*.'

Clown Killah shakes his head. 'I shouldn't leave you two alone.'

'*HYUNG!*'

I clamp my hands over my mouth. One.J's voice came out surprisingly deep, and he has a fearsome look on his face. Celebrity or not, it strikes me as downright un-Korean to shout at a grown-up like that.

Clown Killah mutters under his breath and storms out of the room. When we're alone, a gentle expression returns to One.J's face. Almost shyly, he says, 'I hope I wasn't too forward that night.'

I shake my head no.

'I have something upsetting to show you,' he sighs, brow furrowed.

Uh-oh. Not what I expected.

One.J pulls his phone out of his pocket and shows me a grainy photo. It's of a boy on a Seoul street kissing a blonde girl. You can only see the blonde girl from behind, but the boy is unmistakably One.J, his surgical face mask lowered.

I feel as if my skin is being flipped inside out. 'That's us?'

'Yes.'

'But no one was on the street,' I say in a high-pitched voice. 'We checked.'

'You can't underestimate these *sasaengs*,' says One.J, making a fist. 'The one who sent me this photo is one of my worst ones – she must have a contact at a phone company, because I change my Kakao every two weeks, yet she always finds me. She's making all sorts of ridiculous demands to blackmail me, saying she'll release this photo to the press if I don't take her to a private island, which of course I won't do. My manager and I are doing everything we can to reason with her without telling S.A.Y. about this. If this does come out, don't panic.'

Too late.

'Aren't you worried?' I say. 'Don't you know what happened to QueenGirl?'

'Well, my fans are so devoted that they won't blame me. But I'm worried about you – if people figure out this is you, it'll ruin any hope of a career before it starts. We can't have that. Your talent is too important.'

I look at the girl's white-blonde hair again. That's me, as impossible as it seems.

'I'm ruined,' I moan.

'No, you're not,' says One.J firmly, penetrating me with his amber-lensed eyes. 'Most of the public knows you so far as the purple-haired girl in the MV, and you've done well to wear your hat while YNN has been filming you. If I know this is going to come out, I'll convince the *sasaeng* it's some other girl. Whatever you do, don't confess. *Oppa* will take care of this.'

I flinch a little at the word *oppa*, and before I know it, One.J has leant over and given me a lightning-fast peck on the lips. My mind is racing so fast I don't even feel it. And just like that, One.J slides on his surgical mask and swoops out of the studio.

I can't decide if this moment was romantic – he *is* looking out for me – or totally messed up. Suddenly, I desperately want to be on the roof with YoungBae, where nothing is ever so complicated.

CHAPTER 31

THE QUEEN GIRL

We gather in the big empty ballroom on the fifth floor to practise the group number with all fifty girls to 'I'm Every Girl'. No one can tell I'm the girl singing on the track – my vocals have been autotuned and stacked to sound like fifty K-pop robots, and I have to say: it's not a bad sound. I'd add this to one of my playlists on Spotify.

The fifty girls have been divided into three groups for the group number. I've been named the Centre of Team Cute, which I'm thrilled about; Helena is the Centre for Team Sexy; and Binna's the Centre for Team Girl Crush. Team Two slaying, as usual.

P.D. Choi is back as the director of the broadcast. He shouts into his megaphone from the top of a ladder. 'Cute girls, clear the stage quickly for the Sexy girls' entrance! Girl Crush girls, I want to see cleaner moves! All the girls, Cute, Sexy, Girl Crush! All fifty of you need to be perfectly synced in the choreography at the end, but with your faces, say to the camera, "I'm the only girl on this stage, so vote for me!"'

During our five-minute break, we all sit on the floor and the junior managers and production assistants pass us each a bottle of Elektro Hydrate, CEO Rho's sports drink. 'Take big gulps!' shouts P.D. Choi. 'Say, "*Wahhh!* I've never tasted anything so refreshing!"'

A cameraman closes in on me and BowHee. I take a big swig, but some of it goes down the wrong pipe – and it tastes horrible. But I smile at the nearest camera and widen my eyes with delight. '*Wahh*, that's delicious!' I shriek to BowHee. 'Elektro Hydrate will give me the energy I need to take me all the way to debut!' A producer gives me a thumbs up.

After six more hours of practice on the group number, CEO Sang takes the mic and raises his arm in the air. 'What an exciting time for the most talented and beautiful trainees in all of Korea!'

The cameras in the ballroom are pointed at us from all directions to capture our reactions.

We all cheer wildly.

'In three short days, all eyes will be on you. I'm getting calls from executives and brands from around the world wanting to be associated with this new girl group. There's so much hope for these girls because they are expected to embody not only the standards of S.A.Y. but also the talent, Visuals and global popularity of

SLK. That's why, to host this showcase, I've called in a young woman who already possesses all these qualities. Please welcome . . . WooWee, formerly of QueenGirl!'

My Ultimate Bias of female idols! I thought her career was over! I freak out with the rest of the girls as a gorgeous woman with blindingly pale skin, bright emerald eyes and slender giraffe legs struts into the room.

WooWee joins CEO Sang and bows to the trainees. It takes minutes for us to stop cheering and sit back down; her presence has brought a different electrical charge into the room. But I can't fathom why she's here – until recently, she was signed at one of S.A.Y.'s rival companies.

When we quiet down, she says into a mic, 'It's not long ago when I sat in a similar position that you sit in today. This industry can take you to many unexpected places' – the trainees let out a noise of recognition – 'and if you're strong, you will rise to the top. It's my great honour to help bring in a new generation of K-pop. Keeping that in mind, I have two pieces of news as your host.' The cameras close in on her as she takes a deep, serious breath. 'Although all of you are working so hard to prepare two songs for the showcase, I'm afraid not all of you will be able to perform both. After the first round of performances, only the five teams whose members receive the most votes will continue on to the second night.'

There are cries of shock. I clasp Binna's and JinJoo's hands. We *have* to pass the first night. Obviously, we all want to debut, but our team at least needs to share both of our Stages with the world.

WooWee smiles with compassion and lowers her eyes with an

air of dignified tragedy. 'I know this sounds cruel. It might even seem unfair. However, as I happen to know first-hand, this industry can throw you unfortunate curveballs. Your dreams can crash down around you, through no fault of your own.' Her voice falters. The trainees let out chants of, '*It wasn't your fault!*' and '*Hwaiting!*' WooWee smiles and bows in gratitude. 'Whether you're eliminated after the first night, or you miss the final group by a hair, I just want to tell you not to be too discouraged. It's all about how you find your way back. This is your dream, right?!'

'RIGHT!' all fifty of us scream.

WooWee smiles. 'You kids are so lovely and full of brightness! You inspire *me*. And now, for all of your hard work, S.A.Y. has an incredible treat for you: you will be the first people on the planet to see One.J's new solo MV, "Alien".'

Everyone jumps to their feet and screams again.

'This MV will have its world premiere the night of your first showcase, which is sure to bring even more attention to the lucky girls' debut – and to the lucky trainee who appears in it.'

I get a torrent of pats on the back, the other girls making it clear to the cameras that they don't hate me.

The lights go dark and for the next three minutes, I don't breathe or move. I'm only in the MV for a total of about thirty seconds, but I'm totally enraptured – there's a whole other story-line I had no idea about. One.J performing at a sold-out concert and searching the audience for me, his lost love. Flashbacks to childhood with a kid One.J and a kid version of me – I actually recognize the girl playing Young Me as that adorable junior trainee I waved to on my first day. I have to say, purple hair is *really* my look, and my performance is super believable. Something about the lyrics, One.J's voice and the visuals all came together. I couldn't be prouder to be even a tiny part of it.

I want to create something like this. If you put your heart into it, K-pop – all of this idol business – can make people less alone. It can change people's lives. It's already changed mine.

When YoungBae shows up at the end of the MV, just for a split second, all the girls '*Whoooo!*' but my heart drops.

I've kissed One.J, and if I debut, I'll be swept up into his world – and I want that. But YoungBae will be left behind here, as a trainee. Who knows if he'll ever debut? Will our lives become so different that I'm an alien to him?

I know millions of girls would kill to be in my position, but if I ever had to choose between them, I actually don't know what I would do.

One thing's for sure: I'm not going to let a stupid photo destroy my chances of making my dream come true. My lips are sealed.

CHAPTER 32

IS THIS MY LIFE?

The stylists do one more pass on the Cute girls as we wait in the wings of Seoul Olympic Stadium. The wardrobe assistants fluff our literal tutus on our ballerina-schoolgirl costumes. The hair assistants straighten out my flyaways, which are now silvery purple after Mr Oh bleached and redyed my hair personally last night. No wig needed.

I grab BowHee's hand and press it against my chest so she can see how crazily it's thumping. BowHee takes my hand and does the same with hers; her heart's thumping just as hard as mine.

WooWee already introduced the showcase and did an opening speech. The live audience and the audience watching on TV and via streaming just watched a clip package introducing the fifty girl trainees, why we're the next SLK, and how hard most of us have been practising for years and years. Right now, we're just waiting for the commercial break to end before we do our opening number.

P.D. Choi's disembodied voice sounds throughout the auditorium. He tells the audience to get very quiet until the first girl comes out – 'At that point, go crazy!'

He's talking about me. *I'm* the very first girl to walk out.

The audience goes absolutely silent. After a few seconds of a hush, the P.D.'s voice softly counts down from ten. I close my eyes and try to calm my heart.

'. . . three . . . two . . .'

Blinding lights flash on and the first electronic *THUMP* and *CRASH* shake the floor. I feel the thump in my gut. The audience lets out a '*Wahhhh!*' My recorded voice, sped up to sound almost chipmunk-like, repeats, 'EVERY GIRL! EVERY GIRL! EVERY GIRL!' There's another huge EDM *THUMP* and *CRASH*, the electronic hi-hat drums start to sizzle, and before I know it, the stage managers wearing headsets hiss, 'Go, go, go!' and I feel BowHee shove me from behind.

I step out on to the stage, blinded by the lights, and a tsunami of sound nails me right in the face as ten thousand fans suddenly go nuts. I lip-sync the words and walk fast, not able to see anything and desperate to find the pink X on the floor. We've only rehearsed on the actual stage, which is as big as a basketball court, just one time earlier today. I'm so disorientated that I think there's a possibility I've walked out alone, that none of my fellow Cute girls are actually behind me. I use every bit of willpower I have to keep myself from turning around to check. I strain my face muscles to keep a giant Cute smile frozen on my face.

Finally, my eyes adjust to the bright lights and I find the pink X. When I reach it, I pause. An ocean of fans is going wild, waving neon-pink glow sticks. I spot the cameras, including the one camera that's hanging from wires stretching over the audience, and it swoops down towards me like a robot owl. *Nothing* like the sheets of paper stuck to the rehearsal-room mirror.

My body starts doing the choreography on autopilot. My body knows that I'm supposed to do a spin right now – oh good, the rest of the Cute girls *are* behind me, in perfect formation, no less – and my eyes knows which camera to look at. The Killing Part of our choreography is me standing still and lip-syncing, 'THAT'S ME! THAT'S ME! THAT'S ME!' while the eight girls on either side of me revolve around me, so from above, we'll look like a human propeller. My right eye knows when it's time to do one last wink before skipping down the long runway to make room for the Sexy Girls on the main stage for their verse.

With the hard part out of the way, the Cute girls are off camera for a minute, so I can catch my breath. There's a giant plastic hand in the centre of the main stage squeezing a massive planet Earth, and on each of the hand's fingernails is a different colour and a different girl's silhouette – the group's official symbol. There are giant screens all over the stadium, on which I see Helena, Aram and Luciana – the three main Sexy Girls – absolutely slaying their verse (which *I* sang). *They say the colour white is all colours and no colours at the same time . . .*

There's a mind-boggling number of people in this stadium, but I can't their faces, just their wildly wagging glow sticks. Now I'm less nervous than I was dancing in CEO Sang's conference room – ten thousand screaming fans is a lot less terrifying than five old people scrutinizing you up-close.

The crowd's loving our performance, and somehow they know the song already. They have perfectly timed **fanchants** prepared, which line up with the song's chorus. I see from the corner of my eye that Binna totally smashes her dance solo at the front of the Girl Crush pack, making the fans go wild.

I must be imagining it, but I hear a familiar voice screaming my name. I search the crowd and I spot Umma. I scream 'UMMA!!!' and wave at her like an idiot – I knew she was coming, but I expected her to stand somewhere in the back, not right next to the runway in the K-pop equivalent of a mosh pit! She waves back at me, tears streaming down her face. But Umma's voice wasn't the one I heard. Right next to her is Imani, who's bawling her eyes out.

'AHHHHH, IMANI!' I shout, waving like a maniac. And right behind Imani is Ethan, screaming 'YASSSSS QUEEN!' and snapping at me. His hair is a bright blue, very K-pop boy idol.

How did they get here?! And so close to the start of school! I'm still screaming 'WHAT IS MY LIFE?!' at them when JinJoo elbows me sharply in the ribs.

Oh, right. The final chorus. All fifty girls are now on the runway, so close to our fans. With the good vibes of Umma, my friends and the whole stadium fuelling me, I go harder at the choreography than ever before. *I'M EVERY GIRL, EVERY GIRL IN THE WORLD.*

Pyrotechnics explode all down the edge of the runway. *BOOM BOOM BOOM BOOM BOOM BOOM!* The girls standing closest to the blasts scream and duck for cover; P.D. Choi warned us that the fireworks were coming, but none of us anticipated how huge or loud they would be.

The song ends with all fifty girls with our hands in the air, smoke fogging up the stadium. I bathe in the sound of the deafening cheers and screams and chants of 'S.A.Y.!' washing over me. I close my eyes and wonder, over and over again, *Is this my life?*

My team and I change into our 'Boombayah' outfits in the spacious dressing room backstage. Our wardrobe Concept involves lots of corsets and knee-high boots and elbow-length gloves, all in reflective, wet-looking black patent leather.

I keep my purple hair in a tight, high pony – other Team Two girls have got dye jobs too. Helena, instead of strawberry blonde, now is straight-up white-blonde; I hate to admit it, but Targaryen blonde suits her *much* better than me. Binna has curtains of silvery grey, which looks sick on her, especially paired with black lipstick. JinJoo's pigtails are now Netflix-red, fitting into her whole anime theme. Aram's hair is the same shiny black as always, because why mess with perfection?

The five of us stand in front of a mirror together for a second to check ourselves out. Three months ago, if I saw us in a dark alley, I would have turned around and run in the other direction, wondering for the rest of my life who those five beautiful, terrifying models were.

We make squeaky, rubbery noises as we walk over to the wings of the stage to watch Team One perform 'Dalla Dalla' by ITZY. I squeeze Aram's and Binna's freezing hands in mine – I can feel the nerves in their whole bodies, and my own. I don't know if it's how tight my corset is, but I'm starting to feel sick. I've actually never seen Team One perform – I was too busy getting 'kicked out' of S.A.Y. during the first assessment – but I quickly realize that BowHee has been my biggest competition all along. Just like me, she's on a team with four girls who tower over her, and she's not an amazing dancer, but she makes up for it with tons of energy and bright, funny expressions and an effortless, powerful voice. She adds all sorts of amazing riffs and high notes to the end of the song.

The crowd goes wild for them. One.J, ChangWoo, Wookie and CEO Sang sit at a raised judges' panel facing the stage, and they all heap on the positive feedback. One.J, who looks spectacular with his guyliner, hazel lenses and dangly cross earrings, calls out BowHee's incredible 'charisma' and 'star-quality voice'. A wave of jealousy surges through my veins.

To think, this girl sat across from me at every meal for the last three months.

During the commercial break, my team and I walk out on to the stage and take our positions, me in the centre. I try to catch One.J's eye, but it's as if he's never met me. He's too busy goofing off with Wookie. I know there are probably a few *sasaengs* in the building, but I would hope he'd run his eyes past me even for a millisecond.

The crowd roars as the lights go down, and the big screen behind us plays our team's clip package: moments from our rehearsals, interviews, interactions that the cameras captured over the past week. Our storylines. We're not supposed to turn around and watch – we're in Girl Crush 'Boombayah' mode right now – even though I *really* want to.

The instant the clips end, the opening notes of 'Boombayah' play, which makes the crowd go nuts. We start off with a series of synchronized poses, and then I start my rap.

Tommy will make so much fun of me for my rap – he listens to nothing but hip-hop – but Clown Killah and Manager Kong insisted it's legit. I'm no Missy Elliott at the VMAs; I'm more like Taylor Swift rapping along to Missy Elliott *from the audience* at the VMAs, but my confidence grows when I hear the crowd let out surprised '*Whoooos*'. In the pre-chorus, I have to lie on my back and slide through my teammates' legs, just like Rosé from Blackpink does in the MV. Patent leather isn't great for that move, but I get through it. At the first chorus, an explosion of pink light goes off throughout the stadium. Pink lasers strobe over the audience, the floor of the stage lights up, and the five of us *snap* into our dance break. I lose my mind temporarily as I use my whole body to swing my arms and kick the air like a ninja.

We're getting closer to the eight headwhips, which I know I won't be able to do. Time slows down and an idea jumps into my brain: every time I've stood out as a trainee, it's because I followed my instincts in the moment, whether it was my air sax, deciding to sing 'Yeowoo' instead of my approved song, or voguing at my audition back in New Jersey. Helena will *hate* me for this, but whatever. I've gotta do me.

When the other girls grab their knees and whip their hair as if their necks are meant to spin like tops, I shrug and make a face at the audience as if to say, 'I can't do *that*!' Instead, I twirl my ponytail a few times with my hand.

The crowd bursts into laughter. I wink at the right camera and then jump back into the parts of the choreo I can handle.

For the last beat of the song, my teammates drop into splits and I fall to the floor in a death drop – planned, this time. The whole stadium vibrates under us with roars and shouts of 'Encore!'

We stand up and bow to the audience. The SLK guys and CEO Sang are on their feet. I find Umma, Imani and Ethan again and throw them as many kisses as I can. Imani is cheering so hard.

WooWee, stunning in a sequined black dress, comes out to us with a microphone to ask us each how we feel after the performance.

Aram says, 'It seems to me we worked our hardest. Please vote for me and my teammates, I'm relying on you!' She makes a heart over her head with her arms.

There's a chorus of male voices shouting, '*Yeppeo, yeppeo!*'

When Umma and Abba say '*yeppeo*' to me, it means, '*you're loved*' or '*you're lovable*'. In this context, I'm quite sure it just means, '*you're pretty!*'

WooWee passes it over to the judges. CEO Sang says dramatically, 'Team Two has been the team I've expected the most from, and tonight . . . you exceeded my expectations. Good job, girls.'

ChangWoo says, 'Candace, every time we've seen you perform as a trainee, you did something unexpected, and tonight, you showed the entire world your unique personality. This will serve you well.'

My teammates look at me, confused. A clip of me twirling my ponytail while the other four crush the choreo plays in slow motion on the screen behind us. This time, we all turn to watch, and Helena flashes me a death stare, right there onstage.

I bow to ChangWoo. 'Thank you, *sunbaenim*.'

Still not looking at me, One.J says, 'You five look like you could debut today,' and Wookie says, 'You girls are all gorgeous and talented, but JinJoo, the way you move and sing . . . you're my Bias of this team.'

JinJoo's mouth falls open and she clutches her chest; her life is literally made. She stammers, 'Wookie-*oppa*, you're my Ultimate Bias, can I make you *kimchi bokkum bap* some day?'

It's such an adorable moment that the entire stadium '*awwww*'s.

Manager Kong is waiting for us in the dressing room with bottles of Elektro Hydrate (gross), looking overjoyed. 'You girls did so well!'

As we're changing out of the patent leather outfits into our S.A.Y. schoolgirl uniforms, Helena demands, 'Candace, why did you have to do something extra *again*? You pulled focus from those of us who were actually doing the choreography.'

I sigh loudly as I pull off my corset. I've been ignoring her for three weeks now and it's been working fine.

Helena steps up to me, getting in my face; I'm momentarily stunned by her beauty. With her new white-blonde hair and blue circle lenses, she's serving Elsa from *Frozen* vibes.

But then she opens her mouth. 'Are you ignoring me? Watch yourself, punk! You don't know how to act.'

'Hey, hey, hey, stop that,' warns Manager Kong.

'Leave her alone, Helena,' says Binna, pulling her back. 'Everyone saw us do the choreography for real – Candace just had to do what's right for her. Let's just be proud, OK?'

'I don't care about anything, Wookie spoke to me,' JinJoo says, dazed. 'I can die happy.'

'That's right, girls,' Manager Kong says. 'Just be happy you got to show what you can do. Now, go show your faces in the Viewing Room.'

Changed out of our skintight costumes and back into our S.A.Y. schoolgirl uniforms, we grab our modesty blankets and sit in the Viewing Room, where all the trainees not onstage are supposed to watch the live stream and give big reactions, which will air on the broadcast. A row of seats is reserved for our team, and for the rest of the night, we watch everyone perform, and I'm shook – how are five teams supposed to be eliminated after tonight? Everyone is so passionate, so prepared, so fierce. My team is supposedly a front runner, but I can't say we're that much better than anyone else. I watch ShiHong slay the dance in Big Bang's 'Fantastic Baby'. Luciana looks like a K-pop J.Lo in her team's performance of 'Gashina'. RaLa is a rap machine gun in her team's version of 'Latata' by (G)I-DLE.

We're supposed to be as enthusiastic as humanly possible for the cameras, but I don't have to pretend. I'm a fangirl of all these girls. I whoop, scream and jump to my feet during each Stage. The cameras capture me showing Binna the literal goosebumps on my skin.

Whenever the Viewing Room camera light flashes red, Helena goes from slumping with her arms crossed to fussing over the modesty blankets on our team members' laps, always thinking about her storyline as the helpful, considerate member. Fake, fake, fake.

If we debut in the same group, I might just quit.

CHAPTER 33

INTO THE NEW WORLD (REPRISE)

Less than twenty-four hours later, the second night of the show-case begins with WooWee gathering all fifty girls onstage as the online vote counts are revealed. WooWee says, with many dramatic pauses, that over fifteen million votes were cast in South Korea alone, which incites yelps of surprise.

'Remember, all,' says WooWee in a hushed voice, 'what matters for tonight is team totals.'

Everyone in the stadium is watching with bated breath as the results flash on the monitors.

FIRST PLACE
Team 2: Kim Aram (1,209,345), Candace Park (845,844), Kwon Binna (828,988), Helena Cho (623,112), Chae JinJoo (242,559)

Aram, Binna and I shriek and jump and hug. Our team had the highest votes overall, making us the safest of the safe five teams. Team One is right behind us, with BowHee scoring 972,474 votes.

After Aram, RaLa and BowHee, I have the fourth highest overall votes, and Binna has fifth. If us five are the final group, I'd explode with happiness – our cafeteria table of misfits would be well represented! Maybe this is a sign that Korean fans are ready for a group without the typical, perfect idol types (other than Aram, of course).

'This is really going to happen for you, *unnie*,' I whisper to Binna. 'Ten years.'

She's crying so hard that she can only squeeze my hand back.

I feel awful that JinJoo scored so low – thirty-third place – but things haven't been looking good for her for a while. And Helena in ninth place . . . I expected her to score higher. Well, I guess the Korean public could see through her fakery.

Umma, Imani and Ethan are standing in the front row tonight, and they're all going crazy, crying and cheering. My heart is about to burst.

WooWee calls everyone's attention to some surprising results. Even though RaLa is placed second overall individually – 989,223 votes – the rest of her members did terribly, so they're sixth overall. I look over and RaLa is bawling her eyes out while her teammates comfort her.

They couldn't possibly eliminate the second-biggest vote-getter based on a technicality, right?

WooWee says, 'Team Two, Team One, Team Ten, Team Three, and Team Nine . . . congratulations, you will be able to perform your second song tonight, and you're still in the running for debut.'

Just like that, twenty-five dreams, probably a total of a hundred years of intense training, are wiped out.

I'm shook. I can't help but wonder whether, if RaLa fit K-pop idol standards a little bit better, S.A.Y. and CEO Sang would try to find a loophole to keep her. The eliminated girls, the surviving girls and much of the audience are a blubbering mess.

One.J, his eyes sparking with compassion, says, 'Just remember: tonight's results have nothing to do with your value as people. If becoming an idol is still your dream, never give up. But also remember, achieving your dream doesn't automatically make your life better. No matter what you do, whether you work at a bakery or you're number one on the Gaon Music Chart, our lives are all worth the same.'

There's a murmur of awe from the crowd at his wise words.

'Well said, One.J,' says CEO Sang quickly. 'To all the girls who are not moving on, you have suffered greatly, and S.A.Y. thanks you for it.'

We try to hug the eliminated girls, but they're already being shooed backstage by the producers. I feel it palpably: a line has been drawn between losers and winners.

'And now for the top team: Team Two!' says WooWee.

The stadium erupts in cheers. Ugh, are we really about to be interviewed right now?

'How does it feel being so close to debut?' asks WooWee, putting the mic up to Binna's face. But Binna's too overwhelmed with emotion to answer. The crowd chants affectionately, *'Ul-ji-ma! Ul-ji-ma!'* Don't cry! Don't cry!

Helena steps forward and grabs the mic eagerly. 'Well, it seems to me it's such an honour for us to be one step closer, even though it seems to me we're so sad for the girls who won't be able to perform their second song.'

WooWee looks grateful that at least one girl is game to talk. 'SLK and CEO Sang have said Team Two has stood out all through the trainee process,' she says. 'What do you think it is that makes you guys stand out as a group?'

'Hmm,' says Helena, tapping her chin. 'Well, each member brings such different qualities. Aram brings Visuals, of course. I'd say I'm the mother of the group, making sure everyone's OK and taken care of.'

I want to cough and shout, *Lies!*

'Binna's almost like the dad of the group,' Helena goes on. 'She's very forceful and keeps us all in line. And JinJoo, of course, is our unicorn, our **4D Personality**. So yes, I'd say we all bring something unique to the group.'

'Oh! But it seems you forgot your *maknae*,' says WooWee.

Helena lets out a high, girlish laugh behind her hand. 'Oh my goodness, how can I forget Candace! Yes, our *maknae* brings a certain . . . unpredictability to our group. Without her, we would almost have *too much* peace and harmony among us. What would be interesting about that?'

WooWee laughs a bit uncomfortably before saying, 'Candace, let's hear from you. As the *maknae* of the group, what have you learnt from each of your *unnies*?'

I'm so over Helena right now. I've been trying to take the high road, but between the trainee massacre we just witnessed and

Helena's out-of-control shadiness, my nerves are shot.

'Well, WooWee-*sunbaenim*,' I say, smiling for the cameras, 'from Binna-*unnie*, I've learnt not just dance moves, but respect and integrity in the way she treats other people. She was the first person to help me when I was struggling as a new trainee, and for that, I will always be thankful. From JinJoo, I've learnt to have the courage to be different, and to take criticism and setbacks with strength. And from Aram-*unnie* . . . from the outside, you may think that someone with so much beauty has had things easy, but beneath her loveliness, she possesses resilience and character too.' Aram smiles at me and makes a heart with her arms.

'What beautiful words,' says WooWee. 'And Helena?'

I think for a second. Helena flashes me a warning glare. 'Helena-*unnie* . . . wow, where do I begin? From watching Helena-*unnie* I've learnt how to present an attractive outward appearance to the right people. It seems it will be a very important skill in this industry, and she's excellent at it.'

WooWee nods. '*Wahhhh*, what great insights from a girl so young.' I watch myself on the monitor as I flash finger hearts to the audience. The stadium roars their approval.

Finally, we're ushered backstage to the dressing room to get ready for 'Into the New World'. The eliminated groups are nowhere to be found; for all I know, they've already been bussed away. There's a sombre vibe – Binna, Aram and I are comforting JinJoo, who's devastated by her low individual votes.

'JinJoo, don't give up hope,' Aram says. 'The final line-up won't be based on votes, anyway. You can turn it around with this performance.'

The make-up and hair people rush us into spare seats by the mirror to get us touched up – a lot of us need it from crying. Helena, her face totally dry, is getting changed into her performance outfit, glaring at me the whole time.

I can't stand the passive aggression any more. 'Do you have something to say to me, Helena?' I ask.

She snarls at me in English, 'Candace, of all the shady things you've pulled, that was the shadiest.'

I look at her through the mirror as a make-up artist powders my face. 'I don't know what you're talking about.'

Helena runs up and pushes the back of my chair, knocking into the make-up artist.

'Hey, step off!' I shout back in English. 'Just leave me alone.'

'Oh, and just ignore the fact that you dissed me in front of everyone up there?' she snaps.

All the other girls in the crowded dressing room whip their heads in our direction. I'm mortified. I don't say anything.

'You made me look terrible on national television!' Helena yells.

'You did that to yourself,' I fire back. 'And as always, Helena, whatever I did to you, it's because you deserved it.'

My make-up artist chooses that moment to put down her brush and peace out. I don't blame her – I can't imagine anything more inappropriate right now than the two American trainees screaming at each other in English. I get up and cross the dressing room to a different chair, where a different make-up artist gets to work on me right away. But Helena follows me like an evil shadow.

'Oh my God,' I burst out, switching back to Korean. 'What's wrong with you? Why are you so obsessed with me?'

'Obsessed with you?!' Helena smirks. 'Trust and believe, I'm not obsessed with you. You're not important enough.'

Aram calls out from across the room, 'Come on, you guys, not now.'

'Yeah,' says Binna. 'We've come so far.'

Helena ignores them. 'I just want to know why you've had it out for me since the moment you showed up here.'

'Me?!' I can't help but laugh a little. 'I haven't done *anything* to you.'

'Before you got here and started pulling your little tricks, everything was going great. Your stunt last night and that interview ... that is the *last* time you disrespect me, do you hear me? I'm not gonna let you ruin my life.'

'I've done nothing to you,' I say through clenched teeth. 'It's not my fault you're in ninth place.'

The entire room gasps. That was a low blow, but I've had it. I haven't told everyone she destroyed my hair or sicked her boyfriend on my precious guitar. I get up and pull my costume from the rack. We're wearing soft, delicate rose gold for our second performance tonight.

'What did you say?!' says Helena.

I step into my dress. *Just get through this and hopefully you'll never have to see her again*, I tell myself.

'I'm just saying,' I say, zipping up my dress, 'if you're not happy with how you're doing, don't blame me. I'm not a "threat", remember?'

'I'm not threatened by you, Candace. I'm just tired of how desperate you are to steal attention.'

'*I'm* desperate?! Do I need to remind you who your boyfriend is?'

Suddenly, I'm looking at the ceiling. My scalp feels like it's about to be torn off my head. Helena has my ponytail in her fist. 'LET GO OF ME!' I scream.

The room is in uproar. I'm trying to loosen her grip on my hair, while I'm being pulled by a pair of hands in the other direction. When I finally get my ponytail free, I windmill my arms wildly, making contact with nothing. I feel Helena's nails rake across my cheek before she's pulled away by Binna.

'STOP IT! STOP IT, BOTH OF YOU!' screams Manager Kong, who's holding me back. She drags me across the room and into a chair. The other teams take this moment to flee to the Viewing Room. Helena's in a chair in the opposite corner, bawling into her hands.

'I should cut both of you right now! Do you understand how inappropriate this is? What if an S.A.Y. executive saw this? Or a cameraman? You would be gone!'

A hair stylist shows up out of nowhere to fix my ponytail and a different make-up artist immediately starts dabbing concealer over the claw marks on my face, which sting like crazy. I'm humiliated and furious. That wild animal actually *fought* me. JinJoo, Binna and Aram are all dressed and ready in their lovely rose gold outfits, horrified.

'You still need to go out there and perform,' says Manager Kong. 'But after, you better give me a good reason not to tell the

CEO about this. Because if I tell him, he won't care how well you sing or dance. The biggest cause of idol group disbandment isn't scandals – it's members who can't get along.'

With that threat, suddenly Helena's face is totally dry and she's helping her make-up artist reapply her foundation faster. You almost have to admire the girl.

The stadium is pitch-dark except for a single spotlight on Binna. We hear a high-pitched buzz in our in-ears, which is Binna's signal to start singing. Her voice on the first line sounds a little shaky, unsure.

Guilt sweeps over me; I can't believe I subjected my team to that spectacle right before the most important performance of our lives. I have the second line: I close my eyes and put all the emotions I'm feeling – desperation, regret, remorse, love – into the words. The words echo throughout the stadium into nothingness. You could hear a pin drop.

In the chorus, when all five of our voices come together for the harmony, the cheers swell like a wave. The ocean of pink glow sticks undulates peacefully. To sing without instruments, just our team's voices, I forget where I am and I feel as if I'm connected to them telepathically. When it comes time for Helena and me to make eye contact, I swear she tells me with her eyes, *I'm sorry.* And I say back, *I'm sorry too.*

Before she even gets to it, I know for certain that Binna's going to rock that high note better than she ever has. There's just an overwhelming force lifting this performance up – I know the others can feel it too, as if we're being cradled in the palms of the fans' hands. And just like that, Binna closes her eyes and lets the high note rip. The cheers are so loud we have to wait a full minute to start again.

The song ends and the five of us are holding hands, in full certainty that we made K-pop history together.

CHAPTER 34

CHO HELENA

My final Friday night as a trainee, I see YoungBae on the roof, for the first time in what feels like ages.

'I was starting to feel forgotten,' he pouts.

'I know, I'm sorry. This showcase kicked our butts.'

'Well, you seemed to come out fine. I mean, in my opinion, you were the star of the whole thing. As per usual.'

'You saw?!'

'Yep. They set up a TV in the cafeteria for the boys. We're actually going to the final coronation taping next week though, to cheer you guys on. And to see what could have been, I guess.'

'Ugh, I'm sorry, YoungBae,' I say. 'You *will* debut, I know it. What are you going to do until then?'

We settle on to a bench. 'I figure I might as well stay here and keep training, sign up at an international school. It's not like I'm giving up amazing college prospects back in Atlanta.' He yawns, stretching his arms up at the night sky. 'Plus, I need to make sure you're OK.'

'What do you mean? I can take care of myself.'

'I know. It's for me though.' For the first time ever, YoungBae seems a little shy. He mumbles, 'I guess I've started to feel some *jeong* for you.'

I suddenly feel as if my chest is spawning a colony of multiplying heart emojis.

Jeong.

That's a powerful word. We learnt about it for a full hour in Language class; Teacher Lee said it's one of the most important concepts in the Korean language, but it's very difficult to translate because it's so tied to the Korean spirit. It's what makes Korean ballads so romantic yet so sad. Why K-dramas make you swoon and cry at the same time.

'Jeong' basically means *'love'* or *'compassion'*, but it can also mean *'attached'* – to people, to memories, even to treasured objects. It means that something or someone has got so under your skin, so *fit into the shape of your heart*, that now you have no choice: you have to protect them, no matter how irrational it may seem to others, no matter how much heartache this loyalty might cause you. *You're all in*, basically, in a uniquely Korean way.

I'm speechless. We just sit for a second, and the weight of that word grows.

Then YoungBae pipes up, 'I have a surprise for you!' His usual happy face returns. He runs and grabs what looks like a pillowcase that he stashed next to the rusty door.

'What's in there, YoungBae?' I ask warily.

He mimes giving birth to what's in the pillowcase: a watermelon!

'Ta-da! Happy birthday!'

I literally squeal. 'You remembered my birthday?!'

'Yeah, from that time we talked about star signs. Twenty-fourth August. Virgo. I know your birthday's actually *tomorrow*, but since I probably won't see you ...'

'Where did you get a *watermelon*?!'

YoungBae puffs out his chest. 'It's the baddest thing I've ever done here. You wouldn't believe all the rules I had to break. Anyway, I couldn't steal a knife or a birthday candle, but ... *Saengil cheukka hamnida ...*'

He starts singing 'Happy Birthday' in Korean. It's the most adorable thing anyone's ever done for me, but YoungBae's Korean pronunciation hasn't improved at all, and his singing isn't that good either.

'Hey, YoungBae,' I interrupt, 'can you actually *rap* "Happy Birthday" for me?'

He perks up. 'I thought you'd never ask.'

Starting with a few bars of beatboxing, he raps 'Happy Birthday' in Korean, and even starts breakdancing, using the watermelon as a prop. I double over laughing. This kid's so *extra*. At one point, he decides to attempt a move where he tries to roll the watermelon down one arm, over the back of his neck and into his other arm. It doesn't work and the watermelon splats on the ground, the shell shattering into pieces.

'Oh, snap,' he says, rubbing his head. 'Sorry. I'm still up for eating it if you are.'

'Duh!' I say.

We squat over the watermelon carcass and devour the pieces shamelessly with our hands, spitting the seeds into the lilac bushes.

As he smiles at me with sticky red lips, I realize I'm feeling *jeong* for YoungBae too. Even though One.J is a musical genius and an old soul and gave me the coolest date ever and my first kiss, it dawns on me that he really is an alien to me. Something about the way he yelled at Clown Killah, his carelessness . . . shouldn't he have been more careful on our date, knowing all those *sasaengs* were around?

But YoungBae's right here. He's liked me, just the way I am, since that first day he spoke to me across the Gender Line in Teacher Lee's classroom.

'May I kiss you, Albert?' I ask.

He looks surprised. 'Yes,' he blurts.

I lean over and kiss him, and I learn what 'Red Flavor' tastes like – I never really understood from the song.

'Whoa,' he says, eyes wide. 'I'll even let you keep calling me Albert if you keep doing that.'

We laugh and kiss again. Longer this time. *Definitely* not a Manners Kiss.

'How 'bout this,' he says when we pull away. 'If you debut next week, I'll stay as a trainee here and see if I can debut too. In the meantime, you can try and make me a backup dancer in y'all's debut MV. If you don't debut, I'll quit too – CEO Sang doesn't give a crap about the boy trainees, so I bet he'll let me out. We can go back to America and try to make it there. We can do YouTube collabs and stuff. Deal?'

I bite my lip, suddenly feeling guilt like a medicine ball to my ribs. I think of the line in 'Alien': *You'd hate me for the things I must do to survive.* I should tell YoungBae about the photo. About One.J's kiss.

But One.J said he'd take care of it. He'll never have to know. No one will.

If I become a star like One.J, will YoungBae one day hate me for the things I might do to survive in a world as tough as K-pop? What I've *already* done?

I shake away my guilt. I spit a watermelon seed at YoungBae. It bounces off his chest.

'Deal,' I say, clearing One.J from my mind. 'I choose you.'

YoungBae looks at me quizzically. 'Choose me? What do you mean?'

'Never mind,' I say, shaking my head. 'I have trainee brain.'

He grins. 'At least you get one more day outside for your birthday. Are you excited to celebrate with your mom tomorrow?'

'Yes and no. I did something I might regret.'

YoungBae arches an eyebrow quizzically.

'I invited Helena to come with me.'

Imani and I hug for a full minute, jumping up and down. 'You are officially the coolest person ever!' she screams in my ear, startling all the black-suited Koreans in the lobby. 'MY BEST FRIEND IS A K-POP SUPERSTAR!'

'I was so excited to see you!' I shout, squeezing her shoulders, not quite believing she's real. 'How did you guys get here?!'

'Well,' says Imani proudly, 'I successfully raised enough money for the Korean Culture Appreciation Club to get me and Ethan round-trip tickets.' Then she mouths to me, 'His parents paid,' pointing to Ethan, and I nod and say, 'Ah, got it.'

I hug Ethan too and ruffle his blue hair. 'I'm gagged, girl, gagged,' he says. 'I never thought Candace Park would pull off a death drop before me.'

'How was my form?' I ask.

'Good, not great,' he says.

Savage.

For a moment, I forgot Helena was here. I introduce her, and she bows deeply to Umma and waves to Imani and Ethan.

Imani gasps. 'You are *so* beautiful.'

'Thanks,' says Helena, grinning shyly.

'You were *so* fierce in the showcase,' says Ethan.

On the trip home, Umma fusses over how skinny Helena is and how hungry she must be for a home-cooked meal.

When I brought up inviting Helena to come hang out with Umma and me for our last weekend as trainees, to prove we could get past our differences, Manager Kong immediately approved Helena's departure from the building.

As I could have predicted, Umma was only too happy to take in a stray Korean American girl with no family in Seoul. 'You should have invited Helena sooner!' Umma scolds me. Then to Helena, she explains, 'Sometimes Candace has no manners.'

Ugh.

Imani has planned a jam-packed tourist itinerary for us. We

explore the Ihwa Mural Village in the independent theatre district, sample some live octopus (Ethan passes on that), dip our feet in the foot pools at the Seoullo 7017, visit Poopoo Land, an actual museum about poop and farting (Koreans are obsessed with these topics), and have lattes at a meerkat cafe, which is even cuter than the raccoon cafe. The meerkats nip at most of us but seem to love Helena for some reason, eating right out of her hand.

Afterwards, we go back to the apartment for an early dinner for my birthday, which in Korean tradition always includes *miyuk guk* – seaweed soup. Immediately, Helena insists on helping Umma set up dinner, which Umma refuses, but Helena insists three times; this is the same girl who wouldn't throw out her own trash. Already, Helena's making me look bad. I've literally never helped Umma or Abba in the kitchen in my life, but they've never asked me to. If they did, I totally would.

While they're getting dinner ready, Imani, Ethan and I crowd around Umma's laptop to watch all the performance clips from the showcase, the most popular of which is our a cappella performance of 'Into the New World', which already has eighteen million views!

'Dude, this performance was legendary,' says Imani. 'My children and their children's children will be watching this.'

I scroll through the comments. Most are positive ('QUEENS!', 'Marry me, Aram!', 'This performance is shutting down the internet'.) but there are some horrible ones ('THAT'S THAT SLUT WHO BROKE ONE.J'S HEART!' or 'Kwon Binna is too ugly to be an idol there I said it'.).

'All right, that's it, no more reading troll comments allowed,' declares Ethan.

Imani then opens the S.A.Y. website to start voting for me over and over again. 'Helena, I'm gonna throw you a bunch of votes too, don't worry!' Imani yells.

'Thanks, Imani!' shouts Helena from the kitchen.

I roll my eyes. 'What?' says Imani.

I've never told her Helena and I aren't friends.

'Never mind.'

After everything is clean and put away and Ethan and Imani head back to their youth hostel, Helena and Umma both insist that they'll take the couch in the living room, and after an epic battle of Korean manners, it's finally settled that Umma will take the couch and Helena and I will share the bed. 'You girls need to rest your tired bodies!' Umma insists.

I don't put up a fight, since the whole point of this weekend was Helena and me bonding. In the darkened bedroom, we lie next to each other on opposite sides of the bed in silence for so long I suspect she's fallen asleep. But then she finally says, 'I know JiHoon is the worst.'

I breathe a sigh of relief. 'But then why are you with him?'

'I guess . . . it felt kinda nice to feel like there was someone on my side. I was always completely on my own in there, and he was looking out for me, you know?'

'I get that,' I say, thinking of the chicken strips YoungBae smuggled for me in his pockets.

'I mean, I didn't get that much special treatment from JiHoon, and Madame Jung never knew about us. I never got anything big, but he'd maybe get me some extra fruit from the cafeteria or some really nice treatment samples from GlowSong for my hair.'

'About that . . .' I say.

'I swear, I didn't ruin your hair on purpose,' Helena says quickly. 'I swear on my life. I swear on *debuting*. Madame Jung was the one who gave me that extra bottle to use on you, after she saw your hair at the second assessment . . .'

'Really?! I mean, I knew that lady always hated me.'

'She was always telling me that I was the model foreigner and you were the disrespectful one, a loose cannon who'd hurt the company if you ever got to debut. She was the one who told me there's only room for one American in the group, and I better make sure it's me. After the first assessment, some of the stuff she was saying about you started to seem true . . . so I told JiHoon about the *yakgwas*. I swear I didn't want him to break your guitar. And a few weeks ago, when you stopped talking to me completely, it kinda hurt my feelings.'

I play Helena's and my entire relationship in my head. Is it possible that I misunderstood her intentions all along?

'But Helena,' I say, 'you were insanely shady to me from the jump. You never wanted to talk to me, anything.'

In the half-light, I see Helena frowning at the ceiling. Her white-blonde hair is luminous in the moonlight. 'I guess I've been in no-new-friends mode for a while,' she says. 'The thing is, I told myself I need to debut no matter what – anything that distracts from the goal, including friendships, has to go. I don't have anything outside of debut.'

'That's not true. You're smart and really talented. You could go back to California and slay in other ways.'

'There's nothing for me in California. My mom died when I was ten. I left America to train in Korea when I was fourteen, when I passed the audition for one of the other Big Four companies. When I didn't get picked to debut in that group, my dad told me to come home, but I was so determined to debut that I got myself traded from my old company right into S.A.Y. A year after I started at S.A.Y., I got news that my dad died in a car accident.'

'Oh my God . . . Helena . . .'

'I got permission to fly to California for the funeral, but I had to come right back to keep training. I never even told any of the trainees because I didn't want to seem weak. I thought, if I didn't even get to see my dad for the last three years of his life, I better make it worth it and debut no matter what.' Helena sniffles. 'So I guess when you arrived . . . it all seemed so easy for you. I mean, not *easy*, but you never even learnt the choreography and you could still charm the CEO. And it was like our teammates liked you better than me right away. I don't know, it kind of drove me crazy how it didn't seem like you *need* this the way some of us do . . .'

I reach over and wipe her tears. 'I can totally see that.'

'Anyway, if I was a total monster, just know that I'm out of my mind half the time . . . that trainee life will do that, you know?'

'Totally. And I need to apologize too. I know I can be extra sometimes—'

'Sometimes?!' Helena turns over to shoot me a look.

I laugh. 'All right, don't start with me.'

The next day, Umma drops us off at the ShinBi lobby. Helena gives Umma a longer hug than I do. The next time I see Umma, I'll either be getting on a plane with her back to America or saying goodbye to her as she gets on it alone.

'Candace,' Umma calls after me as Helena and I go through security. 'Actually, both of you.'

Helena and I look back at her.

'If being an idol is really what you want to do,' she says, 'please promise me you won't make it all about looking beautiful and gaining fame. Use those voices God blessed you with to speak for others.'

'OK, Umma,' I say.

'Yes, Mrs Park,' says Helena.

We go through the turnstiles.

'And one more thing,' Umma adds. '*Seoru akyeo-joh.*'

Look after each other.

'Yes, Umma.'

'Yes, Mrs Park.'

CHAPTER 35

RAINBOW ROAD

The twenty-five remaining girls are being held in the big rehearsal room backstage at Seoul Olympic Stadium dressed in pure, virginal white. I look like Kate Middleton on her wedding day, except with purple hair and a dress so short my safety shorts are almost showing.

We've been told that, in the next room over, CEO Sang and other S.A.Y. and ShinBi executives are apparently reviewing the votes and other factors before finalizing their decisions. SLK is out onstage at this very moment, making the crowd go wild with performances of 'Unicorn' and 'Sorry 'Bout It'.

I look around. JinJoo is sitting on the floor, rocking back and forth. Binna, Helena and Aram are in a corner, holding hands and praying. Other girls are pacing, crying, praying too.

Even though I'm tired, I'm achy all over and I'm emotionally spent, I'm calmer than I should be. I know I can go through this ten more times and survive. I've been pushed to what I thought were my limits and I still had a lot more left to give.

A producer pops his head into the room to give us a one-minute warning. 'CEO Sang and the executives have made their decision,' he says.

Just then, Manager Kong pushes past him and storms into the room, looking at her phone, a sheen of sweat making her face sparkle.

'Who is this?!' she demands in a soft but tense voice. 'Which one of you did this?!'

Everyone, already on edge, looks absolutely panicked. Manager Kong demands the cameramen to stop filming and darts to every corner of the room, shoving her phone in each trainee's face. Every girl jumps back from it like it's a photo of a severed arm. JinJoo literally screams when she sees it.

Oh no. I know what it is before Manager Kong comes around to me.

It's a *Korea Radar* article. I clamp my hand over my mouth. The headline reads, 'ONE.J CAUGHT KISSING S.A.Y. TRAINEE JUST BEFORE GIRL GROUP DEBUT'.

The grainy photo.

'Well?!' hisses Manager Kong, shoving the phone further under my nose. 'This is on every celebrity news site in Asia already!'

I just shake my head no like everyone else, thinking of One.J's instructions. *Don't confess.* My blood turns to icicles as Manager Kong continues to make her way around the room.

Of course a *sasaeng* would choose today of all days. I

remember what One.J told me: they don't always want to be noticed for good reasons, they just want to be noticed. What would get more attention from One.J?

With no answers, Manager Kong tells us to go ahead and get ready. 'We have no choice,' she says. 'But just know – whoever this is, never forget: One.J is S.A.Y.'s most valuable product and anyone tarnishing his perfect image will be dealt with accordingly. Madame Jung is on her way to the studio right now.'

I want to throw up, but I try to control my breathing. Rattled, the twenty-five of us line up at the door in the order that we rehearsed. BowHee is directly ahead of me, Binna right behind. We carry microphones that have been decorated to look like bouquets of purple and pink lilacs. We're guided down the cinder-blocked hallways, past the Viewing Room where YoungBae and the other boy trainees are watching, past the dressing room where less than a week ago, Helena and I were fighting to the death.

I tell myself that no one will be able to tell that girl in the photo was me. To the public, I have purple hair. The eighty thousand people who watched my 'Expectations vs Reality' YouTube vid saw a regular girl in New Jersey with greasy black hair. Young-Bae hasn't seen the photos, and if it all hits the fan, I can explain that my kiss with One.J was before I kissed him – that I choose him.

A crew member wearing a headset gives the girl at the front, ShiHong, the green light to walk out on to the stage, and we all follow, met by thunderous applause and cheers. We wave as we sing our second group song, called 'Rainbow Road', written by One.J and Clown Killah. We pass the giant hand holding the

Earth, which has been moved to the front of the stage, and walk down the runway, which is lined by white, pink and purple cherry blossom trees – I can't tell whether they're real or fake, but they're so delicate and lovely.

When I was a little girl
My head was high up in the clouds
I always dreamt of the castle
At the end of a rainbow road

Now that I'm older
My feet are on hard ground
But with you beside me
We can paint this path as we go

It's not the road we imagined
There's been hardship along the way
But our steps leave beautiful traces
When you look back, you'll see
This was the rainbow road all along

By the end of the song, the cheers become so loud I can barely hear myself sing. I look up at one of the monitors and see my fellow trainees, all glowing in white. We look like a dream come to life.

WooWee steps out on to the main stage and interrupts the fantasy, saying that the time has come to announce the five girls who will get to debut. The audience lets out a shriek of anticipation and agony as we line up in rows to the side of the giant hand. There are chants of girls' names. I hear Aram. I hear BowHee. I hear Binna. I hear Candace. It doesn't feel real that so many people I don't know care so much about me.

But then I hear a fan in the crowd shout, 'Get your hands off my One.J, Helena Cho!' And another: 'Helena Cho, how dare you corrupt my One.J!'

I glance over at Helena, who looks completely terrified in her white lace dress and white-blonde hair. Then I wonder: in trying to protect me, did One.J throw the suspicion in Helena? He knew from the first assessment that she and I didn't get along. And it's not lost on me how coincidental it is that right before the showcase, Mr Oh, who gets his orders from S.A.Y., changed Helena's hair to the exact colour I had when I kissed One.J.

What can I do? If I don't get chosen, I'll admit it was me to get the heat off Helena. And if I *am* chosen . . . this might blow over, just like any tabloid story, right?

The lights in the stadium darken. There's explosive, apocalyptic music to heighten the drama.

Before I know it, WooWee is saying, 'The first member of S.A.Y.'s first-ever girl group is . . . Kim Aram.'

Aram falls to her knees, crying, in the row in front of me. I put aside the photo drama and scream and cheer for her, not the least bit surprised; her face was meant to grace billboards and CFs all over the world. After girls pull her back up to her feet, she walks centre stage, bawling her eyes out, where WooWee puts a crystal tiara on Aram's head before directing her to the far-left spot on the podium. Just as Aram steps on to it, the thumbnail of the giant hand lights up, glowing red right behind her.

WooWee reads out, 'Kim Aram, from Ansan, South Korea,

will serve as the main Visual of the group. Aside from her unparalleled beauty, Aram is an excellent actress and strong Sub-Vocal.'

The stadium chants, 'Kim Aram!' There are cries of '*Yeppeoh!*'

Everyone quiets down for the next announcement. WooWee says, 'The second member is . . . Shin BowHee.'

My right eardrum practically blows out as BowHee screams right next to me. I hug her and she's swarmed by the other girls' congratulatory hands. She's vibrating with joy and shock. When she finally lets go, she receives her tiara from WooWee and steps on to the second position of the podium; the index fingernail of the giant hand lights up blue.

'Shin BowHee hails from Daegu, South Korea. She will serve as Lead Vocal of the group, providing soaring vocals and **aegyo** charm.'

My heart sinks a little. There goes any hope, however little there was in the first place, of Team Two staying intact. Plus, BowHee and I, both short Cute girls with big voices, would fill similar roles in the group. I can't tell if I'm devastated or relieved.

'Now the next member,' says WooWee, 'has been hailed by CEO Sang as the female One.J.'

An '*Ooooooooh!*' from the crowd.

'The third member of S.A.Y.'s first-ever girl group is . . . Candace Park, from New Jersey, USA!'

I see myself on the screen in the back of the stadium. I see my mouth falls open, a face of pure shock. Binna screams and jumps, squeezing me tight. 'You did it, you did it,' she shouts, tears pouring down her face. My face on the screen crumples. I bury it in Binna's shoulder. All I can say is, 'Thank you, thank you, thank you, *unnie.'* I look at the screen again – it flashes to the Viewing Room, where all the S.A.Y. boy trainees are watching. YoungBae is front and centre, and he's jumping up and down for me, punching the air.

After getting past a jungle of sweaty hands and hugs, I walk out to the centre of the stage to WooWee's side. 'Congratulations,' she whispers off mic as she places a tiara on my head. I search the crowd for Umma's face and finally spot it halfway back. She's crying and nodding to me, as if giving her approval. I make a heart with my hands.

I step on to my spot on the podium. It's a little higher than the others. The middle fingernail behind me lights up purple, like my hair.

Of *course* I'm the middle finger.

WooWee reads from her card, 'Candace Park, with her unique voice, will serve as the Main Vocal and Centre of the group, bringing to it her American spirit and incredible songwriting ability.'

Then it really hits me: *I'm* Centre?! *I'm* the female One.J?! After all my shenanigans and failures? After all the times Manager Kong said I was a 'big problem'? After all those times The General screamed in my face?

Before I have too much time to bask, the next girl is named: it's ShiHong from Team Three. I don't know her very well at all. She's always stood out though – she's gorgeous, with her tomboy vibe and Peter Pan haircut. WooWee says, 'ShiHong hails from Shanghai, China, and will bring a fierce Girl Crush vibe to the group and top-notch rapping and dancing skills.'

When ShiHong steps on to the podium next to me, the ring fingernail on the giant hand flashes green. I whisper congratulations. She nods to me, the only girl on the stage who isn't boohooing.

'Ladies and gentlemen, I'm afraid there's only one more spot left,' says WooWee dramatically, with a hushed voice. There's an excited groan from the crowd.

I say a silent prayer. Binna can still snatch the final spot; she and ShiHong have similar skills, but they're two completely different types of Girl Crush – ShiHong is more modelesque, Binna is more hip-hop – that could balance out me and BowHee, bringing up our dance cred.

'This final member has been training for a long time and has impressed CEO Sang with her team mindset and hard work. She will serve as the Leader of the group.'

It has to be Binna. Leader? Long training? Teamwork? It can't be anyone else.

WooWee says, 'Please look to the screens for the two contenders for the final spot.'

My eyes dart to the monitor at the back of the stadium. Binna's and Helena's faces flash in split screen. They see themselves and immediately begin sobbing.

My knees give way and I crumple to the podium. *Please* let it be Binna. Even though Helena deserves a spot, too, it has to be Binna. I would never be here if she hadn't taken me under her wing when Manager Kong was ready to give up on me. I would never have survived a single assessment if she hadn't given up hundreds of hours of her own practice time to help me. I can't do this without her.

'And the fifth and final member of S.A.Y.'s first-ever girl group is . . .'

Please, please, please.

'...Helena Cho.'

I sob into the podium. I've never felt anything quite like this, like my stomach has been cut open and my insides are spilling out. *Bae-jjae-ra.*

This feels infinitely worse than if I'd been eliminated myself. Binna is the most deserving of all. Everybody who knows Binna can see her worth. The only explanation for this is that she doesn't fit some stupid standard of beauty.

BowHee and ShiHong pull me up to my feet. I hide my face from the cameras with my microphone bouquet of lilacs – it smells like night-time on the roof with YoungBae.

Binna and the other eliminated trainees are already being shooed off the stage. She looks up at me with her tear-streaked face and raises her fist. She mouths, *Hwaiting.*

As Helena, bawling, steps on to the final spot of the podium holding her tiara in place, the pinky fingernail glows yellow. The entire Earth in the giant hand's fist suddenly lights up, casting spots of light over the entire stadium like a massive disco ball.

Thunderous applause assaults us from all sides. There's also another sound coming from the audience – a bass line.

It's booing.

WooWee says, 'To the nation, the world ... your new top girl group, the absolute ideal of idols, greets you.'

Holding our tiaras, the five of us bow deeply and shout into our microphone bouquets, 'Please expect great things from us!' It's what we were told to say if we were chosen.

There's an explosion at the ceiling of the stadium, and a

torrent of glitter, flower petals, and streamers rains down on the ten thousand fans. Sparks rain down on the stage behind us.

But the booing is persistent. It gives way to a chant that has scattered all over the stadium: 'HANDS OFF ONE.J! HANDS OFF ONE.J! HANDS OFF ONE.J!'

Those blend together with chants of, 'WE HATE HELENA CHO! WE HATE HELENA CHO!' Fans are making Xs with their forearms in Helena's direction.

Helena has stopped crying tears of happiness. Her face is a picture of utter mortification. 'What's going on?' she asks ShiHong frantically. 'Why are they doing this?!'

I look to One.J. His mouth is open. He needs to say something. Why doesn't he take any of the heat off Helena? It takes two to cause a kissing scandal.

CEO Sang is on his feet. He's shouting at P.D., 'GO TO CF BREAK! GO TO CF BREAK!'

P.D. Choi runs out on to the stage, waving his arms.

All the screens in the stadium switch to a CF for Elektro Hydrate.

CEO Sang and One.J rush the stage, flanked by beefy body-guards who bat away female fans reaching for One.J. CEO Sang yanks Helena off the podium by her arm. She screams, dropping her bouquet as her tiara falls off her head.

'You!' CEO Sang booms. 'Get off the stage.'

'CEO Sang,' Helena sputters desperately, 'that's not me in the photos, I swear! I've never been alone with One.J-*sunbae* in my life!'

'It doesn't matter,' he says dismissively. 'The nation believes otherwise. Your image is ruined. Get off the stage!'

Helena opens her mouth in protest, but crew members are already pulling her away. Gasps and commotion from the audience. Helena looks at me desperately before she disappears into the dark of backstage.

The other girls on the podium are just as frozen as I am. Everything we've worked for is falling apart at the last second. CEO Sang and P.D. Choi are shouting. This is all my fault. And I have no idea how to fix this.

'Let's just debut them as four when we come back from break,' says P.D. Choi.

'They're the female SLK,' says CEO Sang. 'We need five. For symmetry.'

Suddenly, WooWee steps between the two men. 'CEO Sang,' she says, her fiery amber eyes glinting, 'debut me now. Make me the fifth member *tonight*.'

All of us girls on the podium gasp. I look at Aram, who's just as shaken as I am.

One of the biggest female idols in K-pop debuting for a *second* time . . . in *our* group?

'But WooWee,' says CEO Sang. 'We were saving you for right before the girl group's first official single, to make the biggest splash in the press.'

'I know the plan was to switch me out for one of these girls in a month,' she says, her voice sharp and impatient, 'but this will solve the problem. You owe me this, CEO Sang. I didn't move heaven and earth to get out of my old contract just to debut in a second group that implodes from a scandal.'

I can't believe what I'm hearing. So S.A.Y. has been planning to knock one of us off this whole time? Replace one of us with WooWee right before our official debut track dropped, just for publicity?

'CEO Sang, this is too cruel,' One.J says. 'You can't play with people like this.'

CEO Sang ignores One.J. He nods resolutely to WooWee. 'This is the best solution. Let's announce this after the break. Helena Cho's announcement was a mistake.'

P.D. Choi nods too. 'It's an unexpected storyline, but it could work.'

'I will act sufficiently surprised,' says WooWee, bowing.

'We're really doing this?' asks One.J in disbelief.

CEO Sang says, 'One.J, when WooWee is announced, you take over as the host. And you girls . . .' He looks at us on the podium. 'You're overjoyed that one of your favourite idols will now be one of your members, got it?'

One.J opens his mouth to say something, looking at me, but I give him a reassured nod. 'Yes, CEO Sang,' I say.

The other girls gawk at me. I give them a smile.

It's become crystal clear to me what I need to do. I gaze out upon the crowd. Umma, concerned, has moved up to the front. She's waving at me frantically to get my attention. I smile and nod to her too. I remember what she said as she was dropping me and Helena off in the lobby: '*Seoru akyeo-joh.*'

Look after each other.

But the word for '*look after*' – '*akyeo*' – also means to '*spare*' or '*ration*'. It means to ration something precious to you, like food or water or iPhone battery life. When you say it about a person, you're literally saying that you want to ration them – spend them with care – make sure they're not used carelessly or wasted. It's what anyone would want for someone they love: for them not to be made to bleed, starve, be lonely or overworked. It's what Umma and Abba have always done for me. It's why I'm strong enough to stand here today.

I look at the three girls standing beside me – Aram, BowHee and ShiHong – and know they feel powerless right now, to have this moment spoilt after years of gruelling work. I think of Helena backstage, how thrown away she must feel; she doesn't even have parents to turn to. And JinJoo. It fills me with shame that in all this time, I was too afraid or distracted to speak up for her; if she'd been allowed to focus on her talent instead of constantly being told to lose weight, maybe she could have shined brightest of all.

Who's really been looking after any of us?

Not anyone at S.A.Y. They'll use and spend us any way they can – that's clearer than ever to me now. To them, our spirits, our youth and our dreams are abundant resources. When they've squeezed us dry, there's more they can take from someone else.

So it's up to me. *I* will look after these girls. It will surely cost me my spot in this group. And if it makes the K-pop fandom hate me, if it makes YoungBae hate me, I'll have to live with the consequences.

When we're back from the CF break, CEO Sang addresses the audience directly. 'We've heard you loud and clear,' he says into his mic, his arm outstretched to the crowd. 'You don't want

Cho Helena as one of your idols. The news of her misdeeds only reached us now. We apologize, and One.J apologizes for his mistake. But we're pleased to announce a change in direction that will surely please all of you. We ask your host – former member of QueenGirl – to debut in this new group.'

There's a huge stir in the stadium. All cameras zoom in on WooWee's face, which is overcome with unspeakable shock. The confusion from the crowd turns to applause. 'Thank you, CEO Sang!' she gasps into the mic. ShiHong and I help WooWee on to the podium as she covers her mouth, sobbing with joy.

'After your past group was plagued with scandal, due to one wayward member,' says CEO Sang, 'may this moment be the closest to scandal your new group ever gets.'

One.J laughs uncomfortably. 'Well,' he says, 'what a turn this moment has taken.'

Cheers and laughter. Everyone's thrilled that One.J has the mic. How quickly One.J has been forgiven for his part in this – not that I think there's anything so wrong with kissing, but why should the girl sacrifice herself? Why is One.J any more important than Helena?

Then it dawns on me. K-pop is no different from Hollywood; the woman always takes the brunt of a scandal. Just like One.J doesn't have haters chanting his name, QueenGirl was the only group that broke apart. HyunTaek and RubiKon are just fine, while Iseul is ruined and WooWee is left to make desperate moves to survive. The unfairness of it all gives me fuel for what I'm about to do.

One.J, not prepared to play host, sticks the mic in Aram's face.

'Aram, do you have any words about this new development?'

Shell-shocked, Aram shakes her head and looks at the floor.

I step forward and grab One.J's mic. 'I have something to say.' My voice echoes throughout the whole stadium.

'Yes, Candace, let's get our Centre's thoughts,' says One.J through a nervous chuckle.

'To be honest, this news is bittersweet,' I say. 'As many of our fans know, there were photos that went up online of you, One.J, and a blonde S.A.Y. trainee kissing. Everyone assumed it was Helena. But it wasn't. That girl was me.'

There's an outcry in the audience. I need to say this quickly before I get pulled offstage – I see CEO Sang jump up from the judges' table. I see phones pop up from the audience to video me. Good.

'In our world, that photo is enough to ruin a career. But if it has to ruin a career, it should be mine, not Helena's. Helena is one of the hardest-working people I ever met, but without even both-ering to search for truth, our company, S.A.Y. Entertainment, threw away this girl without a second thought – like she was worth nothing. As an idol trainee, I'm tired of being treated this way. Why is it that the generation before us gets to decide what we're worth? Aren't we already enough?'

There's a murmur from ten thousand people. My mic is cut off, but Aram quickly hands me hers.

'We're told every day by adults that we're too fat, too ugly, that we didn't work hard enough, that we need plastic surgery. We've been insulted, turned against each other, almost driven crazy – a trainee named EunJeong was driven to the edge from all the pressure. But I just want everyone watching to know that you don't need to look or act like us. We're no better than any of you. We "idols" get lonely, hungry, tired . . . we fight, we curse, we fart, we gain weight, we want love. We're human and I'm tired of pretending I'm perfect. If you want perfect, these amazing girls onstage are pretty close to it. I'm definitely going to be fired after this, but I still know I'm not worth any less as a person. And One.J? One.J is great, but he still belongs to his fans, not me. I'm into someone else, a boy trainee named YoungBae, and I *really* don't believe most fans care that much if their idols date.'

Then I literally drop the mic. Not because I'm cool, but because I'm in a hurry to run away. Away from the cameras, away from the stunned public.

Trouble is waiting for me in the wings of the stage. Madame Jung has arrived at the studio, and I've never seen anyone look more furious. I try to pass her quickly, but her hand flies out. She's backhanded me across the face. I lose my balance, but I fall against a warm, sturdy body.

'YoungBae?' I say, dazed.

'Madame Jung, what are you doing?!' shouts Manager Kong.

I hold my cheek, which is stinging. Madame Jung sneers at me. 'Did I not tell everyone that this one was going to be trouble? Not only has she shamed this company, she's shamed Korea on a global stage.'

'Korea is not K-pop, Madame,' says YoungBae.

'Shut up, you idiot!' she snaps. 'Both of you are out of this company. And I'll make sure you'll pay for the rest of your life for what you just did, Candace. You're in breach of contract – you've shared confidential information, committed slander against the company. ShinBi Unlimited will come after you with all of its might.'

YoungBae and Manager Kong are holding on to my arms as we walk back to the dressing room. There's pandemonium in the hallways. The boy trainees in the Viewing Room seem to be revolting – tearing off the ties of their S.A.Y. schoolboy uniforms, throwing chairs, shouting, 'We're tired of this too!' Managers, production crew and executives are running around in a panic.

'You're so dead,' YoungBae whispers, looking worried for me.

'Do you hate me?' I ask.

'No, I'm proud of you – the real bad girl of K-pop. But it's about to get lit up in here.'

Terror strikes me all at once. What have I done? Will my family and I be paying for this mistake for the rest of my life? Why did I have to open my big mouth? Why did I have to come here in the first place?

I might have just cost my family our convenience store. Our house. Tommy's college. My future.

Manager Kong gets me a cold, wet paper towel from the ladies' room for my burning cheek. 'Come on,' she says. 'We'll get your mom and I'll take you both back to my apartment and figure out what to do next. S.A.Y. isn't going to let you leave the country while they're suing you.'

'Aren't you mad at me?' I ask Manager Kong.

'No, I'm scared for you. You said some things I agree with – to be honest, I've never understood why we had to be so harsh either. I was just doing my job.'

CEO Sang and Umma burst into the dressing room at the same time. CEO Sang lunges towards me and shouts right in my face. I feel flecks of saliva hit me. 'Do you know what you just did, you little brat? Do you know how many millions you just cost me?'

Umma throws herself between us and growls, 'How dare you even speak to my daughter!'

I've never heard this voice come out of Umma before – it's from deep inside, guttural and animal-like. She's dressed in a pink shawl-collared sweater and Crocs, but she has CEO Sang back on his heels. Thank goodness my cheek isn't red.

'Now I see where she gets it from,' spits CEO Sang. 'I'm coming for everything you have and then some.'

'Please try it!' shouts Umma.

I'm so stunned I can't even cry. YoungBae's mouth hangs open as Umma, like an attack dog, chases away a parade of people who've come to scream at me: a ShinBi lawyer, a mascara-stained WooWee, JiHoon, Madame Jung again, at whom Umma snaps, 'People like you give Koreans a bad name!'

Manager Kong has been on her phone this whole time. 'Junior Manager InHee's on her way in a van,' she announces. 'Come with me. My apartment is hardly big enough for one, but we need to get out of here.'

We speed down the hall, Umma squeezing my one hand, YoungBae clasping the other. Aram and Helena come out of a bathroom to chase behind us.

'Candace!' Helena calls after me.

I stop. 'Helena. I'm so sorry.'

I wouldn't be surprised if she clawed my face again, but to my shock, she hugs me. 'Thank you,' she says.

The moment we leave through a back exit, I'm blinded by cameras and deafened by a roar.

'*SARANGHAE, CANDACE!*' *We love you.*

'*HWAITING, CANDACE!*'

'*Yeopeoh, yeopeoh!*'

Young fans are holding up their phones, playing a video of my speech. I hear my own voice say, 'Why is it that the generation before us gets to decide what we're worth? Aren't we already enough?' I hear a chant of 'CANDACE PARK, K-POP WARRIOR! CANDACE PARK, K-POP WARRIOR!' A few kids are holding up photos of a female idol who died last year, after being dropped by her company and harassed by trolls over nonsense 'scandals'.

'*HWAITING*, K-POP WARRIOR!'

Aram flashes her dazzling smile and waves as we push through the crowd into the van. Whatever happens, this girl needs to become a celebrity.

When we're finally piled in the van, Umma squeezes my hand. 'Don't be afraid, Candace. You told the truth.'

YoungBae whispers into my ear, 'You're my Ultimate Bias.'

I'm dazed. Helena is on Umma's phone, her famous finger-nails clacking against the screen as she scrolls. 'Oh my God,' she reads out loud. '#KPOPWARRIOR and #CandacePark are already trending on all SNS. Even in America.' She reads off Korean and English blog headlines.

'K-POP EXECS, LISTEN UP. THIS IS THE MESSAGE

FANS WANT TO HEAR.

'WE ALL THOUGHT IT, SHE SAID IT: K-POP STAR BLOWS UP HER CAREER TO SPEAK TRUTH ON LIVE TV.

'FANS, IF YOU AGREE WITH CANDACE PARK, WATCH THIS VIDEO. BUY HER MUSIC.'

'Did I really just "blow up" my career?' I ask.

'Umm, pretty much,' says YoungBae.

I laugh, and tears spring to my eyes as a massive sense of relief, terror and excitement floods me all at once. Even though I literally threw a grenade at my entire life, and I have to get ready to fight a multi-billion-dollar corporation, I have people on my side: everyone in this van; Binna, JinJoo; and apparently, thousands, maybe millions of people I don't even know.

At that moment, 'Into the New World' by Girls' Generation plays on the radio. Manager Kong turns up the volume. Umma starts singing along. YoungBae beatboxes and the rest of us join in.

I rest my head against Umma's shoulder as we speed down the Seoul streets, recalling that time in our store when Umma explained what this song was about: beginning a journey that's sure to be long and uncertain, yet moving forward with courage, knowing you have a heart full of hope and love.

'Umma, I just thought of something,' I say.

'What?'

I grin up at her. 'No matter what, this is all going to make a killer college essay.'

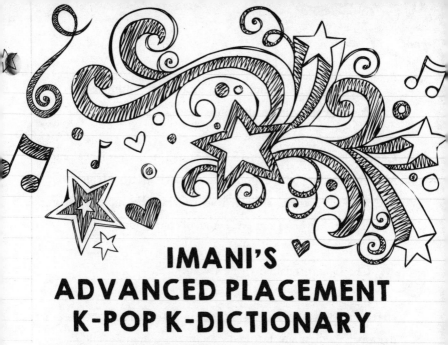

IMANI'S ♥ ADVANCED PLACEMENT K-POP K-DICTIONARY

Hey, girl! Since my purpose in life is to spread knowledge and enlightenment, here are some words that'll come up when you're becoming a K-pop superstar. Whenever you're feeling confused – and you will, cuz K-pop is fab but cray – open this up and think of ME! Love you, bb. Finger hearts x 10,000! <3

4D Personality: A lovable weirdo from outer space. Examples: Jisoo from Blackpink, Park Bom from 2NE1, our beloved Ethan.

aegyo: Oh, goodness, where to begin . . . it's a way of behaving in a so-called cute manner (babyish gestures, whiny voice) to get what you want. Most people, including Koreans, find it cringey, but female idols are expected to know how to do it on variety shows. Practise up, Candace!

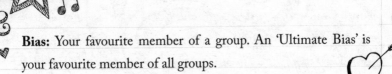

Bias: Your favourite member of a group. An 'Ultimate Bias' is your favourite member of all groups.

Centre: The member who's most featured in performances and MVs. Depending on the group, it can switch up from Comeback to Comeback, or there's an agreed-upon Centre. Examples: Nayeon from Twice, Taeyong from NCT and, of course, One.J. <3 <3

 CF: 'Commercial film', or a TV ad.

chaebol: A massive corporation run by a powerful Korean dynasty . . . these are featured heavily in K-dramas. ShinBi Unlimited, where you're going, is one of the biggest chaebols. It's about to get lit!

circle lenses: Coloured contacts that K-pop idols are famous for.

Comeback: The release of a new single/mini-album/album, complete with its own Concept. Many groups have several Comebacks a year, but some have just one or two per year if we're lucky (ahem, Blackpink).

Concept: The look and feel of a group, song, Comeback, MV, etc. For girl groups, there tend to be two broad categories of Concepts – Cute and Girl Crush – but really, those distinctions are a blurred line, and the possibilities are endless! That's what makes K-pop slap.

Cute Concept: Innocent, youthful, pastel colours, high-pitched voices, cutesy choreo. Some fans, especially in the West, look down on Cute Concepts, but Cute is fierce in its own way!

dating bans: Girrrl . . . K-pop needs to stop with this. Pretty much every K-pop company has a strict no-dating rule for trainees and rookie idols, so they can be 'available' to fans. Yes, a vocal minority of the fandom flips the hell out when idols date, but it's messed up how companies will kick out trainees and cancel contracts over it. Come on, K-pop . . . let idols love!!

Face of the Group: The face you think of when you hear the name of a group. Often the same as the Centre but not always. Examples: Kai from Exo, Jennie from Blackpink and the most iconic FOTG ever, ~*One.J*~

fancafe: An official forum where you can interact with other fans and occasionally idols themselves.

fancam: Footage taken by fans.

fanchant: Chants officially created by K-pop companies for fans to shout during live performances. They're usually a mix of the members' names and the song lyrics.

fansign: It's any stan's dream to be chosen to attend a fansign, where you can meet idols and get their autographs. Secretly, my ulterior motive for getting you to try out for S.A.Y. was so you can get me into SLK fansign events. 😊

finger hearts: A love gesture made by crossing the tips of your index finger and thumb. K-pop idols make this symbol approximately 10,000,000 times a day.

Girl Crush Concept: A girl group Concept that's more fierce than Cute; the epitome of Girl Crush is 'I Am the Best' by 2NE1 or Blackpink's overall vibe.

gyopo: A foreign-born Korean. Examples: Tiffany Young from Girls' Generation, and Candace Park from the much-anticipated S.A.Y. girl group. 😊

Hallyu: 'The Korean Wave', or also Korean Hollywood. Refers to the fact that Korean culture is spreading all around the world because it's amazing. Be proud!!

in-ears: Monitors idols wear during live performances. Idols personalize them with colours and symbols.

Killing Part: The one part of the vocal or choreo that you can't get out of your head, like Twice's 'TT' hands or GOT7's thigh-tap move in 'You Calling My Name'.

maknae: The youngest of the group. Age and titles are important in Korea, so there's kind of an expectation for a *maknae* to be especially cute, charismatic or lovable, and sometimes expected to be the 'mood-maker' of the group. Examples: Lisa from Blackpink, Sehun from EXO.

monolids: Eyes with no crease above them. These are adorbs eyes, just like yours! Not that common with idols, however – notable monolidded idols are Red Velvet's Seulgi and Twice's Dahyun.

music show: Weekly countdown shows where idols debut new music in front of a live audience. There's *M Countdown*, *Inkigayo*, *Popular 10!* and others. Each show has a complex formula for deciding which group or artist 'wins' for the week.

netizens: Citizens of the net. In K-pop, they're an organized and committed squad of Nancy Drews, able to sniff out scandal.

no-jam: 'No fun!' An affectionate-ish way to call someone a Debbie Downer.

P.D.: The director.

 Perfect All-Kill: When a track tops all of Korea's major charts all at the same time. A song has to *really* slap and snatch some wigs to achieve this.

safety shorts: What female idols wear under their tiny-tiny skirts to prevent wardrobe malfunctions.

selca: Selfie!

skinship: Public displays of physical affection between idol group members. It makes fans happy to see!

slave contracts: Horrible agreements that keep idols/trainees under a company's control, sometimes for thirteen years. There are many stories of idols suing to get out of them. You gotta avoid these, Candace!

SNS: Social networking services, or social media.

Stages: What K-pop calls live performances.

sunbae: A 'senior'; in K-pop, this means anyone who debuted before you. You better bow and speak to them formally in public, unless you want Korean netizens to come for you for bad manners. The opposite is *hoobae*, a junior.

surgical mask: Idols (and Koreans in general) wear these to protect from germs, pollution and micro-dust.

Visual: Everyone has their own preferences, but the Visual member of a group is the one who the company/the public decides is the closest to the Korean ideal of beauty.

PLAYLIST

CANDACE PARK'S K-POP PLAYLIST

Dearest future and current K-pop stans, I listened to these songs on repeat all through my trainee period, and I'm *still* not tired of a single one. If you haven't let K-pop take over your entire being yet, I recommend starting with all this fierceness. I dare you not to get obsessed with Korean girl groups after this. You're welcome!! ♥♥

'BOOMBAYAH' – Blackpink

'WHISTLE' – Blackpink

'I Am The Best' – 2NE1

'달라달라 (DALLA DALLA)' – ITZY

'FANCY' – Twice

'Into the New World' – Girls' Generation

'빨간맛 Red Flavor' – Red Velvet

'Genie' – Girls' Generation

'CHEER UP' – Twice

'PLAYING WITH FIRE' – Blackpink

'Bon Bon Chocolat' – Everglow

'Ugly' – 2NE1

'Egotistic' – Mamamoo

'I'm so sick' – Apink

'Oh! my mistake' – April

'Up & Down' – EXID

'Dumb Dumb' – Red Velvet

'LOVE WHISPER' – GFriend

'TT' – Twice

'PICK ME' – PRODUCE 48

'Ah-Choo' – Lovelyz

'As If It's Your Last' – Blackpink

'BBoom BBoom' – MOMOLAND

'Gashina' – SUNMI

'HANN (Alone)' – (G)I-DLE

'BLACK DRESS' – CLC

'Bad Boy' – Red Velvet

Photo by Lauren Perlstein

STEPHAN LEE is a senior editor at Bustle after a five-year stretch covering books and movies at *Entertainment Weekly*. He is a graduate of Duke University and The New School. *K-Pop Confidential* is his first novel. Follow him on Instagram at @stepephan and on Twitter at @stephanmlee.

WITH THE AUTHOR

What interested you in writing a novel about the K-pop world?
A trainee programme at a K-pop label is probably one of the most intense environments on the planet for teens. It's also a place where love is *literally* forbidden. Traditionally, in K-pop, the fans own their idols, so if idols date in real life, it's like they're actually cheating on their fans, and it can ruin careers in an instant. It struck me as such a perfect, high-stakes basis for a YA novel!

Even before the popularity of BTS and Blackpink, I knew it was a matter of time before K-pop truly hit it big outside of Korea. In 2014, *Entertainment Weekly* sent me to Seoul to report on the rise of Korean entertainment. The story was cancelled due to a change in editors-in-chief, but from all the interviews and research I did, it was clear how intentional the entire Korean entertainment industry was about spreading Korean culture all around the world through amazing music, film and TV.

How did you come up with your narrator?

Candace Park came to me right away! I wanted the character to be Korean American without a ton of knowledge about her Korean roots so the reader could go through a discovery process along with her. When she ventures to Seoul, Candace has no idea what she's in for: the cultural and language differences, the cut-throat rivalries, the back-breaking rehearsals, restrictive diets, lack of sleep and the strict rules.

I think there are a lot of children of immigrants like Candace – grateful to their parents but also constricted by their expectations and the paths laid out before them. In the process of training as a K-pop star and meeting all these new people, she learns to use her voice – as a singer, for sure, but as a change-maker and leader too.

What other books inspired you in writing *K-Pop Confidential*?

In a way, this is an adventure story about taking a huge leap of faith into a world that's entirely foreign. There are parts of this novel that might seem fantastical or dystopian, even though all the details are based on actual research (as well as a healthy dose of my own imagination!). In a way, my biggest inspiration was *The Hunger Games*. Kids are literally being thrown into the spotlight in the most demanding environment imaginable – what more dangerous arena is there in real life?!

While the K-pop world is so glamorous on the outside – all that perfect skin, crazy style, fierce imagery – so much effort goes into creating that fantasy. I think the push-pull of the expectation of the perfect image and the reality of what goes into it is ripe for conflict, and I think it's an extreme example of what young people go through all around the world, whether it's fierce competition to get into top colleges, or all the impossible hoops young adults have to go through to land a dream job. With this novel, I want to depict these young people discovering their inherent value, independent of the sky-high expectations adults are putting upon them, and exploring what their true desires are. For so many kids, the road to success can sometimes feel like an all-out battle.

With this book, did you want to address recent issues that have hit the news about K-pop?

It's no secret that many aspects of the K-pop industry need to change. The diets, demand for physical perfection, the ridiculous hours, the public scrutiny – all of those factors have the potential to be incredibly damaging to anyone's mental and physical health.

But it's also important to point out that none of this is unique to K-pop and certainly not to Korea. (I mean, watch any documentary about teen competitive athletes.) It's actually amazing to see young K-pop stars lead an international conversation about mental health and positive self-image. There's a long way to go, but change is possible. Idols are taking more control of the narrative and sharing their stories, and people are listening.

While the book addresses challenges that trainees have to go through, and Candace learns to speak out against mistreatment, the novel is ultimately a celebration of the music, creativity and talent you can only find in K-pop, and the resiliency of these artists. Candace's summer as a trainee is the hardest time of her life, but also the best. I hope she inspires others to chase their dreams, while also speaking out when they see something that's not right. It should never be necessary to sacrifice your values to achieve your goals.

Who are your favourite K-pop groups?

I'm totally 'multi-fandom'! I'm definitely in the BTS ARMY – they're changing the game for a reason! In addition to their amazing music – my fav track of theirs is 'DNA' – I love the message they're spreading to young people, of self-love, mental health and equality. I'm also a big fan of GOT7, who don't get the attention they deserve!

But really, I'm all about the girl groups. I'll always be a SONE and Blackjack, and of the current generation, I can't get enough of Blackpink, Red Velvet and Twice, and I love what ITZY, April, and Everglow are coming out with. My Ultimate Bias would have to be Blackpink but my Bias-wrecker is Red Velvet! Spotify also told me I'm in the top 4% of Twice listeners worldwide, so I'm pretty proud of that too.

ACKNOWLEDGEMENTS

Making *K-Pop Confidential* what it is has been an amazing team effort. In my eyes, everyone deserves to be the Centre, Visual *and* Face of the Group!

To start, endless thanks to David Levithan for the opportunity to debut at Scholastic, the publisher that made me a lifelong reader. Thank you to my brilliant, patient editor Sam Palazzi for respecting the subject matter so deeply and taking my calls right up until your wedding! A huge *gamsamnida* to Barry Cunningham and Jazz Bartlett Love at Chicken House for believing in this book from day one, to my super-agent Brenda Bowen for fighting on my behalf while making this whole process *fun*, and to Dana Spector at CAA for taking this project way beyond what I could have dreamt for it.

Justin Sherwood and Devin Alavian are the best friends anyone could hope for. Your belief and encouragement mean more than I can ever say. Mell Ravenel, it's been such a joy fangirling with you for almost twenty years – I'd like to think we would have been reading this book during freshman Geometry. Luis Jaramillo and everyone at The New School: I couldn't have written this book in three months without everything you taught me; you changed my life. Thank you to Aria Bendix, Arielle Dachille, Jessica Gross and Brian Saladino for being perfect readers. I owe so much to Tina Jordan and Jeff Giles, not only for giving me my first dream job, but for showing me that I'm a person who can make things happen. Thanks to Jackie Bernstein and all of BDG for making work a pleasure to go to every day.

To the talented, resilient young artists who've made K-pop the phenomenon it is: thank you for using your voices to inspire millions all around the world. We love you even more when you're not perfect. *Hwaiting!*

And most of all, thank you to Umma, Abba and Tim for everything good in my life.

PLN 22·01·210